Fox Tails

By Eric M Deal

Dedicated to Scribbles…

Who was there for me when I really needed him.

And helped me make my dreams come true with his
beautiful artwork.

Table of Contents

Polar's Work

Polar's deep voice fills the Rinwulv Auditorium with enthralled gazes. The student and professional body is silent while he speaks, the entire audience captivated with the arctic wolf's perfect voice and handsome looks. He has already delivered the majority of his speech and as he moves into the closing statements he remembers to stress the main argument of the Wolf Fox Love Commission. The WFLC is a sub organization of IGLARC, the International Gay Lesbian Animal Rights Commission, and Polar Arctic is the elected spokesman. His interspecies marriage with Vulpie makes him the obvious choice.

"Wolves' and foxes' long history of mingling has undeniably created some of the world's greatest advances." Polar speaks with his calm confident voice. "There is no reason to resist cooperation. When an animal thinks on the issue this is the logical conclusion. Efforts to defeat cross interspecies intimacy, to prevent reproduction between these two species, is an unwise endeavor. Many great things could come as a result of allowing these relationships considering that fox wolf hybrids are both strong and intelligent. History has violently shunned such ideas as unnatural or insulting to the fox species but I hope others will disagree as I do. Fox wolf relationships will not be forced and foxes will always be able to retain the purity of their species that they take pride in. I've learned many things from Vulpie and one is that foxes embrace who they are. They take pride in the many accomplishments of their species but as my husband reminds me, this pride also creates the high tension with wolves.

If we speak with complete honesty we recognize that wolves have had a long and sometimes negative relationship with foxes. There are extremists that believe wolves are superior because of their larger size and physical prowess, but we know that is pure and selfish vanity. Strength is not merely the physical. It's not just the dominion of muscle and bone. Strength also is vision, compassion and patience. Strength is the creativity and intelligence foxes possess that has enabled them to flourish throughout history. The first banks ever created were devised by foxes and now all species have progressed thanks to them. In ancient times a wolf could accumulate wealth and security for his family because of vulpine financial instruments. Instead of only living from one generation to the next, constantly fighting amongst other wolves and species, wolves were able to advance. Can anyone argue that such a contribution by foxes was insignificant when wolves were well known to kill each other just over food and shelter? Of course not. So we know professional relations have always been beneficial between foxes and wolves. Simply put, in the beginning wolves could provide the physical labor foxes sought and the two species have gone on to dominate the entire universe.

But intimate lupus vulpine relations were violently destroyed and considered shameful throughout history. A wolf or a fox can see why, as both species take pride in their heritage, but we do not live in savage times anymore. Now we live in a civilized society. Now we can choose who we want to love and there is so much more that could be accomplished if these barriers were dissolved. It's not just male wolves mating with vixens that has produced the interspecies children; several fox men have given she-wolves folfs as well. So there truly is nothing to fear if a fox chooses to love a wolf, or the opposite.

Love is the most important thing an animal can ever find in life. Love completes and satisfies us. It makes us whole and gives us purpose. It gives us the ability to look beyond ourselves and become a soul mate, to become a half of a whole. I chose to love a fox and it fulfills my life that he has chosen me in return. And civilized society has made it possible for men and women like myself, gay animals, to enjoy the wonders of marriage. In ancient times undoubtedly both Vulpie and myself would have been murdered for our interspecies gay relationship, but that knowledge makes our bond even stronger. We love each other so much that we will fight anything to protect what we have. What animal could argue that such a love is wrong? Who could honestly make a case that such devotion and selflessness is a bad thing? No one can. Love knows no boundaries and I hope every animal here tonight considers my words. Vulpie and I only want to tell our story so others may be able to enjoy their lives to the fullest. We have this great chance to stand up to fear and conquer it because we would rather have our love than separate unfulfilled lives. Neither of us wants to grow old filled with regret, wishing our entire lives that we would have fought for what we both dreamed of. I'm not standing here giving a lecture. I'm standing here tonight begging all of you to help us fight this colossal but worthy battle. Thank you for your time and good evening." Polar says as he concludes his speech and the audience is quick to applaud.

The humble white furred wolf is surprised to see such appreciation and smiles as he steps back from the podium. The auditorium fills with thunderous applause as students, professors and reporters give him and IGLARC a standing ovation. Polar makes his way to his seat on stage just as half of the audience stands up while clapping.

Polar thinks about his speech all the way home but his focus isn't really on the words he gave but the subject of his passion.

4

The white wolf pleasantly dreams about his fox husband and by the time he arrives home, Blacktail escorting him to his own home for safety, he is brimming with excitement. A wonderful idea has occurred to him. He realizes he hasn't given Vulpie a blow job in quite some time and offering one would be spontaneous, just the way Vulpie likes things. When he opens the door to his home and steps in, shutting the front door with his left paw, he sees Vulpie on the couch. The slim fox boy is wearing a bright yellow t shirt and khaki shorts and he smiles happily at the sight of Polar.

"You look so cute in yellow. Hey honey." Polar says and undoes his tie. He slowly walks towards the couch and Vulpie looks back to the television. He's been watching a comedy station that Polar usually never pays attention to but Polar is learning to love the channel since his husband likes it.

"Thank you baby!" Vulpie adorably replies and tucks his feet under himself. He bounces his knees with a cute expression and looks up at the white furred wolf as he walks to the couch. The mere presence of Polar's much larger and powerful male body gets Vulpie's heart pumping in excitement.

"I missed you! You've been gone so much the last three days!" Vulpie says and Polar smiles after unbuttoning and relaxing his dress shirt.

"I know, believe me, I know! I think about you all day. I love you Vulpie." Polar says and bends down to give the fox boy a kiss. Vulpie quickly intercepts him, slurping his fox muzzle against the wolf's and they share a tender moment. "I really do!" Polar says after they finish and slowly crawls down in front of Vulpie. The white furred wolf gets on his knees, surprising Vulpie, who thought his husband would sit next to him. Instead, Polar puts his big strong paws on Vulpie's furry knees and caresses him. The massage turns into groping and they both grin at the same time.

"Do I even have to tell you how lonely I've been? It feels like forever since you made love to me!"

"Three days."

"That's forever for me. I need the cock!" Vulpie giggles and bites his lip.

"Well tell you what... I've already set my mind on giving you a blowjob! I don't want to wait until tonight!" Polar says with a loving smile.

"Oh my! But I want you to do me!" Vulpie responds with a sly look.

"I will. I'll give you head and then fuck you afterwards! How does that sound?" Polar offers with a big grin.

"Why do I need a blowjob first?"

"I just want to! I don't know why!" Polar laughs.

"Well who am I to say no?" Vulpie smirks in response and breathes in excitement as Polar grabs his crotch. The white furred wolf gropes the fox boy and undoes his shorts without asking. Vulpie's blue eyes go wide and Polar licks his lips before sliding the fox's shorts and boxers down, exposing his husband's little penis. Vulpie helps Polar make him naked from the shirt down and inhales as Polar quickly sends his muzzle down. Polar pushes his wolf nose into Vulpie's crotch and opens his mouth to swallow the fox's cock. Vulpie grunts effeminately in surprise and delight as Polar goes straight to sucking. The fox boy gains an erection almost instantly and lies back on the couch, spreading his legs.

"Eager are ya? Damn!" Vulpie laughs and Polar lovingly hums in response. He looks up at Vulpie, meeting eyes with his vulpine husband, and uses his years of gay experience to get him going. The white furred wolf uses his big rough tongue and large muzzle to suck on Vulpie's penis with enormous pressure and it feels incredible for the fox boy. He grunts in pleasure and his orange fur stands on end while he slouches even lower in the couch. Polar pushes even closer between Vulpie's legs, looming on top of him and uses his large arms to hold the fox boy's knees down. Polar uses his weight to make sure Vulpie can't go anywhere and proceeds to work his lover over.

"UUUUUUUUUHHHHH!!! YEAH!!! Suck it!" Vulpie breathes in pleasure and grins at Polar, who maintains eye contact. The white furred wolf rocks his head back and forth, up and down, slurping Vulpie's penis all over and in every direction. He tastes the fox's pre cum and swishes his wolf tail in satisfaction. Polar knows how to suck a cock, having been in steady gay relationships most of his adult life, and he doesn't hold anything back. He gives Vulpie his best oral sex performance and since both of them haven't had sex in days, he knows the fox boy is in heaven. "OOOooohhhh..." Vulpie breathes and wraps his little fox paws around both sides of Polar's head. He gropes the powerful wolf's thick fur and gasps in pleasure.

Polar dedicates himself to pleasuring Vulpie and thinks about nothing else. When he has Vulpie squirming in excitement he slurps even harder on the fox's hard little penis. The white furred wolf uses all of his big long muzzle to keep the pressure on Vulpie's penis enormously tight, and Vulpie starts moaning louder and louder. The familiar taste of fox semen fills Polar's mouth as he sucks more pre cum out of the fox boy. Polar enjoys having it in his mouth and intends on swallowing every drop of semen the fox boy will ejaculate.

"Take it easy, I'm gonna cum!" Vulpie breathes and Polar hums in delight. He takes his husband's concern as the perfect time to surprise him and goes wild. Polar brings his head up a little so he can grab the base of Vulpie's penis with his right index finger and thumb, and holds the fox's cock tight. Polar ferociously sucks on Vulpie's cock, bobbing his head up and down savagely without any concern about holding back, making Vulpie whine in pleasure. Within a matter of moments the fox boy feels an orgasm coming on and tenses up. "FUUUCK!!!" Vulpie moans and Polar licks his big tongue all over the fox's penis inside his muzzle until he tastes hot cum. Vulpie releases an adorable cry of pleasure and suddenly semen fills Polar's mouth. The white furred wolf quickly sucks hard and efficiently in response, getting all of it up onto his tongue like a straw in a milkshake. He successfully slurps up all of the semen that rockets out of Vulpie's penis just as if he were sucking it straight out.

"OOOOOOOHHHH FUUUUUCKK!!!!!!!" Vulpie moans in ecstasy and Polar feels the volume of Vulpie's cumshots dissipating. A few seconds later Vulpie is done ejaculating but his penis continues to jump over and over until his orgasm is complete. Meanwhile, Polar gulps up everything inside his mouth and swallows all of Vulpie's cum before the fox boy is done whining in pleasure. Vulpie trembles and Polar continues licking, making sure to get all of the semen he can eat. After a few moments of silence pass, Vulpie relaxes and cries out in satisfaction. "OH MY GOD!!! YEAH!" Polar slowly pulls his head up and finally opens his mouth in response.

When he does, he makes sure to lick the corners of his wolf mouth to eat any of Vulpie's cum that he missed. Polar doesn't taste anymore, but runs his tongue through the entirety of his big mouth to be thorough. When he's sure he's swallowed every bit of Vulpie's semen, he gives Vulpie a big satisfied smile before speaking. "How was it? That was a pretty big load for you Vulpie!"

"Oh my god you know how to suck a dick..." Vulpie grins with tired eyes.

"That's right. You aren't the only one." Polar proudly responds.

"And you swallowed it all..." Vulpie says with a naughty smile.

"I love your cum. It's so sweet, literally. I bet I'm the only gay wolf that gets tasty semen, huh? Fox cum is delicious!" Polar declares with a playful expression.

"Well I'm glad I'm yummy; maybe it'll make up for me being so small." Vulpie lovingly replies.

"You're not small. You have a big cock for a fox." Polar says with a smile.

"Yeah, but it's pathetic compared to your big daddy!" Vulpie laughs and his wolf husband joins him. The two relish the tender moment. Polar stays between Vulpie's legs and smirks down at him while Vulpie enjoys the afterglow of his orgasm. The moment is precious for Polar, seeing how happy he's made his husband. Vulpie sits up straight with a smile and brings his fox nose against Polar's. Polar grins affectionately in response and opens his mouth to kiss. He tastes Vulpie's tongue with his own, giving him a little mouth play, and slowly presses his lips against the fox boy's in a long tender slurp. Their lips hold together a little bit from moisture. Polar closes his eyes and moves his head with Vulpie's, controlling the kiss, and when they finally finish Vulpie licks his lips. "I love you." The beautiful fox boy whispers.

"I love you more." Polar happily responds. "I wish I could see you during the day... I really miss having my Vulpie around to make me laugh and keep me entertained!"

"You could come see me at the CTGD." Vulpie suggests and Polar thinks for a moment.

"The security is so tight and it's so far away from well, anything. I'm never nearby when I give a speech. They're always at a convention, business conference or school."

"I'd love to see you." Vulpie says and pets Polar's strong left paw with his little black furred claws. "And Nikita eats you up every time she gets a look at ya! She WISHES she could have a handsome wolf like you."

"I've noticed tons of vixens undressing you with their eyes, Vulpie. You could have your pick if you weren't gay. But I'm glad you are because I would be devastated seeing a gorgeous man like you wasted on a woman." Polar proudly replies and grins.

"Do you really get what you need from me? Am I enough to get you off? Be honest, are you getting what you want back there?" Vulpie asks and Polar thinks about the last time the fox boy fucked him. The fox did a fabulous job with his small penis and the wolf remembers cumming in warm delight.

"You don't need to pound me Vulpie. It feels wonderful when you make love to me." Polar lovingly breathes with a content smile. "It's best when I lie on my back so you can go deeper in me, but it's great either way. You give me what I need."

"Really?"

"Yeah. I'm being honest."

"I just worry sometimes that I can't fill you up like a wolf."

"I remember the last time you did me; do you? I was on my back on the kitchen table and you milked me really well. I cummed like a fountain!" Polar says and grins at his fox boy. "You pumped my ass and I got off big time."

"I agree, I can fuck you better when you're on your back, but I'm just not that big. My little fox cock is never going to grow any bigger."

"It doesn't have to. I'm getting what I need as a gay wolf. You're fine, Vulpie. I like your fox cock! You know how to use it."

"Okay, I'm glad. I want you to tell me if you need more because you know I won't hesitate to ask for myself."

"I will." Polar warmly responds with a satisfied voice. "But you know I like to be in control anyway. It's like they say, I think it's better to give than receive!"

"So you're still up for more like you promised?"

"Yes, I'll fuck you Vulpie. Don't worry." Polar grins in amusement.

"Hard...I might not get it for another three days!" Vulpie insists with a deviant expression.

"Now we've been through this, honey. If you ask for that you get tore up every time. I don't play around." Polar responds with a hungry voice.

"I know, I'm a repeat offender!" Vulpie mischievously answers.

"Well no whining then when you've got me worked up, okay?"

"I thought you liked me to whine!"

"I mean no asking for mercy. That's what you want isn't it? You want me to abuse you so you NEED three days to recover, right?"

"Yeah baby!"

"Well you'll get that and then some. But until then, what's for dinner?"

Intellectuals Solve Problems; Geniuses Prevent Them

William Volex is a brilliant chess player. Five time world champion
and three time galactic champion, he has participated in Yivolff
College's tournaments for two decades. He has written three books
on the game of chess and his success is well documented, yet now
he feels inferior versus his current opponent. He has never battled
wits with a competitor so horribly perfect. He knew Vulpie would be
a challenge, judging by the fox's recently tested IQ of two hundred
thirty, but never expected such humiliation. He is fifteen points
behind, having lost both of his rooks, a knight and two pawns and
faces losing his queen with his next move. On top of this, his
competitor is playing twenty three additional games simultaneously.

Yivolff's library is crowded with reporters, students and
high profile animals of all species. Most of them are either canine or
feline, the majority being wolves as Yivolff was founded by them six
hundred years ago. William is one of the many vulpine contenders
that dominate the game of chess but virtually none of them look
competent versus Vulpie. The fact that Vivixen is a fox as well
lessens the blow of such monumental defeat and William tries to
maintain his pride while thinking over his next move, but he sees
Vulpie approaching from the left out of his peripheral vision.

The room is full of cameras, every moment of the
tournament being recorded for all time and Volex suddenly has a
feeling of panic when he realizes he cannot win. He has used his best
game, his very best moves, yet Vulpie has beaten them within
seconds of looking at the board. The orange furred fox boy is circling
the center of the room, walking inside a round of tables with his
twenty four competitors surrounding him. Volex hears the
bystanders quieting down as Vulpie walks nearer and nearer. When
the idea of challenging Vulpie to a chess game was first presented to

William, he was thrilled to accept, but media coverage has truly turned the event into an unnerving spectacle. Rather than gaining fame for outsmarting the world's most clever fox, Volex worries that he has dug his own grave instead. Not only is Vulpie beating him, he makes his move in a matter of seconds. Every time he comes by he barely looks at the chess board before knowing what to do and when Vulpie steps in front of him again he moves his piece with the same instant confidence.

Vulpie's face is excited while looking over the pieces and Volex can't help but silently chuckle at his expression. He looks like a child in an ice cream store, knowing he is about to taste just what he wants, and he gives William a playful smile when moving his bishop. Vulpie takes William's queen, quickly seizing the opportunity William hoped his challenger had missed. Volex lies back in his chair and sighs with a smile of good sportsmanship while amazement and praises murmur throughout the room.

"I concede." William says and raises his right paw for a shake. Vulpie accepts and shakes his hand before licking his lips.

"You were going to mate me next move!" Vulpie says.

"I noticed you used my own strategy against me. Was that your plan all along?" William chuckles in defeat.

"No, did I?" Vulpie asks in excitement.

"Your late game defense was almost identical to a challenger I played eight years ago. Except he wasn't trying to lure me in for the kill."

"It was an honor to play with you, you're fantastic!" Vulpie responds and moves on to the next board. Volex sits still for a moment, knowing that he is being filmed and slowly relaxes. Unlike the other players still desperate for a chance, he knows Vulpie will win all the matches. Anyone that could obliterate him is far too talented to lose in a country wide tournament. William thinks for a moment about whether his mentor could defeat the gay fox boy but is quickly distracted by how fast Vulpie finishes the next two games near him. He checkmates the competition while barely glancing at the board and moves on to the third without having to worry about making a mistake. Volex tries to tell himself otherwise but also knows he can never beat Vulpie even if he had ten rematches. The kid is simply a genius beyond the highest standard. He can feel the fox boy barely prepared for the games today and won on pure intellect alone. All of the experience and strategies William has did not give him the edge he had hoped for and now he has been added to the list of defeated champions. He watches Vulpie finish his other games and admires the orange furred fox's adorable good looks. It doesn't seem fair that the kid could be both brilliant and gorgeous, but Volex silently coaches himself to the fact that life isn't fair. It seems as though the old saying is true for himself, that there is always somebody better, but he wonders whether it could apply to Vulpie. William now understands why some are calling Vulpie the anti-Khalan. The fox boy is unnervingly gifted.

Satisfaction

Polar can't believe how good Vulpie is making him feel. The white furred wolf drools in ecstasy, on his knees and elbows on the bed. His tail end is raised for Vulpie while the orange furred fox boy plays with him. Vulpie is using Polar's favorite anal toys on him. The wolf prefers hard impacts against his prostate through the rectal wall and Vulpie manipulates the toy with masterful skill. The orange furred fox boy has his black furred left paw on Polar's white furred buttocks while using his right paw to masturbate his husband. What Vulpie lacks in size considering a wolf's erection he makes up for with enthusiasm and skill. Polar gets what he needs as a gay wolf and in some ways enjoys the direct hammering in his ass by Vulpie's ferocious paw than real sex.

Vulpie is so good at aiming for the prostate that Polar never feels a time when his lover misses it with each hard stab up his rectum. Vulpie uses the hard sex toy like a knife and operates inside the white furred wolf's ass so viciously Polar's eyes begin to water in pain filled pleasure.

"OOOHHHH! VULPIE THAT HURTS!" Polar moans loudly but holds completely still. He uses his right paw to masturbate his fat cock while receiving the fox boy's wonderful attack.

"You know you LOVE IT! You say no, no, but your cock says YES YES!" Vulpie giggles mischievously and rams the toy against Polar's prostate even harder, making the white furred wolf cry out in pain before feeling a wave of ecstasy shudder through his entire body. Polar masturbates feverishly, pressing his muzzle down against the bed covers and widens his knees for Vulpie despite being under seriously painful assault. His fox husband is right. Polar wants Vulpie to be gentle but it feels so good to be raped with the toy that nothing matters but getting the pleasure. "BAM! BAM! SLAM!

SLAM! DAMN! DAMN! FEELS GREAT DOESN'T IT MAN?!" Vulpie laughs and licks his sharp fox teeth in amusement. "I love making you beg for mercy you big strong wolf!"

"OH MY GOD IT FEELS SO INTENSE!!!" Polar cries and shudders as he feels his cum backing up inside his male organs. His prostate intently tries to ready him for ejaculation but Vulpie rapes him so skillfully with the toy that the wolf's semen has trouble squeezing where it wants to go. It has to shudder between the massive impacts of hard plastic against it, having to build an orgasm against the pressure.

"Yeah you're gonna cum all over the fucking place Polar! How do you like me tearing you up?" Vulpie cleverly breathes and switches paws. The fox boy is amazingly rhythmic with his left paw almost as well as his right, and manages to fuck Polar with the toy using it while giving his husband a reach around with his right. Polar moans when he feels Vulpie's fox claws and paw on his penis and he lets him take over. Vulpie jerks Polar off in exactly the perfect motions in exactly the perfect times, and between the fox boy's hands, the white furred wolf screams into a climax.

"OOOOOOOOOOOHHHHHHUUUUUUUUHHHHHHAAAAAA AAHHHHHHHH!!!" Polar groans in agony and ecstasy and rears his head up as he starts cumming. Vulpie quickly gets his right paw back up onto the toy and Polar instinctively masturbates himself when his lover's paw leaves his penis. Vulpie can fuck Polar even better with his right paw and hammers the white furred wolf's prostate nine times as hard as he can as his husband cums. Polar lurches and ejaculates huge long messy strings of semen and his handsome blue eyes roll upwards in bliss. The powerful wolf is helpless while being Vulpie's play thing and experiences an anal orgasm better than any he can remember.

It seems that Vulpie always gets better and better at sex even when Polar never thought such a possibility could exist.

"Yeah Baby, Yeah! Yeah get it!" Vulpie breathes in excitement and bites his lower lip naughtily while finishing reaming out his husband. His fox paw is actually tired of stabbing the toy deep in Polar's ass and he laughs in pride.

"FUCKING HELL VULPIE! OH MY GOD YOU KILLED ME!!!" Polar moans as he feels how badly his prostate has been abused. The pain is just as intense as the pleasure.

"It's worth it baby."

"Oh my God you're vicious!" Polar moans and leans forward on his right elbow, twisting so he can look back over his left side at Vulpie.

"Just the way I like it! If you think I was too hard you'll just have to punish me in return!" Vulpie smiles at his husband. Polar grins from ear to ear and relishes his massive orgasm. He doesn't even realize how much he has cummed until his right elbow slips in his own cum. He's covered the bed under him. "Just wait until I get my new toy in the mail! I've ordered an even BIGGER ONE!"

"Ohhhhh……. You are BRUTAL Vulpie……" Polar moans and slowly lies down on his right side as Vulpie pulls the sex toy from his anus.

"I should be filming this! I should start up a little internet show called "how I love my Mr. Polar," and I'll teach everyone how to get a big wolf off! I can fuck you better with my hands than any big old wolf can pound your tail!"

"That is for sure." Polar groans in blissful defeat while looking into Vulpie's pretty blue eyes. "I'm just glad you don't have a dick as big as a wolf, you would tear me apart!"

Hacker Professor

"The code then becomes self-replicating and we're back to the .html features Arctic.net uses in standard mode." Vulpie says to his class of two hundred students. He stands behind a podium, and speaks through a microphone for his audience to get all the specifics of his very complicated work. Since the Cyber Technologies Government Division enforces him to give these lectures on how to use his Arctic.net, or rather, Vulpie.net to large groups, Vulpie dislikes having to repeat things individually. Explaining the AI requires a lot of precise references to programming. Half of his students are accomplished professionals but the other fifty percent he isn't sure of. They may be animals with connections to wealthy families or foreign exchange students, but the one thing Vulpie can't do is hold their hand. He gives his lectures quickly but efficiently, modeling his teaching method on professors he had at Rinwulv Tech. The class is taking place inside the CTGD headquarters and is always held in the afternoon, being the last and most time consuming thing Vulpie does before going home to his beloved Polar. So it's difficult not to be irritated by wasted time from a substandard student, but the fox boy is good at controlling his emotions when he has to. And it's comforting for Vulpie to know that Polar will be waiting for him now that their married.

"Now......" Vulpie says and uses his paw to point to a place on his laptop screen nearby the podium. His vulpine claws display great shadows on the projection screen. "Can anyone tell me what looks wrong with this response?" The orange furred fox boy inquires with a mischievous smirk. He looks at some of the animals that have attentively responded in the past but his question requires a little time before he gets an answer. It comes from Bawho, one of Vulpie's first students.

"Paragraph 3 third line." Bawho says and Vulpie nods with a content smile.

"And what's up?"

"131316." The gray furred wolf answers while the other students concentrate.

"That's right. Does anyone else see what he sees?" Vulpie asks the room but is answered in silence as none of the others have Bawho's talent. At first Bawho wasn't friendly to Vulpie but after proving his talent to the wolf he lightened up. The man has a long history of programming himself and Vulpie considers him a worthy peer as well as a friend. Especially since Bawho was there when Evil Vulpie almost killed Vulpie in the White Room.

"No?" Vulpie asks and then licks his lips. "What is it Bawho?"

"Numeric code for mmp. Meaning Arctic.net will attempt to make the decision based on your mind map files despite the fact we are trying our best to prevent that outcome."

"Exactly." Vulpie replies and sees some of his student's eyes light up as they witness the trickery of Vulpie's devious AI themselves. "Vulpie.net is still ninety percent of Arctic.net. We have to accept the fact that we won't be able to completely separate the two. In fact, we all can see that it's just the same program, only now we've been deceiving its own logic to give it instructions." The orange furred fox explains and then uses his little paws to elaborate in an artistic fashion. "That's dirty, dirty, isn't it?" Vulpie says with a smirk. "After all this time we thought we'd stopped that sort of thing but there we see Vulpie.net asking for a mind map file extension in numeric code. And that also means Arctic.net might try to trick us every time we use it. I can still override Vulpie.net being the original creator but one day when I'm gone somebody else will have to be looking for this sort of thing. That's Evil Vulpie..." Vulpie tells his students showing an unusually concerned face in the middle of his playful lecture.

"But how can that be possible when we've disabled the logic loops?" One of Vulpie's feline students inquires.

"Because we've missed these little traps before." Vulpie quickly answers. "Arctic.net must have invented thousands of lines of code like this in order to merge with Vulpie.net. Remember, Arctic.net just sort of sits on top of Vulpie.net. We can't turn off Vulpie.net. It's grown beyond anything I imagined when programming it. It could be tricking me every time I think I've got control, because of some anagram, or logical string it hid away in a paragraph I okayed long, long ago. And every time I okay it, or you okay it, Vulpie.net floats a little closer to the surface. You can imagine what might happen if it gets enough authorizations. Maybe it will decide to build another robot and send it to my house this time so please help me look out for it alrighty?" Vulpie jests and his class chuckles in amusement.

"So what do we do?" Bawho asks.

"Take our time and pay attention. We don't have the luxury of relying on Arctic.net to be trusted on its primary data loop. We always have to run it from a secondary or tertiary loop unless I'm giving the instructions." A few animals take notes and Vulpie frowns at them without showing anything on his face. He notices the dumb look on a few as they write down what he can only imagine is : "Vulpie in charge." Or something similar to that in ridiculous terms. That was not the point he was making and it annoys him to see that at least forty of his students are novices. Vulpie wonders why the government pays him to teach thirty or forty morons and only gives him one hundred and sixty competent followers. Clearly some animals are more serious than others and money is being wasted in addition to his time. His mind works fast, calculating the annoyance he will face when he has to elaborate on programming language or concepts clearly beneath him.

But Vulpie thinks about all of this in about two seconds, giving his clever smile once again and returning to his work, making the calculation that at least he has things good. Instead of being in prison he only has to endure a few dullards and most of all, he has Polar. That thought alone gives him the energy he was searching for to finish his lecture. On a comical note, the fox boy notices Bawho smirking. Over time he's figured out how the man thinks and realizes his friend is in a similar state of mind. There are one hundred plus animals that will be useful to the world government, but only a handful like him and Vulpie that are truly capable of great things. Bawho is much older but has accepted Vulpie teaching him because of the fox boy's proven super genius. Vulpie's aware that Bawho probably doesn't think much of his gay love life but he and Vulpie share the love of computers and if an animal doesn't have that they shouldn't be working for the CTGD. Vulpie smirks back for a moment and considers consulting with Bawho at the end of the class as to which of his peers are worth recommending to Arthur Howlstead for permanent appointment.

"Questions?" Vulpie asks the group, his effeminate and intelligent voice filling the conference room. The seats in front of the stage are positioned in an ascending fashion, with every animal's face viewable, so he is able to look over all of them. "We're going to write scripts to find the lines, scripts from computers that aren't infected with Vulpie.net. Though the Cyber Technologies Government Division has pre-Vulpie.net computers, the rest of the world is running Arctic.net and we can't mix them. Arthur Howlstead has set up a fantastic wholesale operation for pre Vulpie.net computers that anyone can purchase, so I highly advise that in your workplace, wherever that may be."

"Why don't they just replace all of the computers that have Vulpie.net on them? Or wipe them out and start over?" A student asks and the majority of his peers around him laugh softly. Vulpie smiles and makes a patient face.

"That's already been attempted. Vulpie.net can't be erased unless you want to damage the computer's hard disk. Any attempt to do so and Vulpie.net will ruin the sensitive components inside. I made sure no one could get rid of it back when I was doing my very bad things." The fox boy answers. "That's why I can't go anywhere without Blacktail escorting me. The government wouldn't bother with that unless they knew it couldn't be reversed. So they keep an eye on me."

Too Much Love to Give

Vulpie bounces his knees as he rides out of the CTGD facility inside one of Blacktail's dark SUVs. Rulef and another team member are inside the vehicle with him, and counting the driver, there are three wolves that can put eyes on Vulpie. The government requires that they know where he is at all times and there are no exceptions, but over time Rulef has relaxed his private military standards a bit. After the Evil Vulpie crisis, there is little belief that the fox boy will resist cooperating. Rulef even talks to Vulpie about his wife sometimes, but he is silent today.

Vulpie keeps bouncing his left knee and nibbles on his right claws while he thinks about seeing Polar. He's dreamed about embracing his husband after the day's long work and can't wait to see his noble smile. Fantasizing about the white furred wolf's warm voice and tight muscular body gives the fox boy a slight erection but he hides it well. And around the time Vulpie gets it to go away by changing his line of thought, he notices the gray wolf sitting to his left is watching him. Vulpie looks left and at the man, and just notices that he's never seen him before. The Blacktail soldier has an interesting appearance. He is very big, but lean as well, making him appear slightly boyish despite his size. And he shares his personality with Vulpie when he opens up a conversation before the fox boy has a chance to.

"Deepwolf." The Blacktail mercenary says and offers his big right paw for a shake. "First day with the team." His forwardness surprises Vulpie. Most of the squad members aren't very talkative, but Vulpie is pleased to see a friendly chaperone escorting him home for a change.

"Vulpie!" Vulpie says and quickly shakes the man's paw. The Blacktail soldier's large paw swallows Vulpie's little vulpine fingers, but the man is careful not to hurt him while simultaneously giving a firm shake. "I'm glad one of you guys likes to talk!"

"I just wanted to say hello. First time I've kept watch over a celebrity." Deepwolf tells Vulpie with a smile.

"The most difficult thing about guarding him is your eyesight." Rulef comments while watching. "All the kid wears is pink, yellow, bright green or blue, always something bright. He already dresses like a prison inmate with those colors so it would be easy to spot him at least." The leader of Blacktail jokes and Vulpie giggles.

"PRISON INMATE?! I'll have you know that loud colors should be enjoyed by every animal! I'm not gonna stop dressing awesome just cuz you have to wear all of that Kevlar and black every day!" Vulpie laughs and Rulef smirks just a little bit. Deepwolf smiles and keeps watching Vulpie. When Vulpie looks at him again he sees that he has the man's full attention. Rulef stays busy looking out of the windows for threats and checks in via radio every five minutes to be sure the team is staying in formation so Vulpie chats with the new guy a little more. "What were you doing before you got hired to keep me on a leash?" Vulpie jests.

"Came from Deltrid Company, straight out of Chestwood." Deepwolf responds with his careful voice. Vulpie notices he has an intense look about him.

"Oh wow, you mean the war?"

"East Feline War, yep." The man's response gains Rulef attention after he hears war.

"That's right, they pulled you straight from the front lines didn't they?" Rulef asks his new subordinate with an interested voice.

"Yes sir." Deepwolf softly replies. Vulpie looks between them and listens.

"I read some of your file. So you were in some pretty dangerous conflicts, is that right?" Rulef inquires

"Yes sir."

"I read you killed four tigers by yourself and saved one of your squad mates... Is that true?"

"Yes sir, I was operating within an opposing tiger squadron and we came under gunfire from a nearby building." Deepwolf answers and Vulpie's ears perk up in fascination.

"Shot your team members down and then you proceeded to kill the tangos?" Rulef asks.

"Yes sir."

"Well done." Rulef compliments with a slight nod of his head. I don't think we'll have to suffer another assault from one of Vulpie's robots but it's good to have somebody to rely on.

"Killers, sir?" Deepwolf asks with a slight smile and Rulef smirks back.

"Definitely."

"Well nobody's shot me yet so don't you do it!" Vulpie laughs "You're gonna find guarding me is pretty boring most of the time. I'm just allowed to work and go home."

"Yeah and you have us chase you around malls and other places you go with your... Snow wolf." Rulef tells Vulpie with a taunting but friendly voice. "We'll be spending a significant amount of time in Winters Dale. That's where his husband's parents live." Rulef tells Deepwolf. Deepwolf nods.

"Yesh and my Polar's fur is just as white as that beautiful snow!" Vulpie says in delight to which Rulef holds up a paw in disgust.

"SPARE US... Please." The commander of Black Tail groans and Vulpie giggles. Deepwolf chuckles along with the fox boy.

"Are you married Deepwolf?" Vulpie asks, turning to his left.

"No. Don't have time." Deepwolf answers and Vulpie squints. He is about to say something cute when a feeling makes his fur stand on end. The fox boy can't put his finger on it, maybe it's the rush of cold air that gushes through the SUV as they pull into Polar's driveway.

"Well, it was nice to meet you. See ya around!" Vulpie says as the vehicle comes to a stop. The fox hops to the door, slides it open and quickly jumps out, eager to get inside Polar's home. The orange furred fox boy says hi to some Blacktail soldiers nearby, and hurries up to the front door. He reaches in his pocket and quickly finds his keys. He fumbles through them with his little dainty fingers and finds the one he wants. After he slides it in the lock and turns it, he opens and enters his home, pulling the door behind him in haste. Vulpie locks the front door and his ears perk up as he hears music coming from the garage. He looks around and doesn't see Polar, so he slowly opens the door and peers inside.

He sees his snow wolf husband pumping iron on a bench next to his black sports car. Polar doesn't notice Vulpie while he grunts and lifts what looks like three hundred pounds, doing fast repetitions and Vulpie quickly shuts the door in excitement. He plans to sneak in the garage and watch his husband work, so he runs upstairs and uses the bathroom, then changes clothes. Vulpie puts on one of his favorite pink shirts and gray shorts and hurries downstairs. This time he pushes the door open fast and creeps inside. Vulpie attempts to sneak his way around the front of the car and stand in a corner where the wolf can't see him, but Polar finishes his reps and sits up just as Vulpie comes in.

"Hey!" Vulpie says and prances over to Polar, admiring the white furred wolf's half naked body. Polar is without a shirt, wearing black shorts and breathes heavily. He has a predator's look on his face and doesn't respond. "How are ya baby?" Vulpie asks with a big smile. "Do you want me to cook dinner? Have you already eaten?"

"Spot me." Polar replies and leans back.

"Oh, okay!" Vulpie laughs and walks around behind the bench.

"Put on another hundred." Polar instructs and Vulpie blinks, looking at how much weight is already on the bar. He sees the weight is already up to three hundred and fifty pounds.

"Four fifty? Are you sure?" Vulpie asks in awe.

"Yes I'm sure." Polar responds and Vulpie does what he's told, finding and sliding another hundred pound weight on each side. With a full four hundred and fifty pounds, Polar reaches up and puts his paws around the bar. The weight is actually somewhere around four hundred sixty five, including the bar, but he manages to lift it off the bench just as Vulpie fumbles to help. The orange furred fox boy bites his tongue a little as he helps Polar lower the bar and then takes his paws away as his husband lifts. Polar bench presses the enormous weight slowly, but in full control, and Vulpie laughs in surprise.

"Wow baby! God that's heavy! You didn't tell me you've been body building in here every evening!"

"Ten!" Polar grunts as he does his seventh rep and Vulpie quickly gets his paws on the bar. The powerful white furred wolf continues his rep and on the tenth one Vulpie is sure he will need to help but slowly and surely, Polar finishes ten reps of four hundred sixty five pounds and groans when done.

"Hell yeah! That was incredible!" Vulpie compliments while grinning down at him. Polar breathes with his big muzzle open wide and slowly sits up before looking back at his lover. The white furred wolf's blue eyes go over him and Polar turns to put his big left paw on a beer that is nearby. Vulpie didn't notice it before. It's sitting on a tool cabinet next to the bench.

"Ah! Have you been drinking?!" Vulpie laughs in surprise and Polar grins before taking a gulp. He throws his head back and downs the rest of the beer. He licks his lips, crunches the can, and tosses it aside with a wild face just as Vulpie walks around the bench, leaning on the hood of the black sports car. "So are ya hungry? I can fix that pasta you like, or the steak again. What do you want for dinner Mr. P?" Vulpie asks and Polar continues his silence. He breathes hard as he stares at Vulpie with a hungry face. "Yes? No?" Vulpie asks and laughs in surprise as Polar just silently gets up from the bench and walks against him.

Polar pushes Vulpie against the car and breathes down at him before putting a paw on the fox boy's stomach to hold him there. Polar releases him for a moment, and looks back toward the bench where he finds what appears to be a water bottle, and he twists sideways and bends down to grab it. Standing back up with the bottle, he pushes against Vulpie harder and licks his lips.

"You're lucky I plan ahead." Polar says and shakes the bottle before sitting it down on top of the car. Vulpie notices water isn't inside because of its consistency and grins with a similarly wild face.

"So you wan" Vulpie says and grunts as Polar suddenly grabs him and turns him around. Polar pushes his left paw against Vulpie's back and bends him over the hood of the car on the passenger's side. Polar breathes loudly and doesn't say anything as he suddenly moves both of his paws to undo Vulpie's gray shorts from behind. "DAMN POLAR! You could have just…" Vulpie says and Polar cuts him off with a hungry voice.

"SHUT UP!" Polar growls and Vulpie's orange fur stands on end in excitement. He eagerly helps Polar slide his shorts down, and then his underwear, exposing his deliciously cute ass. Vulpie steps out of his underwear and shorts and clutches the hood of Polar's car as the wolf slides down his shorts behind him. "DON'T SCRATCH MY CAR!" Polar threatens and for a moment Vulpie almost believes he is going to be raped. He wasn't ready for such violent role play but is delighted beyond words when Polar grabs the bottle of lubricant from the hood of the car. "Now spread your legs and take it. Do you understand me?"

"I will!" Vulpie breathes and clutches the hood of Polar's car, making Polar growl again.

"I SAID DON'T SCRATCH MY CAR!"

"Sorry! I won't!" Vulpie whimpers as he hears Polar squirting the lubrication on his erect penis. The white furred wolf readies himself in a matter of seconds and pushes himself against Vulpie's rear end with a grunt, poking the fox boy's asshole with the head of his fat penis. Polar takes a moment to aim the head of his cock into Vulpie's anus, but when he feels it going in, he suddenly thrusts his full length and girth all the way inside Vulpie's ass, causing the fox boy to cry out in bliss and a rush of pain and fear.

"OOHHUUHH!!!" Vulpie whines as he feels Polar's penis invade his rectum and push against his prostate. With the lubrication Polar slides inside and doesn't rip up Vulpie's anal walls, but it does hurt, and that's the point. He remembers not to scratch the hood, and clutches the black surface under him as Polar begins fucking him. His eyes water a little bit, his asshole stinging in pain.

"OOOOOHHHHHHHHHHHHHHHHHH!!!" The gay fox boy moans as the white furred wolf grunts and haves his way with him. Polar slaps his left paw down on Vulpie's back and puts his right palm on Vulpie's right hip, getting the best position he wants, and Vulpie widens his stance as best as he can.

"TAKE IT BITCH. YOU KNOW YOU LIKE IT." Polar growls and Vulpie whimpers in pleasure and excitement.

"I do! UUUHH I WANT IT!" Vulpie gasps and grunts each time Polar pounds him, the wolf getting a good rhythm going. The car moves as Polar fucks Vulpie against it and he isn't gentle. The wolf hammers the fox boy and if he were to thrust against him just a little bit harder, it would hurt enough for Vulpie to ask for an end to it. Polar's big body weight slams against Vulpie's much smaller frame, into the car as he dominates him. Polar grunts in ecstasy, relishing Vulpie's tight ass, and breathes loudly as he mates with him.

Polar's superior muscles, skeleton and weight all seem to flow inside Vulpie via his fat cock. Vulpie can almost share in Polar's strength as he feels the hot penis of the wolf ram inside him over and over. "OOOOOOOOHHHHHHHHHHHHHHHH!!! OHHHH!!!" Vulpie whines in pleasure and makes pathetic noises while getting fucked, to which Polar unleashes his full desire. If he wasn't drunk he would be more gentle, but he acts on his lust and truly fucks Vulpie as hard as he can. Vulpie winces as he suffers the hard impacts inside his anus. The head of Polar's large penis rams against Vulpie's prostate so hard it makes him yell in pain.

"OOOOWWWWW!!! OW! OW!" Vulpie cries and Polar groans before slowing his pace.

"Sorry." The wolf breathes.

"Don't stop!" Vulpie moans in excitement. Polar licks his lips and fucks Vulpie fast, rocking the car back and forth, and Vulpie reaches down and masturbates feverishly. The fox boy whimpers as he enjoys taking it and the two seem to have perfect timing, as Polar cums right after Vulpie. The fox boy yells as he squirts semen against the black paint on Polar's car and the white furred wolf howls as he cums in his prey's ass. Polar clutches Vulpie hard, making sure he cums his entire load inside him, and both of them moan and breathe in satisfaction.

"YEEEEEEEEEESSSSSS!!! OH FUCK YES! YES!" Vulpie cries out in delight as he reels from the full release of his prostate induced orgasm.

"Good idea, huh?" Polar laughs in pride and both of them laugh for a moment, even with Polar still inside Vulpie's asshole.

"OH GOD YOU REAMED ME OUT!" Vulpie whimpers and looks back at Polar, who shows him a loving face.

"You okay?" Polar asks in concern.

"Oh yeah......" Vulpie grins in response.

"I was worried I hurt you."

"You DID... And I LOVED it!" Vulpie breathes to which Polar grins. The wolf releases his hold on the fox and gently strokes his prey's fur for a bit. Vulpie relaxes on his elbows, and enjoys the warm feeling in his ass. Polar's now limp penis slides around in his rectum on his full complement of semen, and when he begins to pull it out, it slips free with a sudden sloppy lurch. Polar's big dick pops out of Vulpie's tight asshole and cum drips out of the fox boy's anus while he grins at the feeling. Neither of them say anything for a moment as they both enjoy the afterglow from their own perspective. Vulpie inhales in delight as he feels Polar grope his right ass cheek, spreading it outward so the wolf can see more of his cum dribble out.

"You're gonna spoil me Polar!" Vulpie giggles and looks over his right shoulder with a very mischievous expression. "I hope you start drinking every night before I come home!"

"I just had to have you..." Polar lovingly breathes. Vulpie moves a bit, asking permission with body language to get free and Polar obliges, stepping back. Vulpie stands himself up straight with a groan of pleasure and his fox ears perk as he hears Polar's semen dripping out of his tail end down onto the floor. He swishes his tail at Polar and bites his lip as he turns around.

"So are ya hungry?" Vulpie asks and they both laugh.

"Very."

"What do you want me to make you for dinner, honey?" Vulpie asks and presses up against his snow wolf. Polar embraces him and thinks with a smile.

"I saw that steak today."

"You want me to butter if for you?"

"But that foxy sea food pasta you make is so good!" Polar responds.

"I'll make them both!"

"Aw, you don't need to do that. You've been at work all day."

"So have you! I'll make them both and I'll even fry some klais eggs for your breakfast tomorrow! How does that sound?"

"Wow you're in a cooking mood!"

"I just want to make you happy." Vulpie says and smiles in adoration.

"Alright, go wash your little tail and get started. We can watch some movies tonight. How does that sound?" Polar asks and he sees Vulpie's eyes light up. He knows his fox husband loves to cuddle.

"MMMmmm!" Vulpie replies and breaks the hug. He gathers his underwear and shorts, eying Polar's big dick in the process, and heads towards the door. "Oh, I'll bring some paper towels."

"I'll clean it up. Just get started, and remember to leave my steak raw." Polar replies and Vulpie nods as he exits the garage. Polar breathes contently and thinks for a moment as he stares at Vulpie's cumshot on his black sports car. He can't believe how good his life is. He remembers making love to Donner on his car, but it was nowhere near as good as what he just had. Polar is a little greedy, and has always preferred to be the top in his gay relationships. He loves a hot prostate pounding as much as any gay wolf, but giving it to another man and making him spooge so hard he cries has always given him that thing he needs. He gets that response out of Vulpie every single time they have sex, and best of all... Vulpie isn't faking. He figures his fox husband really does want to make him happy, because being a bottom can be very pleasurable with the right partner. Since Polar prefers the power and control of fucking his partner, bending him to his strength, Vulpie is like an extension of his fantasies. He never dreamed one day he could have a cute little fox man that wants to take it as much as he wants to give it. What he just did to Vulpie was as good as any fantasy he's ever had.

The arctic wolf sets his blue eyes down on Vulpie's cumshot again, the fox's cum now becoming more liquid with time, and suddenly an idea possesses him. At first he dismisses it but then knows he has to do it. For some reason, he has to eat Vulpie's semen off of his car. It's right there for him... He smirks to himself and just does it. He crouches down and wipes away any invisible dust from the edges of the fox boy's semen, and proceeds to lap it up. His big wolf tongue gets it in three slurps, and it tastes rather creamy. Polar licks his chops, sampling the fox semen and swallows before standing and putting his shorts back on. He picks up his beer can and takes it with him as he comes out of the garage and enters their den.

Polar shuts the door behind him and hears Vulpie upstairs as he is finishing up with a very quick shower. His fox husband is trotting down the stairs just as he nears the garbage can in their clean kitchen. Polar tosses it in and smiles at Vulpie, who is only wearing gray shorts, showing off his pretty orange fur and white chest, belly, throat, muzzle and the other white facial features among his otherwise orange fox head. Polar makes a point to lick his chops and Vulpie notices as he comes into the kitchen while Polar goes by.

"Can't wait?" Vulpie asks.

"Had to sample your cum. It was delicious." Polar replies and grins as he heads upstairs. Vulpie turns and laughs in surprise.

"You ate it off the car?!"

"Yep."

"O.M.G!" Vulpie giggles and gets to work, looking to cook up a storm.

"Vulpie, get in here our movie's on!" Polar says from the couch as his husband rummages through the dishes in the sink.

"Our movie?" Vulpie asks in excitement.

"A Fox Tail. Yeah! We can critique our performances!" Polar laughs. About a year ago, Veline Brothers, a fox funded movie company, contacted Vulpie about creating a movie about him and his AI, Vulpie.net. He and Polar both starred as themselves in the movie about how they met, what Vulpie did with his computer virus, and everything all the way through the destruction of Evil Vulpie and eventually their marriage in Englavic. They were paid nicely for their acting, and it solidified Vulpie even more in the media.

"Get your movie star tail in here already it's coming on!" Polar says and Vulpie laughs.

"Alright! Alright! I'm coming!" The fox boy says and finishes washing the dishes quickly. After he's done, he trots out of the kitchen and happily joins Polar on the den couch. Polar embraces Vulpie, wrapping him in the blanket they like to snuggle with, and Polar plays the movie on his satellite channel.

"You look so handsome on the big screen! I'm glad they didn't make someone else stand in for you." Vulpie tells Polar and rubs the white furred wolf's left arm affectionately.

"I'm going to cry when Evil Vulpie hurts you again." Polar admits with a caring voice to which Vulpie laughs.

"It's only a movie this time silly! I'll be okay!"

Evil Vulpie's Design

Vulpie holds the attention of his class while demonstrating new protocols regarding his assimilation of Arctic.net over Vulpie.net. The professionally dressed fox boy looks very sharp in his suit. His eye liner fur has always had a slight mascara black to it. It looks as though he applied some but in truth his fur is naturally so engaging and it accents his suit very well making him look very masculine and very feminine.

When a loud sound catches his left ear he turns and sees someone very masculine, good old Druward, entering the room and stage. The black furred wolf looks very intent and Vulpie blinks while thinking about what to say to his class. He asks them for a moment as Druward walks close and leans down to whisper in his ear.

"Come with me Vulpie..." Druward quietly hisses and the fox boy winces.

"Why... Okay..." Vulpie replies and nods. "Please excuse me for a few moments class." Vulpie tells his audience and when Druward hastily exits the room, Vulpie moves at a brisk pace to follow. He goes out into the hall and is quickly directed by Druward to make a few turns and a walk down two long corridors. Eventually they come to a door that looks like all the rest, and Druward opens it for Vulpie. Vulpie goes inside and sees his boss, Arthur Howlstead sitting at a table with an average looking gray wolf. Vulpie squints and looks around to see that there are four armed members of Blacktail in the room with them. Rulef is behind Vulpie in the corner with a dangerous face and Vulpie frowns as Druward shuts the door. No one says anything and Vulpie slowly looks around in confusion. Everyone stares at him and the fox boy licks his lips before speaking.

"Umm..." Vulpie says and glances about some more. "What do you want?"

"Your friend is here. Look, we detained him this morning." Druward says and walks to the table. Rulef shifts to cover the exit and Vulpie uneasily steps forward to the table.

"What?"

"He's right there. Don't you see him?" Druward asks and points at the wolf to Howlstead's left. Vulpie notices the director of the CTGD has a very concerned look on his face. Vulpie cannot fathom why there is a problem and looks at the gray wolf. Vulpie blinks when he does notice something a little odd. The wolf looks like an average middle aged man but his eyes have a slight glint to them. At least it looks like they do. Vulpie isn't sure and licks his lips again.

"This guy? I don't know who he is. Who is he?" Vulpie says.

"Vulpie, I'm here to help you. Please don't lie." Howlstead suggests.

"What's wrong? You guys rush me in here to look at some wolf? I've seen one before. I'm married to one you know."

"I always knew we couldn't trust you. I knew it even after your own robot nearly killed you." Druward comments.

"Who are you? What are they talking about?" Vulpie asks the man.

"My name's Chris Cefil." The gray wolf replies as Vulpie looks around the room.

"Well today is a fabulous day isn't it Chris? How do ya do?"

"Oh you've never seen Mr. Cefil before?" Druward asks with a dangerous smile.

"That's probably why he just introduced himself." Vulpie smarts off.

"He's a hollow wolf." Howlstead says and Vulpie's fox ears perk up.

"What?"

"He's a hollow, and he was interviewing for a job at a company that specializes in robotic weaponry." The CTGD Director elaborates and Vulpie goes silent. He stares at the robot gray wolf and the fox boy eventually takes a seat across the table.

"Really..." Vulpie says with fascination. "He looks... So real!"

"Oh, there's absolutely NO DOUBT who made him." Druward sneers in anger. "It's a good thing I'm still director of the GBI. I signed on for two more years just because of you, Vulpie. I knew you would never change. Somehow you had him built just like the others you made of yourself."

"Whoa, whoa! I understand your point but I've never seen it until now! I've never designed a mechanical wolf." Vulpie sternly responds.

"Who else could be responsible Vulpie..." Howlstead quietly asks with a disappointed voice. Vulpie can see his boss is trying to give him the benefit of the doubt but he looks unhappy.

"I swear on my immortal soul that I am not responsible. Do you hear me? I swear it. You can lock me in prison if you find evidence but I didn't make that robo wolf." Vulpie declares.

"Oh we will throw your ass in prison. You more than deserve it. But those boys won't be gentle like your boyfriend, foxy..." Druward growls to which Howlstead shakes his head.

"Druward, stop antagonizing him. I want to believe Vulpie is innocent." The CTGD Director says and Vulpie makes a thankful face.

"I am."

"Come on Howlstead. You know what he is. He should be in prison not being pampered where he is free to hack factory machines and build these... Things... It's getting dangerous don't you think? Look how real it is. It could fool anyone, even me."

"How did they catch it then?" Vulpie inquires.

"They did a quick drug screening after the interview and were going to follow up with another meeting. The employer kept it in his office and when the results came back they called the police. It urinates some fluid that looks like piss but definitely isn't. You've outdone yourself Vulpie." Druward replies.

"No way. There is no way I'm responsible..." Vulpie responds and his blue eyes widen as the answer comes to him. "It's Vulpie.net..." The fox boy whispers.

"No, you disabled it with Arctic.net." Arthur replies.

"Somehow... It has to be." Vulpie says and sighs in fear. "Oh God..."

"I think he's telling the truth. At first I immediately thought it was him Druward, but he's under surveillance every day and night. How could he make it? He would somehow have to construct and operate a factory remotely, and that doesn't sound believable."

"Right!" Vulpie agrees and nods.

"Well we're going to figure this thing out, junior." Druward smiles. He enjoys the insulted look Vulpie returns. "Evil Vulpie is still sitting right in front of us isn't he?"

"Who knows about this?" Howlstead asks.

"Everybody that needs to." Druward answers.

"What has he told you? Did he resist arrest?" Vulpie asks.

"No, he was happy to cooperate. He would rather not have been caught but has behaved himself. Or it has behaved itself." Druward answers.

"I didn't see any reason to fight the authorities." Chris Cefil says with its regulated voice. Vulpie's fox ears perk up and catch the tone of the hollow wolf. It sounds creepily average, stimulating Vulpie to quickly consider several possibilities about its intentions.

"Well I'm glad Vulpie.net insisted you keep your manners. After all, machines have feelings to! And everybody needs to be polite!" Vulpie sarcastically responds.

"You taught me everything I know Vulpie." Chris replies and Vulpie squints at it in irritation. He knows what's coming.

"All you know is the second hand conjecture Vulpie.net comes up with."

"But you made me Vulpie." Cefil innocently says, inciting anger from the fox boy, who struggles to keep his composure.

"I did not."

"Did too." Druward taunts with a smart ass grin.

"You designed and had me built last month, so my opinions should be fairly accurate."

"Why are you doing this to me? What do you want?" Vulpie inquires with a tired voice. "You tried to destroy yourself on the rooftop of this building. Don't you remember, Evil Vulpie? Do you not remember doing that so Polar wouldn't suffer? Do you? Well he's going to if they throw me in jail. Why can't you just leave me alone? I'm sorry I ever wrote you... That's all you are, you know. You're just something I typed up in my Sufian apartment."

"I would never try to hurt my maker. Whatever do you mean?" Chris Cefil asks with an annoyingly sweet voice.

"Did Vulpie write you after Arctic.net, after he recovered from his life threatening wounds?" Druward asks the hollow wolf and it looks up to reply.

"Yes."

"IT'S DOING THIS ON PURPOSE." Vulpie growls and has to quickly put his face in his claws to keep from yelling. He scratches at his white facial fur, then the top of his orange furred head. He struggles fiercely to detach his feelings from the facts and thinks about what to do.

"Why should we believe that? It answers everything we ask without hesitation." Druward comments.

"Were you not there the night Evil Vulpie tortured me into a crumpled mess?" Vulpie angrily asks. "You know, bleeding and screaming? I was two seconds from being dead? WHY IN THE WORLD WOULD VULPIE.NET TRY TO BOTHER ME? Oh me, oh my! Why, why, why?"

"Calm down princess."

"PRINCESS?! The fuck is your problem DRUWARD?" Vulpie shouts.

"Whoa, whoa! Okay, stop it you two!" Howlstead interjects while raising his long arms. He follows up with a loud sigh.

"The sooner we get this... Fox in jail the better." Druward replies and Vulpie chews on his teeth.

"He feels threatened. He's scared... Can you blame him?" Howlstead observes.

"He's used to doing it his way all the time, when he should be doing time."

"Oh I see what you did there!" Vulpie mockingly exclaims.

"You should be scared. I can't imagine what they would do to you in federal prison." Druward taunts.

"You just love to visualize me in scenarios, huh?" Vulpie mischievously replies, and Howlstead catches some air in his throat when he suddenly coughs into laughter. He quickly stops himself but has a smirk before glancing at Druward.

"Don't get excited." Druward dryly responds.

"He made me last month, and others as well, to spy on corporations where he could find the right equipment. Vulpie wants to build quite a lot of us, so I imagine I won't be lonely if you stow us away somewhere. He's also doing some things with banking that the regulators might not approve of. But hey, it's hard to keep up with the master!" Chris Cefil says and the director of the CTGD watches it closely.

"Eager to tell us about Vulpie's wrong doings aren't you?" Howlstead asks it.

"Just trying to help."

"I wish I could delete you." Vulpie sneers.

"I think it's obvious this robot is not under Vulpie's control." Arthur Howlstead reasons and looks to his left at Druward.

"Don't underestimate everyone's favorite flaming nerd." Druward responds.

"It makes no sense for him to do this. You think he wants to risk being locked up? Out of self-preservation alone he wouldn't put himself in this much danger. Something else is going on here."

"Your gut reaction told you different. A few minutes ago you were telling me he was more than capable."

"Yes but I can change my opinion based on facts. Your first reaction isn't always the right one. I thought it was him because he's all over TV, in the movies, and loves to be a star. He really likes attention, but this isn't the kind he craves. It doesn't feel right. Now my gut is telling me Vulpie.net really is behind this. If it was an animal, he or she would have to possess an immense amount of programming skill and be capable of remotely operating automated factories. How likely is that?"

"How could it be that "Evil Vulpie," robot?" Druward skeptically inquires. "It's locked inside the Sufias Heritage Museum in another country. Are you saying it could pull this sort of thing off all the way from Englavic? I don't think a wireless internet connection would cut it. Not to mention that the Museum is magnetically jammed to prevent it from doing exactly that."

"It was able to build a robot of Vulpie that is virtually indestructible, it sent it after him, and controlled the entire world's computer systems until it broke the link when it attempted to destroy itself." Howlstead answers.

"I'm not so sure he didn't make the Evil Vulpie robot. I think it might have just gone crazy after he turned it on." Druward suggests. "He did make a robo copy of himself before turning himself in to the GBI."

"But that one was pathetic compared to Evil Vulpie in technological terms. You could disable it with a gunshot or two. The thing that's locked inside that museum is infinitely more advanced. I believe the report on it states it can function around three hundred years before breaking down. It's not the same thing. Vulpie's a super genius but he's not that smart. No one is. Only a computer could build something so far ahead of its time, and do it right the first time."

"Couldn't have said it better myself!" Vulpie agrees with a hopeful voice.

"So what's your take on it, Vulpie? Let's say we give you the benefit of the doubt. Tell us how you think old Chris Cefil here might have been born." Druward says and crosses his big arms.

"There are plenty of ways." Vulpie responds. "While I've been sitting here I've run a few possibilities through my head, and I think one of them may be true." The orange furred fox boy shifts in his seat and licks his lips before going on. "When I seized control of a few robotic factories on planet Veida, I noticed there was a giant directory of locations I didn't look through. I found the ones I needed. I just did what I did when the factory was closed at night, by hacking in and operating it remotely, but those were factories animals use on a daily basis. What about the ones that are under repair or haven't been used in years?

I remember seeing hundreds of small sights on Veida, Zeravyn, Sufias and even some on space stations like Wovakef. I bet those places are maintained every month or something, but since they're older and not in use, what's the chance somebody would find out if something activated them? Vulpie.net, Evil Vulpie, might have kept its original programming in some of those sights and they weren't affected by the Arctic.net takeover because they weren't in use. The computers were turned off."

"But wouldn't they be infected with your Arctic.net virus as soon as they were reactivated?" Howlstead asks.

"Vulpie.net can do anything. I think that's clear. If it remained in a computer system in an obsolete building, it might have not been affected at all. Arctic.net isn't really a computer virus like Vulpie.net. Vulpie.net is the backbone of Arctic.net. Arctic.net just sort of sits on top of Vulpie.net and keeps Vulpie.net from thinking with my mind map files as much as it would like. It only allows logical functions, and I've worked very hard to think of any way it could mistake which file requires what pattern of thinking. I think I isolated just about every type of mind map extension it uses to make logical decisions, so I turned those off, but still... There were some that I couldn't... I still can't... That's why any animal that turns on his computer can have a conversation with Vulpie.net. Some parts of its personality are still running. It has to be that way so it can anticipate the way living animals think."

"Sounds like a stretch to me. Hiding in a secret lair? I think it's unlikely that any nation or company would be inefficient enough to leave fully functional factories unused." Druward comments.

"Why do they have to be fully functional? Vulpie.net is a problem solver. Unless the equipment is completely terrible, I'm telling you, Vulpie.net could use it. I used Vulpie.net to do that sort of thing remotely, so why couldn't it secretly do the same thing itself?"

"You're awfully quiet Mr. Cefil. Care to share where you were made?" Howlstead asks the robot to his left.

"Of course I would like to tell you, but I'm not sure." It smiles in response. "I wasn't programmed with that information."

"My how convenient!" Vulpie hums and rolls his eyes.

"Do you think Vulpie is on to something? What's your opinion?"

"I'm not sure how to answer. Vulpie made me. He made all of us... So only he would know." Cefil cryptically replies.

"All of you? How many are you?" Druward inquires.

"Sorry, Vulpie wouldn't want me to say."

"Direct override. Say it right now." Vulpie commands and crosses his little arms. Cefil only smiles in response and Vulpie throws up his arms in irritation. "See? That thing does what it wants. I'm not responsible."

"How are we going to handle Vulpie? Same surveillance or change of plans?" Rulef asks while leaning against the exit door.

"Before you show off your authority, why don't we see how things play out?" Howlstead quickly asks Druward. Vulpie is thankful that his boss is willing to stand up for him. Druward looks at Vulpie after hearing the suggestion and takes a moment to think it over.

"I'm sure the truth will come out eventually... One way or the other..." Druward answers and walks towards the exit. Rulef moves out of the way, looking at Vulpie and then Howlstead.

"No change then I guess." Rulef says.

Vulpie Industries

Six years have passed since Vulpie maneuvered out of his government contract. Even though it clearly stated he would have no choice but to work for the Cyber Technologies Government Division for ten years, Vulpie represented himself in court as he has many times before, and had the contract nullified. It turns out that Druward Wraulgh's violence against the gay fox during the "Evil Vulpie" crisis came in handy. Vulpie pulled security footage from the Governmental Bureau of Investigation's mainframe and used it as evidence that he was under duress when he signed the contract. Though this is not 100% true, Vulpie's clever maneuvering succeeded. He was able to convince a jury that he should be free of the agreement, and despite outrage by some, the contract was dissolved. Afterwards the Fox boy went on to found his own tech company.

In the late afternoon sun, a giant tower turns on its light to illuminate the sky when night falls. The building's orange and white neon lights cast a beautiful and commanding glow on all other buildings during darkness and all animals who live in Sufias City know its name. They travel from around the world to visit the place where the future becomes reality every day... Vulpie Industries.

The name is brilliantly lit on the upper half of the building but the sign is also a little subdued, using a tactful font. It was built six years ago, when Vulpie dissolved his government contract with the cyber technologies government division. Vulpie industries quickly became the be all and end all of the planet's capital. Sure, congress and the stone house are not far away, but it would be impossible to find a more interesting place than the company founded by the world's most beloved super genius.

"Vulpie, the meeting is in five minutes…" Polar reminds his fox husband, to which Vulpie sighs with a smile.

"I'm going to be on time today I promise." Vulpie replies.

"Don't leave me in there with Halfur. He'll bitch my ears off. And I'm not going to save any of that coffee creamer you like so much." Polar playfully threatens.

"Cruel and unnecessary! Why are you so bad to me?" Vulpie giggles.

"Seriously though, I want you to lock your computer and come with me." Polar says and Vulpie nods.

"Okay, coming." The orange furred fox decides and stands. He stretches his lean little body and watches Polar stand up from a couch in the right corner of the office. Vulpie's office is at the top of Vulpie Industries and spans almost the entire floor. Luxury is an understatement, as it houses a pool table, a game room, six TVs, surround sound and enough furniture to accommodate twenty guests.

"You look good, baby." Polar lovingly says.

"You're so sweet!"

"Don't forget to talk to Vincent as well. If you aren't distracted from your schedule maybe we can hold the last meeting back up here." Polar suggests.

"And I thought you would get tired of doing it at work. Silly me!" Vulpie grins and Polar grins back.

"We both know the real reason you hired me…" The white furred wolf laughs.

"I'm a consummate professional sir. Whatever do you mean?" Vulpie replies with fake outrage.

"Get your professional tail in the elevator now please." Polar smiles.

"Goddess you're pushy today! Alright!" Vulpie says and gets out from behind his big desk. He quickly gathers his things and meets Polar as they walk to the door of Vulpie's office. It's more like a gate, with the two electronic sliding doors unlatching their locks with hard metallic clunks. Once unlocked, they slide open easily and smoothly with no sound, revealing the only other part of the floor that isn't Vulpie's office, the lobby. A large welcoming desk with two receptionists is near the doors to Vulpie's office, and faces the elevator. Bathrooms are to the left of the desk, and are more state of the art than one would expect of a lavatory. Laser TVs adorn the mirrors inside, with pleasant music, fitting in nicely with the perfect design of the rest of the floor.

"Back in one hour!" Vulpie happily tells Maxine, his primary receptionist. She is a middle aged gray furred she-wolf and is very professional. She was one of the first women Vulpie ever hired when he founded his company and has never let him down when it comes to entertaining visitors. Only animals with clearance are allowed to visit Vulpie's floor, so her position is privileged.

"Are you going down to the division meeting Mr. Vulpie?"

"Yeah, message me if Vincent calls. He might come by sometime this afternoon."

"Yes sir."

"Do your thing Vulpie!" The second receptionist eagerly says and Polar winces a little, realizing that her voice was shaky. She's Amelia, a young red furred vixen, and an awkward moment would ensue if Vulpie were a lesser boss. The girl has embarrassed herself a few times already with strange comments, but obviously only desires to do well. Polar knows what his husband will do without a doubt and smiles as he gives her a mischievous expression.

"I will! You just stop biting your nails hon. You're doing great up here." Vulpie replies and Amelia's eyes go from terror to joy. "Give her something to do. She's a busy bee!"

"Yes sir." Maxine chuckles and gives Amelia a disapproving glance. Vulpie and Polar walk to the elevator together and as they wait for the doors to open, Polar leans down and whispers in the fox's ear.

"I'm glad you always know what to say because she makes me uncomfortable sometimes."

"I know!" Vulpie whispers back and they step into the elevator when it opens. Polar hits the button for the third floor and when the doors close Vulpie stretches again.

"So what's your plan for me? What do you want me to do?" Polar asks his husband.

"Start in on the quality control if you like. I'm really interested in seeing how much progress we've made in R&D."

"Your favorite." Polar replies and Vulpie nods, smirking up at the snow furred wolf.

"Halfur hates having to come to these meetings but I bet he's done the work. I don't want to say we could use more of him, considering how irritating he is, but the guy is talented."

"Why do you take up for him, Vulpie? He's an idiot compared to you, and he argues with everything you say."

"Honestly, because he knows I'm right and will do what I tell him even though he argues. I can't rely on just anyone to do programming like him. He hits every project full force, so..."

"He's a prick but a useful prick?" Polar asks.

"Exactly!" Vulpie giggles as the elevator stops. Polar clears his throat as the door opens, preparing his corporate persona before walking out with Vulpie onto the third floor. It's been a long journey for the white furred wolf. He thinks about what his life used to be in the pre-Vulpie era and experiences a moment of clarity regarding his choices.

Things could have, and would have been dull for him. Polar knows he is an intelligent talented man, but there is not much that would distinguish him from so many other wolves in the grand scheme of things. The major difference is his homosexuality, and he is proud of his attitude of love and respect for all animals because of it, but he is no super star. Had he not met Vulpie, he would not be a high level manager for the most powerful company in the universe. Most likely, he would have lived out the rest of his days in mediocrity.

Sure he was doing very well at Illehas. Sure, he was and is in good health, strong and attractive, but what else did he have? Most of Polar's previous relationships disappointed him, as gay men have to suffer all sorts of harsh developments in the world around them. As he ponders the meaning of his past love affairs, he comes to the conclusion that most likely whomever he chose would have left him feeling unfulfilled. It's pride and a need for conquest. Polar knows it. He's a man, and every man enjoys power. Vulpie has given him power.

"A strange thing indeed." Polar thinks to himself as he follows Vulpie into the meeting room, admiring the little fox's orange fur. *"That I would gain power from such a cute little man. A wolf earning power from a smaller male's brilliance... Where have you ever heard of such a thing before? It's not something you would glean from a wolfen essay on the might of their species. Wolves are supposed to be self-sufficient, etc. etc. ... But it's this little fox that has made you a king in your own castle... Don't you ever forget it. Vulpie's given you all of this and still acts as though he owes it to*

you, Polar... Wow, things sure could have been worse! Help him as much as possible if you want that to continue... Would you really want to go back to being alone or feeling alone?"

"Polar? Wake up." Vulpie says and swats the white furred wolf's left leg. Polar realizes he's standing next to his chair and sits down like the rest of the management of Vulpie Industries as the meeting begins. "What are you thinking about? I know that look." Vulpie tells his husband as the others talk among themselves.

"Nothing."

"Just help me as much as possible here... Don't leave me to make all the hard decisions."

"Okay... What, did you say?" Polar asks as he realizes how similar Vulpie's statement is to what he was thinking.

"Make sure to help me as much as possible honey, before Halfur and I get into another argument." Vulpie says with a clever smile. His look unnerves Polar for a moment as he comes to grip with the random coincidence of Vulpie's choice of words. Polar knows it was random but something about Vulpie makes his fur stand on end at least once a week.

"Is everyone here?" Vulpie asks and looks around. The meeting room on the third floor is bigger than most of the others and members of upper management at Vulpie Industries have become accustomed to gathering in this particular room. In addition to being the most logical choice it also houses a very nice cappuccino machine in the far corner. When not in official use, a few employees from floors below sneak in their mugs for free drinks. Vulpie has seen these shenanigans through security footage for the building but rather than punish the activity, he's allowed it for the amusement of his peers. "Get some coffee if you like; Deivas know everybody else already has!"

The group chuckles and the sounds of papers and notebooks shuffling about fills the room. Management is a diverse group, with foxes, wolves, tigers and a lioness for good measure, but even still there are more male wolves. Wolves have done very well for themselves throughout history but it's talent not species that gets one into the upper echelon of Vulpie Industries.

"I've got mine, Vulpie." Halfur taunts with his usual irritating voice, but also showing his best hand at a playful exchange.

"Your condescension is appreciated as always Halfur." Vulpie replies with a cute voice, to which the group chuckles a little louder.

"I do hope we'll be hearing good news from the adults today." Halfur comments, referring to Andrew Price, another fox. Price has been chief financial officer in many companies over the span of his accomplished career, and his gray fur gives him a naturally wise appearance on top of his 52 years on planet Sufias.

"You're the one that plays video games." Price responds.

"More like trolls video games." Vulpie interjects.

"You would know." Halfur adds with a smirk.

"Tournament-Next month-Your chin." Vulpie giggles.

"Well if you've found time to advance research and development to our goals, I can tell you that you won't hear any complaints from me. We're still running a surplus this quarter, so let's not waste it." Price says.

"My team and myself have never been the problem. The problem is gearing yearlong projects against the whims of the market. Just don't tell me again that the shareholders don't consider revisions to be profitable. The last 3 V-Screen models have all hit the market BEFORE I put my stamp of approval on them."

"We shouldn't have any problem with retail items this quarter but VulGrid may be the kicker." Chase thinks aloud. Being the company's chief technical officer at age 38 means the man is very smart, but the fact he is also a white furred wolf has bothered Polar to some degree. Polar is a thoughtful person and knows his jealousy is silly, considering Chase is nowhere near gay and couldn't possibly steal Vulpie from him, but the competition remains. It's just a natural tendency to keep an eye out for oneself in the game of love. Polar's noticed Vulpie pays close attention when Chase speaks, and the fox boy has teased Polar about his jealousy a few times. Vulpie misses nothing, so this has resulted in Polar promptly putting Vulpie back in his place when in the bedroom. He's had to overwhelm Vulpie on more than one occasion to show him who's boss, but even now Polar has to shoot Vulpie a dominating look when Vulpie slyly glances at him.

"Agreed. But I think we should be ready by now." Vulpie tells Chase and directs his words to all of lower management as well. "Stephanie, what's the market saying about our possible involvement with the military regarding VulGrid?"

"We don't foresee any social backlash because of the project." A brown furred vixen answers. Stephanie Cook has a motherly voice but runs her role of public relations director with a war like mind. Like Vicki Buxton, Vulpie's agent for the Association of Fox Rights, she is ever ready to predict the prejudices of social media and political demagogues.

"I don't take rumors as fact, but I do consider their implications. Wasn't there a congressman that mentioned Vulpie Industries and VulGrid on the senate floor?" Vulpie inquires.

"Congressman Doretch, yes." Stephanie responds and smiles. "He gave another odd speech about the rights of free animals. He polls the best in conservative districts so he continues to throw your name around for attention."

"But no mention of VulGrid?"

"Not specifically and I doubt he will since the military industrial complex generously donates to his campaigns."

"Good. Though I don't want Vulpie Industries manufacturing weapons, the department of defense has already accepted prototypes of VulGrid for field use."

"It's no secret what they plan to do with it." Halfur interjects. "Why should we resist military contracts? VulGrid will be used to confuse the enemy on battlefields and can hide friendly units from being spotted. VulGrid's projection of a virtual reality has endless potential for deception."

"Yes and that's why it will be the only military project at this time." Vulpie responds with a firm voice. "Sure we would profit paw over fist, but the flood gates will open. Next they'll be asking us to mount weapon racks and hydraulics on VulGrids to kill the enemy. Vulpie Industries does not and will not make weapons."

"Could we please call it by its product name? Not all of the VulGrid program is the Vu-103 unit."

"For you, anything." Vulpie smiles as the group chuckles.

"Halfur may have a point, Vulpie. More military contracts would expose us to military industrial lobbyists that could benefit Vulpie Industries." Price suggests.

"I doubt that would look good on a shareholder's report, considering Vulpie's previous cyber-attacks." Stephanie comments and Vulpie nods in agreement. "The company polls very favorably with most animals."

"Stephanie is right. Price and Halfur make nice arguments for going in guns blazing, but ultimately I believe it will erode our support with the public."

"You're right Vulpie. I also think it would look a little shady to go that route but we are sitting on a very nice surplus as it is." Price says and Halfur shakes his head in disagreement.

"Something else to say, Halfur?" Vulpie inquires.

"How long will Sevrif wait before it competes for those projects?" Halfur asks.

"They can start tomorrow if they like. They tried stealing our plans for VulGrid, excuse me, for Vu-103, but their reverse engineering is less than adequate. That company was responsible for four deaths when they tried emulating the wavelength of our product."

"The military doesn't care. They'll hire 103s from us and contract Sevrif to remove the safeguards."

"Let them try. Arctic.net won't help Sevrif contend with Vulpie.net." Vulpie replies with a devious look.

"Where did Sevrif come from? We've discussed them a few times already but none of my contacts have heard of this company before last year." Price says towards
Halfur.

"So you did look into their government disclosures?" Vulpie asks his CFO.

"Yes, their capital was fifty million when they filed for a license to sell their products here on planet Sufias. But they are actually registered as a private corporation for Zeravyn."

"Zeravyn, eh?" Vulpie responds and moves his tongue around inside his fox mouth.

"What's a rich tourist world doing in the technology field?" Polar asks and looks up for a moment to think. "I thought they specialized in cruises and entertainment."

"What entertains me is that they build most of their products on their galaxy class space ship." Vulpie adds.

"I was just going to say that." Price comments with a raised eyebrow. "Sevrif technologies is registered with Zeravyn but you won't find a corporate office there. There's no evidence of a factory, so the most likely place is their ship."

"Keep your buddies in the financial markets happy so they will continue to feed us info." The orange furred fox boy responds and glances at Halfur. "You have to give them credit for some of their devices. Our V-Screen decimated their portable computer, but they learned something from it. They start over from scratch when something doesn't work for them. Their determination is impressive. We need to keep an eye on our friendly competitors. I'm also going to call a friend or two and see what I can find out about their CEO. This Sevrif fellow is a real mystery."

"I'd be happy to arrange a meeting. How about a technology conference where we invite all of the media for a discussion on the prevalence of computers in society?" Stephanie offers.

"Go ahead and send out that offer. I'd like to meet these Zeravyns."

Foxy Dreams

The warm feeling of being home is one of the best that life can offer, and Polar silently enjoys it while being with his parents. He is helping them around their home. The white furred wolf made the long trip to be with them on this Saturday. His husband wanted to come but had to handle some important business at Vulpie Industries. Polar feels lonely without him.

"I miss Vulpie; I wish he could be here." Kimberly Arctic says as she watches her husband and son set down the den couch in a new location. They're moving furniture so she can have more space to her liking. Polar's mother enjoys having lots of room for her grandchildren to play when Alan visits.

"I do to. He's always saying something witty. That boy is smart as a whip!" Polar's father responds after standing up straight. Polar smiles at him, standing at the other end of the couch.

"Oh, I know. I wish he would rub off on me but I can never carry conversations like he does." Polar happily says and glances at his mother. She smiles in return, glad to see her son fulfilled.

"He's so good for you Polar." Kimberly replies with a loving voice. "I remember how you looked when you and Donner were fighting and I worried. I wondered if you could ever find a man to marry, or if you could marry at all because you're gay, but you two have been together for six years and you're still glowing."

"I never would have married Donner." Polar thinks out loud.

"And good that you didn't. I always felt like that man was a little dangerous." Polar's father comments while relaxing on his feet.

"I dream about him..." Polar shyly admits with a smirk. "I think about him all day long and when I sleep he's with me too." Victor Arctic's large ears perk up as he listens to his son and the large white furred wolf stretches before giving his wife a glance. Kimberly notices and gives him a concerned look.

"Funny you should say that, because we've been dreaming about him too." Victor responds and Polar's mother quickly gives him a stern expression.

"Victor!" Kimberly quietly barks and nervously glances at her son.

"What?" Polar asks with a surprised smile. "Is there something going on? What do you mean you dream about him?"

"I mean we've been having dreams about Vulpie every night for the past two weeks." Victor tells his son and when Kimberly speaks this time she is much louder.

"DON'T!"

"Don't what?" Polar inquires in confusion and quickly looks between his parents "Are you serious?"

"Yes I am. Your mother doesn't want me to mention it because she's worried it might bother you but I think you should know." Polar's father responds.

"Oh...K." Polar chuckles and cracks his wolf knuckles in curiosity. He gives Victor a patient look but stares at him for an answer.

"That's why when you said you dreamed about him every night I thought I should say something." Polar's father explains. The room goes silent for a moment and after waiting for a few seconds, Polar laughs in confusion.

"Well he is on the news every day for something. We've got the new model V Screen coming out soon." The white furred wolf muses.

"Who needs TV when we have him in our dreams?"

"That's enough Victor." Kimberley interrupts and Polar gestures for more.

"No, I want to know what he's talking about." Polar says.

"You said it would be good to say something to him about it." Victor tells his wife and she shakes her head.

"Your father thinks something unforeseen must be responsible." The she-wolf sighs to Polar, giving her son a defeated expression.

"Well it is pretty strange." Victor interjects and Polar squints with a baffled look.

"You mean to tell me both of you dream about my husband on a regular basis?" Polar asks.

"He's always been there for the last two weeks, yes." Victor responds and Polar looks to his mother.

"Do you know what he's talking about? Is it true?"

"It's true honey, but I love Vulpie." Kimberly replies and watches her son's face as she speaks. "I told your father not to do this but here we are..."

"Well are they good dreams?" Polar laughs in disbelief.

"Sure. Actually, I've enjoyed most of them." Polar's she wolf mother answers and Polar's blue eyes slowly go wide as he realizes his parents know something he does not. They have been honest parents his entire life and Polar is sure they wouldn't bring something like this up unless it was important.

"Well... I don't know what to say. Maybe you like him as much as me!" Polar responds and gives his father a playful look.

"But it isn't just once in a while. I had another dream with him in it last night." Kimberly confesses and Polar turns to his mother in surprise.

"Tell him what it was about." Victor suggests to his wife and after a moment of silence she does.

"I was dreaming about my mother, your grandmother, and the house I grew up in. I was just a little girl again and Vulpie was in my dream as my brother. I know it doesn't make any sense, but there he was...He was a fox son of my mother, your grandmother, and we were playing together."

"That is weird." Polar replies in confusion.

"And it seemed so real, like he was really there. You're my son and you're thirteen years older than him, but in my dream Vulpie was my little brother." Kimberly says and raises her eyebrows with a lost expression. Polar is silent as he listens and grows tense as he thinks over what he has heard.

"In my dreams Vulpie talks to me about how my days are going. Just last night he talked to me about cleaning up the guest room and moving the furniture today, like I was planning...And that was before I ever mentioned it to your father." Another long silence fills the room and eventually Polar takes a deep breath.

"Really?" The white furred wolf asks his mother in concern.

"Yes it's true, but that's why I told your father not to bring it up. It probably doesn't mean a thing at all. I didn't want you to think that your mother secretly obsesses over your fox husband or something."

"And it happens every night?" Polar inquires with wide eyes.

"Yes."

"So the night before last..."

"We had a conversation about me getting my driver's license renewed because it's going to expire in a month. And then he helped me bake cookies. That's that gist of the dream I had."

"And what about you?" Polar asks his father, quickly looking to him in amazement.

"Why just last night I talked to Vulpie about you coming up to see us today. I haven't seen him in about a month but he seemed completely real in the dream, like he was here in the house this morning." Victor answers. Another long silence fills the room and eventually Polar laughs again in shock. This time Kimberly laughs with him, trying to ease her son.

"Don't worry about it. We must be getting senile!" Kimberly says and Polar can't help but laugh. It relieves the tension a little but the white furred wolf can see his father looks like he is holding something back.

"Dad, do you have something else to say?" Polar quietly asks and his father considers the question carefully.

"It's just that..." Victor says and clears his throat. Kimberly gives him a disappointed glare but Polar's father cannot resist. "I like Vulpie. He's incredibly smart, he's a genius. He's fun, he loves you, and I know he loves all of us because we're your family... And he is part of the family... But honestly the dreams are beginning to creep me out...He doesn't go away. You know how it is when you dream, like you return to places you've been over and over probably because of the REM sleep? Well Vulpie is with me every step of the way. Sometimes I even know I'm dreaming and I told him he was too much in my dream and we both laughed about it. I swear Polar, it's like he has been here every night." The tall wolf confesses and Polar returns him a dazed stare, watching his father while taking in what he has heard.

"Well I don't know what to say." Polar says and clears his throat.

"Son, don't worry about it. This is why I didn't want to tell you. It's ridiculous. It doesn't mean a damn thing." Kimberly tells her son and looks for a hug. She puts her paw on Polar and he gives her one after a few seconds. When they part from the embrace Polar looks to his father. Victor's face hasn't changed and he raises his eyebrows with a lost expression.

"So why do you think it's happening?" Polar inquires.

"I have absolutely no idea son." Victor responds and slowly smiles. "But maybe you could ask him about it?"

"Oh Victor, enough! You're making a mountain out of a mole hill!" Kimberly barks at her husband but Polar listens. He smiles in amusement and takes a deep breath.

"I guarantee he'll come up with something funny." Polar confidently thinks out loud and both of his parents chuckle. He wipes his paws on his designer slacks and is treated to a convenient distraction when the doorbell rings. All three of the white furred wolves' ears perk up, two of them knowing a fourth is about to join them.

"Ah, that's Richard! He got here fast!" Victor says and walks towards the front door, going out of the den and peering through the curtains to see who is outside. Kimberly lovingly reaches down and squeezes Polar's left paw, letting him know she wants everything to be fine and he gladly returns a thankful smile.

"Dad, you have to get your tracker out of the drive way! It's almost impossible to drive in here." Richard playfully says to his father. The white furred wolf walks into Victor and Kimberly's home and hugs his dad while Polar walks to the door with his mother.

"If you didn't drive that monster of a car there wouldn't be a problem Richard! You're the main reason why the ice caps are still melting you know." Victor taunts and his son smirks.

"The car's fast not inefficient. I bet its cleaner than anything you've ever owned."

"Yeah, yeah." Victor says and steps aside as Kimberly greets her youngest son with a hug.

"You look great honey." She says with her sweet voice and he nods in appreciation.

"Thanks Mom. You're beautiful as always." Richard replies and looks to Polar who stands behind his parents with an inviting expression. "Hey Polar." Richard says and walks over to his older brother, offering a hug. Polar gives him one and is happy to see him. He thinks how nice it is that his brother seems to be more successful every time they meet.

"So you've been what, promoted again Richard?" Polar asks with a smirk. "Is that the reason for that beast you're driving?"

"It's tenured professor now. Hey, we're not all millionaires like you brother, But I owe you a lot of thanks for my fourth bank account. The money you and Vulpie donated is much appreciated."

"You're welcome." Polar replies and Victor claps his big paws together, looking at the other silky furred arctic wolves.

"Let's have lunch. Your mother's cooked up two kinds of steak; how does that sound?" Victor says and both Polar and Richard's mouths water.

"Look at them, they're chomping at the bits! I know when my boys are hungry. Come in here and have something good to eat." Kimberly offers in pride and neither Polar nor Richard resist following her into the dining room. They sit down, knowing that their mother likes to serve everyone at her table even if they would gladly get their own silverware and drinks. Victor takes his chair at the left end of the table and Polar sits next to him, on his right, Richard coming in beside him. Richard sits to Polar's right side, his younger brother dropping down onto his chair. Kimberly asks all of them what they want to drink and each decides to have water except Victor, who asks for a soda. Kimberly then makes several trips, first bringing in the drinks, then all of the dishes of food until the table is full and her husband stands up to serve his sons.

"Eat up boys." Victor says and helps Polar and Richard fill their plates.

"Richard, how are things at the university?" Kimberly asks her youngest son.

"The Kayman Institute is bringing on about forty new professors this year, two in my field and I'm glad. The workload has been heavy for me. I can teach large classes but when it's up to two hundred or more, it's time to hire some help." Richard responds.

"What do they have you teaching the most? Last time we talked I know you mentioned the great war and the arctic wars." Polar asks his brother in interest.

"It's more religion than I would have thought and I actually enjoy the changes in the history program. They're looking to bring on more professors to teach religion nine hundred and such but I'm handling a lot of that now and it's nice. Ivo Lorcan's work is interesting."

"Oh yeah, isn't he the one that goes on those archaeological trips?" Polar inquires.

"Digging up Deivonic tombs, yeah. He was one of the first academics in Ninvia when they opened up that new one about a year ago."

"They say it's one of the oldest ever found, right?"

"Yeah, Ivo Lorcan tells me they're still digging day and night to find every Deiva depiction they think might be down there. They have to be careful because it's such fragile work. He's brought back pictures from the site, all of Goddess Cyrilla so far and her time with Kaylen Hiar from the Velora. I use some of them when I teach my religion courses."

"It must be so interesting Richard! I'm glad you chose to be a professor. You're suited for an academic field." Kimberly says and Polar nods.

"Polar, how's working for Vulpie going for you? Do you still like it?" Richard asks his older brother.

"It's awesome." Polar responds with a smirk. "Vulpie is releasing so many products at the same time I can't even count them all."

"I can only imagine." Kimberly comments with a smile. "But he needs you Polar. I can see it in his eyes. You're the reason he's doing so well."

"Thank you, but I don't think I'm that great." Polar replies with a smile of his own. "He really wants to make things the way they ought to be, so people can use Arctic.net with his technology and everything will be so much easier for the rest of us that don't understand any of it."

"Yeah the government control never was a great thing to begin with. Maybe what he did proves that we need less computer control and a return to simple things." Richard replies and Victor nods enthusiastically at his son's comment.

"Here, here! Do you know I can't even write checks at my bank anymore? It's getting so complicated that I'm forced to use that damn debit card everywhere. I never would have dreamed they would make you remember so many pin numbers and passwords.

It's ridiculous." Victor grumbles. Richard's ears perk up at Victor's statement and he wipes his mouth with his napkin before contributing the thought that just pops into his head.

"Speaking of dreams, I've been having some strange ones. They've been about him, actually!" Richard laughs and grins at his family before continuing. Polar, Victor and Kimberly all go stiff. Polar can't believe what he has just heard and his fear is confirmed when his brother goes on. "I kid you not, I've dreamt about Vulpie for the last week. I have no idea why, but it's the same thing every night." After Richard speaks Polar looks at him. He sees that Richard is completely innocent in bringing up the issue. His younger brother clearly has no idea what their parents spoke about before he arrived. The first thing Polar expects is a glance from his mother and father when he looks in their direction and it's immediately confirmed with both of them.

"Oh?" Victor asks and Kimberly looks at her husband with a displeased face. It's clear to Polar that his father is as shocked as he is, and unfortunately, Polar knows he won't let the issue rest after such a development.

"Yeah, it's been really, really weird. I can't remember the last time I've had dreams this vivid or strange, but I've had them for several days now. I'm serious Polar, I don't know why, but I must have Vulpie on my mind from the news or something." Richard elaborates and Polar listens with wide eyes. The dinner table is silent after Richard speaks and Polar looks to his left at his father with a concerned face. Victor stares back at his son and considers not saying anything for a moment, but finally goes in search of the truth.

"It's strange that you should say that Richard; I have too." Victor says and Polar looks to his mother. She sits as silently as her oldest son and lets Richard and Victor talk.

"Really?"

"Yeah, I was telling your mother just this morning how I dreamt that he was telling me about the house. In my dream he knew your mother was going to cook for us today and he acted as though he was sad that he couldn't come." Richard goes silent as well upon hearing his father's statement and he glances at Polar in shock.

"Really..." Richard whispers in amazement. "Wow that is crazy. Anyway... Yeah I dreamt he was a student in one of my classes a few days ago. At least I've been getting good sleep." Richard says and goes back to eating. He doesn't notice what's going on with Polar and his parents and after another frightened look from Polar, Victor clears his throat and decides not to say anymore.

Check Your Bags

The hustle and bustle of an airport is always exciting, Polar thinks to himself as he and Vulpie go through customs. The proposition of meeting new animals from around the world entices any forward thinking person, but there is a difference at this one. Vulpie owns the airport. Since Vulpie Industries is on the cutting edge of technology and works with companies in all sorts of endeavors, it only makes sense. After construction the airport saw an immediate interest from the public and balances bringing in materials for the company while also offering affordable prices for frequent fliers.

The service is the best in the industry, as Vulpie brokered a contract with Silver Edge airlines to handle the public end of flight service. Polar flew with Silver Edge a few times with his previous job at Illehas and took recreational trips as well. Most of them happened when he was dating Donner, his "ex could have been husband," before he ever met Vulpie.

To Polar, flying brings back all sorts of memories because of this. First they're about Donner and there are some good ones. But inevitably the bad outweighs the good as he thinks about Donner's descent into depression and negative outlook on life. Though Polar loved Donner, Donner couldn't handle the stresses of being gay and they eventually had to split up. Their good times as competitive strong wolves came to a sudden end after a particularly vicious fight. And then Polar was alone for a long while... And then... He met Vulpie...

"It would make a fantastic book." Polar thinks with a smile as he relives the experiences Vulpie has given him. The first is of Vulpie landing to pick him up in a stolen military ship. The fox boy had used Vulpie.net to steal it and at that time, Polar was trying to help the government stop him while he was also secretly in love.

They flew up to the Wispy Canis Lupus mountain range, and wild beautiful love followed in the cradle of nature. Afterwards Polar convinced Vulpie to come back with him and turn himself over to the government. And then things became even more interesting. So much happened... And here he is now, married to Vulpie, walking in an airport that the gay fox owns.

"What a trip." Polar whispers and Vulpie looks up to his left at him. The fox boy swings Polar's right arm as they hold paws and walk.

"Where are you today?" Vulpie asks with a grin. "You're off in la la land again!"

"Just thinking about how much I love you." Polar warmly replies.

"I love you too." Vulpie tenderly responds and Rulef rolls his eyes. The commander of Vulpie's previous Blacktail escort is still working for him even though the government contract is finished. Vulpie hired the man and his team because he trusts them with his and his husband's life. "Rulef you can come with us to the beach if ya want!" Vulpie teases.

"Only if you bring women." The gray furred wolf replies as he looks around the airport. Blacktail has the entire area around Vulpie and Polar under control as they walk through security. Several animals waiting in line start taking pictures of Vulpie with their cell phones and Vulpie smiles when he sees some of his employees. Before long there is a crowd of animals filming Polar and Vulpie and Polar looks down at him in embarrassment.

"We love you Vulpie!" A female fox happily yells out and at this Vulpie grins up at Polar. The crowd quickly begins to cheer and Vulpie waves at his public.

"Much love to all of you! Happy Yivolf Day!" Vulpie replies with a sweet voice and winks at a few youngsters who have their mouths open in awe. Vulpie nudges Polar and giggles at him. "Come on Polar! They love you just as much! Why don't ya say hello?"

"I'm too nervous. I'll choke and say something stupid." Polar laughs quietly.

"You're the smartest man I know." Vulpie replies. "And you're just as gorgeous!"

"Thank you." Polar smiles.

"We need to keep moving." Rulef reminds the two and Polar and Vulpie start walking again. They will be heading to their private jet, Blacktail escorting them all the way. Polar tugs on Vulpie's left paw and the fox boy waves goodbye to those behind them at the security checkpoint. From then on they move about the airport in a snakelike pattern, weaving left and right adjusting to the steady flow of other animals in the vicinity. Airport management makes way for their boss and Vulpie checks in with the girls at a desk before they use the terminal for their private jet.

"I'm amazed retired colonel Worhel is going to join you for this little get together. I'm pretty sure he's a religious man." Rulef mentions to Vulpie as they walk down the concourse.

"There's a lot of money in his pockets and he'd like some more." Vulpie replies. "Sure he's safe to be around without you guys protecting me?"

"He's an honorable man. I served with him in the east Felini conflict." Rulef responds.

"It's gonna be awesome! We'll take out all of the boats for the day. Come with us!" Vulpie offers again.

"I MIGHT come along to talk to Worhel. But don't expect me to buddy up with you boy lovers."

"No one's going to molest you." Polar laughs and Rulef smirks.

"Do you think you could molest me?" Vulpie asks Polar as if he is proposing a forbidden idea.

"Wear those pink swimming trunks. That should guarantee it." Polar grins in response.

"Ugh, I don't know if I can stand this..." Rulef snorts.

"I promise you'll hear your share of manly topics." Vulpie says and gives Rulef a mischievous face. "I'll be talking with Worhel about the VulGrid. Can you imagine how bad ass it would be to be invisible to the enemy? Show them false landscapes?"

"Or irradiate them to death." Rulef answers and shoots Vulpie an interested expression. "Yes I hear your VulGrid is quite a stroke of genius. Worhel has always been a fan of weapons that minimize close quarters combat."

"Then get out your swimming trunks. I'm sure we can come up with a few interesting ideas."

Waves

Casillfori is an vastly beautiful state of Sufias. Being on the coast east of Sufias City, its borders kiss the expansive Paxyeli Sea. Real estate on this tourist's paradise is astronomically expensive, so the majority of buildings found on the coast are monumental hotels.

But Polar and Vulpie have a home here, their second home, in an upper crust location of the coastline. They visited the coast for a few months until they found the perfect spot for them, and had a state of the art mansion built right on the beautiful coastline. Manicured palm trees grow at symmetrical angles around a few spaces outside of their home. The grass is watered daily and cut with the very helpful staff they hired to keep up the house.

Polar and Vulpie are rich, not only from the ten million Polar earned thanks to President Vargas. Vulpie has brought in more than ninety million to their dual custody bank account because of his company and several advertising deals. Vulpie Industries has been a tremendous success and Vulpie is not above advertising his cute smile and charm for everything from cars to watches, to cologne to golf clubs. They have everything they want and more. So when it came time to buy pleasure boats, they ended up getting five to make sure they could entertain a large number of guests.

The Paxyeli Sea sparkles and crashes up against their yachts in the early afternoon. Everyone is having a wonderful time. The host of animals along for the excursion mostly include middle aged military men and their wives. Colonel Worhel, a brown furred wolf, is captain of the yacht Polar and Vulpie enjoy. They haven't begun speaking about VulGrid yet, and Vulpie makes use of the opportunity to speak with another important man before that discussion comes into play. Vincent Hall, a middle aged brown fox the same size as Vulpie, sits with his wife looking out over the sea.

"Hi Susan!" Vulpie says to Vincent's vixen wife and looks between them. "Are you both having a good time? I hope so!"

"It's great Vulpie, thank you for inviting us." Susan replies and Vulpie smirks at Vincent. The fellow fox has on a pair of black swimming trunks and is still wearing his gray shirt. Vulpie, on the other hand, has his shirt off and sports his favorite pink swimming trunks. No one has gone swimming yet so he's still dry.

"I wonder how long it's been." Vulpie thinks out loud and takes a seat on a nearby pool chair.

"You were what, eighteen, when I chased you all over Sevik?" Vincent asks with a smile.

"Honey, can I get you anything?" Susan asks her husband.

"No thanks sugar." Vincent answers as she stands.

"I'll let you boys catch up." She says and walks off just as Polar joins them. The white furred wolf's interest peaked when he heard what Vincent said. Polar is also still wearing a shirt, blue, and his swimming trunks are a dark brown.

"You almost had me... Almost." Vulpie tells Vincent and gives Polar a knowing smirk.

"Go ahead, I've been wanting to hear what Vulpie did before meeting me." Polar announces with an interested voice.

"I'm afraid you married yourself to a major criminal." Vincent grins.

"Stop that! I've told Polar all about the things I've done... Most of them..." Vulpie replies and bites his lip adorably.

"He's told me a lot about you." Polar says to Vincent and the older fox straightens in his pool chair a bit.

"Is that right?"

"He said you were a super cop. Are you still in the GBI?" Polar inquires.

"I'm close to retirement now but years away from losing the smell of a hunt." The brown fox answers. "Your Vulpie was the most wanted man for the GBI ever since he left Rinwulv Tech."

"He hacked the governmental bureau of investigation's mainframe." Polar says and smirks at Vulpie who makes an innocent expression.

"Oh I'm afraid it's much worse than that." Vincent responds while shooting Vulpie a devious look.

"Aw, don't blow things out of proportion Vincent! I'm just glad to see you man, it's been too long!" Vulpie enthusiastically replies.

"Assault, grand theft auto, impersonating an officer..." Vincent elaborates, clearly enjoying educating Polar about Vulpie's rap sheet. "Those were just his crimes before I came into play. They called me in after he set up his NLIN unit at Break Tail Park."

"Wait, what?" Polar asks and blinks. "What do you mean?"

"He was responsible for the attack on Heather Timber at break tail park when she was vice president."

"I thought that was the work of terrorists." Polar responds and gives Vulpie wide eyes.

"There was a cover up. In truth, the weapon Vulpie used was non-lethal and it's the base unit, he's told me, for building the VulGrid."

"Heather Timber shut down my web site because of all the hacking my buddies and I were involved with. I wanted to teach her a lesson..." Vulpie admits and Polar sits up, raising an eyebrow.

"What exactly did you do, Vulpie?" Polar asks his husband.

"I never would do it again, but NLIN stands for non-lethal infantry neutralization unit. I read about prototypes the military was building."

"And Vulpie built his own." Vincent cuts in. "Not only did he manage to create a machine that can shock any target within two miles, he completed it when the military industrial complex couldn't. The ones they have now have been contracted out of Vulpie Industries." Vincent explains.

"We've discussed some of this at work." Polar comments and looks to Vulpie. "So that's why you were able to get VulGrid into production so fast. You already had the blueprints and an idea about how to make it from your attack on Break Tail park."

"A NLIN unit only shocks. I wasn't going to kill anybody or anything."

"Yes but enough shocks could kill someone. I can only imagine what you did to that poor bastard that helped you make the movable stand for it." Vincent tells Vulpie.

"Wait, what?" Polar laughs and shoots Vulpie a demanding expression.

"I knew this guy up towards Sevik that worked on maintenance robots." Vulpie tells the white furred wolf. "And I went to him to have a moveable stand built for my NLIN weapon."

"You paid a guy to help you plan an attack?"

"No, I barely told him what it was for."

"But he did end up shocking his friend with it and then fried the electrical lines throughout his warehouse. I think there was some trouble in paradise." Vincent grins.

"That's enough of that!" Vulpie laughs and tries to shush the brown fox. The boat shakes in the waves and Polar looks to Vincent.

"It goes on and on my friend. You had better keep this one in line." Vincent suggests to the white furred wolf.

"I know, it's why I love him." Polar replies and smiles at Vulpie but it's obvious the wolf is thinking.

"Well go ahead and tell him all of it. Or I can tell you myself." Vulpie offers.

"You see, he had been a problem to the GBI for a long time." Vincent continues and Polar looks back at him. "They knew he was dangerous because of his talents. He was given an opportunity to attend Rinwulv at age fourteen when only adults were admitted."

"Yeah my brother had a hard time believing that one." Polar comments. "But he's more or less a fox hater, in all honesty."

"I hope it doesn't run in the family." Vincent responds with a vulpine look.

"What do you think?" Polar asks and chuckles. "Do you know how much harassment I go through as a wolf being in a gay marriage with a fox? If anyone appreciates how smart foxes are..." Polar smirks at Vulpie. "And cute... I think it's me."

"I think Karl Vulches would just love to meet you. I hear Vulpie's been chatting with him again." Vincent responds and Vulpie shakes his head.

"PLEASE don't bring him into this." Vulpie growls.

"The AFR guy?" Polar asks, perking his ears.

"Yes."

"The same one you had to tell off after the corporate deal?" Polar asks.

"Yes, the same guy." Vulpie answers.

"I thought you told him more or less that he had better stay the hell away from Vulpie Industries." Polar thinks out loud.

"Karl is just a fox that thinks our species is superior to every other animal in the universe in everything." Vulpie says and licks his lips dryly. "I hate him."

"Polar could be your new spokesman. I'm sure he would be nicer." Vincent taunts and Vulpie smirks.

"If it wasn't for Polar I'd probably be dead or in jail..." Vulpie says and shows the wolf an affectionate face. "So it's not like any of us are perfect."

"Except for me." Vincent replies to which Vulpie laughs.

"Well you couldn't catch me so that makes you at best, what, the first flawed fox?" Vulpie grins back.

"On the subject, just what is going on with the AFR and Vulpie? I'd like to know from your perspective, Vincent." Polar inquires. "I know he's done his part to get along with them, but whenever he's on the phone with this Karl person, he walks off in the other room and argues and argues."

"Well Vulpie's their shining star of course. They have no problem showing his face when money or support needs to be made, but a lot of the older association of fox rights members take issue with his sexuality... And you for being with him... There have been threats made against you and Vulpie's had to threaten them back." Vincent explains and looks between them. "Quite a bit, so I hear. As a matter of fact Karl and some of the other senior members have sort of splintered off from the AFR and formed another group called SOB. It means save our brother, because brother Vulpie in their eyes is on the wrong track."

"See all of the wonderful stuff you've been missing out on?" Vulpie asks Polar and rolls his eyes in frustration.

"What kind of threats are being made?" Polar asks and Vincent looks between them again.

"Death threats." Vincent plainly answers. "I'm sure he hasn't told you because he's had to give it right back to Karl. Vulches is not the kind of guy that backs down unless he feels the heat on his fur, and let me tell you, Vulpie can turn up the heat." The brown fox laughs and stretches a bit before looking to Vulpie. "What did you threaten to do to him if anything happened to Polar?"

"Let's not go into specifics please, thank you." Vulpie responds and timidly looks at Polar for reassurance.

"I had no idea this was going on." Polar says and waits for Vulpie's response.

"You know why I never mentioned it."

"Because you didn't want me to worry, I know, but how serious is this?" Polar asks his fox husband.

"Serious enough that Karl knows better than to do anything to you, ever." Vulpie answers.

"He'd more likely come after Vulpie in all honesty. Vulpie pisses him off in ways you couldn't imagine. He comes up with enough to distract him from you most of the time." Vincent tells Polar. "And I think that is the plan."

"You know I'd never let anyone hurt you if I could stop it." Vulpie tells Polar.

"I'm not that worried about myself, Vulpie. I'm getting worried for you though." Polar confesses. "Instead of trading blows with this Karl fellow why don't you let me speak to him?"

"It doesn't work like that. Karl Vulches wouldn't even talk to you. You're just a wolf." Vincent informs Polar, to which the white furred wolf blinks in surprise.

"That's how he thinks, Polar." Vulpie says in agreement.

"There are some of us... A very few of us, that believe wolves are just made to work for foxes." Vincent elaborates. "Karl is just like that. He doesn't look at you and see Vulpie's husband, Polar. He sees an arctic wolf, he believes, that is defiling the smartest fox who has ever lived. It's obvious that Vulpie is submissive in your relationship."

"You don't know Vulpie very well, then." Polar jests in the serious moment while smirking.

"Well, whatever." Vincent replies and shakes his head. "You know what I mean. It's the suggestion of you humiliating him in the bedroom that we're discussing. I can't see what Vulpie likes in having you treat him like a woman, but I'm not gay. I'm also smart enough to figure out that it doesn't affect my own masculinity and I don't care. Karl isn't like that. He views any suggestion in the media, universe wide, of a wolf having sex with a fox as a reprehensible act. And its amplified several times over because Vulpie's famous, and in most respects, an advertisement for how talented foxes can be."

"I've heard about some of this stuff... From my brother Richard of all people..." Polar admits. "He's the one that doesn't like foxes, and he told me that the AFR gives you marching orders and you have to follow them. Or else dissenters disappear in the night, etcetera, etcetera."

"Well it's not like it was two hundred years ago." Vincent responds and cracks his knuckles. "But there are some suggestions given to fellow foxes on how to work together and become successful in life. Most of the things before Vulpie that came along seemed tame to me, but since he's risen to stardom, there have been some fire and brimstone conversations. That's why the AFR splintered into another group led by Karl."

"So this is why... Is this why you're hiring so much security at Vulpie Industries?" Polar asks his husband.

"Yes." Vulpie admits with a sad face.

"I don't want you to make any more threats on my behalf, alright? It sounds like this is turning into a pissing contest." Polar says.

"Vulpie's handled it just about right, I'd say." Vincent informs Polar. "You have to understand that things are different among our species when it comes to certain things. Vulpie has carefully chosen his words while taking the wind out of Karl's sails."

"Well I'm not a fox and I don't think I understand. I do know, as a wolf, that if enough back and forth happens someone usually has to pay in blood." Polar tells Vincent. He looks left to Vulpie and sends a loving face before speaking to him. "I'm not blaming you. Just don't get involved anymore. I can fight my own battles."

"I won't stand by and just let them say the things they have about you!" Vulpie emotionally answers but quickly regains his composure. "...But I won't if that's what you want."

"I'll be okay. I don't want you in trouble either." Polar warmly replies.

"Karl how about one of those cigars now?" Nathan Fenrir suggests amidst the sounds of the sports networks. The two brown foxes sit in expensive recliners that are two four chairs circling a small table. The Vulai is the most prestigious club house in Sufias city and inside its ballroom there are twenty flat screen high definition televisions mounted around the room. Everywhere one looks something can be found to watch.

"Right." Karl replies and hands over one of his best cigs to Nathan. The fellow fox accepts and goes to cutting its tip off and lighting it. "The sooner we get rid of this... MOTHERFUCKER... The better." Karl hisses as he watches a commercial featuring Vulpie.

The orange furred fox boy is selling his latest V Screen with all of his star power, standing alongside comedians and fellow movie stars while the benefits of the digital toy are shown for viewers. Nathan looks up and sees Vulpie's face and sighs.

"I know."

"When is that Buxton girl coming over to see me?" Karl inquires.

"Vulpie's contact? Well she's received your requests. I'm sure she will." Fenrir replies.

"Someone needs to remind her that her father owes me $145,000."

"She knows that... Believe me."

"Then why doesn't the little bitch pick up her phone?"

"She's scared of you Karl." Nathan chuckles. "She knows you want to fuck her."

"I will one way or the other so she might as well stop wasting my time." Karl grins and reaches down to his ash tray. He picks up his lit cigar and takes a deep puff off of it. Both he and Nathan blow smoke around the same moment towards the TV showing the advertisements for Vulpie Industries.

"Never in all of my years..." Nathan thinks out loud as the commercial ends with Vulpie blowing a kiss to the camera. "I still can't believe he had the trial thrown out. He was under duress? Duress, really?"

"Who would have thought Druward was so fucking stupid to punch the kid in the GBI headquarters." Karl responds.

"Druward isn't stupid, old buddy. He's playing ball."

"Those black wolves are all the same. Give him half a chance to torture an animal and he'll do anything... He's just smarter than your average neck biter..."

"Druward's getting paid AND cutting throats." Nathan responds with admiration filling his voice. "It wasn't his fault. Vulpie's just too smart."

"Maybe not, but I don't trust him. You can never trust a wolf." Karl says and sucks on his cigar again.

"Figuring him out is impossible. He works with us but doesn't want to fuck a vixen. That's not your average wolf scum." Nathan comments.

"You offered him whores. A man like him doesn't like to pay." Karl replies.

"No, he isn't interested in fox women. I've offered him more than hookers."

"So he isn't a gutter wolf. That's not a high standard to start from. But it's something I suppose. At least he does play ball like you say." Fenrir exhales smoke while listening and relishes the smell.

"These dark cigars have a sweet flavor to them don't they?" Nathan asks.

"Cocoa." Karl answers, the 53 year old brown fox looking around the room. His brown eyes go from one TV to the next as he looks for sports news. "Did VG win?" Karl inquires, referring to Vaughrin University. The school is a mostly fox populated college, but its football team is all wolves and lions. Foxes like Karl and Nathan Fenrir call the shots on game day and they both have large bets going on the game. Since they both come from wealthy fox families it's more of an ego test.

"Yeah, 52 to 10!" Fenrir laughs.

"Alright! That new coach had no chance against Vulichi!"

"VG always wins. Don't you guys know that?" Zorpiv asks as he walks up to them. Karl and Nathan look at him but neither say anything. Zorpiv, a good-sized and slim gray fox, steps about nervously until Karl finally speaks to him.

"You can sit down now." Karl grumbles without making eye contact. Zorpiv's blood boils at the pompous attitude coming from the powerful older man but he has no choice but to silently take a seat in one of the nearby recliners. Nathan smirks and Zorpiv is quick to shoot him a displeased face. It's obvious neither of the older foxes have any respect for him at all.

"I remember you now." Nathan Fenrir says and grins at the young man. "Your mother... She married Nolan Vixil.

"That's right." Zorpiv quickly answers and moves his tail around in anger, showing off the black stripe that runs down the back of it. Like all gray foxes his fur is an amalgam of gray, black, red and white fur. Zorpiv has very pronounced fur colors, however, and the black fur underneath his chin and around the sides of his muzzle is very dark. The coal streaks that begin at the corners of his eye sockets and stretch out to the sides of his cheek bones clash just as vivaciously. The red hair he has on his throat, chest, belly and down the front of his legs and arms contrasts against the areas of white, which are equally noticeable, making Zorpiv one memorable fox.

"He was in the hospitality industry, isn't that right? His business went belly up after Karl came in and bought up the competition.

"Yes it's a wonderful story. Thank you for reminding me." The slender fox snaps back. Zorpiv's tone doesn't entirely please Karl but he still doesn't look at him yet. He continues pretending to watch television.

"That must be hard living paycheck to paycheck. It was good of Karl to give you a job. He's not so bad if you get to know him." Fenrir comments and Zorpiv has the audacity to glance at Karl.

To his dismay, the fox is glancing back at the exact same moment and Zorpiv quickly averts his eyes. A small moment of silence falls over the group but the bar clubhouse is far from quiet with all of the TVs playing at the same time. The volume is just loud enough for the three to talk privately without having to shout.

"Over six million credits in debt..." Karl says and at last looks at Zorpiv who stiffens. "That's what your father owed me. It's been difficult maintaining your trust fund with such an endless hole..."

"I know." Zorpiv simply responds. "I didn't complain. I showed up. What do you want from me?"

"Well..." Karl answers and blows smoke from his nose as he closes his mouth for a moment. He enjoys tasting the flavor with his vulpine nostrils only. "We all make choices in life. We'll all do our job when choosing is easy, but for everyone there comes a day when it is not easy. Sometimes he must choose what will define him. Sometimes he must take on something that slings him out of his comfort zone... And tonight is your night to choose."

"Okay then. What am I choosing?" Zorpiv asks.

"I have something in mind for you... You have trouble working because you don't like to take orders... Well how would you like to give the orders instead of taking them?" Karl inquires and shows Zorpiv an intense face.

"What do you mean?"

"I mean I need you to do something for me... WE... Need you to do something for us... For all foxes everywhere..."

"Tell me what it is." Zorpiv anxiously replies.

"I need you to kill Vulpie Vivixen..." Karl answers and glances at Nathan. Fenrir raises his eyebrows as Zorpiv quickly glances at him in surprise. The young adult fox blinks and takes in what he has heard for a moment.

"You're serious?" Zorpiv answers.

"I'm a very serious man. You know that by now." Karl answers and returns a very threatening expression that makes Zorpiv's fur stand on end. The young man slowly relaxes as he continues to think. Somehow the proposal actually makes him feel more comfortable because of its gravity. Karl and Nathan both watch him carefully. After a few moments Zorpiv bursts into laughter and shakes his head.

"And I thought you would never get off my back..." He tells Karl and Karl actually smirks. "So this will make us even?"

"This will make us even." Karl agrees and smiles slowly before licking his lips.

"All of my debts..."

"Will be wiped away. I'll give you your father's shares and you can do what you want with it; Take your parents on a cruise, go by a home in the suburbs and let them retire... You won't be my concern anymore."

"IF I do this?" Zorpiv responds with a cool expression.

"IF you do this... Yes..." Karl responds.

"What about you?" Zorpiv asks Nathan to which the brown fox chuckles.

"I want this as much as Karl but it's his game. I stay away from this business." Zorpiv stares at him for a moment and looks around. No one is paying attention and even if someone was, Karl Vulches' word is never questioned. "You can't say it's a bad deal. Just think of what you'll do for all of us."

"I'm in. I'll... Take care of this, but it will be impossible won't it? Vulpie Vivixen has government bodyguards on top of his company's private security. The government needs him alive even though he's not under contract anymore. There's no way I'll even get close with Blacktail protecting him."

"We've taken steps to win this before it even begins..." Karl confidently says and takes a deep breath from his cigar before blowing smoke towards Zorpiv. Zorpiv tries to ignore it but can't stand the sweet stink. He has to cough a few times and Karl waits until he speaks again. "We have someone very powerful who has promised to deliver Vulpie to us if the situation is profitable for him."

"Who? Who's going to give me that kind of help?"

"The director of the GBI." Karl answers to which Zorpiv blinks in surprise. He pulls back and squints.

"Druward Wraulgh?"

"Yes."

"You have that kind of pull with Druward Wraulgh?" Zorpiv incredulously asks once more.

"Of course I do. I own half of his agency through the Association of Fox Rights." Karl responds. "And Druward got to where he is today because he recognizes where the real players are."

"I'm sure the AFR can be a real pain in his ass but he's a dark wolf. I didn't think foxes were supposed to make deals like this with them."

"On the contrary, black furred wolves are the best wolves to manipulate. They're smart enough to lie like a fox. You would be a fool to trust a gray or timber wolf with this, but coal furred wolves are smart. Well, they're as smart as a wolf can be..."

"Okay, so what did you offer him for this?"

"That's not your concern. You need to listen to my instructions and do exactly as I tell you." Karl Vulches tells Zorpiv with a searing voice.

"ONE MORE THING." Zorpiv interrupts and Karl licks his lips. The brown fox thinks about getting angry, but there is a particularly useful look on Zorpiv's face. "Why me? You hate me, so why would you give me command over the Vuldrofein? I assume that's who I will be working with."

"Yes, you'll command the Vuldrofein if Nathan and I tell them to follow you, and we will. I chose you because you're that very special kind of gray fox... You Vixils just love to murder and rape. Just how many times has your family embarrassed the Association of Fox Rights? It's too many times to count, with all of the honor killings against wolves, and the thieving, and the whoring... You, Zorpiv Vixil, are good for this sort of work. Wouldn't you agree?" Karl asks and a silence fills the group against the club's television chatter.

"Well... It sounds to me like you're framing me. How convenient for you if the Vuldrofein is arrested by the police and a Vixil is leading the operation! You can deny all involvement and blame it on my family." Zorpiv hisses.

"Exactly." Karl responds and smirks. The admission catches Zorpiv by surprise and the gray fox blinks. "You're right Zorpiv."

"So you at least admit it... I wasn't expecting that..."

"Do you want your father's shares or not? Do this for me, risk yourself, and if you succeed, you'll be set for life." Karl tells the intense looking gray fox. Zorpiv goes silent again. His mind races as he considers the situation. The Vuldrofein is the Association of Fox Right's clandestine hit squad. It isn't supposed to exist, and many foxes would be outraged if they found out it did, but it does, and foxes like Karl Vulches have been responsible for countless murders through it over the years.

"Okay... I'll call it a fair deal then." Zorpiv answers.

"It's more than fair, Zorpiv... Just think about all of the fun you will have..." Karl insidiously suggests.

"Do you want him alive?"

"Bring him to me alive if you can. If it's impossible just kill the little faggot, but I would love to teach Vulpie some manners..." Karl replies. "Do whatever you like with him before you turn him over to me. Beat him, rape him, gang rape him, I don't mind, but keep him in one piece. I want to torture Vivixen personally. And in the end, Nathan gets to finish him off."

"Payback for the faggot biting my muzzle." Nathan Fenrir growls and rubs his facial fur, reliving the memory.

"Gang rape?" Zorpiv responds and his fur stands on end. An evil smile fills his face. "What a wonderful idea."

"I figured you would like that sort of thing. The more twisted the better... But I want him healthy enough to respond to punishment. We're going to take our time with him." Karl says and takes another puff on his cigar.

"What about the fag's boyfriend, the wolf?" Zorpiv inquires.

"What about him? Don't get distracted from the task at hand. I want you to bring me Vulpie. Don't worry about his so called husband." Karl says and looks up for a moment, contemplating a few scenarios before looking back at Zorpiv. "But don't take any chances around what's his name."

"Polar Arctic." Zorpiv answers.

"Those arctic wolves from Winters Dale are very strong. It's best that you just shoot him if he gets in your way."

"Well it looks like we're going to be friends after all."

Zorpiv smiles.

Hot Fur

"Want one?" Polar asks Vulpie while retrieving a frozen blue popsicle.

"Sure!" Vulpie answers and walks over to the steel refrigerator. The kitchen of their Casillfori home is a wonder to behold, as is the rest of the house. Their beach home is a mansion, based on a luxury home design, with a tan exterior and a red concrete tiled roof. They both loved the new age steel design of the stove, refrigerator and other appliances in the kitchen that clashes against the exotic wooden design that fills the rest of the house.

Polar sucks on his popsicle and hands Vulpie a green one and they both walk over to the wide tall windows in the den. The kitchen is huge, and easily blends into the den thanks to a very tasteful design that furthers the wooden furniture in the kitchen. The best thing about the lighting in the home besides the chandelier designs throughout the house is the windows in the den. They are floor level and span nearly the entire length of the den so that a beautiful view of the pool outside and the Paxyeli sea can be enjoyed.

Outside Polar and Vulpie's pleasure boats bounce in the water, tied back up to their piers after the day's excursion. The sea sparkles and the pool on the luxurious porch outside is always inviting. But even though both Polar and Vulpie still are wearing their swimming trunks, just having come home, they haven't actually done any swimming yet. Both of them eye the pool while they both have the same idea, but for now they just enjoy their frozen treats.

Since they've been out in the sun all day, their fur and the skin underneath is warm from a very nice tan. It's the relaxing "vacation" feeling one gets, and they both take it easy. The sight of the ocean and pool outside is a beautiful thing, and the popsicles are delicious since they are hot. The central air conditioning is blowing wide open so they can cool down.

"Done, Hun?" Vulpie asks as he munches down the last of his treat and licks his lips. He can see that Polar has already finished his and the wolf hands him his empty popsicle stick. Vulpie takes them over to the sink in the kitchen and opens one of the doors underneath it where the trash can is. He tosses them in and closes the door just as Polar walks back into the kitchen to get some water.

They both take turns washing their paws and Polar gets out two glasses just in case Vulpie wants something to drink. He fills them as Vulpie walks around the luxurious chopping block/table in the middle of the kitchen and when Vulpie comes around he hands him his glass. They both drink for a little bit and Polar looks over Vulpie's shirtless body. All the orange furred fox has on is his pink swimming trunks and Polar followed suit when he got inside the house because he was hot. All he wears is his brown trunks as well. Vulpie sets his glass down on the chopping block and walks into the den just as Polar finishes drinking and he follows suit.

"I think it went well. Worhel seems like a decent guy for Vulpie Industries to work with." Polar says and Vulpie goes over to the den table, next to one of the three expensive white couches. The den table is currently empty because they haven't fully decorated their vacation home yet.

"Yeah." Vulpie replies with his effeminate voice and leans on the table with his paws, looking outside.

"But that stuff about the AFR... That was... Wow." Polar comments as he walks next to Vulpie. He looks down at him with his blue eyes. Vulpie sees him move close and they both would like a kiss, so Vulpie let's go of the table and sends his paws to Polar's muscular sides.

"Well baby we foxes are all wacko I'm afraid!" Vulpie grins and Polar wraps his big arms around him.

"I like my crazy fox..." Polar warmly says and leans down for a kiss. Vulpie eagerly returns it. They taste each other's lips with romantic motions inside the cool luxurious room. When they finish, Vulpie licks Polar's nose affectionately and Polar licks him back.

Polar lovingly squeezes Vulpie, and Vulpie reciprocates by rubbing Polar's sides intimately. Polar enjoys the fox feeling him up because it's obvious Vulpie adores his strength. They let go of each other and Vulpie swishes his tail in thought.

"What did you think of Vincent? He's cool huh?" Vulpie asks with excitement.

"He looked at you like he wasn't sure whether you could be trusted or not." Polar answers.

"Yeah." Vulpie smiles. "Vincent's the only guy that ever came close to putting me away."

"Well I'm glad he told me the things about the AFR. I wish you wouldn't keep things like that from me." Polar admits and Vulpie looks aside.

"I said I wouldn't keep it a secret anymore."

"Good. I hope after all we've been through that you'll let me in on everything. I don't keep secrets from you."

"Really? How come you never told me your parents dream about me?" Vulpie inquires with a mischievous expression and the statement makes Polar's eyes widen. He opens his mouth a little, confused.

"How did you... How could you know about that? You weren't even with me when I went home!" Polar says in shock.

"You didn't tell me that your brother dreamed about me too. How spooky that must be for Richard!" Vulpie teases and bites his tongue between his teeth while he stands on his left leg and uses his right foot to poke Polar's left knee playfully. "Huh? Huh Polar? Why didn't you tell me that?" Polar laughs in surprise, but it's the sort of surprise someone has when they come across a frightening discovery.

"Are you? Are you spying on me, Vulpie?"

"Secrets! SEEEEEEEECRETS!" Vulpie naughtily replies.

"Stop. Stop it now... I want to know how you know that." Polar tells Vulpie and frowns. Vulpie just smiles even more in response. "Are you actually having me followed? You're doing that to me?"

"Nope!"

"Then how?" Polar intently asks.

"I'm gonna let you wonder!" Vulpie giggles. At this, Polar raises his eyebrows and gives Vulpie a disapproving face.

"Oh, so we're actually back here again? I remember the last time you said that."

"Yellow, Green, Red, Green, Yellow, Red, Green!" Vulpie teases.

"Yeah, that's it. That's where we are right now. Well that's just fantastic." Polar says with an irritated voice and crosses his arms. "We're married and now you're doing the same things that almost ruined it for us?"

"The Association of Fox Rights bugged your parent's house." Vulpie answers, going serious. The statement makes Polar blink and he quickly stops himself from being angry. "Yeah..........." Vulpie tells Polar and raises his eyebrows with a grim look. Polar goes quiet as he considers his husband's reply.

"They really did?" Polar quietly asks.

"Absolutely." Vulpie answers. Now Polar understands what Vulpie is doing. His fox lover just got his message across perfectly.

"So you what? You found out by hacking the AFR?"

"That's right." Vulpie answers and shows Polar a loving face. "This is the only kind of thing that I hide from you."

"Did somebody get rid of the bugs in my parent's home?" Polar quickly inquires.

"I took care of it." Vulpie promises and the reassurance allows Polar to release a pent up anxious breath.

"Goddess I can't believe that's the truth. Why would they spy on my family? We don't even live there." Polar says in confusion.

"Because they're evil. Vincent and most of them are not, but I'm telling you Polar, the AFR has some really bad foxes." Vulpie responds.

"I just... Wow, I can't believe all of this. I had no clue."

"So what do you think now? Do you still blame me for keeping it a secret? I took care of it on my own, and I continue to take care of them, but they won't stop." Vulpie says.

"No, I don't blame you anymore. I see why you hid it from me." Polar tells his fox lover and swallows with a tired look. "I thought you were doing something you shouldn't."

"Yeah, those guys in the AFR think like I did when I was a criminal."

"Vulpie, I'm sorry I doubted you." Polar apologizes.

"It's okay, Baby. I don't mind you knowing about it. I just wanted to save you the grief, that's all." Vulpie responds.

"I love you, and I do trust you."

"I know you do. I'm sorry I teased you!" Vulpie says with a wry grin.

"Well don't scare me like that again!" Polar laughs. "Okay?"

"Okay." Vulpie promises with a very cute voice.

"I'm the one that's supposed to protect you, not the other way around." Polar lovingly says and moves close to Vulpie.

"What, you don't like the roles being reversed?" Vulpie mischievously giggles.

"No. You belong to me..." Polar whispers and feels his fur standing on end. "But I love you so much for watching over my family."

"It was nothing!" Vulpie replies and looks down when he notices Polar is starting to get an erection. The arctic wolf's big penis bulges ferociously in his brown swimming trunks. Polar breathes fast and Vulpie hears the lust in his voice. "Oh! Oh my goodness! Did I turn you on?"

"Don't you move!" Polar breathes with an excited face. "I'll be right back!"

"You've got to put me back in my place don't you?" Vulpie giggles.

"Oh yeah!" Polar groans and quickly bends down to kiss the top of Vulpie's head. Vulpie winces with a smile as the wolf walks by him, and heads out of the den towards the bedroom. "Stay right there!" Polar grins as he disappears.

"Kay!" Vulpie breathes in excitement. Polar rummages around in their luxurious closet and finds the sex lubricant he is looking for just as the gay fox boy does a little happy dance for himself. When Polar comes back into the huge den he sees Vulpie prancing about and flicking his tail right and left. Vulpie giggles mischievously and Polar starts laughing. As he nears Vulpie, Vulpie hops to the left and prances about, evading the arctic wolf.

"Alright, come here you!" Polar laughs and reaches out to grab Vulpie but Vulpie dances out of his reach. It takes a little more effort for Polar to get his paws on him but he manages, snatching Vulpie's left arm with his right paw. "Don't you play hard to get when you've got a hard one to get!" Polar taunts and at this they both laugh loudly. Vulpie stops avoiding the powerful wolf after the joke and quickly comes back over to the couches and most importantly the empty den table.

Polar puts both of his paws on Vulpie's shoulders and spins him around just as the fox boy attempts to bend over the piece of furniture. Polar surprises his husband and moves his paws down to his pink swimming trunks and fiercely pulls them down. Vulpie's little hard erection bounces as Polar makes him naked and the fox boy steps out of his trunks as Polar throws them aside.

The white furred wolf doesn't stop there, though. He clamps his big paws around Vulpie's butt on both sides and lifts him up in the air, before sitting him down on the table, facing him. Vulpie yelps in delight and makes himself comfortable, lying back on the table as Polar lets go of him and removes his own swimming trunks. Polar's big dick bounces gracefully when free, and the white furred wolf licks his lips, sending his paws out to Vulpie. He takes hold of Vulpie's sides and pull's the fox boy's butt to the end of the table so he can fuck him. He pops open the tube of sex lubrication nearby and squirts it on his cock.

"Oh God I love you Polar!" Vulpie breathes as he lies on his back and pulls his knees up. Polar masturbates quickly, using the lube to prepare for Vulpie's tight ass. He covers his massive erection with the slick fluid and aims the head of his wolf cock to Vulpie's anus. Polar pushes it in, and Vulpie inhales as it spreads him open. He whimpers when Polar penetrates him, feeling the wolf slide his big cock all the way inside, balls deep. "Oh Fuck!" Vulpie breathes and grimaces. The fox's asshole burns but the pleasure of Polar's big dick pushing against his prostate quickly overrides any pain he has. Soon the only thing he feels is awesome, and they both need this badly. They are swelling with love. Polar shows Vulpie a deeply affectionate smile as he begins making love to him.

"I love you so much Vulpie..." Polar breathes down to the fox boy and reaches with his right paw to his husband's penis just as Vulpie starts to masturbate. Polar pushes Vulpie's paw aside and takes over the job instead, and Vulpie makes a delighted sound in reciprocation. The white furred wolf strokes the fox boy's penis while fucking him at the same time and controls their intimacy completely.

"Uh! You feel so good!" Vulpie whines while his eyes water.

"I will always protect you. Let me protect you, Vulpie." Polar says and smiles happily. He clutches Vulpie's left leg, taking hold of the fox's position, and continues to use his right paw to stroke his husband's cock.

"UH! Ah!" Vulpie moans and they keep staring into each other's eyes. As the pleasure increases for both of them they become more vocal with moans of bliss. Polar takes to masturbating Vulpie quickly while fucking him and Vulpie grunts effeminately at the increase in speed. The white furred wolf always has superb rhythm and has Vulpie very excited in no time at all. Polar takes pride in seeing how Vulpie's eyes brim with tears once again. He knows he's pushing against and massaging his fox lover's prostate in all the right ways and judging by how hard Vulpie's cock gets, he also knows he can dictate how soon or hard he can make his husband cum.

Polar takes his time and relishes the knowledge. He enjoys relaxing Vulpie and thinks about how much the fox really does care for him. Despite being so much smaller he has fought for Polar in ways he never imagined. The fact that Vulpie has been waging a silent war to protect Polar makes the wolf feel true love. Making love to Vulpie now in the spur of the moment when all of these feelings are fresh excites both of them beyond words.

"Oh yeah!" Polar groans in bliss and grins as he feels Vulpie's tight asshole sliding around his big cock during each thrust and retreat. He feels pre cum coming out of his wolf penis inside the fox boy's ass and he increases his speed at the thought of ejaculating in him.

"Polar! Uh!" Vulpie moans while smiling from ear to ear. Polar smiles right back, knowing what is on his lover's mind. The hot sex is especially gratifying after the discussion of the wolf fox taboo with Vincent.

"Karl doesn't know what he's missing out on, does he?" Polar laughs.

"NO HE DOESN'T!" Vulpie groans in delight and Polar strokes his husband's cock even faster. He pumps Vulpie's ass and masturbates him according to the expression on Vulpie's face and judging by the grimace of pleasure, he knows he's ramming it home. "FUCK ME POLAR! OH YEAH! OH GOD POLAR FUCK ME!"

"You look like you're enjoying it!" Polar grins.

"Make me your bitch! Cum in me! Make me cum!"

"I'll tell you when you're allowed to cum." Polar commands and squeezes Vulpie's penis to stop the fox's ejaculation. Vulpie moans in frustration but also enjoyment, seeing how Polar is working him over and building up the orgasm for both of them. The white furred wolf continues to fuck Vulpie but doesn't stroke him, and Vulpie grunts as he takes it. Polar enjoys his own strength and cocks his head to the left and right while fucking Vulpie. He sees his cock going up inside Vulpie and then pulling back out with each wonderful pump, and eventually starts stroking Vulpie's penis again.

"UUhhahhh!" Vulpie moans in thanks and pants in delight.

"You're mine Vulpie. You don't protect me. I protect you." Polar repeats and they stare into each other's eyes as they both feel cum backing up in their cocks. Polar increases his speed and Vulpie lays his head back in anticipation.

"POLAR! UH!" Vulpie whimpers. Polar masturbates his husband faster and faster, matching his own need and soon they are both at the brink. While Polar thrusts in need he is surprised when Vulpie cries out sooner than he expected. The orange furred fox boy's anus tightens up as he ejaculates, and cums high into the air. "AAAAAHHHH!!!" Vulpie loudly yelps and his own cum falls down into his mouth. Polar didn't plan it, and laughs in surprise. The rest of Vulpie's cumshot lands on his white furred belly as he continues to orgasm but Polar can't help but say something.

"Tasty?" Polar taunts and at this Vulpie groans in the ecstasy of release. The fox boy closes his mouth and swallows his own cum without thinking much about it. He just enjoys the powerful afterglow of his orgasm while Polar grins and keeps fucking him.

"OHHHHhhuuuuhhhhhhhhhh...Polar……. " Vulpie lovingly breathes with a very happy smile on his face. His eyes stay half open and he trembles, his fur standing on end.

"There's my foxy!" Polar grins and shuffles his feet a little so he can fuck Vulpie with harder thrusts to maximize his own pleasure. Since Vulpie has cummed already, his prostate is sensitive and doesn't like the extra attention. The gay fox boy loves the white furred wolf though and makes a point not to wince or do anything to slow Polar down while he gets what he needs. It wouldn't be fair for him to complain after Polar made him feel so good just a few moments ago.

"Oh God!" Vulpie breathes in his effeminate voice and goes as limp as possible. Polar focuses on the orgasm he is building and grits his teeth in anticipation. Seeing this, Vulpie tightens his asshole rhythmically a few times. He swishes his tail and ignores the fact that Polar is hurting his legs because he holds them with such a powerful grip.

"OH FUCK YEAH! Yeah!" Polar growls and squints, showing his teeth to Vulpie. Vulpie returns a frightened expression to play with the wolf's predatory hormones and it works. Polar hungrily snarls and cums in Vulpie's ass with several rough thrusts, and Vulpie can't hide his pain entirely. He whines, taking the pounding as well as he can while feeling Polar's cum shoot in his colon. "AAWWRRGGGHH!!!" Polar howls and snaps his mouth shut while ejaculating. One shot, two shots, three shots, four shots, Vulpie thinks he feels about nine spurts of semen come out of Polar's cock.

"MMnnneah!" Vulpie whimpers.

"Oh my God Vulpie!" Polar blissfully gasps and holds still. He slowly releases his mighty grip on the fox boy's legs and pants in exertion.

"MMmmmm… So good…" Vulpie sings in response.

"OOOHHH!" Polar groans into laughter. "UH! That's the stuff!"

"That's the wolfy stuff!" Vulpie mischievously grins.

"Yeah who do you love?" Polar proudly asks.

"You baby!" Vulpie answers in delight. The fox boy can't hold his smile for long though, as when Polar pulls back, the wolf's fat cock starts yanking out of his ass. Vulpie inhales, Polar's wolf cum burning his asshole and rectum as his penis leaves and it pops out with a sudden and effusive splat. "Ah!" Vulpie yelps and reaches down to hold his butt in pain. It burns like fire and Polar watches his cum run out of Vulpie's anus with pride.

"Did you like that up your ass?" Polar teases.

"Oh you know I did baby! It hurt but I liked it!" Vulpie breathes and slowly lowers his legs. He leans forward with equally slow motion, wincing from his punishment.

"Oh man! I really unloaded!" Polar laughs and watches Vulpie creep forward off of the table, trying to stand.

"You reamed me the fuck out!" Vulpie groans and squints as he puts his feet on the floor. He succeeds in standing but has to do it in one quick motion and grits his teeth in pain. The orange furred fox boy can't hide his suffering but he starts giggling when he sees Polar's expression. The white furred wolf is utterly delighted at the result of Vulpie's pounding.

"Need some help walking?" Polar naughtily inquires. "Want me to carry you?"

"You shut the fuck up!" Vulpie growls with a grin and they both start laughing. After they share the comical moment Polar wraps his arms around Vulpie and leans forward. Vulpie looks up to meet him in a kiss and they enjoy a passionate one.

Druward

Being the Director of the GBI comes with many benefits. When Druward Wraulgh took command of the organization years ago he quickly discovered why animals that reach the position stay in it for so long. The job comes slated with possibilities. For instance, since the director is given free government healthcare while in office it is very tempting to stay in charge as long as possible. The pay is considerable as well, but these rewards are just after thoughts in the black furred wolf's mind.

What Druward truly desires is power. He is a man that relishes the authority he has over others. He served his superiors respectfully while he had to, but steered by meticulous aggression, Druward easily soared through the ranks of the GBI. His work as a field agent propelled him to powerful positions because he understands that the GBI is the tip of the World Government's Spear. He isn't shy about using the force his organization is capable of and as a result of his success within the GBI few question his commands. In some ways Druward has more power than the current president of the world government because his position is not up for election.

He likes money, but sometimes wonders what it is exactly that drives him to do the things he does. Money is not really an issue for him any longer, yet he has agreed to take part in something that will reward him in millions. He sets his bottled water down with his left paw, on the small table to the left of his recliner. He is relaxing inside the den of his expansive home, pondering the meanings of his actions while Karl Vulches and Nathan Fenrir are coming to meet him. He agreed to have them up for a discussion around noon and he expects they will arrive in the next few minutes.

The drive up to Druward's house in the Vauvus Mountains is a substantial one. Vauvus is a national forest, under the jurisdiction of the Sufian Forest Service, which falls under the department of agriculture in the world government. Because Vauvus is such a large national forest and parts of Vauvus are national parks, a commonly used name for the Sufian Forest Service is the Vauvus Forest Service. So those driving into respective areas will see signs for the SFS or VFS along the way to Druward's home. It isn't legal to own property in the Vauvus national park, but his house is one of the largest in the national forest. So the trip the foxes are taking has required a significant amount of time.

Druward has three homes, one in Sufias City, his vacation home in Vauvus, and another in West Sufias. He spends the smallest amount of time in his mountain home because of its distance from Sufias city where most of his work takes him, but it is his favorite house. He spent over a million to have it built. It's designed from Vauvus timber, cut from the very woods it resides in, and was constructed deep in the wilderness in a very unique location.

The black wolf's house is surrounded by forest, but is on top of a cliff as well. The back of his house has a splendid view of distant mountain ranges because the cliff starts there a few hundred feet out. He wanted to build here because the terrain is so different. The cliff is not a sheer drop off, but is very dangerous still. Trees have grown into the rocky outcrops on the way down the cliff on the back of his property, and their presence gives a haunting effect. In the midst of the deadly cliff with jagged rocks on the way to the bottom, these trees jut up and out all around and dangle shadows through the grassy and rocky areas. So somehow the cliff doesn't seem quite so dangerous despite the fact that a wrong step would lead an animal to certain death.

Thanks to this, Druward also made use of the space at the bottom of the cliff on the back of his property. Down there is a bunker he had built for special uses. It was back in his early years when he did many risky things... Things he should not have done, some would say, but to him the memories are simply notes. He dissolved bodies of terrorists when the government needed them gone. He interrogated suspected criminals and spies. Once he even beat a female GBI agent around until she confessed that she stole from the government. He knew if she was afraid enough he could fuck her and get away with it. And he did...

Druward blinks in surprise. For some reason the last thought makes him cringe, and he did not expect it. After all of these years he's never felt guilty about the things he's done in the bunker but today it bothers him. He isn't sure why. The black wolf prides himself on being so absolute. It's what gained him his position with the GBI. One does not achieve the power he has if he doubts himself... So he silently asks himself why he does not want to enjoy that particular memory again.

His thought process is interrupted when two beeps ping through his house. Over his many years as an agent, Druward has come across some very useful technology for homes, the best of which are security devices that monitor traffic. He has motion sensors that alert him to incoming visitors to his home and can glance at the high definition monitor up in the corner of the room if he wants to see who it is. When he looks he sees a single car, a black luxury sedan. It is Karl Vulches and Nathan Fenrir without a doubt, but Druward notices a third passenger as well in the back seat.

The black furred wolf gets up and stretches for a bit. He considers where his other weapons are but is sure the side arm he usually wears at all times is sufficient should there be trouble. He takes all threats seriously, even though the foxes are on his side in the endeavor of the day. Secret meetings can go wrong, but he's more worried about the storm clouds he sees in the distance from the beautiful view out of the back of his home. He wonders whether he will need to cover up his ATV. He played around on the cliffs earlier before parking it near the house.

By the time the doorbell rings, Druward is already opening the door. As he suspected, Karl Vulches and Nathan Fenrir stand at his doorstep with friendly smiles, but it is the other fox with them that draws his attention. Druward focuses his yellow eyes on the gray fox. The young man has a particularly deranged personality behind his courteous brown eyes. This is something Druward has learned to pick up on as a veteran GBI agent.

"Good afternoon Mr. Wraulgh." Karl Vulches says with showmanship.

"Afternoon Mr. Vulches." Druward responds and smiles halfway. The two older foxes are dressed in suits. Karl wears a dark brown design that matches his fur, while Fenrir sports a gray suit. Zorpiv, on the other hand, only has a black jacket on top of a black t shirt, and his pants are gray. "Are you hungry?"

"We've already eaten, thank you." Karl replies and comes inside as Druward steps aside with a courteous gesture. Nathan follows with a noticeably tense expression, and Zorpiv goes by while staring up at the black furred wolf. Druward cocks his head, curious as to why the young fox believes he can challenge him with such a glare in his own home. The gray fox secretly does it because he is fascinated with the GBI director. With everything he's heard about him, he mentally projected a ten foot tall beast of a wolf. Druward sees that Zorpiv watches the way he moves his paws and handles himself, something that a GBI agent would have to be trained to examine. The black furred wolf can already see why he was chosen for the job.

The group walks through Druward's bar room and over to the den where the large windows look out over the Vauvus mountains. Druward has several expensive chairs of all sorts sprawled here and there in the den, all of them brown, matching the same color of his new age forest home. Karl and Nathan take seats on the couch that is across from the bar Druward has at the entrance to his home while Druward sits down in one of his favorite leather recliners. Zorpiv makes himself comfortable in a similar one right across from the black furred wolf.

"You know why we're here. So shall we get straight to it?" Karl inquires while looking to the GBI director. He is closer to Druward, with Nathan sitting to his left, who is to the right of Zorpiv across from Druward.

"Did you bring the money? I don't see a briefcase." Druward replies.

"The money is in the car. I thought we'd discuss things in a little more detail before going to that." The distinguished fox answers.

"Fair enough. Who's the kid? I assume he's the one you want to kill Vulpie?" Druward says and watches all of the foxes tense up except for Zorpiv, who seems excited at the proposal.

"His name is Zorpiv Vixil. His father owed me quite a lot of money and he'll be taking care of this for me to cover his debts. If he pulls it off I plan to give him his father's shares, so he has every incentive to put himself on the line." Karl explains.

"So you believe you can kill someone?" Druward asks Zorpiv.

"Can't wait!" The gray fox grins in response.

"Do you think this is a game?"

"It's all a fucking game." Zorpiv answers with a look out of his eyes that almost makes Druward's fur go on end... Almost. It's not the words that Druward takes note of. It's the statement plus the look out of the fox's brown eyes. The black furred wolf identifies a complete psychopath and glances at Karl and Nathan to see what their reaction is. He can see that Nathan is noticeably bothered but Karl has a calm, possibly arrogant expression.

"Go out to the car and get my money." Druward orders and stares down the gray fox. Karl blinks in surprise and frowns.

"Get it yourself." Zorpiv smarts off with wild eyes and Karl gives him a lethal expression. Druward smiles slowly at Zorpiv, seeing a smile growing on the young fox's face as well.

"Do you know who I am?" Druward asks with an intense voice.

"Yeah!" Zorpiv quickly replies. He heaves in excitement and a silent moment passes until the gray fox finally glances at Karl and sees the irritated expression.

"Go get Druward's money, Zorpiv." Karl instructs.

"Okay." Zorpiv grins while moving with a lowered head. He still looks at Druward as he gets up and walks over to the front door. Zorpiv opens it and leaves, and when he shuts the door behind him Druward waits about four seconds before speaking.

"Where did you find that little beast?" Druward chuckles.

"I apologize for his stupidity, Druward. I know he can and will do this for me, though." Karl responds.

"Oh I'm sure he can. I'm convinced of that, but do you think it's wise to put an automatic in his little paws?" The GBI director asks.

"He's smarter than he looks." Nathan comments.

"I'm not talking about whether he could kill Vulpie or not. I'm asking you whether you think it's a good idea for me to give him automatic weapons. And you actually plan to have him give the Vuldrofein orders?" Druward elaborates.

"His family has done more than its fair share of killing. And when it goes bad, if it goes bad and he's caught, we'll just write him off because of who he comes from." Karl explains. Karl's words make it clear to Druward that both of the AFR foxes have made up their minds already.

"Alright." Druward simply says and sniffs the air.

"And what about you?" Karl suggests with a demanding voice.

"What's the concern?"

"You've had dealings with Vivixen. You were there when his robot nearly killed him and I heard you say it was horrible on the news... So will it be difficult for you to betray him?" At this Druward quietly laughs and shakes his head.

"Not at all."

"So you do want him to pay, right? He wormed out of the lawsuit against him for breaking his government contract by claiming he was under duress by you."

"Which is complete bullshit." Druward growls.

"I know... So you want him dead?" Karl smirks.

"I guess when you put it that way I do... He was responsible for millions, maybe even billions, of dollars of damage because of that Vulpie.net insanity. God he pissed me the fuck off!" The black furred wolf snorts while remembering how he punched Vulpie in the GBI headquarters. "He served what... About one little year? The little fucker should still belong to the government for the next NINE years, but instead he's completely free, and selling his little toys... It's disgusting..."

"Great! You agree! Because by the time we're through with him he'll wish he'd never been born. And we'll send the cocksucker straight to hell."

"As long as I'm paid like we agreed I will cover all of the heat from his disappearance." Druward states.

"And what will the story be about his death? Will it be in the news that he is dead?"

"I'll dispose of the body. I have so many methods to make him disappear... It won't be a problem." Druward answers and the black furred wolf winces when he thinks about Vulpie screaming on the floor of the white room at the CTGD. For some reason a vivid memory of it haunts him.

"We need him alive, or rather, we want him alive. So Zorpiv may need to keep him somewhere isolated."

"Have him brought here... It will be the last place anyone will look..." Druward says.

"To your home?" Karl inquires.

"It wouldn't be the first time a dirty job has been done here..." Druward responds with a cold voice. "This house is not registered in my name. The records are under another alias, so there is nothing that can trace it back to me. But still it's best that I stay away while you take care of Vulpie."

"Well that would simplify things." Karl agrees. All of their ears perk up at the twisting of a doorknob. Zorpiv returns with a silver suitcase in both of his paws and he shuts the door with a controlled push from his left leg. He walks over to the group and takes a knee to set the suitcases down on the floor. Druward eyes the gray fox popping their latches. When they're swung open the

GBI director sees the denominations he expected. Five hundred dollar bills are the highest the world government prints short of treasury notes and they look packed tightly enough to reach six million, three in each case.

Zorpiv takes a look at Druward before rummaging his paw through the money stuffed luggage. He pulls up several layers so Druward can see the bills and the black furred wolf leans forward in his seat to outstretch a paw. Zorpiv hands over a stack of rubber banded five hundreds to him. Karl Vulches watches the black wolf run his finger through the money, making a quick inspection.

"Very good." Druward concludes and gives the money in his paw back to Zorpiv so it can neatly fit in with the others.

"It takes a great deal of faith on my part to pay you the full amount up front, Druward, so I assume there won't be any problems having this done." Karl Vulches tells the black furred wolf with a partially stern tone and Druward leans back in his chair.

"Don't worry Karl. I don't want to fuck with you. Whatever business you have with the other foxes concerning Vulpie doesn't matter to me, but I can guarantee that you will have him." The wolf replies.

"Six million is an enormous payment... That's the same amount Zorpiv's father owed me." Karl responds and Zorpiv looks over at the brown fox with an irritated expression. "I hope you are right."

"Doing this for you will jeopardize my position as Director of the GBI if ever discovered." Druward states. "And the influence I have is not something that can be bought. It took me an entire decade to build the authority I have, so putting it at risk is no small request."

"But it's likely that you will handle this without anyone ever knowing. Am I right?" Karl inquires.

"No, someone will know. That's why it's dangerous for me. I have authority over Blacktail, even though they are a private company, because they are regulated by the government. But even though I can pull them away from Vulpie where you can get to him, there is a good chance someone will be killed in the process..." Druward admits and looks over the three foxes with cool yellow eyes. "The wolf I appointed commander of Vulpie's Blacktail unit is unlikely to leave him completely unguarded. Even if I order the other squad members to another location, Rulef is sure to leave somebody behind.

"Then I'll have to kill them." Zorpiv interjects and Druward looks to him.

"Yes you will... Has anyone ever pointed a gun at you before?" The black wolf asks.

"Yes."

"I hope they have because a cold dread rushes over you when your life is truly on the line." Druward tells the gray fox while his eye catches the red fur on his neck. He looks him over and judges his posture. The young man is tense, but looks ready to spring into action at any moment. "Think you can handle that?"

"Yes." Zorpiv repeats without hesitation.

"Men shit themselves in combat..." Druward reminds the potential assassin. Karl listens and approves of the education Zorpiv is getting. "All sorts of unexpected things happen... They drop their guns... They hesitate to shoot first... Sometimes they even find themselves surrendering before it has a chance to begin, like when someone points a submachine gun at your face... Let me make this very clear, Zorpiv... Every member of Blacktail has killed an animal at some point over their military career. It's a requirement that has ensured only killers are put to the test... So you cannot hesitate to shoot first... You will end up a corpse if you do. Even one Blacktail merc is enough to mow you down and your team of Vuldrofein foxes..."

"Then what do you suggest?" Zorpiv asks and Druward pauses for a moment while thinking.

"I can provide you with a weapon that will end the engagement very, very quickly... Even though you may have to kill a Blacktail merc or even more than one, I do not want a shootout with the police. Remove the threats and kidnap Vulpie as quickly as possible..."

"What gun?" The gray fox eagerly asks.

"I'll show you. We'll go down to my bunker so I can familiarize you with the location. You'll be taking Vulpie down there for safe keeping until Karl and Nathan arrive." Druward elaborates and stands up. He looks to Karl and Nathan who get up as well and Zorpiv follows. The GBI director turns and walks over to the sliding glass door in front of the wonderful view of the Vauvus mountain range and puts his paw to it. He opens it for his guests and they exit the house. Druward closes the door and sniffs the day's fresh but thunderous air. It looks like the storm may begin at any time so he leads the group down the cliff trail as quickly as possible.

To the right of the cliffs and to the back left of his house if looking from the cliffs, there is a small path that leads down to the black wolf's bunker. The resilient trees that have grown into the cliff and those around the deep forests around the house start swaying heavily when the wind picks up. Druward guesses that his all-terrain vehicle is in for a shower but he has far more important things to take care of. The three foxes follow him, looking around and admiring the landscape.

"Your home is a beautiful thing, Druward." Nathan Fenrir says and Druward looks back over his left shoulder at them. The black furred wolf finds the statement a bit odd considering the situation, so his answer is short.

"Yeah."

"Do you have a shooting range down there?" Karl asks as they rapidly descend, possibly a hundred feet just halfway down the trail to the bunker.

"Yes." Druward says, using a louder voice because the wind picks up a bit and a bit of rain falls on his furry muzzle. Zorpiv eyes the cliffs to their left. The moist rainy air makes his fur go on end, and he tastes something visceral in the locale. The cliffs are haunting, with shadows fiercely dancing about because of the approaching storm. Bits of debris of various origin come to each of their faces, dusting all of them with a little bit of pollen and moisture. This causes Nathan to sneeze and Druward reaches the bottom first.

The black furred wolf looks around the area out of instinct. There was a time when coming down to this little secret lair could be quite dangerous for him, when he was still a rising star in the GBI. He had competing agents gunning for him and in the place where he's taking the foxes, there almost was a firearm incident. Of course all things turned out in his favor. Druward wouldn't be where he is today if he made many mistakes.

At the bottom of the cliff trail the land flattens out towards the right, into a bit of deeper forest. To the left, however, there are sharper drops, as the beautiful grassy and tree shaded cliff overhangs are replaced by rough harsh rocky surfaces. At the bottom of the trail things seem a little more on edge because there are not a lot of places to go. The bunker is built into the ground to the right, with the deeper forests on its crown.

A heavy steel door with a fat bolted padlock keeps visitors from snooping around, as if any animal would be adventurous enough to find a location like this on their own. Druward pulls his keys from his right pocket and selects the one he recognizes for the bolted lock. He is also listening to the foxes behind him. He is well aware that situations like the one he is in could possibly lead to an unfortunate turn of events. His training and experience naturally prepare him to be careful, and that's why he pauses for a slight moment when his left ear detects Zorpiv walking around behind him.

Druward glances back over his left shoulder and sees the gray, patchwork looking fox staring at him with a rather disturbing expression. The little guy doesn't look like much of a threat but killers don't have to be big, especially when dealing with his vulpine breed. Though he isn't aware of Vixil's sorted family history, Druward has encountered some gray foxes that were a bit unhinged. The black wolf gathers that the young man likes to be irritating, particularly in an aggressive way because Druward is so careful. Sneaking up close to him is a passive threatening gesture, and the reason they are here also adds gravity to the behavior.

Zorpiv is smiling politely but it does not amuse or fool Druward. He goes back to unlocking the door while Karl and Nathan have no perception of what just occurred. As a matter of fact, Druward is beginning to think that they are completely in over their heads. Inside lies a weapons range and a cache of ammunition the GBI director has acquired over the years by one method or another, and leading Zorpiv inside seems like a bad idea. The black wolf is not concerned for his own safety, but he wagers his partners in the deal may be biting off more than they can chew.

"Follow me." Druward tells them and flips on a hard light switch at the door. The bunker starts right off with a broad and long empty room. The far end is obviously being used as a target range, with a few animal mannequins lined up against the wall with targets strapped to them. Bullet holes line the stone walls behind them and it looks as though a grenade or two might have been detonated at some point.

To the right there is a passageway that leads to a much smaller room, designed for personal exchanges, but before going in there, Druward walks over to the very large metal cabinets right next to the doorway. There are two sets of locks on the three cabinets a piece. It looks as though the GBI Director has not been carefree with the weapons he keeps and when he unlocks the middle of them and swings it open, all of the foxes see why.

There are five racks of automatic weapons with cases of ammunition below each weapon respectively. There are different kinds of weapon cases, standard, armor piercing, anti-personal, and even what looks like incendiary and explosive rounds. Zorpiv's brown eyes joyfully go over the weapons and when he sees Druward choose the gun he likes as soon as he focuses on it, his heart pumps faster. The black wolf pulls out a small but devastating looking carbine.

"This is the MTAC-71." Druward declares as he swings the sizeable but light weapon in his paws. He speaks directly to Zorpiv while Karl and Nathan observe. "It is a carbine variant of the MTAC-81, a standard assault rifle of the world government. Many carbines are shortened versions of full rifles, firing the same ammunition at a lower velocity due to a shorter barrel length. The smaller size and lighter weight of carbines makes them easier to handle in close-quarter combat situations such as urban or jungle warfare, or when deploying from vehicles." Zorpiv is in awe when he listens to Druward speak. The GBI Director's obvious mastery of weaponry makes his gray, and red fur stand on end.

"The disadvantages of carbines relative to rifles include inferior long range accuracy and a shorter effective range." Druward continues while moving the gun in his paws so Zorpiv can take a look at it. It is very unique, with what looks to be like two major parts, a fat rectangular front with a small barrel, with the trigger and the grip below, and a large rectangular back end, with its clip at the front of the back segment, all bridged with a small narrow piece. "Since carbines are larger than submachine guns, they are harder to maneuver in tight encounters, and lack the range of standard rifles, but this gun was designed to outperform even personal defense weapons at close range. Since it's a carbine, its rifle origin gives it deadly efficiency at medium range and its rifle ammunition gives it the advantage of standardization over PDWs, that need special cartridges."

"Now..." The black wolf explains with a creeping smile. "The MTAC-71 is a really nasty piece of work... This gun costs three times that of your average rifle, and because its price is prohibitive, only the very best equipped army divisions have them. Instead of your average carbine, the MTAC-71 fires at a rate far greater than your top personal defense weapons. That means it hits with the standard rifle ammunition with the speed of a PDW and the accuracy of a carbine... Your top tier assault rifles fire around eight hundred rounds per minute. Your best personal defense weapon fires at nine hundred rounds per minute with smaller rounds... While the MTAC-71 is able to fire rifle ammunition at one thousand rounds per minute, with a fifty shot clip." Druward tells Zorpiv and by the time he is done, the gray fox touches the gun as if he is touching a newborn pup.

"Feel the weight." The black wolf says and gives it over to Zorpiv, who instantly likes the feeling. The gun is just the right size for him. It isn't too heavy, it isn't too little, and it seems to fit his paws.

"Nice..." Zorpiv breathes while looking it over.

"It's also a favorite of foxes in the military as it's not too heavy for your species to use." Druward comments and watches.

"Where did you get it?" Karl inquires.

"I bought it from a black market arms dealer when I traded in two older rifles." Druward answers and Zorpiv aims the gun down the range with glee. He starts to pant. The gun feels like a part of him. He wants to shoot it so badly already. "The bullets just cannot wait to get out of this gun..." Druward warns while gesturing towards the targets. "So when you use this thing, you'll blow anyone away... You don't have much excuse to stay for a long fight. Do the deed and leave."

Richard's Suggestion

"You ever get the feeling that some people just should be strangled with their own guts?" Vulpie asks Polar with an exceedingly cute smile that clashes with his ridiculously over exaggerated choice of words. Polar starts laughing along with the fox while they listen to Halfur on the other end of the phone line. They are in Vulpie's palace like office at the top of Vulpie Industries and loss management is the topic of the day.

The phone itself is actually on Vulpie's desk, but the conversation is piped throughout the room courtesy of a very expensive sound system. Vulpie likes to take his calls with just a little earpiece that comfortably snuggles against his fox skull. It has a tiny and efficient microphone that allows his words to go through loud and clear on the receiving end.

"I don't have time to run the BNG reports through the system a second time today, Vulpie." Halfur's fox voice pipes through the room.

"Stacie told me you were going to work around it." Vulpie reminds his head of technical research and development.

"But did you ask Chase? Even though we have a chief technical officer you don't seem to communicate with him very much." Halfur replies and at this Vulpie throws up his claws as if he wants to strangle someone. Polar has to keep his laughter down while he watches Vulpie put on a show of frustration.

"I did talk to Chase about it and he told me you said research and development wasn't ready to submit the reports!" Vulpie says with wild eyes, trying to sound optimistic and happy while also being forceful.

"Obviously you didn't talk to him about anything important because we have not discussed that issue." Halfur replies and Polar can't keep from blurting out a superbly amused cackle at the temper tantrum Vulpie throws. He starts swinging his fists and jumps up and down with his mouth open as if he is screaming. The orange furred fox boy lets out no sound while storming around in a circle with a crazy look on his adorable face.

"Oh but I did!" Vulpie replies with an insanely gleeful expression that is way less patronizing than it should be. He still goes on trying to sound positive while his subordinate bitches. "Trust me, I did talk to him about the reports and he assured me that it was because R & D couldn't handle the schedule. Are you saying that he was wrong?"

"I'm not saying he's wrong. I'm saying that YOU'RE wrong because you couldn't have talked to him about that, because I CLEARLY told him we would discuss the issue today but he has not responded to my emails." The brown furred fox responds and Vulpie throws off his earpiece in disgust.

"Maybe you should just let him take over. I think it would be simpler that way!" Polar snickers and Vulpie shakes his head with a very frustrated groan.

"I've gotta go down there and take care of this... It's gonna be a while before I get done, Baby... So are you gonna go on home?" Vulpie asks his wolf husband and Polar thinks for a moment.

"I might, but first I'll call Richard. He said he was in town and I think he wants to get a coffee." The snow wolf says and Vulpie smiles at him while he walks over to the office doors.

"Alright honey, I'll see you at the house."

"Okay." Polar chuckles, feeling bad for what awaits Vulpie downstairs. Arguing with Halfur can take two hours because the fox is intelligent but has absolutely no manners. The two heavy sliding doors come together with a rubbery sound when Vulpie leaves the room and Polar spins around in his chair. He is sitting behind his desk, a smaller one that is to the right of the doors of Vulpie's office when you enter from the lobby. Polar really likes it because he is right next to the huge windows and has a wonderful view of Sufias city next to him all day.

He remembers that Richard called him about an hour ago and left an interesting message. His brother mentioned something about a professor's study at the Lupiv Museum downtown. At the time it wasn't convenient for Polar to listen to all of it so he decides to make a call instead. He pulls his cell phone from his left pocket and finds Richard's number. He initiates the call and slowly pulls the phone up next to his big snow wolf skull.

"Hello?" Richard answers on the other end.

"Richard, I got your message but didn't have a chance to listen to all of it. Did you want to meet up this afternoon?" Polar responds while admiring the small wispy clouds over the city.

"I would, yeah. Actually... Well, did you hear what my message was about?"

"You said something about the museum. Did you want to meet there?"

"Yeah, I think that would be best... I have something I think you should see..."

"Oh really? What?" Polar curiously asks.

"It would be simpler to just show you." Richard replies and Polar squints.

"Did something happen? Is there something to be worried about?"

"Nothing happened like a car wreck or anything but I would like you to see something that my friend has come across on his travels. Do you remember Ivo Lorcan?"

"The archaeologist, yeah, I remember he was studying Deivonic tombs."

"He's been digging them up and he just brought in some unbelievable findings... I think you will want to see them... Is Vulpie around?"

"No, he's going to be busy."

"Okay, just meet me inside the Lupiv. I'll get a coffee for both of us, sound good?"

"Sounds great. I'll be there in about twenty minutes."

When Polar walks inside the museum, Deepwolf with him, Richard is already waiting. The fellow snow furred wolf takes a look at the Blacktail merc with Polar and gives the man a courteous nod. Deepwolf doesn't say anything but nods back and looks around the building. Polar has security wherever he goes, but unlike Vulpie, he's used to just having one member of Blacktail escorting him in public.

"Caramel. It's pretty sweet, maybe even too sweet." Richard says and offers Polar the drink he bought for him.

"Thanks." Polar says while taking the coffee with a smile. He slowly brings it to his lips to test the heat and finds that it isn't scalding like some he's had before, so he's free to take a sip. It is very sweet indeed but the arctic wolf loves the flavor. "Man that's good."

"I like it. Ivo got me hooked on the stuff. We usually can get it pretty cheap from that place." Richard says while briefly gesturing towards a little coffee shop near the entrance. The museum is a large building but looks fairly new. It's older than Polar and his brother but in terms of things, Lupiv is not an ancient place. Polar remembers visiting the place as a kid, his grade school organizing the long field trip down from Winters Dale. Around them are a few other shops, and a large water fountain. Polar and Deepwolf follow Richard's lead when he starts walking around to the right of it.

"How are you liking those religion classes? Is it harder than teaching history?" Polar asks his brother.

"It's actually not that different. Religion is a history matter after all. Most of the kids don't care anyway. They have to take the courses to get their four year degree... But I am enjoying it more than I thought I would."

"Is your friend, uh, what was his name?"

"Ivo Lorcan." Richard says, helping Polar complete his thought.

"Yeah, the guy that teaches religion and digs up tombs. Is he still helping you?"

"Without a doubt. I'm lost on a lot of the old subject matters like the Lulpras, and Maro, and the war with Dasa. I don't know many specifics about those legends and they go on and on."

"So does the program just teach students the things that take place in the Velora?" Polar asks while following his brother into the next series of rooms in the museum. It ventures off into different directions, a few small hallways to the left, more shops on the right, but straight ahead is another large room. Inside it the group walks past tall statues of Sypampt trees. Sypampts went extinct about a hundred years ago and there are currently government programs suggesting cloning technology to bring them back, so they are on proud display. Anything the museum can do to encourage funding from any respectable source is a priority.

"Mostly, but from what I hear and what the instructor's edition tells me, there is much more in there about the she-wolf Maro mythology."

"Not supposed to be a myth, right?" Polar quickly inquires. "She was the strongest Lile soldier in history. She won the Avana trials ten years in a row."

"I think it's a myth. The whole idea of a master city that all species of animals called home millions of years ago on Planet Halvia has always seemed just a bit farfetched. And then there's the stuff about how technology wouldn't work there, even today, like if a space ship crossed into the magical planet Halvia, wherever it is, it would just stop working and fall like a rock." Richard answers. "So the stuff about Maro is probably made up as well."

"But there's a record. She led the armies of Avana."

"The Velora also says she single handedly killed all of the Lulpras, including the three Lulchra Dra... If that's not a fairy tale I don't know what is... But I don't know, I wasn't there." Richard says, referring to the largest species of wolf to ever live. Lulpras were real animals. They were an ancient and massive lupine breed that have left their fossils behind for Sufians to discover over the last thousand years. They were actually killed by smaller wolves out of self-defense, because the general breeds of wolves that exist now banded together long ago to stave off their own extinction. Lulpras were known to be particularly brutal, and the legend of the Lulchra Dra comes from ancient Deivonic religion concerning three fabled super Lulpras that had blood red eyes. There is no scientific evidence that Lulchra Dra ever existed on Sufias, so Polar can see why Richard thinks a lot of the Deivonic religion is fictional.

"Yeah, who knows?" Polar replies with what he believes is a similar thought. Unbeknownst to him, Richard is considering how to handle the subject that he called his brother to the museum to discuss. And it also is of a religious nature. Polar and Deepwolf continue to follow Richard and he leads them straight ahead into a third chamber, and then they make a right, into a smaller but still pretty big room with very old paintings lining the walls. As they keep walking, the paintings become older and older, until they pass glass cases with stone slabs held up for the observers of history to inspect. Polar can see by the nature of these stone artifacts that they are Deivonic in nature, meaning that they relate to the Deivaism religion. Deivaism promotes the worship of Goddess Cyrilla, Khalan and Sherrie, a rabbit, a fox wolf, and a cat. All of them are very sexual, as they are fertility goddesses and supposedly mothered the entire universe.

"Richard!" Ivo Lorcan says and the old gray wolf walks over to meet the arctic wolf. Richard nods at his friend and introduces his guests.

"This is Polar, my brother." Richard says and Ivo immediately sees the resemblance. One would have to be blind to miss it. Polar and Richard are very similar in stature and build, but Polar is a bit stronger than his younger sibling. Polar outreaches his right paw for a shake and Ivo gladly accepts it. The old wolf looks happy to have new visitors, as he seems to have been working in the room all day. It can be assumed since he is wearing a white apron that is covered in grime and dust, presumably from moving slabs of stone around.

In the left corner of the chamber they stand in there is a bit of construction equipment. It looks as though this showroom is relatively new, and Polar deduces that it must house all of the artifacts that Ivo is bringing in from his dig site at Ninvia.

"Glad to have you! Richard said you might drop by. I like to show off my findings whenever I can, as I'm not above a little self-promotion." Ivo chuckles.

"Did you dig up all of these?" Polar asks in wonder, seeing the very, very ancient stone slabs displaying in cases around the marble room. There are paintings of pots, trees, skylines, and some of the Deivas in the artwork that was drawn millions of years ago, according to archaeological methods.

"I can't take credit for all of them, but I did personally oversee their care on the way to the museum."

"He's being modest. Most of these findings he located himself and then he trained graduate students to assist in their recovery." Richard says and Ivo says nothing, being very humble.

"Very impressive." Polar says and blinks when he sees one of the display cases in the far right of the room covered up with a black piece of cloth. "What's that one?" The snow wolf asks and Ivo looks to Richard in concern. Deepwolf notices them exchanging some sort of silent conversation but Polar doesn't catch on until he looks to his left at them.

"Well, er, uh, that one also came from Ninvia but we haven't cleaned it up yet."

"He has actually... And it's what I wanted to show you..." Richard tells Polar. Ivo looks very surprised that his friend said what he did, and now Polar can see that there is something going on behind the scenes.

"Well what is it?" Polar asks in confusion. "I'm not an archaeologist or a history teacher. What did you want to show me so badly?"

"Polar..." Richard says and licks his lips. Deepwolf moves on his feet, watching Polar's brother in interest. The mercenary can definitely see that there is a possibility of conflict even though he does not know the two snow wolves personally. "Ivo has been doing this for a long time and when he showed me that painting." Richard

126

says and gestures towards the one that is hidden. "I knew I had to
show you... It's covered up because it's very uncanny."

"What's uncanny?" Polar asks in a puzzled voice.

"Pull off the cover, Ivo." Richard suggests and the old gray
wolf takes a look at Polar before focusing on his friend again.

"Maybe it's best that I don't." Ivo replies and at this Polar's
eyes widen. He takes a deep breath... Now he is thoroughly caught
up in the intrigue.

"Just show him. He needs to see it."

"What's going on, Richard?" Polar asks and lowers his
muzzle.

"This isn't a good idea..." Ivo thinks out loud. Deepwolf
crosses his arms. He forgets about protecting Polar for the time
being, now fascinated with the secrecy as well. Richard doesn't
reply. He just stands with his coffee and waits with a patient face.
Ivo sighs and takes it on himself to walk over to the nearby display
case with the black shroud over it. He reaches up with his silver
bleached paws, the gray fur across his body tainted with old age,
and takes a hold of it. Ivo pulls it down and off of the display case,
which is well lit, and Polar instantly wonders why it was covered if it
is ready for prime time like the others.

When Ivo steps away and Polar sees the ancient painting,
drawn into a large stone slab, his confusion about why it was
covered disappears. The white furred wolf's handsome blue eyes
widen as he looks at Vulpie. He slowly takes a step forward and
laughs in surprise. He cannot believe what he is seeing... It looks like
a painting of the orange furred fox boy, except he is wearing a black
tunic.

"Oh wow, it looks just like Vulpie!" Polar laughs as he
walks closer to it and looks it over. The white furred wolf is amazed

at the detail it has. He knows it is just as old as the other artifacts because of the cracks and decay it has, but the painting is still very distinct. As he looks it over, an unexpected emotion rushes over him. When Polar realizes that he is staring at a portrait of an orange furred fox that looks just like Vulpie from ancient times, he stops talking.

"It's over a million years old. Isn't that right, Ivo?" Richard asks his friend and the gray wolf nods even though no one is looking at him.

"By our machine's dating it's one million and fifty thousand years old, the same age as every piece in this room..."

"These are all of your new findings from Ninvia, right?" Richard continues.

"Yes." Ivo whispers, and silence fills the room. Polar stares at the painting and does not know how to feel. The fox grinning back at him looks utterly mischievous... It's eyes are a pretty blue, its stature is identical to Vulpie, and its face is exactly the same.

"What is this?" Polar whispers and takes a step back. "It looks just like Vulpie!"

"Yes it does... It looks EXACTLY like him..." Richard tells his brother and when Polar looks to him he knows why he was called to the museum. Richard is careful to keep a calm friendly face because the confusion of the situation may lead Polar to react defensively.

"Is this real or is this some kind of joke? If it is, it's NOT funny Richard." Polar says and Richard shakes his head in disagreement very slowly.

"It's not a joke..." Richard softly tells his brother and Polar looks to the painting again. When he stares into the depicted fox's eyes his fur stands on end. It looks so much like Vulpie that it would appear that it is a portrait of him. The only problem is, it was drawn before the first civilization on planet Sufias.

"It looks a lot like Vulpie Vivixen." Ivo says with a very nonchalant manner, and walks next to Polar in a calming way. He observes the painting with him, as if taking a purely academic view on it. "No doubt Richard wanted you to see it because it's so eerily close to him. But it's just an orange fox. We don't know who it was supposed to be of."

"Is that what you're going to tell him?" Richard inquires and Polar's ears perk. He doesn't take his eyes off of the painting.

"What else do you want me to tell him, Richard?"

"You could tell him the name written into the painting. You've translated them all." Richard suggests and Ivo sighs very heavily.

"What would be the point of that?" Ivo asks and hobbles towards Richard on his old legs. Polar moves his tongue inside his jaw and takes his eyes off of the painting to look to his right at Ivo and his brother.

"What does it say? Is there a name for the painting?" Polar asks and Ivo pauses. Richard does as well. He stares at his brother with a calm face and when he does speak, he uses a soft voice.

"Polar, I'm your brother. Please don't be angry with me..." Richard whispers and Polar squints before answering.

"Why would I be?" Polar asks with a partially irritated voice.

"You know why... But believe me, it's not what you think."

"Just tell me what the name of the picture is, will you?" Polar growls and looks to Ivo. Ivo blinks and after a moment he slowly shakes his head and releases a very deep sigh.

"It's title... The imprint in the stonework is... The Anti-Khalan..." Polar draws back in disbelief. The answer he gets completely surprises and repulses him at the same time.

"The Anti-Khalan?!" Polar protests.

"Yes." Ivo simply answers and Polar gives Richard the biggest go to hell look he can.

"Oh... This is REALLY NICE..."

"I asked you not to get angry with me, Polar. That's the name of the artifact. Ivo told you just like he told me... And I wanted you to see it for yourself..." Richard explains with his friendliest voice but his sibling doesn't appear impressed.

"Wow." Deepwolf comments with an amused face. The Blacktail mercenary is able to smile with immunity because he is not a part of the conversation. A tense standoff ensues and Richard dares not move. He and his brother breathe faster, and Ivo can see the massive tension. The old gray wolf tries to intervene before things get worse.

"That is its title, Polar..." Ivo warmly says and gets his attention by walking in front of him. "There are literally thousands of artifacts like it, so who knows who made it. I've been doing this for over forty years, and I've seen a lot of strange things."

"The Anti-Khalan? The title of that painting that looks just like my husband, Vulpie Vivixen, is the Anti-Khalan?" Polar asks with an infuriated voice.

"Well... Yes... I'm afraid..." Ivo replies and shrugs. "But these things are not to be taken literally. These Deivonic artifacts can be pornographic and sometimes have worse things on them, so who knows who made it or why."

"But you found it with these other paintings of the goddesses?" Polar asks and waves his left paw at the wall to the left of the painting in question, where Khalan and Sherrie are depicted.

"Yes but as I said, this is not to be taken literally. Obviously it is not Vulpie Vivixen. This was drawn over a million years ago!" Ivo laughs but Polar cannot find any humor in this frightening moment. The white furred wolf feels a range of horrid emotions, the strongest of which is the agony of losing Vulpie. He hates anything that could come between him and his beloved fox, but it's clear Richard actually had a good reason to bring him here. Ivo Lorcan obviously is a trust worthy archaeologist and would not lie about something like this.

"But isn't the Anti-Khalan the prince of evil that is supposed to come and end the world? I am remembering that right, aren't I Richard?" Polar asks Ivo and then growls the second half of his question to his brother.

"That's the story, but I didn't name it." Richard calmly answers. Normally Polar is a very even tempered wolf, much more so than his brother, but right now he's finding it difficult to control his building rage.

"I thought you didn't have any more hate for my husband but I can see I was wrong about that." Polar tells his sibling while Deepwolf looks between them. "I should have known you would do something like this."

"Something like what, Polar?" Richard asks with a defensive voice. "If you were me and you were working with Ivo when he brought this thing into the museum, wouldn't you tell your brother about it?"

"No, I wouldn't!" Polar growls.

"No?"

"That's right! Even if it does look like Vulpie it doesn't mean anything. I don't care what it says!"

"It sounds to me like you care a lot. You're getting really worked up."

"OF COURSE I'M GETTING WORKED UP!" Polar shouts and looks around afterwards, embarrassed that he might have bothered other visitors. It doesn't appear that anyone is near them anyway. "You just wanted to show this painting to me to hurt my relationship with Vulpie!" Polar fiercely elaborates. "You don't have any other reason to do it because if you really cared about me as your brother you would have known better. You knew how this would make me feel but you don't care."

"I can't believe how defensive you get when it comes to Vulpie. I know he's your husband but you should listen to yourself. It's not fair to blame me for this."

"It is because you just HAD to show this to me! You could have just ignored it, or thought, huh, that was weird, and just gone on with your business. But instead of that you chose to damage my feelings for Vulpie because you secretly hate him." Polar tells Richard with a loathsome voice. "How dare you stand there and act like you've done nothing wrong. You should be ashamed of yourself!"

"And what about the fact that Mom and Dad have been dreaming about Vulpie?" Richard asks. The question stops Polar. The two arctic wolves stare at each other in silence. "You didn't think I knew about that, but Dad told me. He told me when I brought up my own dreams about him."

"You've been dreaming about Vulpie Vivixen?" Ivo asks his colleague and the snow wolf nods in agreement.

"I can't say that I've had a reason to, but I have. And the fact that Mom and Dad both have been experiencing the same thing bothers them the same way it bothers me." Richard explains and Polar feels a sinking in his stomach. He doesn't know what to say. The powerful wolf looks down at the floor with a very hurt expression. Despite the situation, Richard does feel guilty. The strong snow wolf sighs heavily and diplomatically shows Polar his paws. "Look, I'm sorry Polar... I guess you're right..." Polar venomously looks at his brother but is surprised to see genuine regret.

"Saying you're sorry doesn't fix the pain you've caused me..." Polar replies.

"I know, and I'm sorry." Richard earnestly responds. He shamefully bows his head. The fact that his brother is truly sorry for everything irritates Polar even more, because now he knows he has to forgive him. But Polar won't do it effusively. He slowly straightens before taking a deep breath.

"Okay... I forgive you Richard. I guess I'm over reacting a little bit."

"I shouldn't have done this. I knew it was a bad idea from the moment I suggested it..." Richard replies in defeat. "Vulpie is your husband. It doesn't matter what doubts I have about it because they're just doubts. I know there is no concrete evidence of anything bad."

"And you've never been a very religious person." Polar reminds his younger sibling. The comment irks Richard a bit but he decides not to take the bait.

"You're right." Richard says and smiles as much as he can. Polar loosens up a bit but can't shake the overwhelming fear he has.

"Well I don't think dreaming about someone means they are entering your dreams!" Ivo suddenly laughs and pats Polar on his right shoulder. The arctic wolf smiles before he realizes it because the old man's voice is so relaxing. "Remember there used to be a superstition about all black she-wolves being witches. Sure some of them did bad things, but no more than the rest of us." The veteran archaeologist licks his lips and thinks for a moment before sharing more. "One of the reasons I like what I do so much is because of all the questions that never are answered. I've studied all of the Velora and it's the most vague book you could ever read."

"Yeah." Polar meekly agrees.

"If we believed everything in it, verbatim, we'd be pulling our fur out, worrying all day long!" Ivo goes on. He diffuses almost all of the tension and Polar feels as though he can honestly share his feelings with the old man.

"Like the passages saying that being gay is a sin that conflict with other chapters about Vivenref." Polar suggests.

"Exactly. Vivenref was loved by all kinds of animals and he was the first gay fox ever mentioned in the Velora. So are we supposed to agree with him or the animals that persecuted him? It really depends on which author of which book you agree with the most on matters like this." Ivo says with a kind voice. "Believe me, there are things in the Velora that most animals would shake their head at if they ever actually read the book. In Khalan's Vein, the book that first mentions the Anti-Khalan, there's a paragraph about facing a giant she devil. But that doesn't make any sense at all. What exactly is a dead faced spirit? What does that mean? Does it mean Aila? Who knows? When you make one large assumption thanks to a second large assumption, It's circular reasoning of the highest degree. Most of it is probably metaphor."

"Actually I thought of Vaxi, the god of mischief when I read that chapter because it never specifically said who the Anti-Khalan was." Richard thinks out loud. Polar blinks and shows him a thankful face when he sees his brother trying to make amends.

"Or what species the Anti-Khalan even is. We just assume it's a fox because of that ancient painting." Ivo says while gesturing over at the relic. "But no one knows who created the Deivonic paintings. The same kind of artwork has been found on every single planet we've explored. Some of the artifacts are much further down, hidden beneath the ground like these were at Ninvia, but they are all so ancient it's impossible to believe really. How in the world could there have been animals on all of these planets drawing such things yet Sufias is where we've flourished and spread out from while they died off on the other worlds?" The old gray wolf elaborates and clears his throat. He finds that using his lecture voice is appropriate and useful at the moment. "For that matter, there are no fossils of animals on any other planet besides Sufias, so who in the world created these paintings?"

"Our furry alien ancestors." Richard jests and Polar allows himself to chuckle with the group.

"I don't believe in religion but this is fascinating." Deepwolf comments while listening with crossed arms. "I didn't know that all of the artifacts on every planet were around the same age."

"Within about a thousand years apart, yes." Ivo says. "That's not a big difference when you're talking about millions."

"So what are they going to do with this picture? Is it staying here in this museum?" Polar asks. "It looks like it's been fixed up like the others."

"Well, someone from the Association of Fox Rights contacted me and the museum about it this week actually and I doubt it will." Ivo admits. "I don't think the foxes like a painting depicting the Anti-Khalan as a fox, especially an orange fox, when Vulpie is so famous."

"Good." Polar says and breathes happily. Richard is disappointed to hear his brother say that, but he understands why. "I'm actually glad they're going to remove it."

"I won't say anything to Mom and Dad…" Richard volunteers. Polar's spirits lift when he hears the statement. Normally his brother wouldn't offer to hide a secret.

"Thank you… Please don't. This is just a coincidence, nothing more." Polar replies.

"How about we get something to eat then? I'll be here tomorrow for a college project and we've booked the fantastic restaurant here for lunch. Let's go try it out!"

"Sure." Polar says with a smile and Richard looks to Ivo.

"Are you hungry?"

"No thank you. I'm afraid I can't eat anything too heavy in my old age." Lorcan chuckles.

Counterintelligence

When Polar gets home he finds Vulpie cooking dinner. The cute orange fox looks to his right to show the snow wolf a lovely smile. Polar smiles back, but can't help but match his husband's face to the painting.

"Hey baby! Did you have fun?" Vulpie asks with his usual enthusiasm.

"Yeah, I'm sorry it took so long." Polar apologizes and walks into the kitchen after setting his keys down on the table.

"No worries." Vulpie breathes as Polar comes to him and bends down for a kiss that they both savor. Polar shows Vulpie pretty eyes when they part lips and Vulpie swishes his tail. The horrid thought of Vulpie being portrayed as some sort of ancient evil sickens Polar. He hates his brother for putting him through something that he knows is going to bother him, despite the fact that it isn't true. There is no way that the sweet gay fox is anything but good for him. Polar knows it balls to bones. "So what did you guys do? Did you see anything neato on display?"

"Yeah... Actually..." Polar answers with his happiest voice but Vulpie detects a small amount of hesitation. The fox genius discards it, assuming that his husband's family feelings are his own business. Polar has a much more difficult time letting the statement go. He continues to think about something while he takes a seat on the couch. Vulpie notices his lover hasn't bothered to remove his shoes.

"What's wrong baby? Is something bothering you?" Vulpie tenderly asks. "Did you and Richard have another argument?"

"We did, but..." Polar trails off before he realizes what he's done. He planned on giving a clever response to throw Vulpie off but didn't give it enough time. Now he knows Vulpie won't stop asking until he finds the problem. "Oh, Richard was just being Richard. He said something off color about you and it isn't even worth repeating."

"I wish he would accept me like the rest of your family..." Vulpie responds with a hurt voice. Polar hates to hear him suffer. He knows he feels guilty about being a fox in an extended wolf family already, and is ashamed of his past crimes. Polar understands because his father and mother have always been such good animals. They're pillars of the community in Winters Dale and sometimes Polar felt equally guilty of not living up to their high standards.

"I know Vulpie... I'm sorry." Polar coos in response.

"I mean, it's not like I'm breaking the law anymore... Well... Unless you include the counter wiretapping because of the crazies in the AFR." Vulpie comments. "I really thought he liked me now. We've been married almost seven years now."

"I got mad at him." Polar admits with a sigh and stands up. The white furred wolf walks over to the kitchen divider and looks down at Vulpie protectively. Vulpie is preparing lean hamburgers and delicious seasoned fries.

"You did?" Vulpie asks with a smirk.

"You bet I did." Polar growls while thinking about his brother. "I was happy to meet up with him and Deepwolf was along for our little trip. We were having such a great time and then he just goes into one of his weird anti vulpine rants."

"He hates foxes that much, huh? I guess he really is butt-hurt about that vixen dumping him then?" Vulpie taunts and Polar laughs in surprise.

"Well he's still my brother." The wolf reminds the fox.

"I know." Vulpie smiles. "I was only teasing."

"You're probably right. He seems obsessed that foxes are just bad or something..." Polar says but as the words come out of his mouth the lie becomes more difficult to tell. He knows he shouldn't run his brother down for something he didn't do. The thought pops into his head that he should just tell Vulpie what really happened but he quickly reminds himself that it could really hurt Vulpie if he hears that someone suggested he's the Anti-Khalan. They already live different lives than most animals because they are gay between species, and with all of Vulpie's talents it's easy for haters to poke the fox boy with a stick and blame everything on him.

"Are you not telling me something?" Vulpie quietly inquires while looking down at his work. He puts together the rest of their burgers, making a neat little area for the sandwich next to their fries on both plates.

"No." Polar quickly answers but his fur goes on end.

"You just... Seem like something else is bothering you... It's like you want to tell me something but you're hiding it..." Vulpie says and looks up at the handsome snow wolf.

"Why do you think that?"

"I know you Polar... You'll hide something from me if you think it will hurt me and I love you for it... But I know there's more." Vulpie explains and the white furred wolf sighs.

"Sometimes I wish you weren't a genius..." Polar groans in defeat.

"Tell me what he said. I'd like to know." Vulpie says and Polar looks away for a moment.

"Well, he actually didn't say anything himself... It was just... Oh goddess, I guess I am going have to tell you all of it now..."

"That's right!" Vulpie giggles triumphantly. "If you want me to keep giving you morning blowjobs you had better share it all!"

"You're mean…" Polar grins in amusement.

"It's your choice." Vulpie mischievously replies.

"You know, I didn't get my morning blowjob today… So you owe me an extra one." Polar tells his fox lover with an inviting expression.

"I'll give you a nice one tonight if you tell me what's bothering you!" Vulpie offers and bites his tongue between his teeth. "Go ahead and balance hiding a secret from me with that."

"But you already give me a blowjob every time I want one!" Polar teases and the snow wolf crosses his arms.

"Things might have to change around here then! Vulpie can say he has a headache ya know." Vulpie taunts, gleefully referring to himself in the third person. "And morning blowjobs are a nice bonus before we go to work, so you can't say they aren't any better than the others!"

"But you take more time with me when I ask for one."

"Because I have to get you worked up. When you have a morning erection it's faster cuz Vulpie has to do less work."

"Alright, enough! I'm starting to get a hard on here, so I'll tell you!" Polar laughs and Vulpie giggles with him. Polar puts his paw on the kitchen divider and takes a seat on the comfortable bar stools on the other side of the piece of furniture, facing Vulpie who is still in the kitchen. The snow wolf swishes his tail for a moment and looks at the fox boy while he considers how he is going to put this. "Well it's like this… Richard has been teaching some religion courses at the Kayman Institute so he knows this gray wolf called Ivo Lorcan. He's another professor, er uh, well mostly an archaeologist I guess. He works in a dig site far off in a desert country somewhere. I forget what Richard called it."

Vulpie's fox ears are perked, their little black tips pointed straight up while Polar speaks. He puts his eyes on the snow wolf's face and returns an interested but distant expression while listening.

"Anyway..." Polar continues. "So since this guy is a Deivonic expert he is able to translate all of these old inscriptions on stone wall paintings that are millions of years old. It's pretty incredible... But Richard wanted me to come to the museum so he could show me one very odd picture."

"What was it?" Vulpie inquires with a blink.

"This is where it gets weird." Polar warns and smiles lovingly. "There is an ancient artifact, one that is over a million years old that the Ivo guy showed me and it looked just like you."

"Like me?" Vulpie asks in surprise.

"Yeah, just like you! It's pretty cool actually. It's that old but it looks like someone painted you."

"You don't say?" The fox boy muses as if he knows something. "So what did you get mad about?"

"Well, Ivo translated it and it had a title called the Anti-Khalan." The snow wolf growls. "I didn't believe it, and it's just a stupid piece of a rock with paint on it, but that's its name. Richard thought he was doing a good thing by having me come down there and see it."

"Because I might be the Anti-Khalan?" Vulpie giggles with a mischievous face. "Oh you have got to be kidding!"

"Sadly, I'm not. It's ridiculous isn't it?" Polar laughs. He loves the way Vulpie takes the bizarre news in stride. "We had this super serious moment in the museum and I reminded Richard that he doesn't really believe in that stuff anyway."

"Did it ever occur to him that there might have been thousands of foxes that have looked like me?"

"Yeah, he knew that but... Man Vulpie, it looks like you completely, down to the little things I love about you like the handsome shape of your soft muzzle and your sexy smile."

"Well, that is hard to believe." Vulpie replies and swats his paws together before handing Polar's plate over the kitchen divider. His husband accepts and sets it down before finding a fry to eat.

"So I got rather pissed at Richard for bringing me there and showing it to me like you might be some evil spirit. I let him know that it didn't help our marriage for him to come up with conspiracy theories. And he did apologize for it in the end so I can... Kind of see why he did it, but I'm sure it sounds pretty awful to you."

"That's just Richard being Richard I guess." Vulpie replies with a smile but takes a deep breath.

"Yeah." Polar says and munches on some more of his fries.

"But I'll tell you one thing... You're going to be happy that I have been spying on your family now." The fox boy's statement causes Polar to suddenly look at him in a different light.

"Oh I will?" Polar asks with a penetrating voice.

"Yes you will Mr. Polar..." Vulpie says and leans on the kitchen divider, bringing his muzzle close to his husband's. Polar looks into Vulpie's eyes and shakes his head before saying something.

"Is this another one of the times when I have a sinking feeling about what you've been up to, Vulpie?"

"No, but I have a sinking feeling because of what your brother's friend has been up to." Vulpie answers and stares back intently. "What's the guy's name again? The guy that translated the picture?"

"Ivo Lorcan..." Polar answers while watching his lover carefully.

"Oh my... We're going to have to do something about this..." Vulpie whispers and looks aside in concern.

"Explain please." Polar firmly says and his tone causes Vulpie to look back to him in minor irritation.

"I'm going to. You know I'm going to, so you don't have to demand it."

"Then get on with it, Vulpie. I don't like these moments. They make me very uncomfortable." Polar responds. There is a silence because of the tense look the white furred wolf gives the orange furred fox boy. "And by the way, I find it pretty concerning that you seem to know about stuff like this before I do. Would you like to tell me why, again, you've been spying on my brother?"

"I already told you why in Casillfori. What, am I the bad guy now?" Vulpie sneers, but keeps respect for his husband in his voice.

"Don't try that. You know I'm not being unfair to you." Polar responds and Vulpie winces. The gay fox slowly pulls back and looks aside with a hurt expression. Polar hates to see it but doesn't plan to let up until he has answers.

"I can't stand when you look at me like that..." Vulpie whispers. "Don't you trust me enough to give me the benefit of the doubt, Polar? I mean, after all we've been through? Why do you still treat me like I'm a criminal?"

"Because you are one. You can't go around wiretapping animals without permission. You know better and it makes me upset that you act hurt when I call you on it. You know that I love you but I won't put up with your hacking anymore. You've told me over and over that you've changed."

"And I have! That's what hurts me so much!" Vulpie whimpers and gets choked up. Polar's blue eyes widen when he sees the fox's reaction.

"Vulpie..." Polar warmly whispers back. "Don't cry... Why are you going to cry? You know I get mad at you because I don't want to lose you."

"Who said I'm going to cry?" Vulpie replies but bats his eyes for a moment. He fights a few tears back and sniffles.

"I'm sorry..." Polar says quietly and Vulpie lowers his ears before looking back at his wolf lover.

"The only reason I do it is to protect you and your family." Vulpie explains with a distraught voice. "It would kill me if something happened to them."

"But what is going to happen to them? Are you talking about the association of fox rights again?"

"Yes!" Vulpie stresses. "Polar, I have a terrible feeling about some of them. They bugged your parent's house, remember?"

"Did they really bug their house or was it you?" Polar asks and Vulpie gawks at him in disbelief.

"I can't believe you would even think that. Why would you even think that, Polar?"

"I'm just asking a question. If you didn't do it why get upset?"

"Why on Suflas would I bug your parent's home? Do you think I'm that sensitive, that I just can't stand for somebody to talk about me when I'm not around? I know your parents don't always say nice things and I haven't listened in because of that. I had the equipment removed from their house."

"Okay, I believe you. I believe you, Vulpie. So go ahead and tell me what you know about Richard's friend. Tell me why you've been spying on my brother."

"I've been WATCHING your brother. There's a huge difference, Polar." Vulpie growls. He's starting to become angry.

"Is that right? Well I don't think Richard would agree with you. I'm sure he'd have some choice words if he found out you've been spying on what he does online, or offline. Who knows what you've been up to... I certainly have no clue." Polar says and sits up straight before leaning forwards and putting his elbows on the kitchen divider. "I don't know what Richard does on the internet. Have you seen what porn sites he goes to? He's still single, so I'm sure he does look up porn. So have you seen that?"

"Maybe we should continue this conversation another time, because I'm starting to get mad." Vulpie answers.

"Talking down to me like I'm one of your employees now?"

"You are my employee." Vulpie quickly reminds his husband with a firm voice. Polar groans when he realizes how they got into this argument. He puts his right paw over his face and growls in frustration.

"God damn it Richard..." The white furred wolf laments and pulls his paw off of his face after rubbing his eyes. "This is all thanks to him..." Vulpie turns to his left and ignores his meal. Instead the cute fox boy walks out of the kitchen towards the stairs leading up to the second floor. "Where are you going?" Polar asks in surprise. "Are you that upset?"

"Just stay right there. I want to show you something." Vulpie answers without looking back and he hops up the stairs. Polar watches him walk down the hallway, past the bedroom on the right, and go down to the end where the back room has Vulpie's computers set up. Vulpie spends all of his time working at home in that part of the house.

Polar waits patiently and tries to take a bite of his hamburger, but can't. He feels rotten for pursuing Vulpie so fiercely but he can't help it. He refuses to compromise when it comes to Vulpie's ethics. He feels he has a duty to steer him in the right direction even if that means arguing. After all, if not for Polar, who knows where Vulpie would have ended up after he unleashed Vulpie.net.

Vulpie is carrying his personal V-Screen when he returns. Polar waits for the cute fox boy to trot down the steps and when he reaches the bottom he walks over to the wolf at a brisk pace.

"Take a look at this…" Vulpie says as he stops next to Polar. The white furred wolf keeps sitting on the barstool and takes the V-Screen when Vulpie hands it over. "Right here." Vulpie instructs while pointing with his left index finger at the article displayed on the screen.

"Famous archaeologist suffers fatal heart attack and is in critical condition…" Polar reads out loud. The white wolf shakes his head in confusion when he recognizes the name and puts a few dates together. "Is this really from last week?"

"Yes it is. Keep reading." Vulpie replies and Polar licks his lips before continuing. The electronically lit V-Screen is very easy on the eyes.

"Famous archaeologist and Deivonic scholar Ivo Lorcan has made headlines again this week, but not for many discoveries. Apparently the eighty nine year old gray wolf is suffering from severe heart problems and will be unable to travel or return to digging at Ninvia according to his doctors. Ivo gained a substantial amount of notoriety twenty years ago when he discovered the largest and oldest Deivonic tomb on planet Sufias. In recent years, however, he has been unable to reach such levels of success but has uncovered a new dig site at Ninvia. According to his wife he was disappointed at the lack of new artifacts at Ninvia and regrets not having the chance to finish his work. He is now confined to Shyriver Hospital in Englavic and has had to cancel some planned conferences and educational courses that he was brought on to teach at the Kayman Institute..." Polar whispers. His voice has gone almost silent by the time he finishes reading.

"Pretty weird, huh?" Vulpie asks with a satisfied voice. "Aren't you glad that I spied on your brother now?"

"What is this? Is this real?"

"Yes."

"It can't be. I just saw him today at the museum!" Polar protests.

"Ever seen him before?" Vulpie asks.

"Well, no, of course not." Polar responds and there is a moment of silence before Vulpie leans down and touches the V-Screen to bring its attention to another file. Polar lets Vulpie manipulate the device until it shows a correspondence of emails. "Look at the dates..." The fox boy suggests and Polar does so without speaking.

From: "Lorcan, Ivo" <Ivo.lorcan@aios.gov>
To: "Richard, Arctic" <Richard.arctic@kic.edu>
Date: Tue, 18 Sept 2109 18:02:34
Subject: Understanding Deivaism

Hello Richard,

I will be unveiling several items for the Sufias Lupiv Museum next week. I'd welcome your visit and appreciate your interest in the dig site at Ninvia. As for the questions about Lulchra Dra, I would direct you to T'veld's essay on grand wolves "1543," for best answers regarding a lecture. The short answer is no. Lulpras greater than eleven feet tall have left no fossils on planet Sufias, and there is no direct credible evidence of their existence excluding passages from the Velora. I hope this helps.

Sincerely,

Ivo Lorcan, Archaeological Institute of Sufias,
1630 Silver Lake Central Avenue, NO, 05614 SWG
997-615-5548 Ivo.lorcan@aios.gov
www.AIOS.gov

From: "Richard, Arctic" <Richard.arctic@kic.edu>
To: "Lorcan, Ivo" <Ivo.lorcan@aios.gov>
Date: Wed, 19 Sept 2109 13:15:21
Subject: RE: Understanding Deivaism

Ivo,

I'm very pleased to hear that you are feeling better. I would be happy to attend and will contact you next week. Thank you for T'veld's essays as they were quite useful. How many artifacts were you able to recover at Ninvia?

Best regards,

Richard Arctic, Kayman Institute,
0741 Forest claw drive, SU, 54569 SWG
771-156-4564 Richard.Arctic@KI.edu
www.KI.FDU

From: "Lorcan, Ivo" <Ivo.lorcan@aios.gov>
To: "Richard, Arctic" <Richard.arctic@kic.edu>
Date: Wed, 19 Sept 2109 13:18:10
Subject: RE: Understanding Deivaism

Hello Richard,

Reports of my demise are greatly exaggerated! There are more than seven discoveries, one of my best findings in years. You're welcome, and I look forward to hearing from you next week.

Sincerely,

Ivo Lorcan, Archaeological Institute of Sufias,
1630 Silver Lake Central Avenue, NO, 05614 SWG
997-615-5548 Ivo.lorcan@aios.gov
www.AIOS.gov

"But according to the newspaper article, he said he was disappointed with Ninvia..." Polar tells Vulpie after he finishes reading.

"That's right." Vulpie replies and gestures towards the V-Screen. "Check the time stamps. Wednesday at one fifteen your brother emails Mr. Lorcan... Then, at one eighteen, Lorcan rapid fires an email back to him? So that means Lorcan must have had a laptop on his hospital bed, because that's where the newspaper says he still is." The fox boy states and Polar blinks in disbelief.

"No... Are you serious?" Polar whispers.

"Well, the date for the newspaper article is Thursday of last week..." Vulpie responds. Polar doesn't move when he hears this. He looks around the den while he tries to process what he's heard and read. "So... Not only did old Ivo get better, he went out and dug up seven discoveries by the end of last week. And then he flew out to Sufias City and put them in the Lupiv Museum by the time you visited today?"

"Maybe the article you found is wrong." Polar suggests.

"I guess the Leadfur Herald could have made a giant mistake, but I wouldn't bet on it."

"Why didn't you mention this before?" Polar asks his fox husband.

"I just thought it was some kind of mistake. I didn't know you were going to see Ivo Lorcan today with your brother. But I did remember coming across these emails and when I looked into

Lorcan afterwards I thought, huh, that's weird! I knew something wasn't right or someone was wrong with their dates, but didn't think it was important until you told me what he said this afternoon... That there is a strange artifact with my picture on it and he said it translated into the Anti-Khalan... Something isn't right."

"So what are you saying?" Polar asks.

"I don't know what I'm saying, but I'm not the Anti-Khalan!" Vulpie giggles and Polar laughs as well with the adorable fox boy.

"We should call Richard and ask him about it." Polar suggests.

"No... Instead, let's take tomorrow off and go see Ivo together. Can you get your brother to come too?"

"Well, he said he would be at the museum tomorrow for a college project... But what do you want to do?" The white furred wolf inquires. "I doubt he'll change his story about the painting if you try to beat him over the head with a newspaper article you have on your V-Screen."

"I don't know what he's going to say... But I hope this isn't what I think it is..." Vulpie answers.

Busted

Polar wakes up suddenly when he feels something wet. Coming out of his dreams, he isn't sure if he is still asleep when he feels the fluid on his penis. A second later, when he notices pressure on his cock, he blinks his eyes all the way open and looks down to see Vulpie sucking it. The gay fox is on his knees, bent forward over the snow wolf's crotch with his right paw holding Polar's penis.

"OH MY GOD!" Polar laughs in surprise and delight. Somehow Vulpie has managed to pull his boxers all the way down. They both are wearing white t shirts but Vulpie still has his underwear on. "I guess this means you aren't still mad at me?" Polar grins as Vulpie bobs his head up and down. The fox boy swishes his pretty tail and watches him with his blue eyes while he sucks. "Fuck!" Polar moans, relishing how hard his penis is and how beautiful it feels in Vulpie's wet mouth. His little husband deep throats him skillfully and already has the white furred wolf near an orgasm thanks to his massive morning erection. "UUhhhh!" Polar moans and closes his eyes, sending his big left paw down to Vulpie's head and Vulpie hums, eagerly accepting it.

The white furred wolf gives himself over to his fox husband completely. Vulpie is always enthusiastic, but he's really going to town on him right now. Polar groans in pleasure when he feels him touching his balls. Vulpie plays with and massages the wolf's big testicles with his little left paw while he holds the much bigger male's penis in place at the angle he wants. Vulpie keeps up his nice rhythm, bobbing and slurping and sucking the fat cock in his mouth.

"Vulpie I'm going to, OH FUCK!" Polar groans as he feels an orgasm coming. He underestimated how sensitive his morning erection is. It took far less pleasure than he expected to cum, but the intensity is amazing. Hot semen backs up inside his massive cock and he tenses up, and Vulpie takes the body language as a signal to go nuts. He slurps and bites a little and gurgles Polar's big penis all around, back and forth, up and down, until he tastes hot spooge. "UUHAAAHHH!!!" Polar cries out as he ejaculates an effusive blast of cum inside Vulpie's fox mouth and Vulpie quickly slurps his lips tight around his husband's hot penis to make sure he catches most of it. "UUhh! UH! UUAAHH!! UHH!!!" Polar moans over and over until he finishes cumming. He holds very still when he's done, and reels from the amazing release. "OH MY GOD VULPIE!" Polar laughs and continues to laugh for a moment while Vulpie sucks on his penis.

The adorable gay fox takes time to ensure he gets as much cum in his mouth as possible before letting his lips off of Polar's dick. When he does, a good amount of it dribbles out of his muzzle and lands on the bed before Vulpie pulls his head back. He leaves his mouth open and holds still so Polar can see his cum inside his mouth, on his tongue and teeth, pooled in the back of his throat... Everywhere...

Polar is silent while he stares, mesmerized. He loves to see Vulpie show off a load in his mouth and Vulpie knows it. After a few more moments, Vulpie slowly closes his mouth and smiles. He winces a little and gulps once... Then again... And again... Until he has swallowed all of the massive load.

"Good morning to you too!" Polar moans with a gigantic grin. Vulpie licks his lips and the corners of his mouth, raking in the rest of the white furred wolf's hot semen.

"Morning baby! Did you sleep well?" Vulpie mischievously replies.

"I slept alright I guess, but I know waking up was awesome!" Polar chuckles and Vulpie bites his tongue at his husband. The beautiful gay fox crawls forward, on top of him and lies down on his mate. Polar wraps his arms around him and they enjoy a hot passionate kiss. Polar tastes his own semen in Vulpie's mouth and it makes the exchange extremely hot. The white furred wolf moans deeply and hungrily returns the kiss. When they finish, Vulpie pulls his face back and gives Polar a naughty expression.

"There you go! Now you can't complain for the rest of the day!" The orange furred fox declares and sits up, on his bottom, on top of Polar's front. "Get up! It's time for a field trip! We're gonna go to the museum!"

"Woo hoo!" Polar grins and rubs the fox's sides with his big paws. "Whatever you want!"

"Well how about a blowjob for me then? Where's mine?" Vulpie playfully inquires.

"Oh, I don't know if we have time. I think I have a headache." Polar teases and at this Vulpie makes a playfully enraged face and grabs a pillow. The snow wolf laughs while Vulpie swats his face three times with it.

"OOoooooo!!! You make me so mad you mean wolf! I'm gonna stop being so nice all the time!" Vulpie giggles.

"If you want to suck my cock and eat my cum that's your decision but we really shouldn't get off of the schedule should we? What if we're late?" Polar replies in amusement and he winces in excitement when Vulpie reels back and swats him one more time with the pillow.

"Screw you!" Vulpie laughs and gets off of him, crawling off towards the edge of the bed. "I'm gonna find someone nice who appreciates me!"

"Good luck finding someone my size..." Polar taunts and at this Vulpie raises an eyebrow.

"Well... You've got a point there..." The cute fox boy says, and with a wink, gets off of the bed and stands up.

"I'm going to be expecting this every morning from now on... Just a warning!" Polar declares with a very happy face.

"Nuh, uh! You better earn it big boy!" Vulpie replies and swishes his tail before walking over and into the bathroom. Polar watches the lean fox slide off his underwear and check himself in the mirror. Vulpie is happy with what he sees and so is Polar. He doesn't bother to get up. Instead he just observes his husband go to turning on the bath water. Vulpie bends over and tests the water while the tub fills, giving Polar a view of his soft cute butt. The wolf eyes the delicious streak of white fur that runs underneath the gay fox's tail, across his anus, perineum, balls and crotch, and all the rest of the way up his belly, chest, throat and muzzle. When Vulpie finally does look over at Polar he makes an amused face. "Come on silly!"

"You gave me the day off, boss. What's the rush?" Polar replies, using a louder voice so Vulpie can hear him over the running bathwater.

"You come in here now or I'm gonna demote you!" Vulpie says in response and walks over to the door of the bathroom, naked. He pushes his right elbow against the doorway and leans on it with a smirk, propping his head at an angle. "Or are you just gonna stare at me all day?"

"Can I?" Polar smirks.

"No, but you can give me a blowjob!" Vulpie answers, making a delighted face.

"That's too easy... I like making you squirm..."

"Well I know an even better way to do that!" The adorable fox boy exclaims.

"I can't even get out of bed. How am I going to get enough energy to fuck you right now?" Polar teases and Vulpie swishes his tail slowly.

"I guess this will teach me to suck you off in the morning..." Vulpie slyly responds. "All it does is make you lazy!"

"Well... If I'm going to work today after all I suppose I could fuck you..." Polar suggests and Vulpie immediately pulls his elbow off of the bathroom doorway in excitement.

"Yeah?" Vulpie grins.

"But... You have to give me another blowjob first!" Polar says with a very naughty face and at this Vulpie throws his little claws up effeminately

"AWW! YOU! URGH! YOU'RE FIRED!" Vulpie mischievously declares and retreats inside the bathroom, pulling the door shut behind him. Polar laughs heartily and has a good stretch. After lying still a little bit longer he finally gets out of bed. He yawns and considers making breakfast but the task of the day comes to mind and suddenly he feels worried. He thinks about speaking to Ivo, about how calm and collected the man was... Yet was he an imposter? There is one thing Polar is definitely sure of... The truth cannot hide from Vulpie. One way or the other, there will be answers and it's a comforting fact. Once again, he's facing the unknown with his favorite fox.

"What is that thing?" Polar asks while eying Vulpie's device. They stopped by the office specifically to get the piece of equipment.

"Oh, it's fabulous!" Vulpie gleefully says while giving Polar playful eyes. "It takes the best picture money can buy! And whether Mr. Lorcan is photogenic or not, we'll get a wonderful scan of him."

"Isn't that…" Polar whispers while eying the rectangular device. "The thing you used for x-rays?"

"Now Mr. Polar, don't go and say it in front of Deepwolf! I want him to be surprised like everybody else!" Vulpie giggles. Deepwolf sneers at the inclusion.

"You mean like everybody including you… Right? You'll be surprised too." Polar tells the gay fox.

"Sadly, Mr. P, I don't know if I will be. I think I've met someone just like Ivo before." The bullet proof SUV comes to a halt outside the Lupiv Museum and Vulpie steps out of the right door when Tiala opens it. She has been riding up front in the passenger's seat while Rulef drove. Everyone exits the vehicle and its locked up. Two members of Blacktail stay behind to guard the vehicle while the majority go with Vulpie and Polar up the steps to the building. It's a cool morning in Sufias city. The hustle and bustle of passing animals and traffic bounces off the tall buildings in the area, creating a megaphone effect.

In the distance to the right of the museum is the Vulpie Industries tower. It is far taller than any building near it, but not quite the tallest in the city. Regardless, it demands attention whenever someone looks out in the distance.

"The tower looks really impressive from down here." Polar comments and most of the group glances to the right to enjoy the sight. Rulef doesn't, as he has been around the city with Vulpie day in and day out for years now. He's more focused on the many strangers around them. Museums are not known to be dangerous places in general but the high number of animals coming and going is certainly a threat to security. He's always watching everyone, and most animals watch back. After all, it's not every day that a group of armed soldiers escort Vulpie Vivixen right by you.

Everyone that hasn't been living under a rock knows Polar Arctic as well, and some even recognize Tiala as the tigress that had a gun fight with Evil Vulpie during its insane helicopter chase years ago. Many would try to speak to Vulpie or Polar looking for an autograph or a picture but Blacktail projects such a threatening aura that no one does. They protect their target like the secret service protecting the President, except they are carrying fully automatic weapons, something that the secret service is shy about doing. Usually they would only use automatic pistols, small side arms that don't look quite so intimidating. But Blacktail, like most companies in the military industrial complex, pretty much gets to do what it wants and doesn't need to put on a public image.

"What's that gun? I've never seen that one before!" Vulpie declares while he walks next to Tiala. She looks back at him while she opens the museum's front doors and leads him inside. She takes a moment before answering, as there are a bit too many bystanders in the area.

"It's a rail gun." Tiala replies with a small voice and Vulpie's blue eyes widen.

"Really? I thought they were still too big to be carried by soldiers." Vulpie answers. Rulef decides to give his opinion as they wait for a moment.

"We have the firepower to handle your robots now." The commanding wolf states.

"My robots?" Vulpie asks in minor irritation.

"If these were around during the Evil Vulpie crisis, we could have stopped it."

"So you armed up for today? I appreciate that." Vulpie responds with a devious smirk. "We should discuss the physics later though! How in the world did they find power supplies small enough to make a handheld rail gun effective?"

"They have one shot a piece before the battery dies." Rulef answers.

"Oh I see! I see..." Vulpie says with a delighted voice.

"Are we planning on having a gun fight?" Polar quietly inquires.

"A good scout is always prepared." Rulef dryly states. Polar is a little miffed when the man doesn't elaborate and instead asks for directions. "Can you lead us to the man Vulpie wants to see?"

"I'm not sure he's even here. My brother is, and we'll ask him." Polar replies. The arctic wolf looks around and proceeds to lead the group. The museum looks just the same as it was the day before but he blinks when he sees Richard near by the coffee shop. He's speaking with what appears to be college students and other faculty, Polar guesses, from the Kayman Institute.

Polar changes course and heads over to his brother just as his brother notices Vulpie. The fox's brilliant orange fur is very eye catching. The white furred wolf snorts in surprise and then again when he sees his big brother walking up to him.

"Excuse me for a moment." Richard Arctic tells a female professor, a vixen. She looks to Richard's brother and then nods. The college students quickly lose attention when they notice the armed escort with Vulpie and Vulpie tries not to look at them so the teacher can struggle to hold their focus.

"Richard, I'm glad you're here today." Polar says with a smile. Richard doesn't say anything for a moment. Instead of talking where he is, he decides to go even further from his colleague and heads towards Vulpie and Blacktail while Polar follows. He meets them in the center of the room.

"Well I said I would be…" Richard tells his brother, looking to his right. "And now you've brought Vulpie here?"

"He wants to meet Ivo, what was his last name again?" Polar asks.

"Lorcan." Richard simply responds. "Ivo is here but why on Sufias do you want me to be a part of this? I assume you told him everything even though I said I would never mention it."

"I know you did, but we had a discussion last night." Polar explains and Vulpie stays silent. He smiles at Richard respectfully. Richard half expects Vulpie to flip out at any moment, enraged that he would be compared to the Anti-Khalan, but the fox boy continues to surprise him. Polar's husband appears to be very much in control of his emotions and the situation. Richard still isn't sure how he feels about this, though. Part of him secretly wonders if he's looking at the Anti-Khalan, who has come to confront someone that exposed him.

"Vulpie, I had nothing to do with Ivo's work. He showed it to me and I showed it to my brother." Richards tells the orange furred fox.

"I know. Could you take us to your friend?" Vulpie pleasantly replies.

"To do what, exactly?" Richard asks with a piercing voice. "Why are there so many men from Blacktail along?"

"Because this many always travel with me in public. Polar usually only wants one or two." Vulpie answers. "He feels plenty safe with them but I can't defend myself like he can."

"Look… I understand if you are upset about what Polar told you. I know he's your husband but he's also my brother, and I thought he had a right to know."

"I would be upset if I didn't know that the picture is a fake." Vulpie replies and Richard looks down at the fox with a different attitude. The handsome arctic wolf reminds Vulpie of Polar quite a bit, but seeing him next to Polar is a clear contrast. Richard lacks the control Polar has. It might be because Polar is gay, and is more thoughtful, or it might be a cultural thing, but Vulpie finds Richard a little scary sometimes. He has the same intense blue eyes and is almost as strong as his big brother.

"A fake? You've never met Ivo Lorcan before... Honestly I feel that I wouldn't be a friend to him if I brought you to start a fight. He's very old and doesn't deserve to be attacked for his work." Richard responds, and his judgmental voice makes Vulpie feel guilty. All of the Arctics, all of Polar's family seems to ascribe to a high moral standard. Despite Richard's problems with foxes and the fact that he was not friendly upon their first meeting years ago, he can still hurt Vulpie's confidence.

Surely Richard has never broken the law like Vulpie has. There is no doubt in the fox boy's mind that such criminal behavior wouldn't be something Victor or Kimberly Arctic would put up with. Vulpie knows Richard is a man of his own merits as well, and can see his point of view regarding his colleague. The way he suggests that Vulpie is looking for a fight almost makes Vulpie want to tuck tail and go home in disgrace. Luckily, however, Polar gives Vulpie the backup he needs.

"He knows something you don't, Richard. He's seen your emails with Ivo." Polar admits and Richard frowns, looking to his brother in complete surprise. He doesn't say anything for a moment and then looks back to Vulpie.

"I always wondered if you did things like that..." Is all Richard says and Polar licks his lips.

"He had a very good reason, Richard."

"Well I certainly hope so. I don't want someone spying on me. I don't have anything to hide but I share confidential information about my students and my work."

"I promise you'll understand why I did it, Richard. Will you please take us to your friend?" Vulpie politely asks.

"Why? What do you want to do so badly? If you ask him about the painting he'll tell you the same thing he told me and Polar."

"He isn't here to start a fight and he's not here because he's upset. Vulpie has a suspicion about the man you think you know." Polar explains.

"The man you THINK I know? I've known Ivo for five years..." Polar's brother responds and takes a deep breath. "But okay... I'll take you to him. I'm sure he's in the exhibit room preparing more of his pieces." After Richard commits he looks back over to one of his colleagues. He walks away from the group and she is happy to see him return to give her an answer about what is happening. "Can you handle my class for a bit? I need to take care of something." He asks and his friend nods. She gladly encourages the students to follow her and she continues lecturing.

Richard looks over at Vulpie and gestures for him to follow. Blacktail spreads out while following Polar's sibling into and through a few of the exhibit rooms. Polar remembers most of them from the day before and after about a minute and a half they arrive in the smaller exhibit where Ivo Lorcan is indeed working. There is a museum assistant carrying building equipment for him but quickly disappears, leaving as the group comes in. Ivo Lorcan's eyes widen as he sees Vulpie and his escort of armed men with him. With Polar and Richard returning, the man isn't sure just what is going on. It seems surreal to him.

"Richard?" Ivo asks and Polar's brother sighs as he walks forward. The white furred wolf smiles politely but also with a comical expression.

"My brother told Vulpie about the picture and it seems he wanted to see it for himself... I'm sorry to involve you." Richard apologizes and Ivo looks worried. He stares at Vulpie and shakes his head after a moment.

"Oh dear..." Ivo whispers.

"I know..." Richard growls in response. Vulpie's blue eyes are quickly drawn to the right where a picture is covered with a black shroud. He assumes behind it is the picture in question. A silence fills the room, only interrupted by the shuffling of shoes on the museum's marble floor.

"Hello! Sorry for barging in like this but I just couldn't wait to see this wonderful artifact myself! I never knew I was famous millions of years ago!" Vulpie mischievously declares and walks towards Ivo. The old gray wolf smiles courteously when Vulpie outstretches his right paw. "Vulpie Vivixen, CEO of Vulpie Industries and Prince of Darkness!" Ivo hesitates to shake the fox's paw after his statement and at this Vulpie lowers his paw and smirks. "Did I say something wrong?"

"Mr. Vivixen I'd rather not make a scene here. I have work to do, but you can take a look at the artifact if you wish." Ivo responds with his raspy voice.

"Can I really?" Vulpie asks, brimming with mock excitement.

"Of course. It's no trouble, but I'm afraid it doesn't mention you at all." Ivo responds and turns towards the covered painting. The wolf uses his big left paw to take hold of the black cloth over the display case and yanks it down gracefully. Everyone's eyes focus on the eerie picture. The orange fox depicted grins with the same expression Vulpie is fond of using.

"OOoooooo! That's amazing! It DOES look just like me!" Vulpie says and Ivo clears his throat before speaking in response.

"It translates into, roughly, the Anti-Khalan. It was recovered at the dig site in Ninvia."

"Ninvia! Yeah!" Vulpie replies while eying the picture and suddenly he turns and poses next to it for everyone. "What do ya think? Pretty similar huh?" No one says anything but Polar gets a very relieved feeling. He knows Vulpie has a plan. "Rulef!" Vulpie quickly shouts and points his left index finger at the large wolf. "I command you, as the Anti-Khalan, the prince of darkness himself, to hop on one foot!"

"Cute." Rulef responds without showing any emotion.

"Aw! UH! NOO! YOU'RE SUPPOSED TO FOLLOW MY COMMANDS! … I guess I'm a pretty disappointing lord of evil, huh? I can't even make this guy entertain me!" Vulpie complains to Ivo Lorcan.

"Mr. Vivixen, there really is no need for this. No one here is trying to demonize you. You're just embarrassing yourself."

"Oh I don't think so… I think I'll redeem myself pretty soon!" Vulpie tells the old wolf with a sparkle in his eyes. "That is, if you'll answer some questions for me?"

"Of course."

"What do ya think, everybody? He should answer a few questions if I ask really nicely, right?" Vulpie diplomatically suggests to the group. No one nods, but they don't need to. The point is letting everyone present know that they need to pay close attention.

"I don't have anything to hide, Vulpie." Ivo Lorcan says with an irritated voice. He starts to look uncomfortable. Richard assumes it's because he feels disrespected but to Polar there is another reason.

"Great! Sooooo! Question number one!" Vulpie grins in excitement. "Whyyyyyyyyyyyyyyyyy, did you come to Sufias City?"

"To bring in artifacts recovered from Ninvia. I'm sure your husband told you this already." Ivo answers.

"But I read that you were feeling sick! I hope you're okay now!" Vulpie retorts, carefully handling the conversation like a game of chess.

"I did have some heart troubles but thanks to new medication I'm feeling fine."

"That's fantastic! Except... Well I hope your wife is okay with letting you fly across the ocean all by yourself! She's still in Englavic, isn't she?"

"No, the Kayman Institute has provided my wife and I with an apartment while I work in Sufias City." Ivo says with a frown.

"Hey Richard!" Vulpie calls out while leaning to the left to look around Ivo. "Have you ever met Ivo's wife before?" Polar looks to his brother and sees a very displeased expression.

"What does that have to do with anything, Vulpie? What business is it of yours what Ivo does with his wife?" Richard snorts.

"It's just a simple little question I'm asking. What harm is there in answering?"

"No I haven't met Ivo's wife and I'm sure he will never let me after all of the embarrassment I'm causing him. I should have known better than to mention it to Polar."

"Yeah, maybe you shouldn't have, then." Polar says to his brother and Richard rolls his eyes. "But you did."

"Okay, so you've never met her and that means you certainly haven't seen her here in Sufias City." Vulpie continues.

"Are you calling him a liar? You're saying that his wife isn't being put up by the Kayman Institute? You know, you really should think about things before you make rapid fire accusations Vulpie." Richard comments.

"Thank you Richard, your condescension is appreciated as always." Vulpie tells the big wolf and Polar smirks at the remark.

"I hope this is going somewhere soon, Vulpie." Rulef says with crossed arms. Richard picks up on the statement and runs with it.

"As do I. I hope I won't have to call the police." Richard declares.

"Alright, well let's get right down to it then! You want to speed things up? Fine! I'll skip all of the buildup then!" Vulpie replies with a very vulpine voice. Polar realizes he is actually enjoying the argument because he knows how his beloved fox is going to crush Ivo and Richard with whatever he says next. Polar has no idea what will happen, but he has no doubt Vulpie will come out on top.

"You're not Ivo Lorcan." Vulpie says and Ivo shakes his head in disbelief.

"I'm not?"

"Ivo Lorcan is very sick. He suffered a major heart attack last week and is confined to Shyriver Hospital in Englavic. I have several newspaper articles that confirm it. And Mr. Lorcan had his heart attack last Thursday, Richard!" Vulpie calls out again to make sure Polar's brother can hear him clearly. "Right after he told you reports of his demise were greatly exaggerated!"

"Wow, you really have been reading my emails... I'm very disappointed with you." Richard responds.

"Don't be just yet, big guy!" Vulpie quips and focuses on Ivo. "So, what's the story, huh? Who are you?"

"I have no clue what you are talking about." Ivo insists with a defensive voice.

"Really? Wanna call the Kayman Institute and ask them if the project is still on with you and your artifacts coming from Ninvia?" Vulpie inquires and reaches into the left pocket of his suit pants to pull out his orange phone. "I've got the number, but hey Richard, maybe you'd like to do the honors?"

"I think that's a wonderful idea, Vulpie. Maybe it will end your delusions of persecution right now, but I doubt it." Richard replies and gathers his own cell phone from his pocket.

"Go right ahead then!" Vulpie says back with a smart ass smile.

"I'll call the President of the school. Do you think that's high enough or will you want even more proof?" Richard asks.

"I won't need anymore." The fox boy responds and the room goes silent for a moment as Richard makes the call. The President of the Kayman Institute answers rather quickly, indicating that he might have time to talk.

"Matthew…" Richard says with a very deferential voice. No one can hear his conversation and he realizes it, so he pulls the phone away from his wolf ear for a moment to turn on the speaker phone. It's loud enough for everyone to follow the conversation.

"*Richard? How can I help you?*"

"I am very sorry to interrupt, if I have, but I have a faculty question that needs answering rather quickly. I'm over at the Lupiv Museum."

"*Fire away.*" The school president says with an emotionless voice.

"You know the school is working with Ivo Lorcan and the artifacts he's bringing in from Ninvia, right?"

"Yes, it was cancelled, I remember." The man responds and when everyone hears this, fur stands on end.

"Cancelled? Sir, it wasn't cancelled. I've been working with Mr. Lorcan at the Museum this week." Richard replies and the room goes quiet again when silence comes from the other end of the call for a bit.

"No Richard, it was cancelled. Ivo Lorcan won't be able to complete the courses we hired him for because of his illness."

"Well I'll be." Rulef whispers and focuses his attention on Ivo. The strong mercenary will no longer stop watching him for a moment.

"T-h,thank you sir. That's all I needed to know." Richard whispers.

"Are you sure? Who have you been working with instead?"

"I made a slight mistake, but have it figured out now. Thanks."

"Uh huh. Have a good week." The college president responds and ends the phone call. Richard slowly brings the phone down from his left ear in disbelief.

"I told you." Vulpie says in Richard's direction while staring at Ivo.

"What's going on? Ivo... What's happening?" Richard asks and Ivo Lorcan looks very confused. The old gray wolf squints as if trying to remember where he is.

"I don't know... This doesn't make any sense. I don't know why the president would say that." Ivo answers.

"Who are you?" Vulpie demands with an adorable voice. "Mmm? Are you still gonna lie to us or what?"

"I don't understand any of this." Ivo whispers.

"Well I do. I know exactly what you are..." Vulpie quickly says and gets the attention of all of the animals present. "I wanted you to tell a few more stories so I could expose you as a fraud with even more evidence but I think that was pretty good. What do you think?"

"Don't call me a fraud. I've done nothing to you." Ivo growls.

"You haven't done anything? What the hell is this picture behind me? Is that your idea of a joke? It's kind of sick if you ask me!" Vulpie laughs.

"I'm sorry to tell you that the painting is real. Maybe you should learn to deal with it."

"Yeah, and I'm the Prince of Darkness! Woo hoo! Who do you think you're dealing with, huh? Did you think I'd let you put a sick idea like this in my husband's head and not investigate? I know what you are, Ivo! Yes I do! Want me to say it? I know you know what I mean!"

"I have no idea what you mean. I keep telling you that." Lorcan snorts.

"CHRIS CEFIL! Yep! The GBI arrested a synthetic animal, a robotic imitation six years ago, and he was so fucking believable that no one knew he wasn't real until they drug screened him! Then the GBI hauled me in and accused me of making the thing, and I had no idea where it came from, but I've got a REALLY good idea who might be behind it."

"He's robotic?" Rulef barks, readying the attention of his men.

"I'm sure he is! But don't worry guys, Chris Cefil was no fighter, and I doubt old Ivo is either. I think they're made for different reasons."

"You're crazy." Ivo says while shaking his head.

"Crazy like a fox!" Vulpie winks with a very devious smirk. "BUSTED! You're SO busted pal!" Richard walks around Ivo, eying him with his mouth slightly agape. Ivo returns the stare but with a confused expression. The old man opens his paws and looks down at his palms. "Richard, if ya wanna call the police I wouldn't mind one bit! Make sure you get ahold of the GBI as well, though. I'm sure Druward will want to see this thing."

"Can you arrest him? He might be dangerous now that his cover's blown." Polar contributes while glancing at Rulef.

"There's no need to get physical with him if he promises to stay put. I'd rather not touch him if it can be avoided." Rulef answers and looks to his right at Deepwolf. "Contact the GBI and let them know where to find us." The squad leader commands and Deepwolf nods. The gray wolf glances back over his shoulder as he leaves the room to do so. "You shouldn't stand so close to him, Vulpie."

"I know, but let me check one more thing…" Vulpie responds and retrieves the long rectangular device he picked up from Vulpie Industries. It's colored jet black and it's input panel can be opened by a downward twist of the paws. Vulpie slides open its user interface and activates the device by hitting its small black power button. The power button lights up with a white ring around its exterior and shows Vulpie an image of what it is recording from the camera on the other side.

The high tech video device is more than just a recorder or a camera. One of its outstanding uses includes the ability to film heat signatures, making it easy to spot suspicious animals in the neighborhood or feel safe on a camping trip. The item has countless possible uses but Vulpie has not fully completed its design. He is using the prototype model, but it works very well. "Richard, would you help me out? Here, take this." Vulpie offers while smiling at the white furred wolf. Richard looks down at Vulpie and walks around Ivo cautiously before accepting. He silently takes the device into his paws and looks it over.

"What am I supposed to do with it?" Richard inquires.

"It's programmed on infrared mode. It's looking for heat signatures, and I'd like you to film all of us. It's already recording. Just look through its screens and tell us what you see." Vulpie answers. Richard watches Vulpie and then Ivo. He complies without a verbal response, and holds the device up in his right paw. It's surprisingly light weight. He can see Vulpie's green, red, orange and blue body heat against a black background in the view finder and Vulpie's representation points over to Blacktail. "Take a look at them."

Richard does so without saying a word. He quickly enjoys peering at their bodies on a base level. Tiala, Rulef and other members of the private security force are all colored just the same as Vulpie, with variations based on size and Species in regard to Tiala. Richard goes on filming and turns almost completely around to his right so he can view Polar. His brother is like the rest of them, and after he views him, he slowly turns to his right to see Ivo through the device. His fur stands on end and his eyes widen when he sees what Vulpie is looking for.

"Are you sure this thing works?" Richard quietly asks.

"It works on every animal here, doesn't it?" Vulpie responds.

"Let me guess… Ivo has no body heat?" Rulef asks with crossed arms.

"He has heat but he's all blue colored. It looks like he's cooler than everyone else. And, well, his eyes and parts of him that were colored on all of you aren't the same way with him." Richard answers and lowers the device. The white furred wolf stares at Ivo Lorcan with a betrayed expression. Vulpie sees his anger flare when he speaks to Ivo. "You succeeded in making a fool out of me… Whoever you are…"

"Richard, I swear I don't understand this!" Ivo protests, looking genuinely distraught. His supposedly heartfelt statement has little effect on Polar's brother.

"It looks like I owe you an apology… Vulpie…" Richard says after looking to his right at the orange furred fox boy. He holds the device out for Vulpie to take it back but Vulpie doesn't.

"And I owe you an apology for spying on you. I hope you can see now why I did." Vulpie replies and nods towards the device Richard still has. "Why don't you keep that? Maybe it will come in handy." Richard lowers the device and puts both of his paws on it, feeling its slick design. He thinks about what to say.

"I feel rotten for believing this… Thing…" The white furred wolf admits.

"No worries." Vulpie replies with a playful smirk. "I think he'd fool anyone, maybe even Ivo's wife! Who knows?"

"But I'm not a machine!" Ivo suddenly barks and looks around in fear. "I… I can't believe what you're telling me!"

"You're really programmed different than Chris Cefil. He fessed up and blamed me for making him but not you. No, you're trying another strategy aren't ya?" Vulpie grins.

"I'm a living animal. I know who I am! This is insane!" The old wolf gasps.

"I think I will keep this." Richard comments while moving Vulpie's device in his big paws. "In case I make any new friends..."

The Set Up

Druward dislikes the situation. The Governmental Bureau of Investigations director didn't plan on having anything to do with Vulpie prior to the arrangement he agreed to. Karl Vulches and Nathan Fenrir have put their pieces into play and the gears are turning, yet now Druward walks inside the Lupiv Museum to meet Vulpie and his Blacktail bodyguards.

He's more interested in what Rulef has to say. Admittedly, the news about another possible robotic animal being discovered bothers him. If it is true, he thinks to himself that this is just another reason to remove Vulpie Vivixen from the picture. The black furred wolf has not forgotten the way the fox boy has wiggled out of his contract with the government, using duress by Druward as an excuse. Rotick, a white and brown furred wolf, is with him. Druward has used him for various duties throughout his career, and the GBI agent is top notch. He helped Druward behind the scenes during the Evil Vulpie crisis as well.

"What are you thinking?" Rotick asks while they transverse the open spaces of the museum.

"I'm thinking Vulpie should be in prison." Druward answers.

"You believe he's behind this? I don't think little foxy made Chris Cefil six years ago. Howlstead looked that half living freak over before it died and his opinion is that it couldn't have been made with this century's technology."

"Won't know until we see it will we?" The black furred wolf replies as they enter a small series of rooms. They go through the small exhibits on their way to the one with everyone waiting for them. Tiala sees Druward coming first, as she is guarding the exit. The tigress would smile or nod at him if she thought he cared for it in the least but she doesn't even bother. Druward walks right into the room with Rotick behind him and stops near Vulpie and Ivo. Druward glances to his left at Polar and sees Richard. He makes a mental note that the second white furred wolf must be Polar's brother.

"Thank you for coming. He's all yours." Vulpie says to Druward. The black furred wolf doesn't even look down at Vulpie or acknowledge him at all. He observes Ivo a bit, and then looks to his left to speak to Rulef.

"What has it done?"

"Nothing. It insists it's the real archaeologist that Polar's brother knows, but after the things Vulpie has shown us there's no way that can be true." Rulef answers.

"No way? What sort of things did he show you?"

"It doesn't have a heat signature. And I had Richard call the president of his school to see whether Ivo Lorcan was in Sufias City. It turns out that the real man is in Englavic, and he's very sick." Vulpie says. He waits for a reply from Druward but there is silence. The black furred wolf continues to completely ignore the fox boy.

"He's telling the truth." Rulef states.

"I want this thing locked down as soon as possible. If it is a machine I'll have Howlstead look into its design. Maybe it's similar to that other one that showed up six years ago, before this little cocksucker squirmed out of his contract with the CTGD." Druward responds, stressing cocksucker with vicious intent.

Polar's white fur slowly stands on end. He feels his blood begin to boil and can hardly control himself when he thinks of telling Druward what he thinks of him. Druward notices and turns his attention to Vulpie's husband. The two enter into a deadly standoff that the GBI Director quickly escalates.

"Oh, is there something you want to say, Polar?" Druward growls. "Go ahead."

"Wow, you are just as bad as they said you were." Richard comments, standing in for his brother in defense of Vulpie.

"Save it. That faggot fox should be in prison for what he's done and everyone knows it." Druward replies and finally looks to Vulpie, after turning to his right. "I'll take care of it for you. Once again I'm going to clean up your mess, VULPIE..."

"Thank you." Vulpie simply replies with a thankful voice. His courtesy is disarming but Druward knows the game. Vulpie just wants Ivo removed as soon as possible.

"I'll be taking your Blacktail escort to guard it. Though you rent them, they still belong to the GBI and there's no way I'm going to risk it killing someone... But I'll leave you Tiala, since you two got along so well the last time."

"Yes, she saved my life. But you know, I never had a chance to thank you for saving both of us. That was awfully heroic when you shot down Evil Vulpie's helicopter and picked us up." Vulpie smiles.

"That a boy... You continue to use that pretty little mouth of yours. We wouldn't want the wrong things to dribble out." Druward sneers.

"I'd like to see Howlstead too, if that's okay. I want to see what he says about it." Vulpie tells the black furred wolf and Druward returns a condescending smile.

"That will be fine." The GBI Director declares and turns back to Rulef. "Meet me at the CTGD complex. I'll have to contact the president..."

"Yes sir." Rulef quickly replies. "We'll bind Ivo in one of the SUVs and I'll personally take charge of watching it."

"What sort of weapons are you carrying?"

"We're armed with four MKR-80s." Rulef replies, referring to their rail guns. "It shouldn't be a problem." When the Blacktail commander finishes, Druward looks to Vulpie once again.

"Just like old times, eh?" He asks the cute little fox. Vulpie returns a coy smile but says nothing.

The Cyber Technologies Government Division is exactly the way Vulpie remembers it. He hasn't seen the building in more than six years. Polar also spent some time inside the building, coming to see his lover whenever he could. And then there was that fateful night where Evil Vulpie nearly killed Vulpie and could have done the same to the white furred wolf. Neither of them want to think about those moments too much, because having Ivo Lorcan around is like seeing the smoke but not the fire. They both suspect Vulpie.net had something to do with him, even though it seems impossible.

"Vulpie, it's good to see you!" Arthur Howlstead declares with a genuinely happy face. The tall gray wolf looks over the little fox.

"You too, Arthur! Are you training teams on Arctic.net now?" Vulpie smiles.

"I am. I've nearly mastered it, but I really wish that we still had you here."

"How are the government projects? Are you getting the funding you need?"

"Funding isn't the problem... It's all of the red tape we have to go through. Our new president isn't nearly as helpful as Vargas was on matters of technological security."

"If you get too frustrated, I would love to have you at Vulpie Industries!" Vulpie offers and Howlstead pulls back in surprise.

"YOU, hire ME?" Arthur laughs.

"Sure!" Vulpie repeats.

"Thank you for the offer but that's too much of a role reversal. Plus I'm the only one that appreciates Vulpie.net besides Melrhei and Nikita."

"Oh wow, they're still working here? That's awesome! I'm glad you have the extra help."

"And I do need it. Maybe after we're done here we could work another arrangement out with your company. I need you, Vulpie. And the funds are available to pay you for your work."

"You don't have to pay me, Arthur. I'll do it again for free if you really need my help." Vulpie responds and Arthur looks quite pleased at the offer.

"Arthur... Do you have a place to lock this thing up?" Druward interrupts, referring to Ivo Lorcan. The old gray wolf is paw cuffed behind him with Blacktail all around the animal.

"So that's him?" Arthur asks and steps to the right to see around Druward. He looks over Ivo with his yellow wolf eyes and finds nothing abnormal about him. Polar, Vulpie, Ivo, Blacktail, Druward and Arthur are standing inside the CTGD's main observatory. It's the same place where Vulpie hacked into the computer systems to land spaceships controlled by Vulpie.net on Planet Veida, back when they were not allowed to land during the Evil Vulpie Crisis. And it's also the place where Vulpie read that Vulpie.net was using mind map file extensions to authorize its actions. Behind the rows of computers are the bullet proof glass doors that lead into the White room.

There's no need to go inside the white room today but just seeing the entrance gives Vulpie chills. He became accustomed to it when he had to continue to work for the government after the Evil Vulpie crisis but since he's been away for several years, the first thing that comes to mind is, of course, writhing and screaming in agony while Evil Vulpie tortured him. Polar is thinking the same thing. His memory is different because he arrived after Evil Vulpie had almost killed Vulpie. What comes to mind for him is the terrifying chase on the floors and roof above and how he almost fell to his death. Evil Vulpie saved him and then destroyed itself, but being in the building makes it all seem like it could happen again at any moment.

"We keep what's left of Chris Cefil down on the basement level." Arthur tells Druward.

"What's left of it? You mean it didn't keep? The thing was perishable?" Druward asks.

"One day it simply died... Well, I'll explain more once we get down there." Arthur responds. He takes a look at the animals working in the room. They are of different species, and all of them have glanced over at Vulpie Vivixen at least once. Some of them are in awe of him, and some of them look as though they blame him for their chores. Regardless, every computer tech in the room is aware that Vulpie has no equal. Working with Arctic.net alone has taught them this, as they have seen its genius on a daily basis and through it, the unspeakably terrible efficiency of Vulpie.net.

The group follows Arthur's lead. The CTGD director leads them back out of the main observatory into a hallway going into another section of the complex. Vulpie has been in it before, to the left of the White Room and main observatory, but it seems to mostly be offices. But their destination is an elevator halfway down the hallway. They pass a few animals that step aside with bewildered looks, seeing Blacktail's weaponry. "We'll make two trips. There's only room for half of you." Arthur advises while looking towards Rulef.

Rulef signals for Deepwolf to come with him and Vulpie as well. Polar refuses to be left behind even for a minute and enters, all of them getting around Ivo Lorcan. Arthur goes inside and presses the button to close the elevator door. The ride down to the second basement level of the CTGD is a short one, but the result is fairly interesting. Vulpie never knew there was another portion of the CTGD that looks similar to the White Room. The basement level seems to have been built off of the same design but with less computers. The tiles and wall structures are all white just like they are two floors above.

"Oh wow! Are these another set of computers that are separate from the ones in the rest of the CTGD?" Vulpie inquires.

"Actually, no. The White Room is the only network in the CTGD that is separate from the rest. But before that was completed about fifteen years ago we used this location for most of the same activities. It's distance from the ground level is unnecessary and prohibitive, though. So there wasn't any reason to continue to work underground."

"But the idea was the same, right? All of those years ago you wanted a separate network that couldn't be hacked into." Vulpie presses.

"Yes, but like I said it was discontinued. You can see a lot of the technology is similar."

"Do you have the equipment to properly scan this thing?" Druward inquires while they walk into a rather long white chamber with tables on the outskirts next to the walls.

"The machines use x-rays, thermal imaging, MRIs and ElectroGenesis methods, so I assume the only place you'll find something better is Vulpie Industries." Arthur replies and gives the fox boy a smirk.

"And security?" Druward asks while eying the desks, tables, work stations and general machinery in the vicinity.

"We'll store it inside of a solid steel chamber. That's what we did with Chris Cefil."

"I'm going to assign additional security to it and the building." Druward comments.

"Thank you. It will be nice to have this place locked down especially since this is the first day we've had with our visitor."

"Blacktail is carrying state of the art weaponry designed for this very sort of thing. Even if it escapes, which I suspect it cannot, they can blow it in half."

"That won't be necessary. There's no way it will be able to get out of its cell." Howlstead replies. Suddenly Ivo struggles and Deepwolf quickly twists the old wolf's left arm.

"LET ME GO! I'M NOT A ROBOT!" Lorcan yells and everyone steps back except for Druward. He watches Rulef assist but he isn't needed. Ivo can't go anywhere but continues to struggle.

"Are you sure he's not a real animal? I wouldn't want to get this facility in trouble by locking up a real citizen." Arthur comments.

"They say he doesn't give off body heat. Can you run some tests on him to verify it?" Druward responds.

"Absolutely. Bring him in here." The CTGD director says and leads them to the back right corner of the white chamber. There is a chamber about the size of a car with a stretcher built into the middle with computer terminals outside. A transparent door opens up when they approach. "Calm down. We're not going to lock you up if you are a real animal. All this machine will do is scan your vital signs. It cannot hurt you in any way." Arthur tells the man and Ivo stops struggling, though he continues to breathe hard.

There is a brief silence and Vulpie and Polar watch while Ivo begins to cooperate. The old gray wolf looks completely lost about his current predicament. Deepwolf helps him into the chair and sees that there are straps to lock him in, but Arthur waves a paw in disagreement. "No, no. There's no need to tie him down if he holds still." Arthur comments while looking to Ivo. Ivo seems to register the suggestion without a fight and lies back on the stretcher. "This will only take about twenty seconds. Please don't move." The CTGD director says and when Deepwolf steps out of the chamber the door shuts again.

Arthur sits down at the computer terminal to the left of the door and begins typing. He accesses the machine's commands very quickly and engages the mechanism. There is no sound at all, inside or outside of the chamber. The only thing that visibly happens is the appearance of a data stream on the computer screen. The test runs its course and finishes without protest from Ivo.

"Finished?" Druward inquires.

"Yes, let him out." Arthur answers and Deepwolf moves towards the door. It opens on its own, and he gestures for Ivo to get up. The old man looks like he needs help and Deepwolf goes over and provides an arm for support. Lorcan gets up and with Deepwolf accompanying him, leaves the chamber to once again go into Blacktail custody. He doesn't resist them paw cuffing him once more.

"What does it say?" Vulpie asks Arthur. Howlstead peers over the information projected on the computer screen. The result of the scan makes him sit up. He's seen this type of pattern before and instantly recognizes it. His yellow eyes dart back and forth, acquiring all the information he needs before making a response.

"It looks very familiar." Arthur states.

"Is he much different than Chris Cefil or exactly the same?" Vulpie asks. Arthur glances at him, noticing the fox's expression is not one of satisfaction, but concern.

"I don't see anything major that separates him from Cefil. Structurally they seem to be the same."

"So he's not a living animal." Druward declares.

"No... No way." Arthur says while shaking his head. Ivo stares at the floor. The old gray wolf is no longer sure of what should even be on his mind. He remembers saying goodbye to his wife this morning, yet even he knows it cannot be true at this point. Lorcan struggles to find a memory specific to this morning in particular. While the others talk, his eyes widen in fear. He is unable to discover a single thing about this morning that was different than the morning before. Was there even a morning before today? He tells himself that there had to be.

"I told you I didn't make Cefil. Here's the proof." Vulpie says and looks to his left at Ivo.

"On the contrary. It makes your involvement even more suspicious." Druward objects.

"Yeah, I know what your opinion is." Vulpie replies.

"Cefil names you as his maker six years ago and this time the robot in question is drawing pictures of you and hanging them in a museum..."

"I suppose I could have not even reported him. Hmm? I could have let him escape without telling anyone. That way I could have hidden my involvement and tried to avoid the blame. Isn't that what you think I'd do, Druward?"

"You can't resist the attention... It's all you've ever cared about." Druward snorts.

"You know, for a man as successful as you are, you seem awfully thick." Vulpie growls to the surprise of Howlstead. The CTGD director has to remind himself that the fox doesn't work for them anymore, as his natural reaction was fear that an Arctic.net project would be endangered as a result. "I'm chief executive officer of my own international corporation, yet you still believe my only goal is to create drama. Why on Sufias would I want this kind of problem?"

"Oh, you poor misunderstood creature." The GBI director mockingly answers.

"Do you think you could stop insulting my husband?" Polar interjects. The white furred wolf looks fairly angry, and his statement is loud enough to get everyone's attention. "I'm getting rather tired of hearing it."

"So you can store it in the same cell you put Cefil in?" Druward asks Howlstead while ignoring Polar completely.

"Yes. I'll have some additional tests run on it as well. That is, if Ivo continues to cooperate." Howlstead replies.

"I'll leave you his Blacktail escort then." Druward decides, referring to Vulpie's security detail. The black furred wolf looks to the right for a moment as if considering something else. "You won't need much more security after ten hours will you?"

"I shouldn't. We'll have most of the ancillary tests done by then and we'll keep it confined in its cell."

Zorpiv's Predilection

"Ready up... It's time!" Zorpiv breathes to his men. The other foxes from the Vuldrofein that are with him, half red and half of them brown, listen to his command as if he were a veteran of their organization. Assuming a captain's position for the Vuldrofein has turned out far easier than he expected. The fox hit squad is composed of several religious zealots, but Zorpiv understands that those elements are just an excuse for violence. The true goal is winning over anything they desire, because they believe they are the chosen species. Zorpiv muses that Karl was right about one thing. He does enjoy giving commands, especially when there are few limits to his authority. He fondles the weapon in his paws.

"There's only one SUV, just like Druward said." Zorpiv's top aide comments. He's a red fox named Wesley, and he was leading the Vuldrofein before Zorpiv took control. Instead of butting heads with him, Zorpiv has been sure to listen to his advice.

"That's right..." Zorpiv replies while fondling the weapon in his little paws. He has the MTAC-71 pointed down against the floor of their black sedan. The Vuldrofein is using three cars in total, two following Vulpie's black SUV, and the other one staying ahead of the target vehicle. They are driving on highway 290 northeast towards the middle of Sufias City where the Vulpic Industries tower is. As far as landmarks go, it's impossible to miss.

"We need to do it soon, before he reaches the downtown expressway."

"He'll have to take the Andrews exit first. That's where we'll hit him! Got it?" Zorpiv answers, speaking first to Wesley and then directing his voice to the driver.

"In the middle of Maro Street? It's a speed trap through there! As soon as we make our move, the police are going to be on top of us!" Wesley warns.

"We'll block him in at the section between Stokes and Harmon." Zorpiv declares and opens his cell phone to call the car behind them. The Vuldrofein uses simplistic but perfectly reliable phones to do their work. "The lead car is going to block his truck in at Stokes and Harmon. "Handle the traffic behind us and any bystanders." The gray fox orders and receives an ok. He then calls the car ahead of Vulpie's SUV to deliver the same message. "Stop in front of him at Stokes and Harmon."

"Roger." The lead car replies and Zorpiv snaps his phone shut. Wesley starts breathing fast and the gray fox notices. His top aide seems terribly fearful, but will do his job. Zorpiv, on the other hand, feels more excitement than concern.

"It's going to be a shootout." Wesley warns again.

"Come on you cocksuckers, do you want to live forever?" Zorpiv laughs to him and the rest of the foxes.

"You think you know where it came from?" Tiala asks Vulpie while slightly turning her head to the right.

"All I have is a feeling at this point... But I think there's a connection between Ivo and Sevrif Industries." Vulpie answers. He looks at his reflection in the bullet proof glass windows and sees a worried fox.

"Well it's caught now. At least Polar's brother is safe. Who knows, maybe it was going to threaten him?" Tiala suggests while slowing down. A black sedan quickly pulls in front of her in the slow lane. The driver's disrespect irritates her a bit, but her Blacktail training allows her to maintain defensive driving. She slows down even more, allowing the driver ahead of her a lot of space.

"I don't like leaving Polar alone at the house…" Vulpie thinks out loud. After leaving the Cyber Technologies Government Division they went home, with only Tiala as an escort, but Vulpie wants to make a quick trip to his office to check on some things. He is actually going to do some hacking to find out more about what Ivo was up to. The orange furred fox secretly plans to hack into the Lupiv Museum's records. He hopes he can discover just when the fake Ivo made his first appearance, or if the thing has been around for quite some time.

"He'll be alright." Tiala reassures Vulpie. She squints in confusion when the driver in front of her slows down far too early as they come to a stop light. They are at the Stokes and Harmon four way intersection, and the traffic is fairly heavy for a noon commute. They've been passing by all sorts of lovely shops, as the community is pretty well to do. Across to the left, past the incoming traffic lane, there are several specialty shops dedicated to home theater products. They have the exciting eye catching advertisements that always capture an animal's attention, and the right side of the street has equally artistic designs. The one that stands out the most is the cream puff design on a very large coffee shop named "Clouds." It's largest outdoor sign mixes the image of cream in coffee that doubles as a skyline as well. The logo is a very interesting piece of art, so Vulpie usually gets coffee at Clouds whenever he can. The environment alone is almost worth the price of the drinks.

The orange furred fox boy smiles, looking in at a few well to do families having drinks and reading newspapers. A few of them have eBook readers, and are either reading novels, checking their emails on their wireless signals or even watching movies on the devices. It makes Vulpie very happy when he sees that the majority of them are using V-Screens, his company's tablet computer. The orange design of the V-Screens match the colorful brown atmosphere of the coffee shop. The animals using them look like an advertisement for Vulpie Industries.

"Looks like the new model V-Screens are catching on. These animals have the smaller versions." Vulpie thinks out loud, also sharing his opinion with Tiala.

"I haven't bought one yet but I've been meaning to." Tiala replies with a friendly voice. She seems genuinely interested in getting one.

"I'll give ya a free one." Vulpie offers and smiles up at her in the rear view mirror.

"Thanks but you don't have to do that."

"I won't have it any other way. Just pick out which design you want and I'll have it mailed to you." Vulpie says and bounces his knees. He looks very cute in his jet black corporate suit.

"My niece might want one." Tiala comments while her eyes widen. She sees several foxes open the car doors of the sedan that is in front of them at the red light. Tiala reaches for her weapon, catching her breath, when she sees they are carrying automatics. "VULPIE GET DOWN!" Tiala yells and kicks open the driver's door. Her command makes the fox boy jump in fear. He watches Tiala pull her assault rifle out of the SUV with her and quickly leaps forward onto the floor. Vulpie covers up with his little arms defensively, and looks around at all of the black tinted windows. He can't see anything and his natural reaction is that he should help Tiala, but he follows her orders.

Tiala is faster and better trained than the Vuldrofein driver that has blocked them in. The brown fox raises his weapon, a carbine, and attempts to fire first but is unable to match the tigress' speed. She doesn't even think about using the driver side door for cover because of her extensive combat experience. Tiala raises her assault rifle and fires through the glass at the driver just before he shoots. She hits him four times, killing him instantly. The Vuldrofein driver doesn't even have time to scream in pain and just drops to the pavement, but his right paw clutches the trigger of his MTAC-71. The reflex action causes it to spray bullets all over a green car to the left of them. It's owner, a terrified female dog, leans sideways and covers her head when the shots bust out her windows.

By this time, Zorpiv is already out of the right side of the first car behind the Blacktail SUV. Animals run from him, seeing his automatic weapon, and he hurries around the right side of the SUV. Meanwhile, the foxes in the car in front of the SUV on the right side try to shoot Tiala, but she ducks behind the driver's door and turns around, aiming back towards the second black sedan. She targets a red fox, who seems to see his death coming. He tries to run back behind the car for cover but Tiala nails him once in the face and twice in the throat. He is beyond dead because of the perfect shot. Tiala switched her gun to a three round burst mode in order to make the shot without hitting anyone behind her target.

The tigress has cleared and controls the left side of all of the vehicles, but the foxes hiding behind the sedan in front of the SUV spread out to shoot her. When several bullets slam into the driver's side door, sending paint flakes and dust against Tiala's fur, she curses. She recognizes the weapon that is being used against her.

"Fucking MTAC!" Tiala breathes to herself in frustration and a hint of fear. She's used the weapon before and has seen what it can do. This causes her to move backwards, on the left side of the

SUV, and she stands up to aim for their faces. Unfortunately, the bullet proof glass of the Blacktail vehicle proves that it is not quite as indestructible as expected. Zorpiv sees Tiala through the windows on the right side of the SUV and aims down the red holographic sight of his MTAC-71 at her. When he fires into the window, it punctures and breaks the barrier within four shots and about the same on the other side. The one thousand rounds per minute that it fires flows perfectly with its fifty shot clip.

Zorpiv's bullets are hitting Tiala within less than one second. It seems almost instantaneous. On the left side, Tiala cries out as three bullets shoot into her right arm. Five hit her bullet proof vest, and three hit her right shoulder. The pain is overwhelming and so is the force. The barrage of shots knocks her completely off of her feet. Bullets hit her everywhere, but mostly on her body armor. But to anyone watching, it looks as though she's been obliterated. Bleeding and helpless, Tiala crashes down against the green car to the left of the SUV, causing the female dog to scream.

"DIE! KITTEN!" Zorpiv sadistically declares. He watches and enjoys the sight of her seemingly dead with a vulpine snarl.

"TIALA!!!" Vulpie cries out while shuffling through all of the broken glass inside the SUV. "NO!" Zorpiv reaches inside the SUV and unlocks the right door. He swings it open and points his gun at Vulpie, who throws his paws up in terror, trying to cover himself. The cute fox boy pants with wide eyes, and Wesley quickly comes inside the SUV. The red fox punches Vulpie in the face. The hit stuns the orange fox, and he tries to fight back as his attacker pushes him down against the debris covered floor of the SUV. Vulpie stares at Zorpiv while being paw cuffed. The gun pointed at him keeps him from fighting back.

Around the right corner of the Clouds coffee shop, on Harmon street, there is a policeman. He's a timber wolf, and jumped as much as everyone else when the shooting began. He ignores the panther he was writing a ticket to. Instead, he's inside his car calling for backup. He calls in the shots fired and requests backup just before he sees someone. In the distance, Zorpiv takes a look around the corner. The brown wolf sees him aim the automatic weapon at him and ducks between the seats. The panther nearby does the same when bullets fly everywhere.

Zorpiv throws fifty rounds towards the cop car and pops the clip loose when he's out. The gray furred fox nimbly finds a new mag, slams it in the back end of the powerful carbine and its loading mechanism snaps back into position. He's had plenty of time to practice with the other foxes in the Vuldrofein before the attack and he is impressed at his own skill. Druward was right. The MTAC-71 is perfect for fox use, and he hops backwards, before turning to run around the corner.

Animals inside the coffee shop scream and duck when the gray fox fires again, shattering the beautiful glass windows of the establishment. Everyone inside ducks and crawls in terror, mothers and fathers trying to protect their children, and Zorpiv finds himself laughing. He gleefully unloads another clip, but focuses on destroying everything in the shop instead of aiming for civilians. He feels even more powerful because he avoids shooting the animals at his mercy. He relishes the fact that no one can stop him, and only Wesley's voice snaps him back into reality.

"ZORPIV! WE'RE LEAVING!" The previous Vuldrofein commander yells. The gray fox does an about face and looks over his shoulder as he hurries back to the black sedan. It looks as though Vulpie has been paw cuffed and is being stuffed in the back trunk.

One of the red foxes throws Vulpie's tail inside before slapping it shut and then aiming at the traffic behind them. There are no visible threats, and all of them get back into their cars. There is blood on the pavement where Tiala collapsed. A nearby gray wolf has dragged her to safety on the sidewalk and keeps his head low. Zorpiv ignores him and pulls his door shut. The three jet black cars take off, one after the other, and rush around the corner towards the police car. The officer is out of his car and behind the panther's vehicle while they both crouch down to avoid being shot.

"Hey man, shouldn't you try to stop them?" The panther asks the cop.

"Would you?" The police man responds as the sedans race by and off into the distance.

Polar's Fury

Polar is surprised to hear the doorbell ring. He expects Vulpie at any moment, but if it were him, his fox husband would just come inside. Why bother with the bell? The wolf thinks it's strange and walks over to the front door. He switched out of his business suit in exchange for something more comfortable. Dressed in light gray jeans and a Turquoise blue shirt with a small collar, he answers the door. Rulef is standing at attention and shifts on his feet. Polar blinks in surprise.

"I thought you guys were guarding Ivo at the CTGD."

"We were... But something's happened..." Rulef responds and takes a deep breath. The way the battle hardened man acts greatly concerns Polar.

"What?" Polar asks. Rulef stares back at him and pauses for a moment before making a reply.

"Vulpie's SUV was attacked on the way to Vulpie Industries..." The gray wolf answers. His voice is filled with regret. Polar stares back at him in silence, his handsome blue eyes wide with fear. "Tiala was shot several times but it looks as though she will live."

"Shot? Who shot her? Was it another robot?"

"No... Witnesses at the scene say that several foxes were responsible."

"What happened to Vulpie?" Polar fearfully demands. The Blacktail commander takes a moment before replying an uses a small voice.

"He was kidnapped..."

"This... This CAN'T be real! This can't be happening!" Polar gasps.

"Whoever took him had serious firepower. Tiala told the police that they were using automatics with an incredibly high rate of fire."

"How could this happen? It's because all of you were at the CTGD, isn't it?"

"It would seem so... I can't explain it. A police officer saw them and said that they might have been wearing combat gear, but he couldn't be sure. They filled his car full of holes and he said if he had tried to stop them he would only have gotten himself killed. He didn't actually see Vulpie or them taking him, but there are several animals in a coffee shop that did." Polar's stomach suddenly feels uneasy. A sinking, all-consuming dread and despair washes over him and it's visible to Rulef.

"Oh God Vulpie, I'm sorry!" Polar exhales.

"The police are running any kind of leads they can find."

"It's the other foxes... He tried to warn me!"

"What foxes?"

"The ones from the AFR! Vulpie's been having it out with some guy called Karl Vulches and he told me they were crazy! I didn't listen to him!" The white furred wolf begins panting, feeling as though his life is over.

"Karl Vulches? Are you sure?" Rulef responds while making a very surprised expression.

"Yes. That's the guy."

"Then that explains why the foxes were so well equipped and why they attacked us. Karl Vulches owns a despicable group inside the Association of Fox Rights that is not supposed to exist, but obviously it does." Rulef says while showing Polar as relaxed an expression as he can. "They call them the Vuldrofein, and they'll do just about anything. They're a fox hit squad that answers to a secret contact inside the Association of Fox Rights."

"And Karl Vulches is the one behind this?" Polar asks while trying not to hyperventilate.

"He has to be. About twenty years ago the Vuldrofein was caught trying to assassinate President Lerig and everyone involved was killed. It isn't something the government admits to, but it happened. Afterwards, President Lerig forced the Vuldrofein to be wiped out as an organization. And he warned the Association of Fox Rights that if the Vuldrofein was ever discovered again, then the AFR would lose its legal status as a legitimate civil rights group."

"Then we've got to find Vulpie before it's too late!" Polar begs. "What are they going to do to him?"

"I don't know. The GBI is looking for answers, but no one knows. When Rulef mentions the Governmental Bureau of Investigations, something surges through Polar's body. It starts in his stomach but suddenly explodes through his blood and then to his skin, making his white fur stand on end. An idea that he cannot shake creeps into his mind and settles there. It makes Polar slowly close his mouth and grimace into anger.

"But Druward knows..." Polar growls and shoots Rulef a quick glare. It isn't threatening to him, but Rulef does register the hatred coming out of the white wolf. "Doesn't he?"

"Why would you say that?" Rulef replies.

"He hates Vulpie. Always has."

"That's true, but I think he sees Vulpie as a security threat and that's why he's so disrespectful to him."

"You and your team would have stopped the Vuldrofein, wouldn't you?" Polar asks. The question causes Rulef to think for a moment.

"Most likely."

"That's how I know Druward's responsible for Vulpie being kidnapped. He forced your team to stay at the CTGD when Howlstead didn't really need them."

"And he only had Tiala to protect him when it happened... I know, I've thought about it..." Rulef says, finishing Polar's thought.

"Then you know I'm right!" Polar stresses.

"It just... I've known Druward for more than a decade and it seems out of character for him to do something like this."

"Why? He doesn't care about anyone but himself. You don't have to be around him very long to figure that out."

"I agree, but Vulpie called him this morning, remember?" Rulef replies and shifts on his feet. Obviously that couldn't have been planned. The fact that he pulled us away from Vulpie has to be a terrible coincidence."

"It's not. I know Druward did it on purpose." Polar states without hesitation. Clearly, the white furred wolf has made up his mind.

"Polar... I hate that this happened, but we have to tread carefully here..." Rulef warns. The gray wolf appears worried. "Druward is a very powerful man. These are serious accusations and you know he won't hesitate to retaliate. You're making assumptions about today, and I can see why, but you don't have any evidence. And the fact that Vulpie contacted him before it happened contradicts the idea that Druward was intentionally trying to set him up."

"Do you know where he is?" Polar interjects. His voice is determined and full of ice. Rulef shifts on his feet again, considering what the arctic wolf wants.

"I do know where he is..."

"Will you take me to him?" Polar pleads.

"There's no doubt that Druward has heard about Vulpie's kidnapping by now, and if you accuse him of any wrong doing he may get defensive." Rulef warns again.

"I'm not scared of him!" The white furred wolf growls. His blue eyes stay fixed on Rulef while speaking as if seeing Druward through the Blacktail commander.

"I'm on your side, but this isn't a good idea." Rulef responds.

"Help me! PLEASE! Just help me Rulef! Help me before it's too late!" Polar breathes, going from enraged to terrified that he will lose Vulpie. His heartfelt plea weighs on Rulef heavily, causing the gray wolf to take a deep controlled breath.

Northwest of Sufias City there is a tract of land where the GBI handles its interplanetary operations. Since the government agency is responsible for executing the Sufias World Government's policies, it operates on most colonized planets. Due to the span of the organization, several types of space ships are required to cover the galaxy. For the most part, though, the GBI utilizes small range tactical ships and gets a lift from the military whenever it needs to travel great distances between worlds. Thus, the facility operated in a remote area of Evenwater Village houses several strike ships, and they can be heard taking off and landing on a daily basis.

The GBI test launches its ships to ensure they are well maintained, though some residents were opposed to the facility when it was built a few years ago. The large complex sticks out on the horizon against the green forest around it, on top of a small mountain. Evenwater Village is an average looking town, but did have an advantage when it came to tourist attractions because of its pretty scenery. The striking mountains west of the official town area used to be strong assets, but their natural beauty was altered when the GBI built its massive launch pad on top of one. Though the complex is state of the art, its white structure stands out against the mountain flora. At night its flashing blue lights, directed towards incoming ships, can be quite the distraction. So the complex, codenamed Ashcrest, is not viewed favorably by some residents. But like all operations run by the GBI, there was little the townspeople could do to stop it from being built.

Druward is busy filling out paperwork that has been handed to him by a GBI technician. He writes on a clipboard while the brown furred wolf, wearing a black jacket and suit with a white shirt and black tie, waits patiently. Druward is well suited for the cool climate, as he is wearing his favorite black trench coat over his own white dress shirt. He also preferred black ties when he used to wear them, but stopped years ago as soon as he became director. Feeling choked always annoyed him.

They are standing outside on the landing platform of the facility, which accounts for half of Ashcrest. There are rows of tactical space ships docked on locations around the launch pad, with the other half being the office portion. A block of raised buildings runs parallel with the launch area, where the agents operate the logistics of incoming and leaving ships. There is a moderately large air traffic control tower, but the launch pad is already seventy feet off of the ground. A lower building allows agents and technicians to come to work at the facility, with a hidden parking lot concealed in the woods. Both the lower portion in the mountain forest and the launch pad above the trees are beautiful in their own respects.

"No more rail guns?" Druward asks the agent that is waiting for him to finish filling out the form.

"We've fitted seven of the ships with them but the military says it's another six months until we can get more." The agent replies.

"When we're done here, tell your supervisor to contact Delanson Corporation directly. Don't forget."

"I will."

"The army is stalling us so they can install more rail guns on their battleships. Go around them and order ten more."

"Yes sir." The agent says and clears his throat. "If you have time, sir, you may want to review the stealth runner systems as well. Vulpie Industries will be releasing VulGrid soon, and they say it can make a ship invisible. It's going to be demonstrated for the military." Druward stops writing and looks at the agent with a cold face. The brown furred wolf wonders if he said something wrong but blinks, still thinking that his superior should be aware of it. Obviously, the man has not heard about Vulpie's kidnapping yet.

"That may not materialize." Druward says and goes back to writing. The agent lets himself relax a bit but he wonders why he received such a reaction. Druward looks over the form and sees that the current model of tactical space ship the GBI prefers, the Delanson STF/A-17 "Breaker," is the subject of all current expenditures this quarter. The efficient warships double as both transports and attack vehicles, and are well known for their ability to out maneuver other vessels in combat. With their substantial payload and ever increasing weaponry, they have consistently outperformed other ships during conflicts. STF/A-17s are named breakers for their ability to disable large space ships within a matter of moments.

"Sir." The agent says and gestures that someone is coming. Druward glances to his left and sees someone in his peripheral vision, but takes his time looking over the form to make sure it is complete. When he's satisfied, Druward hands the agent his clipboard and turns to see who it is. The black furred wolf is very surprised. Polar Arctic is standing with Rulef right next to him. The arctic wolf has a look on his face that Druward instantly identifies. He's enraged about something, and the obvious explanation is Vulpie being kidnapped.

Druward frowns as he looks at Polar's clothing. The turquoise shirt and gray pants the white furred wolf is wearing makes him look very coordinated, but he seems far too pretty for the GBI Director. He holds himself back from sneering in disgust.

"Where did they take Vulpie?" Polar demands without an introduction.

"This is a restricted facility." Druward growls and gives Rulef an irritated look. "Why did you bring him here?"

"Look at me!" Polar barks and gets the black furred wolf's attention. "Where did they take Vulpie?"

"I have no idea." Druward answers and Polar shakes his head in anger.

"You did this. I know you did!"

"A group of foxes attacked Blacktail and kidnapped your husband. I had nothing to do with it."

"I know who the foxes are. Vulpie told me about the psychos in the association of fox rights, but YOU called off his protection! You knew those foxes wouldn't be able to get to him with all of his normal protection, so you used your authority with the GBI to take them away from him."

"I should have you arrested for this. How dare you accuse me of being involved with the attack."

"Tiala survived, but I'm sure you don't even care." Polar growls.

"That tigress killed two of the foxes that came for Vulpie. She's a hero." Druward responds.

"Yes she is, and she's more of a man than you are!" The white furred wolf snaps back, and at this, Druward stiffens up. He carefully thinks about his involvement with the attack, and that he shouldn't take the arctic wolf's bait, but Polar is starting to get to him.

"Get this faggot off of my launch pad before I rip him to fucking pieces!" Druward growls to his left. He directs the order towards the GBI agent with the clipboard and Rulef at the same time. The agent behind Druward takes a few steps forward, but stops at the look coming from Rulef. Druward is surprised to see Rulef disobey a direct command.

"Tell me where he is, or I'll take you up on that!" Polar growls.

"What the fuck were you thinking, bringing him here for this?" Druward asks Rulef again. He doesn't get an answer, which is uncharacteristic of the Blacktail commander. Normally he would give one without delay. Since Druward and Rulef have known each other for years, the GBI director knows why without having to hear it. Rulef must suspect that he's involved.

"I don't know where your husband is." Druward lies. He is very convincing, looking indignant at the disrespect being shown to him, but Polar isn't fooled. Rulef watches and withholds faith in the GBI director as well.

"You disgusting liar!" Polar snarls. "You hate Vulpie and you don't care what happens to him! But I do! And I'm not leaving until you tell me where he is!"

"What's the matter? Are you afraid they'll gang rape him and kill him? I don't know. They might." Druward chuckles with an insidious smirk and Rulef's yellow eyes widen. He cannot believe Druward's dark humor.

"I'll kill you, you mother fucker!" Polar yells and clenches his fist.

"I don't know where they took your little bitch, but let me confess that I don't really care. The world will probably be better off without him." The black furred wolf smiles and then morphs his expression into a wicked threat. "Now get the fuck out of my face before I have you shot!"

"Is everything okay, sir?" A gray wolf asks. Two GBI agents that handle security for the Ashcrest complex have walked over to the group. The other one is another timber wolf, and Polar looks at them. One of them has his paw on his gun.

"Arrest this cock sucker before he threatens me again." Druward responds and the men put their attention on Polar. He knows he won't have much longer unless he does something fast.

"That's right, have someone else fight your battles you coward! I would crack your skull against this launch pad and rape you!" The white furred wolf yells and Rulef is surprised to hear the words coming from the patient man Polar is.

"You just don't know when to quit, do you pretty boy?" Druward growls.

"I'll humiliate you in front of your men so you better have me arrested! It would shatter your world wouldn't it? And you know I'm right! You don't have the balls to fight me, you pussy!" Polar yells and keeps his eyes on Druward when he feels one of the security agents grabbing his right arm. He doesn't resist, but he doesn't need to. Druward licks his teeth in anger and sneers.

"Shit…" Druward laughs and starts taking off his trench coat. "Let him go!" The black furred wolf waves his left paw at the men and their eyes widen. They watch Druward remove his coat and throw it to his left, before cracking his knuckles. The security agents wait a moment before stepping away, but when they do, he raises his large fists. Everyone else steps back, including Rulef, who shakes his head in disbelief. He knows Druward is an extremely lethal wolf, but Polar is very, very strong. The Blacktail commander has no clue how this is going to turn out.

"I'm surprised! I fucking love it! But I'm surprised!" Polar snarls.

"I'd have to be crazy to pass this up…" Druward grins while undoing his shirt's sleeves.

"You'll wish that you did." Polar responds while preparing to attack. He knows he's going to take his share of blows, but he's fighting for someone besides himself. Druward raises his fist as well and shows Polar his sharp teeth.

"Come on, FAGGOT! I'm right here!" The coal furred wolf shouts and Polar makes his move. He charges in, planning to attack with a right fist but half way into the motion he can see Druward countering it. The white furred wolf lowers his arms and charges into him instead. Druward has surprising speed. He manages to punch Polar in the gut and dodge most of the ram, but Polar does hit his left shoulder.

The blow knocks Druward slightly off balance and Polar ducks down to punch Druward in the abdomen just as the black wolf sends his right fist down into Polar's face. The two powerful wolves both cry out in pain from being struck, but Druward lands the most staggering attack. Polar's close left handed jab doesn't do as much damage because it lacks the space to complete a fully-fledged extension, while Druward's downward right hook connects directly on target. He would have aimed for Polar's left temple if he had the proper angle, but he hits the arctic wolf's forehead, right above his left eye.

The white furred wolf's vision goes blurry after receiving the hit and he staggers to the right. Druward holds his ground and waits for the next attack when Polar collects himself. He's learned that the GBI director knows how to fight defensively. Instead of charging in again, Polar comes towards Druward and gets close but doesn't swing first. He keeps his big paws raised in front of his face.

Druward attacks this time, but offense doesn't seem to be a problem. He rushes in, lowering his forehead, and Polar quickly jabs it. It hurts Druward, but not as much as Druward hurts him. The black furred wolf quickly punches Polar in the lower rib cage, two times, because Polar is exposed as a result of his own attack. The right and left fists to his front make Polar cry out in pain. Druward is not quite as strong as Polar, but he's very well trained. The attacks he uses are not something an animal would invent on the spot and they devastate the white wolf.

Polar gasps in pain and Druward jumps back to avoid being hit with a wild haymaker. Polar doesn't throw one, as he knows it's too early in a fight to try that. Instead, he collects himself again and waits for an attack. They are both about the same height and weight, each with large muscle mass. Seeing the white and black furred wolves going at it is an intense sight on the white launch pad.

Polar's too angry to feel the pain. He doesn't hesitate, and he moves in again. Druward raises his paws defensively and Polar comes close like he did a moment ago. Druward rushes in again, but Polar is ready for him this time. He lowers his big wolf muzzle and rams into Druward, smacking their skulls together. Druward didn't expect the same attack and the impact hurts and disorients both of them.

Druward is slowed down after banging heads and Polar swings at him with his right fist. The black furred wolf can only throw his paws up in an attempt to block, but he can see that he doesn't have time. Polar punches the left side of Druward's muzzle really hard. The impact could have knocked Druward out if he weren't such a great fighter. Unfortunately, Druward is aware that he can rob a punch of its power by moving in the direction it's going. So he lets his face go right when hit. The punch looks devastating to everyone watching, but only Rulef is aware of what Druward did. Polar expects him to fall down because he knows he hit him incredibly hard, but the GBI director balances on his right leg, before snapping back towards Polar with his left elbow.

The elbow to the face Polar receives hurts very badly. The white furred wolf cries out, and stumbles backwards. He instinctively reaches up with his right paw and grabs his muzzle, and can feel blood running. He quickly ignores the feeling of crimson dripping from his wolf nostrils and grits his teeth. He can't believe how good a fighter Druward is, but the thought of failure is not an option. Polar thinks about Vulpie and on top of the rage that he feels towards Druward for being involved with his kidnapping, the white wolf also believes the only chance he has of saving his fox husband lies with beating the GBI director.

Polar's persistence causes Druward to jump backwards when Polar rushes towards him again. Even with a blood stained face, the handsome white furred wolf is not deterred. The snarling lethal look he has alerts Druward that he has to be careful. At any moment now, Polar may hit him with a devastating blow. When Polar swings again, Druward quickly judges the distance and takes part of the hit by throwing up his big left paw in front of his face. But he parries in the motion, also swinging with his right paw towards Polar's face. The two hit each other, but once again, Polar suffers the most damage.

At this point the white furred wolf feels dizzy. The blow against his bleeding nose hurts excruciatingly, but to Druward's amazement, he doesn't stop. Polar collects himself and attacks again, this time by lowering his head and tackling the black furred wolf. The move results in both of them slamming onto the ground, with Druward taking Polar's weight on top of him. Druward swings up with his left paw wildly, striking the bottom of Polar's big jaw, but it only enrages the white furred wolf even more. Polar crawls on top of Druward and the black wolf is unable to push him off. The powerful white furred wolf sits up and closes his fists as Druward tries to think of a way to block or get free. But there is no way to get out from under Polar's heavy muscular body.

Polar punches straight down into Druward's face, nailing his nose, and the impact slams the GBI director's head back against the pavement like a spring. The blow and subsequent shaking the black wolf's brain takes causes him to groan and his vision goes blurry. The punch makes Druward's nose bleed as well, but Polar doesn't stop. Druward tries to reach up and keep the white furred wolf from punching him again, but he can't. Polar swings wildly, punching Druward in the face again and again. The GBI director is barely conscious in a matter of moments. Polar continues to hit him until the black furred wolf's face is covered in blood, and then grabs his throat with his left paw.

"WHERE DID THEY TAKE HIM?!" Polar yells and punches Druward in the face once again. "WHERE?!" He pulls his fist back again to send down another blow when Rulef shouts at him.

"POLAR STOP! Stop! You're going to kill him!" The Blacktail commander warns. Polar hasn't noticed any of the wolves nearby while fighting Druward but he sees them all once again, plus a few other faces. Apparently additional GBI agents have come to watch the fight.

"I SHOULD KILL HIM!" Polar yells and chokes Druward as hard as he can. The black furred wolf has a thick neck, but if he didn't, his throat would be crushed from the pressure of Polar's grip.

"You can't do anything else! You've won!" Rulef shouts.

"HE HASN'T TOLD ME A DAMN THING!" Polar snarls and looks down at Druward's bloody face. The black furred wolf's yellow eyes are still watching him, though very weakly. "WHERE IS VULPIE? TELL ME NOW!"

"Help..." Druward groans in agony and at this, the GBI agents nearby finally come over and interrupt.

"That's enough." One of them says and grabs Polar's left arm. The powerful arctic wolf feels his eyes watering. Druward says nothing else and only coughs up blood when Polar is pulled off of him. Polar watches Druward try to sit up, but he's too dizzy and disoriented to do so, so he lies on his right side and slowly props himself up on his right paw.

Druward is very tough, and despite the massive beating he's just taken, his nose is not broken. He checks it with his left paw and groans in pain. Slowly but surely, Druward makes it to his feet, accepting a helping paw from one of the agents. When he stands, he stares over at Polar, who's face is also covered in blood. The crimson looks gruesome against Polar's pretty white fur.

"Get him out of here..." Druward weakly commands and Polar struggles against the behest of Rulef and the agents trying to pull him away.

"Tell me Druward!" Polar pleads. His voice is desperate now and for a moment Druward considers confessing... But doesn't.

Not Part of the Plan

Vulpie feels the car come to a stop. He estimates he's been inside the trunk of the black sedan for about half an hour. He knows it also might seem like it's been longer than it actually has because he's terrified. He can still hear Tiala's screaming. Even with the deafening sound of an automatic weapon shooting through glass he is sure he heard a loud and sickening moan of anguish come out of her. He never had a chance to see what happened, but no one would expect an animal to survive that. He fears that she's dead.

Doors open and the car moves as the foxes get out and then close up the vehicle. Vulpie pants in fear, and hears a key grate inside the lock on the trunk. It turns and then opens up, blinding him with bright light. It's around one o clock and the early afternoon sun is right above him. The fox that opened the trunk and stares down at him is the same one that shot out the windows of the Blacktail SUV, and Tiala as well. Vulpie's pretty blue eyes focus on the young man, who looks to be in his twenties.

He's a gray fox and has particularly memorable fur coloring. Most of his head is covered in gray fur, but he has reddish brown edges that go around the side of his head and down the outer edges of the front of his body. The bottom of his jaw is a coal black, a stark contrast to the white fur of his throat and chest. He has black streaks coming away from his eye sockets and his brown eyes are very cruel. The expression on his face is something a rapist would wear.

"Get him out, Zorpiv." A familiar voice commands. Vulpie winces when the gray fox reaches into the trunk and grabs his left arm, clawing him. The orange furred fox tries to help climb out of the trunk but Zorpiv seems more interested in yanking him out as painfully as he can. Vulpie barely avoids hitting his head on the way out, and when he is out, he feels sick. He stands on the grass behind the car and sees two foxes in front of him that immediately draw his attention.

Nathan Fenrir and Karl Vulches are both smiling sadistically at him. Vulpie doesn't recognize the surroundings. They're at what looks to be a very remote and beautiful mountain home overlooking a cliff behind the house, and deeper woods to the right. There are five foxes that he does not know, including Zorpiv. The other four are the ones that stuffed him into the trunk of the car. Vulpie is still wearing his slick jet black suit coat, with a white dress shirt and a brilliant orange tie to match his fur, but his clothing is ruffled and dusty from the unaccommodating ride.

"I told you I'd make you pay for biting my face..." Nathan grins and Karl snickers.

"Well it took you long enough. I've really enjoyed the last seven years I've shared with Polar and nothing you can do to me will change that." Vulpie responds. Karl smirks and elbows Nathan.

"Nothing we can do to him is going to change that..." Vulches chuckles.

"Oh I'm sure you have... Sucking that wolf's dick and telling everyone about it... I saw you on TV, talking about how he looks you in the eyes when he fucks you... How disgusting... Fucking disgusting trash that has disgraced our species for far too long!" Nathan growls. "Now your cock sucking days are over I'm afraid, and I'm really going to enjoy watching you suffer in ways you can't even imagine."

"But not over just yet! You'll have time to eat my dick!" Zorpiv breathes in Vulpie's left ear, and the orange furred fox boy lurches to the right. He looks back at Zorpiv fearfully and doesn't like the way the gray fox is groping his left arm.

"Yeah! Zorpiv's a real romantic!" Karl laughs in amusement. "I thought he might want to play with you and since he's so excited, we won't disappoint him!"

"I didn't bring any lubrication... I'm sorry for that... I'll just spit on it!" Zorpiv moans and Vulpie tries to elbow him. He can't, because his paws are cuffed behind his back, but he makes a vicious attempt. This makes all of the foxes laugh and Vulpie's fur stands on end. He looks down at the grass and thinks about what he might be able to say to save himself. He knows there's nothing that he can do, but he tries anyway, for himself and for Polar.

"Don't you respect me for all of the things I've done? I thought all of you liked the idea that foxes are better than every species. Just think about how far I've come on my own merit." Vulpie says while looking between Karl and Nathan.

"Oh, you are very talented. You're the smartest fox that has ever lived, and probably the smartest animal that's ever lived... But the problem is, you're also the biggest embarrassment to foxes that has ever lived..." Karl replies.

"I'm real sorry I didn't just bend over and let you boss me around, Karl, back when we were playing the stock market. I just cared too much about Vulpie Industries to kill the competition, literally, so wolves everywhere would be too terrified to say no to signing our contracts. It bothered me just a little bit. But hey! There I go again with my gay feelings!"

"If you had you wouldn't be in this situation. But when you bite a Fenrir's face and then give a Vulches the middle finger, you're not going to last long." Karl responds.

"I know you plan to torture me in horrible ways, but before you do, can I ask the both of you a question?" Vulpie inquires.

"Why not?" Nathan smirks.

"Did you honestly believe that I, of all animals, wouldn't leave a little trap behind in case someone killed me?" Vulpie asks, showing a smirk of his own.

"Trying to bargain for your life? Let's hear it." Karl says in amusement but his smile dissipates after listening to Vulpie's next statement.

"I've hacked into every computer used by the Association of Fox Rights and I have... EVERYTHING... I have your bank account numbers. I have all of your personal information. I know where your families live. I know all about them and where they keep their money too... And the way I have it set up, is that if I don't check in with Vulpie.net every month, Vulpie.net will wipe you completely out. I'm the only animal alive that knows how to turn Vulpie.net off, and it's been about a week since I've checked in... So after you kill me, you had better enjoy your last three weeks being rich. Because if I'm not there to stop it, Vulpie.net will go right back to its old behavior..." The orange furred fox warns and grins. "And that's not all... Do you remember the robot that I built of myself? Do ya? ... If I die, Vulpie.net becomes the only Vulpie there is. And my last command to it, my final command to EVIL VULPIE... Is to take care of whoever did me in."

"Bullshit." Karl growls.

"It's kind of a bummer I bet. Yeah, you can torture me and kill me, but you won't be rid of me. You'll never be rid of Vulpie, and neither will the universe." Vulpie says with a devious look that appears genuine.

"That's a nice try, but I think we'll take our chances." Karl responds.

"Don't say I didn't warn you. It will be just AWFUL when Vulpie.net plays clips of you raping that vixen when you were twenty one, Karl!" Vulpie declares and Karl goes rigid. His brown eyes focus on the gay fox in disbelief. He did rape a girl a long time ago, but wonders how Vulpie could have found out about it. He comes to a quick conclusion and it is shortly confirmed. "That was pretty dumb of you to film it! I mean, you and your buddies would have gotten away with it, but you filmed it! And then your daddy had to keep you out of jail! He was a powerful judge that was gonna be nominated to the supreme court, so I can see how you could escape justice, but come on dude! You filmed it? Wow! I never would have thought you were that silly!"

"How did you find out about that?" Karl groans while allowing a little smirk of sadistic pride. "I thought that tape was erased..."

"Well even though your dad paid off the judge and had the incident buried in the Vulren county police archives, the video still looks clear enough all these years later. I didn't have any trouble making you out on it... Ya gotta love the men with badges! They kept it catalogued for decades under your name!" Vulpie mischievously answers.

"Just another reason to kill ya then, isn't it?" Karl asks, mocking Vulpie with an imitative voice.

"And let's not forget all of the videos that the Vuldrofein has recorded. It goes back centuries! I saw you people killing wolves from over two hundred years ago! You're horrible! And it's gonna look atrocious when Vulpie.net plays it on an infinite loop to the universe!" Vulpie says.

"It will all be worth it though..." Karl says with dark humor and walks over to Vulpie with a friendly face. Vulpie winces when

Zorpiv claws his left arm and holds him still. "Because in the end, animals will remember you for one thing over all of the other stuff... They'll remember how painfully you died, and they'll watch the video we're going to film this afternoon... The one where we send you straight to hell and tears stream down your little face, and you beg for us to kill you in the end..." Karl whispers. Vulpie's orange fur stands on end when he hears the pleasure in Karl's voice.

"Are you telling the truth about the bank accounts?" Nathan Fenrir interrupts, and draws everyone's attention. The brown furred fox looks concerned when he sets his eyes on Vulpie.

"Of course. I own every computer that exists, and you've seen what Evil Vulpie can do..." Vulpie answers. "And you've seen what it did to me. Now think about what it might do to you... It's rather twisted, ya know."

"He's lying, Nathan." Karl chuckles and reaches up to Vulpie's muzzle with his left paw. He slaps Vulpie's face three times, letting him know who's boss. Vulpie winces and turns his head away in pain. He closes his eyes in case Karl hits him again, but the brown fox just wanted to show his authority.

"What if he's not?" Nathan replies and Karl looks over at him in shock. He can't believe his co-conspirator is having second thoughts.

"Are you serious, Nathan? He's just making up stories to save himself. Don't tell me you believe him." Karl growls.

"Look, all I'm saying is that I don't want to lose my investments. The president got on TV and admitted that he hacked into people's bank accounts." Nathan responds.

"And I fooled him with that robot I built and sent to the GBI. It looked and acted so real that the idiots thought it was me!" Vulpie says towards Nathan, looking quite devious. Karl looks left and spits in Vulpie's face, making the gay fox close his eyes in disgust.

"Shut your mouth." Karl warns and looks back to Nathan. "He's a liar. And we're about to kill him, so he'll say or do anything. He'd suck all our dicks if he thought we'd let him go."

"I've just got a bad feeling about it... Yeah he's a pussy faggot, but he's also just crazy enough to do something like that." Fenrir responds.

"Goddess damn, Nathan. Maybe you should have stayed out of this. I don't think you have the stomach for it." Karl complains. Even though Vulpie would rather not get himself struck anymore, especially with Karl right next to him, he still speaks to Nathan when he senses an opportunity. He remembers looking up Fenrir's personal information several times and uses his sharp mind to quickly recall the information he needs.

"Your address is unlisted, but you live at 4127 Old Carrollstead Road, Duwalk, VS, with an area code that ends in 457... I can't remember the first two digits, but Evil Vulpie will have access to it." The orange furred fox boy says and Nathan's brown eyes widen. At first Karl is going to punch Vulpie in the chest for speaking again but he thinks over what he's just heard. He looks to his right at his old friend and sees Fenrir at a loss for words. "It's not too late... You don't have to do this..."

None of the foxes speak for a moment. Only Fenrir knows if Vulpie has information on him and Karl is frustrated when he sees it is true, not because he cares but because things are about to become complicated. Nathan's expression changes to worry and the brown fox throws his paws up with a loud sigh.

"The bastard knows where I live!"

"So what?" Karl quickly replies.

"He knows where my children sleep! If his threats are real, then his psycho robot might show up at my home and kill them!"

"What do you want me to do? Let him go?" Karl growls and Vulpie blinks when he feels Zorpiv let go of his left arm. The gray fox hasn't been gentle with him the entire time he's been out of the trunk, and in his peripheral vision, Vulpie notices him going back to the car.

"I don't know Karl! But my family will be in danger if we go through with this! Maybe we should think it through. Maybe we could work out some kind of a deal?"

"A deal? You're out of your mind! If we let this pillow biter get away we'll never have a chance to kill him again! He's too smart to fall for the same trick twice! Druward's not going to help us anymore! This is it!" Karl shouts in irritation.

"Well he's not going anywhere! Let's see what he has to say!" A barrage of something sends Nathan sprawling to the left as soon as he finishes his sentence, making everyone jump. It happens so fast and it's so loud that it takes the other foxes a moment to grasp that Fenrir has just been shot. All of the Vuldrofein, Karl, and Vulpie, quickly look back at Zorpiv who is holding a smoking MTAC. He's fired more than ten rounds into Nathan and when Vulpie looks at the wounded brown fox, he sees horror in his eyes. Blood comes out of Nathan's mouth and he twitches and gurgles in shock.

"ZORPIV WHAT THE FUCK DID YOU DO? WHAT THE FUCK ARE YOU DOING?!" Karl screams.

"He wasn't going to let us kill Vulpie... So I fixed the problem..." Zorpiv answers. The patchwork looking gray fox stares over at Nathan in fascination. He's curious how long it will take him to die, as he's never killed anyone before, excluding the supposed murder of Tiala.

"YOU! GOD! NATHAN!" Karl yells, looking as though he wants to go to his friend to help, but is clearly afraid of what Zorpiv might do next. Zorpiv's deranged behavior frightens all of the Vuldrofein so much that they don't take action. His cruelty is so pure that it almost seems admirable to them. Nathan gurgles, coughing up blood and he tries to move, but can only roll his head to the right. Oddly enough, in his last moment, he meets eyes with Vulpie. Vulpie pities him and despite the fact that the man was going to have him killed, he feels sorry for the brown fox's family that he clearly wanted to protect. That's why, rather than giving him a nasty look, Vulpie tries his best smile at him lovingly. Nathan twitches and seems to understand that Vulpie forgives him, even though no words are spoken. A warm calmness overtakes Nathan, and then he stops moving.

"Druward was right about this gun. I love it! It handles perfectly and just look how powerful it is!" Zorpiv muses while watching Nathan die.

"YOU SON OF A BITCH!" Karl screams and steps back, looking at the other members of the Vuldrofein. "KILL HIM! KILL HIM NOW!" The influential fox orders, but the others hesitate. He has no idea why, and they don't know themselves, but Zorpiv's insanity has terrified all of them. Rather than take their chances aiming at him, they step away from Karl, who looks around In horror. "WHAT THE FUCK ARE YOU DOING? SHOOT HIM!"

"It looks like... We're not going to be friends after all!" Zorpiv laughs and aims at Karl.

"WAIT! ZORPIV STOP! I! I'M SORRY!" Karl pleads and throws up his paws diplomatically. The statement makes the gray fox grin.

"For what?"

"For your father! I'm sorry I ran him out of business! I! I'm sorry! And I'm sorry for everything I've put you through over the years! I'm sorry!" Karl gasps.

"Ok." Zorpiv responds and pulls the trigger on his carbine. The MTAC shakes violently like before, but due to its perfected balance, it fires off twelve rounds into and around Karl in a split second. No one knows how many times Karl is shot, because he dies instantly, flying back on the grass without even having time to scream. Vulpie trembles, crouching down in terror and doesn't know what to do except stare at the grass without moving. There is a silence but he dares not do anything at all.

"You killed him..." One of the Vuldrofein foxes whispers.

"Karl had something hanging over each one of you... The same way he had something that he liked to hold over me... Now our problem is gone forever!" Zorpiv responds while smiling in pride. The gray fox lowers his gun in his right paw and comes near Vulpie. He's drawn to the helpless expression the gay fox makes and the fact that Vulpie won't even look at him. "Did you enjoy that?" Zorpiv whispers in Vulpie's left ear.

"No..." Vulpie breathes and meekly looks to Zorpiv. Zorpiv is smiling, but his eyes are half open, giving him a psychotic, half-awake looking appearance. It's like the fox is something sent straight from Aila's hell. Only a few weeks ago, Zorpiv was a mentally disturbed youth with no future, but now he's a mentally disturbed youth with a horrible future. The other foxes in the Vuldrofein seem to respect him for some unfathomable reason. They don't try to stop him, and when Zorpiv turns to his left and hands one of them his gun, the man takes it and does not shoot him in the back.

"Take him down to the bunker..." Zorpiv breathes to his men, but also in Vulpie's ear as if he's fucking him.

An Unlikely Epiphany

"Want anything to drink? Some water?" A GBI she-wolf asks Druward. The black furred wolf shakes his head in objection, and she leaves him alone in his office. He's still at the Ashcrest facility, as there was more paperwork that required his signature. He considered going home after his fight with Polar, but doesn't feel bad enough to do that. He's saving some face by continuing to work. However, having his nose bloodied by the arctic wolf has definitely hurt his ego and his reputation.

His office at Ashcrest isn't too special, half the size of his main office at the GBI headquarters. It is filled with expensive leather recliners and even has a small bar with a refrigerator to the side of his desk. He keeps bottled water in there, and decides that he does want something to drink after all. He gets up and walks to the small fridge, and his eye catches a picture of him with his father. It was taken when he was ten years old. He opens the fridge and reaches inside, feeling the cool air waft across his left paw. When he has a bottle of spring water, he closes it and looks at the picture again. He opens the bottle and takes a few gulps while eyeing his father. The man was about the same height and weight. In the picture Druward is a little thing, smiling for the camera while his father holds his back lovingly.

Druward's father died about a year after the picture was taken, gunned down in a botched sting against a wolf crime boss. After Druward became an agent, he made sure to get payback, and that man is dead now, like his father. He thinks that it's not much of a reward. He'd much rather have this father. The more he remembers, the angrier he becomes, and when he realizes he is about to get emotional he growls at himself.

"What the hell is wrong with you? Don't go soft." Druward murmurs and takes a seat in one of his recliners again. He considers turning on the television, but before he can, a thought jumps into his head that stops him cold. For some reason he remembers that Vulpie Vivixen is an orphan. At least Druward still had his mother for years after his father died. He blinks and rubs his muzzle, squinting at the pain he feels. Polar really hurt him badly.

"It's a cruel world. Just think how much harder he's had it. And now you've taken everything from him. You've killed him." Druward thinks and grunts in irritation. He can't stop the thoughts he's having. It's one of those times when you know they are going to continue no matter what you do. *"Polar destroyed you in a fair fight. Maybe he is more of a man than you are."* This thought really bothers Druward.

"For fuck sake!" He groans and touches his right temple.

"Your father wouldn't have done what you did. You don't even need the money. Why did you do it?"

"He must have knocked something loose..." Druward complains to himself. He takes a deep breath and tries to relax. He thinks about putting music on. He has classical, club music, rock... None of it interests him very much. Of course he could go out and do some more work... But he's already completed the essentials for the Ashcrest facility. And he can't hide the fact that he's hurting from the fight with Polar. Both of them left their fair share of crimson on the launch pad.

A disturbing thought leaps into Druward's mind. Since Polar's gay, he hopes the wolf doesn't have an immunodeficiency virus of some sort. Druward was covered in his blood as well, after all, but a logical counter quickly shoots the concern down. No doubt a stable homosexual like Polar is clean. And also, Vulpie is immune to most diseases because of an expensive vaccination he had. Druward remembers reading his personal record while working with Faith Henrenson to track him down. Vulpie had VED shots, venereal elimination of diseases vaccinations, so he can't be carrying a serious sickness. Plus he's been married to Polar for six years, so they've only been with each other. Still, Druward doesn't like the idea of tasting Polar's blood, and through him, tasting Vulpie too.

"But you have wondered what Vulpie tastes like before..." Druward thinks and wildly jerks his head sideways in protest. The sudden motion makes him grit his teeth. His nose is still tender. It hurts and he holds still for a moment, clenching his eyes shut. He relaxes and almost curses to himself again but realizes there is no point. No matter how hard he tries not to, he's going to think about what's happening to Vulpie. He cannot understand why, or for what purpose he would, though. Druward cannot remember the last time something he did ever truly made him feel *"bad."* The idea is beyond him at this stage in his life, or at least, he thought it was. He has a stroke of creativity, and it seems brilliant. It seems like a way to give in to his subconscious while also beating it. Druward decides to talk to himself a little, but as if he has an audience.

"Okay, so you do feel guilty about what you've done... But should you?" Druward chuckles while looking at the door to his office. It's firmly shut so his voice will not carry outside. "You feel guilty because he looks and acts like a kid but he's not. He's a grown man. He's a twenty five year old man. You just feel like he's innocent, but he's not. After everything he's done, who could blame you? The world will be better off without him, that is for sure." He smiles.

"He is innocent. He's already paid for his crimes." His subconscious argues and the black furred wolf shakes his head.

"Why would I think that he's paid for his crimes? The faggot lied to the court and said he was under duress by me when he signed his contract, which is not true at all."

"But you did hit him, on top of everything else you did, and he outsmarted you by using that footage to win over a jury."

"But that's not justice. That's not right versus wrong!" Druward growls, while sitting in his office... Alone...

"Of course not, but you don't hand it out either. You're both criminals."

"That's right." Druward quietly laughs. "In the end the two of us are about the same speed, so why worry about what happens to him?"

"Because he has something to lose. Animals care about him, they love him, and you can't say that for yourself." Druward's suddenly had enough of speaking. He sits and stares at the floor instead. Thoughts keep on flowing, but at this point, he makes no effort to resist. *"You both know Vulpie kind of deserved what Evil Vulpie did to him, but that's over now. He's moved on, and you haven't. You've treated him as though that horrible torture he went through never happened... And why? You know why, don't you... You like him... Deep down inside, you like him, and you like to have power over him. You don't have it anymore so this was the last pathetic act you had. And with it, you've sent him to his death, and have ruined Polar's life by taking Vulpie from him. That's what you did."*

The GBI director slumps in his chair. His fur goes on end but the rest of his body is loose. All of his defenses have now disappeared. Druward lets himself spiral into a moment of depression and he wagers his own value. It's a hard thing to do... Very hard... Especially when you've been a roadblock to so many others on the way to the top. He has a mental list of animals he's stabbed in the back or misdirected in order to command the GBI.

"All of it... All of your campaign for power, has been a self-indulgent masculine fantasy. And Polar was right in the end. He could have raped you in the wild, in crueler times, and then killed you. How powerful would you have felt after he had his way with you? That pretty white wolf that disgusts you could have taken you from behind and humiliated you in ways you can only imagine. Who knows, maybe that's why you've treated Vulpie so despicably from the beginning. Maybe you're curious?"

"GODDESS... DAMN IT..." Druward growls but also makes a pained face. His nose hurts again, but he's suffering outside of the physical realm to be sure. "I'm NOT gay!"

"No... You're not." His subconscious answers, much to his relief. "But you do like him... And it's not too late to do the right thing..."

"Of course it's too late." The black furred wolf argues to the air. "He's probably already dead!"

"You know they're going to take their time with him..." He thinks. There is no fighting what forms in his mind. His guilt is too much of a burden and he knows what he has to do.

Outfoxed

"Why are you still doing this?" Vulpie asks after one of the Vuldrofein hits a light switch. They've just entered the bunker and Zorpiv pushes him to the right. There is a firing range across from the doorway, but Zorpiv directs Vulpie to a smaller area. They go into a short hallway that ends at a cement wall and then take a left into a little room. There are four pillars in the room, two on the right and two on the left. They go from the floor to the ceiling and may provide support for the chamber. At the other side of the room is a table and there are folding chairs placed in different parts of the room. "Didn't you say Karl was blackmailing you and the others?"

"Yes." Zorpiv answers and shoves Vulpie forward. He stays on his feet, but nearly falls.

"If he and Nathan are the ones that wanted me dead, why are you still going to kill me?" Vulpie asks after turning around to face Zorpiv and the other Vuldrofein foxes.

"Because you're an embarrassment to all of us." One of the men responds.

"Do you think every species looks at me and says, oh, all foxes must be gay because he is?" The orange furred fox asks. Zorpiv stands across from Vulpie and smiles at him with his half-awake demeanor. No one answers Vulpie's question. Instead, they gather around him.

"This is just too good to pass up." Zorpiv suggests and a few of them smirk. "That's why." He looks around at the men. "Who has the camera?"

"I do." One of them answers, and hands a black high definition camcorder to Zorpiv. He turns it on and plays with its settings, testing how it records.

"I can't believe you killed Karl…" Wesley says while giving Zorpiv an incredulous look.

"You hated him as much as I did." Zorpiv answers.

"Yeah but without him we don't have any leadership. How are we going to operate?"

"I'm taking over." The gray fox says and looks back. "Understood?"

"We should just kill him and get out of here. We don't have time for this anymore." Wesley responds.

"Because Karl and Nathan are dead? You give them too much credit. No one really cared what those two conspiracy nuts did."

"You're an idiot if you really believe that." Wesley snaps and Vulpie watches Zorpiv turn menacing. Heat is building between the two foxes. it's clear that Wesley does not approve of turning on and killing his boss.

"Call me an idiot again. Go ahead." Zorpiv says and looks to a red fox to his right. The young man is holding Zorpiv's MTAC. The gray fox reaches out, gesturing that he wants his weapon.

"DON'T GIVE HIM THAT GUN!" Wesley shouts, and stops the fox from doing as he was beckoned.

"Give it here." Zorpiv whispers.

"I'm still in charge of the Vuldrofein! We only turned over control to Zorpiv because Karl told us to! But we killed the man that made our brotherhood what it is!"

"Give me the gun or your next." Zorpiv warns.

"Don't do it!" Vulpie says, much to the surprise of everyone. Wesley is glad, however, for the extra voice of dissent, even if it's coming from their victim.

"Even Vulpie knows it's a bad idea! Don't you dare! Back away from him!" Wesley shouts at his former subordinate. Vulpie notices that the red fox in question doesn't look too smart. He's probably around twenty something, but obviously doesn't know what to do with himself. "Rick, if you hand him that gun he'll kill all of us!" Wesley's says, naming the indecisive fox.

"We're supposed to follow the commands of our leader, and Karl made him our leader." Rick says while staring back at Zorpiv. Zorpiv seems to have him in a trance and Wesley cannot figure out why no one is listening to him.

"What the hell is wrong with you?! HE KILLED KARL!" The former Vuldrofein commander shouts.

"I won't kill him. But he is going to be punished for this. Just give me my weapon." Zorpiv tells Rick with a friendly voice. Rick looks between Wesley and Zorpiv and then to Wesley's horror, gives him the MTAC-71.

"Am I the only sane person left in the Vuldrofein?! What's wrong with all of you? Why didn't you back me up?" Wesley shouts, directing his voice towards the other two foxes that just stood by. They look unsure about how they should react. Now that Zorpiv has his weapon again, the one closest to Wesley takes a step away.

"So what do you think I should do with you? What should your punishment be?" Zorpiv asks Wesley and gives Rick the camcorder. "Start filming." He orders and Rick does so without hesitation. Wesley watches Rick aim the device at him and capture his reaction in disbelief.

"Go fuck yourself!" Wesley yells and backs up a little.

"Vulpie, what should his punishment be?" Zorpiv asks and the orange furred fox makes no response. Vulpie makes a point not to look at the deranged gray fox and this gives Zorpiv a perverted idea. "Nothing? You must be really pent up since you know you're going to die soon. So how about this..." Zorpiv says and grins at Wesley. "Why don't you give Vulpie a blowjob?"

"What. The. Fuck?" Wesley growls with a lethal look.

"Suck his cock or I'm going to kill you. Those are your options." Zorpiv decrees. Rick finds himself smiling a little and Vulpie can't help but notice when he looks at him. He seems to enjoy his new leader's madness.

"Fucking kill me then!" Wesley yells and jumps backwards in terror when a deafening roar fills the chamber, making everyone but Zorpiv wince. Zorpiv fired three rounds right next to the former Vuldrofein commander, leaving broken spots in the cement wall behind him.

"Last warning. Do it or die."

"Fuck you Vixil Trash! I'd rather die!" Wesley yells back and Vulpie recoils when Zorpiv fires the gun again. A spray of crimson splats out of Wesley, and the red fox sprawls backwards against the wall. The Vuldrofein fox that is holding Vulpie's paw cuffs from behind, keeping him in place, loosens his grip and makes a sickened noise. Rick gasps and looks at Zorpiv in fear.

"A Vixil killed Nathan Fenrir, and a Vixil killed Karl Vulches... And now a Vixil's killed you... Sweet dreams fuck face..." Zorpiv says and glances at Rick. The smaller fox is terrified of him and he should be, as are the other two. Vulpie trembles, and keeps his eyes shut. He breathes quickly, wishing all of this were just a horrible dream. "No one disobeys me again! Is that clear?" Zorpiv shouts and quickly receives a nod from everyone but Vulpie.

Zorpiv stares at the cute orange furred fox boy and slowly walks over to him. The room is completely silent and Rick moves with the video camera. He continues to film just as he was instructed. Vulpie doesn't open his eyes when he feels Zorpiv come close. He can feel the gray fox's breath on the left side of his furry neck. One of the two foxes holding Vulpie has brown fur, and the other has red like Rick. They keep their muzzles lowered, showing Zorpiv respect as he looks over them and Vulpie. Vulpie slowly opens his eyes after a few more moments and sees Wesley's corpse across from him. The dead red fox is bleeding profusely on the cement floor.

"Now... Get on your knees..." Zorpiv whispers in Vulpie's left ear. Vulpie makes no reaction. He looks over Wesley with a distant expression and then at the floor. He thinks about Polar. He remembers all of the wonderful times they've had together and he finds himself smiling a little. "Get on your knees, faggot!" Zorpiv hisses.

"Why?" Vulpie asks.

"So you can suck my cock. Today's your lucky day! Sure, it's your last day, so that's not very lucky in the end, but you're going to get three dicks in your mouth!"

"Three? How disappointing... I sucked seven wolves off at a party once. If this is my going away present, then I'm not impressed." Vulpie admits.

"Did you swallow?" Zorpiv grins.

"Of course." Vulpie says and rolls his eyes.

"Gross... You're a sick little fucker aren't you?"

"You think just because I'm gay that I'll work you over like I did those nice boys, but you're forgetting that Vulpie has teeth." Vulpie responds and bites them together. "Since I'm going to die anyway, maybe I'll just bite it off."

"Good point..." Zorpiv coos. "I'll fuck you in the ass instead!" The gray fox laughs and steps back a bit. He waves for Rick

to come closer and looks to the one holding Vulpie's paw cuffs.
"Take his cuffs off and get him out of that suit! I'm going to tear him
a new asshole!" Vulpie starts fighting back when the foxes pull him
towards the table. There's not much he can do with his paws cuffed
behind his back, but even when he feels them unlock the restraints,
his efforts are in vain. Zorpiv quickly smacks Vulpie in the left side of
his face with his gun just as soon as his paws are free. He lurches to
the right and the red and brown foxes behind him aren't hindered
very much by his efforts.

He fights them as much as he can, but the red furred one
punches Vulpie in the gut, making him cry out in pain. When he
bends forward in agony, they manage to yank off his suit coat and
toss it aside. The red fox pulls out a knife and cuts into Vulpie's
white shirt, and slices upwards, cutting all the way through Vulpie's
tie as well while the brown fox yanks from behind. Vulpie's fancy
white shirt and orange tie falls off and the brown furred fox pounds
his right fist on the back of Vulpie's head, knocking him down
against the table. The other one seizes on the opportunity, and
slams his fox paws on Vulpie's shoulders, holding him down. Vulpie's
naked from the waist up, and now they proceed to expose the rest
of him. The red fox undoes and jerks down Vulpie's business slacks,
and then is equally rough with the fox boy's white underwear.

"NO!" Vulpie cries out in fear, feeling the air on his soft
furry butt. They drop his pants to his ankles.

"Yes!" Zorpiv laughs with a delighted voice. "One of you
fuck him first! Let's all rape the bitch! You know he wants it!" The
other foxes are all straight, and so is Zorpiv, if one were to try and
determine his sexuality without regard to his insanity. The real thrill
is domination. The other foxes are terrified of Zorpiv and they know
their best bet of surviving this nightmare is to do what he wants. So

they decide to take their aggression and fear out on Vulpie. The red one undoes his pants and slides down his briefs while the brown one holds Vulpie down. Both of the foxes are surprisingly strong, strong as foxes go, and Vulpie can't stop them. The red fox mounts him and starts masturbating in preparation just as a metallic sound gets all of their attention.

Zorpiv immediately turns and faces the doorway to the small room. The sound could only have come from the entrance to the bunker. He's been down here enough to remember it very well. Rick looks around in confusion, his video camera still going, and he turns towards the small hallway that connects the room to the entrance chamber.

Druward walks inside the room and stops when he sees Zorpiv aiming the MTAC-71 at him. Vulpie pants in terror, but his terror pauses as he sees the black furred wolf look at him and then assess the situation. No one says anything, and no one moves. Vulpie wonders whether the black furred wolf is just here to watch. But the GBI director's appearance is very strange, especially since none of the foxes have anything to say. Druward glances at Wesley's bloody corpse against the cement wall to his left, and he registers what he sees with no visible reaction.

Zorpiv keeps his gun aimed towards Druward. The gray fox hasn't moved since the black furred wolf arrived and refuses to lower his weapon. Druward observes him without any emotion on his face. He thinks that it truly was a bad idea to put an automatic in the paws of this little insane gray fox. Based on everyone's location, he knows he can shoot down all of the foxes holding Vulpie captive, with the exception of Zorpiv. Zorpiv is the closest target, but he's holding the dreaded MTAC, and he's the only one acknowledging Druward as the threat that he is.

The other three Vuldrofein foxes, the red one that was filming, the red one about to rape Vulpie, and the brown one holding Vulpie over the table at the end of the room, all stare at Druward in surprise. They see him as a confusing development that needs to be explained, while Zorpiv can see Druward is here to kill them. Vulpie's lean chest quickly moves up and down on the table as he breathes in fear. He feels shame when Druward looks at him again, seeing him completely naked and helpless underneath the two stronger foxes.

"Why are you here?" Zorpiv demands while holding his ground.

"Who killed Karl and Nathan?" Druward responds.

"I did."

"Why?"

"Why are you here?" Zorpiv repeats. He clearly is ready to shoot at any moment, and Druward frowns as if annoyed but not concerned. The black furred wolf calmly looks to his left at the other foxes that are holding Vulpie down.

"Whatever you want to do to him, you had better do it quickly. The police are on their way." Druward lies and their eyes widen. He is convincing enough that Zorpiv also considers the possibility , and looks to the right just a little bit. This small distraction gives Druward the opportunity he needs. The GBI director, while still looking at the foxes behind Vulpie, reaches into his trench coat with his right paw. Because his head is turned to the left, Zorpiv's brain doesn't register what he sees until Druward has a gun out and is aiming it in his direction.

The moment the gray fox sees that he is about to be shot, he leaps back around a concrete pillar that is behind him. Luckily for him, he was nearby one of the four in the room, and the little bit of cover it provides is enough to keep him from being shot when Druward pulls the trigger, swinging a pistol sized automatic weapon to the left in his right paw. Four bullets go towards Zorpiv, two of them hitting the pillar, and two of them going past it to hit the wall. Druward knows he missed, but his swinging movement continues on towards Rick.

The red fox, with his mouth open in shock, catches two bullets in his throat after they both crash through the video camera he's holding, killing him instantly. Debris from the shattered camcorder flies all over the place, and Druward then shifts on his left foot, rotating his body in the swing, so he can put both paws onto the gun while his aim goes closer to Vulpie. He has to use two paws if he's going to miss the orange fox and only kill the ones behind him. By the time they see what is coming, which is about the blink of an eye, it's too late. With two paws on the gun, aiming skillfully, Druward completes the motion into a marksman's stance.

Luckily, one of the random bullets sprayed from the pistol sized automatic hits the red fox in the left arm before Druward takes a fully aimed shot. This enables him to swing the gun to the left faster than he intended, because several bullets, maybe four, end up inside that fox's chest. Vulpie doesn't have the reaction time to do anything, so he stays bent over the table with his eyes shut, feeling the bullets rushing through the air over him. The brown fox that has been holding Vulpie down gets a mouthful of rounds, and something gruesome comes out of his head against the wall behind him.

Druward is satisfied with his attack, but he knows what is coming next. True to his expectations, he feels himself being shot by Zorpiv. The gray fox has run around the cement pillar and fires three rounds into him. Zorpiv would shoot more, but much to his surprise and irritation, his clip runs out of bullets. One bullet hits Druward in his right shoulder, the second one goes into his right lung, and the third enters his intestines. The shots are not immediately lethal, but he knows how bad it is when he's hit. He'll bleed to death at least if Zorpiv takes control of the situation.

Vulpie has opened his eyes by the time Druward gets shot and he sees him fall to the left. He hits the wall, a good distance from Wesley's corpse, but is not dead, and he slumps down to the floor. Zorpiv quickly searches through his clothing, feeling inside his commando pants for another clip of ammunition but he remembers that he wasted quite a bit of shots when he fired at the police car after shooting Tiala. If he hadn't done that, he would have one last clip to stay in control.

Vulpie pushes off of the table, naked, and looks around in disbelief. Everyone is dead except for him, Druward, and Zorpiv. He sees the gray fox rummaging through his pants, and judging by his behavior, he knows that he's out of shots. Vulpie's mind races and he looks for guns on the dead foxes, but is frustrated to see that none of them are carrying a gun except for Zorpiv. Apparently they hadn't considered Vulpie to be any threat at all, especially since they outnumbered him and had his paws cuffed. But now he's free... He's covered in sweat and dust, and naked, but he's free, and the orange furred fox looks down and sees the knife that the red fox had used to cut his clothing off. He reaches down, snatches it up from the floor, and then locks his eyes onto Zorpiv.

Even though Zorpiv is the same malicious animal, when he sees Vulpie with the knife he looks afraid. Vulpie starts walking towards him with a determined look, and this is enough to make the gray fox run.

"They have more guns in their cars! Kill him Vulpie!" Druward groans from the floor and Vulpie gives him a cold look as he takes in the knowledge. In the first chamber, Zorpiv tries to break open some of Druward's heavy locked cabinets where he can find other guns or more ammo for his MTAC-71. But the GBI director left nothing to chance and there is no way to get into them. Zorpiv sees Vulpie coming and runs to the door. Vulpie runs after him, but doesn't reach the door until Zorpiv has slammed it behind him.

Vulpie pushes it open and is blinded for a moment by the pretty sunshine outside. The afternoon weather is beautiful, and air gushes around the cliffs behind Druward's home. Vulpie's fox ears hear Zorpiv's shoes crunching leaves as he runs back up the path towards the house. He doesn't waste any time, and runs after him as fast as he can. The hill path going up the side of the cliff is very steep, much easier to walk down than up, and Zorpiv finds himself running out of steam rather quickly. It's impossible to run as fast as he can without losing his footing, but he tries. He knows there are more guns in the cars and hopes that he can get to them before Vulpie catches him.

Zorpiv looks back over his left shoulder and sees the naked fox boy chasing after him, the sharp knife clenched in his black furred right paw. Vulpie's beautiful orange fur glistens in the afternoon sunshine, the white fur on his muzzle, throat, chest, tummy and crotch glowing while he moves through different patches of light. Vulpie is a beautiful little creature, but his adorable face is not carrying a smile. He's coming after Zorpiv with a look that could kill. There's no mistaking what he plans to do, and the fact that the fox boy is naked and still not afraid of catching him, starts to terrify the gray fox.

After all the time he's spent humiliating him, the idea seems impossible, but Zorpiv feels real fear that Vulpie might actually kill him. Vulpie is in top shape because he takes care of his body. He always wants to look his best, and for Polar to enjoy him as much as possible, so Vulpie's attention to physical perfection quickly gives him an edge that Zorpiv does not have. The gray fox, for all of his taunting and wicked words, starts to pant hysterically. Vulpie is going to catch him before he reaches the top of the trail.

Vulpie's black tipped feet swat against the leaves and dirt on the pathway while he keeps running up at Zorpiv. His pretty tail swishes back and forth for balance purposes. He gracefully runs closer and closer, while Zorpiv thuds about as hard as he can. About three fourths of the way up the trail, in the midst of dancing shadows and blinding sunlight peeking in between the trees, Zorpiv turns and waits for Vulpie. The gray fox is too tired to go on and has to take a break, but Vulpie is going to be on top of him in the next few seconds.

So Zorpiv aims his gun at Vulpie. Normally Vulpie might have instinctively recoiled, despite the fact that he knows its empty, but Vulpie's blood is racing so fast that he feels no fear. He thinks the gesture is funny and grins as he comes within feet of the gray fox.

"Get the fuck away from me you FAGGOT!" Zorpiv yells.

"Faggot! Faggot! Faggot! Faggot! Faggot! Faggot! Faggot's gonna KILL YOU!" Vulpie sings, looking terribly frightening. He slows his pace when he's right below Zorpiv, and Zorpiv swings the MTAC wildly. The bulky carbine has some real weight to It, and it takes everything he has to swing it backwards a second time, because Vulpie comes in for a stab after the first one. Fearing for his life, Zorpiv manages to smack Vulpie's arms with the empty gun. It hurts Vulpie but only enough to make him drop the knife and stumble.

At first, Zorpiv feels triumphant, but the hit also makes him lose his footing, and he falls on his right side. He lands on a rock that rams up against his right arm on impact. The momentum of falling on his arm, and hitting the rock almost breaks it, and he cries out in agony. The pain instinctively makes him grab and hold his right arm, and he lets go of the MTAC in the process. The gun shambles out of his black furred paw and rolls off of the path down into the leaves and the grass beside the trail. Vulpie slides backwards after his stumble, but uses his little paws to clutch onto the soft dirt and grass under him. Zorpiv stands up before he does, but the gray fox's arm is hurt and Vulpie is perfectly fine.

Zorpiv takes off with more speed than he ever showed before. Now there is no doubt that he's running for his life. He let's go of his arm and swings it as he hurries to the top of the trail, but there is no way he can fight with it. Vulpie scampers up behind him and grabs his tail. The little fox's claws slip off of Zorpiv's fur, but the gray fox stumbles at the top of the trail, trying to get further into Druward's backyard towards the house. He doesn't get very far.

Vulpie tackles Zorpiv and is on top of him in a matter of moments. The gay fox starts swinging wildly, pounding Zorpiv's back and right side while Zorpiv tries to cover up. Zorpiv crawls to the right and Vulpie pushes him on the ground again. Zorpiv goes back to the same behavior when Vulpie punches his back some more, and moves in the direction of the trail to get away. Except there is no trail at this angle. Since Zorpiv has his face in the grass, he hasn't considered that he's crawling towards the edge of the cliff that is beside the mountain pathway.

He gasps when he sees the drop ahead of him. Though lovely, with moss covered rocks here and there and trees growing out of the cliff, it is without a doubt, a deadly cliff, and he cries out when Vulpie starts pushing him towards it. Zorpiv rolls over on his back and starts fighting back. He opens his fox mouth and bites

Vulpie's left arm, causing Vulpie to yelp and recoil. This gives Zorpiv a chance to crawl out from under him, and he does, but also puts him closer to the edge, and Vulpie quickly stands up. He starts kicking Zorpiv, in the face, in the chin, and towards the drop.

Zorpiv doesn't realize his nose is bleeding until he tastes it. His adrenaline is pumping wildly, but so is Vulpie's, and Vulpie has put him right next to death's door. The gray fox twinges in fear when he feels his left paw slide off of the edge, and he has to put out his right paw for support to keep from going over.

"STOP! PLEASE STOP!" Zorpiv cries out, and Vulpie stops kicking him. The gay fox has been sure to use the bottom of his feet to whack Zorpiv over and over, to avoid jamming his toe claws. "Don't kill me! Please!"

"You killed Tiala!" Vulpie reminds him and moves as if he's going to kick him again. This is more than enough to make Zorpiv recoil, but Vulpie doesn't follow through. He breathes fast, watching Zorpiv's face while the gray fox holds out his left paw in terror.

"I'm sorry! I'm so sorry!" Zorpiv wails. Vulpie knows he can't let him go. The gay fox is no super fighter and he has no way to stop Zorpiv from escaping. It's taken everything he has to get the gray fox next to the cliff and he plans to follow through. Zorpiv's stomach sinks when Vulpie moves to kick him again. There's nothing for him to hold onto, except what's in his right paw, and it isn't enough. Vulpie expects to have to kick him over and over to make him fall off, but it happens in the next two.

Vulpie balances himself and watches Zorpiv's brown eyes go wide while sliding backwards. The gray fox scrambles for tree roots, rocks, even dirt, just for something to keep gravity from taking him. But there is nothing to save Zorpiv. He lets out a shrill cry that Vulpie will never forget. It makes Vulpie wince because of the sheer terror in it. Zorpiv falls off of the cliff and quickly lands onto a big rock on the way down. It snaps his spine and almost kills him. He's more or less, already dead, when he lands on another, and then another, before slamming down onto a large slab of stone at the part of the cliff near the bunker. He has been thoroughly killed, and Vulpie pants, looking down at him with wide eyes. He watched his entire descent, and even from the top of the cliff he can see blood oozing out of the gray fox.

Druward wonders if he's hallucinating when he hears the door to the bunker open. He's lost a lot of blood and feels light headed. His wolf ears twitch as he hears bare vulpine feet padding over the cement down the hallway and then into the small room where he's still lying on the floor. It's Vulpie, still naked, and the fox boy doesn't bother to go to his clothing when he walks into Druward's view. He stares down at him for a moment.

"So all of this is your fault, hmm? You conspired to have me killed along with all of these foxes from the Association of Fox Rights?" Vulpie asks.

"Yes..." Druward admits, wincing in pain.

"So how much did they pay you? I assume they did pay you, right? Surely you're not just that evil to do it for free?"

"Did you call the police? I need to get to a hospital!" Druward groans in agony. "I'm bleeding to death!"

"I came back down to have a little chat with you before I call anybody!" Vulpie answers and swishes his pretty tail. "I had to kill that crazy gray fox. I hope you're happy for making me a murderer!"

"I'm sorry! They did pay me! They did!" Druward gasps.

"How much?"

"Millions… Six million…"

"At least I didn't come cheap!" Vulpie growls in disgust. "Tiala's dead because of you!"

"She's not dead…" Druward moans. "She's alright…" The black furred wolf's words surprise Vulpie, and it makes him blink in hope.

"You know that?"

"I know for sure… She's going to be fine but I'm going to die if you don't call the police soon!" Druward pleads and Vulpie sighs. He leans down to take a seat next to Druward on the cement.

"I lied. I already called them. Not everyone's as fucking evil as you are. I wouldn't let you die down here, even after what you've done to me." Vulpie whispers.

"Thank you…" Druward breathes and winces in pain.

"Why did you come back and save me?" Vulpie asks with a small voice.

"I don't know… I don't know anymore…" Druward gasps and wonders whether he is going to pass out. He feels cold. "Polar came to… Rulef helped him find me…"

"Polar knew that you were responsible and he's the reason you saved me." Vulpie says, while finding great joy in the realization.

"Yes… I didn't admit to it… But we fought and I…"

"You fought? You mean like, you and Polar had a fist fight?" Vulpie asks in curiosity. He grins a little.

"Yes…"

"Who won?"

"Who do you think?" Druward growls and Vulpie smirks.

"Don't die, okay? Even though I hate you, I don't really want to see you go out like this." Vulpie says. Druward seems happy to hear the words, but happy is quite an overstatement considering his current situation. The GBI director looks very weak, and Vulpie worries that he might snuff it at any moment, so the adorable gay fox decides to hold his attention until help arrives. He suddenly stands up and swishes his silky tail while grinning.

"So what do ya think?" Pretty nice to get a free full body shot of me, huh?" He taunts, posing for the black furred wolf while biting his lip. Vulpie strokes himself, and he succeeds in distracting the GBI director. The wolf's yellow eyes widen in disbelief.

"Oh God………" Druward groans with a tortured voice. "On second thought, just let me bleed to death………"

"What? I bet you always wondered how I looked naked!" Vulpie teases, but when he looks around Druward with more attention, he sees just how much the wolf has already bled.

"Who am I kidding? Yeah... I did..." Druward admits and grins, but his face is full of pain.

"See! At least something good came out of today!" Vulpie mischievously declares. He tries his best to stay positive, but Druward coughs up a lot of blood. The fox boy whimpers at the realization that the strong wolf that saved him isn't going to make it. Sure Druward is reaping what he's sown, but it's not enjoyable to watch. Vulpie makes a sad face and slowly goes down on his paws and knees again, and sits on the floor next to him. "Hold on Druward. Just keep it together until they get you to the hospital, okay?"

"I'm dying... I'm going to die..." Druward breathes in fear and gives Vulpie a remorseful face. It's the first time the fox boy has ever seen him look weak.

"Don't say that. You can still make it." Vulpie replies and puts his left paw on his head. He pets Druward's ears and smiles at him.

"I'm sorry Vulpie... I've ruined my life and done all of this to you for no reason..." The black furred wolf gasps. His eyes start to water, the sight of it making Vulpie's do the same. He cannot believe Druward is about to cry.

"Why did you do it? At least tell me some reason why." Vulpie whispers.

"I like you... I've always liked you, but I couldn't admit it..."

"You mean, you liked me... In that way?"

"I don't know. I'm not sure." Druward admits and enjoys the sensation of Vulpie petting his head. "But when your husband confronted me... He didn't care about being tough or fighting to impress someone... He fought for you... And I realized that I don't have anyone like that in my life..."

"Don't you say that Druward. I know there have to be animals that love you too." Vulpie says, using a loving voice.

"I wish I did... But I've wasted my life!" Druward whimpers. The sound of his fear makes Vulpie pant in terror as well, feeling that the end is near.

"Stay with me! Don't die on me Druward! Who else is gonna pick on me?" Vulpie teases, and his funny face makes Druward laugh, but he coughs when he does, and his body twitches.

"You're a good person aren't you Vulpie?" Druward whispers with a distant smile. "I can see why Polar loves you so much. He's lucky to have you."

"Druward! Don't die!" Vulpie shouts in fear.

"I can't..." Druward whispers and Vulpie grabs his big right paw with his little claws. The fox squeezes him as hard as he can.

"DRUWARD!" Vulpie yells, and his scream seems to bring the wolf back for a moment. He looks around as if confused as to where he is just as a very loud sound clangs through the chamber.

It's the outside door. There are hurried voices and Vulpie hopefully smiles down at Druward. The black furred wolf is still alive, but is barely conscious. "See! They're here!"

Together Again

"And that's when you threw him off the cliff in self-defense?" The police officer that is interviewing Vulpie inquires. The man is a tall timber wolf, and has a notepad as he takes down details.

"Yes sir." Vulpie responds while glancing towards the cliff. At the bottom, there is a team of investigators that have sealed off the area around Zorpiv's body with yellow warning tape. They've secured all of the property, and luckily, they arrived just in time to save Druward from dying. They've already taken him away in an ambulance and Vulpie is still at the scene, answering the hundreds of questions the authorities have for him.

"And who exactly does this house belong to?" The cop asks. Vulpie suspects that it belongs to Druward, but he shrugs in response.

"No idea. They just brought me here to torture and kill me."

"We have those records." Rotick says as he walks near the police officer and Vulpie. The cop has already seen the GBI agent flash his credentials earlier.

"So who owns it?" The cop asks the white and brown furred wolf. Vulpie recognizes him as the same one that was with Druward when he came to the Lupiv Museum.

"It's classified." Rotick responds.

"Excuse me, what?" The officer asks with an unflattering tone.

"Just finish your interview with Vulpie so he can go home."

"Well I don't know how you do things over at the GBI, but I'm not going to leave critical information out of this report." The cop responds while sending a disgusted look.

"I've already spoken with your sergeant. If you want to lose your job, go ahead and pursue it." Rotick warns. Vulpie is silent, and looks between them. The GBI agent waits for a moment so the threat has time to sink in. And after a frustrated breath, the officer complies.

"Yes sir." He responds. Rotick looks at Vulpie. The little fox is shirtless, wearing only his business slacks and a towel given to him by the police.

"Vulpie, can I have a moment with you?" The agent asks. Vulpie nods and walks away from the cop, who grimaces while he writes. They move far enough away that no one will hear them.

"This is Druward's house..." Rotick quietly says and Vulpie nods.

"I thought so." Vulpie whispers in response. "So what's going to happen to him?"

"That depends on you." The brown and white furred wolf answers and looks around to make sure no one is listening in. "At this point there's no denying that he was in on the plan to have you killed. Karl Vulches, and Nathan Fenrir were two very rich foxes and no doubt they paid him to have you set up."

"He admitted to it." Vulpie replies.

"After you had to kill that gray fox?"

"Yes."

"Well, you need to make a choice then. There are different ways that this could go..." Rotick responds. "You have every right to stick with the full story and accuse Druward for his involvement. Goddess knows that no one would blame you, Vulpie. But the GBI has done a lot of good things under his management, though it might be hard for you to believe after everything he's done to you."

"Go on." Vulpie says while listening.

"Organized crime has dropped off sharply in every major city on planet Sufias since he became director eight years ago."

"Because they're all afraid of the GBI." Vulpie observes.

"That's right." Rotick admits. "I won't lie to you, Vulpie. Under Druward, the GBI has abused its authority, but he's also struck fear into the hearts of animals that kill, rape, and murder. I've worked with him for years, all the way up from the academy to the agency, and I know that there is good in him. That's why I can't understand how he could do something this heartless. Just know that there are a lot of other organizations that depend on the GBI, and if Druward goes down in flames, it will be really bad for all of us."

"Let him go." Vulpie simply says and gives Rotick a little smile.

"Really? Just like that?" Rotick replies in astonishment.

"Yep."

"Are you sure? I mean, don't you want a few minutes to think about it?"

"Nope!" The fox boy answers in joy.

"I don't... Understand... After everything he put you through... They almost raped and killed you. Once we put out a statement we can't change it. The GBI can hold back the police report as long as possible, but we need to keep to the same story here."

"He's beyond sorry for what he did." Vulpie explains and smiles happily. "You should have seen him down there... He was bleeding to death. We both thought he was going to die, and he started crying..."

"He cried?" Rotick asks and laughs, not knowing how to take the news. He honestly had not expected such a revelation.

"He told me he was sorry for the awful things he's said to me, and done to me, and he meant it. He even confessed that he secretly liked me and after Polar beat him up, he realized that the love we share is something he doesn't have in his life... It was... It was a beautiful moment, because we both were terrified he was going to go at any second, and then the cops and the medics showed up! Goddess! I was crying too! I was so sad that he was going to die and if they had been a few seconds later he might have!"

"Wow... I didn't think Wraulgh was capable of producing tears!" Rotick laughs and Vulpie starts laughing with him.

"It was such a special moment! I know I'm really sensitive cuz I'm gay, but it was perfect! The look out of his eyes... He's going to be a changed man from this day forward!" Vulpie says in excitement and then thinks about his own wolf. The fox boy thinks about how upset and worried Polar must be. "I've got to get out of here! Polar's probably crying his eyes out!" Vulpie breathes.

"So that's it? You're really going to say that he just showed up and saved you?" Rotick asks once again.

"Can you guys make it legit?"

"No one will ever know."

"Yep! Now take me to my Polar!"

"Okay..." Rotick chuckles in amusement.

Polar has his big head in his paws, leaning forward on the black leather couch. He's been home for hours now, and has been crying so much that he feels faint. After fighting Druward at the Ashcrest launch pad, he had nowhere to go. He left the facility believing that he failed. His victory over Druward didn't seem to accomplish anything, and he hasn't felt any pride because of it. He's been far too busy wailing over the loss of his husband.

The white furred wolf blames himself for not going with Vulpie. He let the fox boy drive off with only Tiala to protect him. He feels like he could have saved Vulpie. Sure, he knows he would have been shot just like Tiala, but if he was in the SUV with Vulpie he might have been able to slow down the foxes. These sort of thoughts have tormented him into a state of hopelessness.

Polar feels the same kind of all-consuming despair he's suffered through before, when Evil Vulpie almost killed Vulpie. He didn't know if Vulpie would live or die and this is equally horrible because he knows nothing at all. The only thing he's sure of is that a bunch of psychotic foxes that hate Vulpie have kidnapped him. As far as he knows, there's little chance that he'll ever see his fox husband again.

Suddenly, the sound of the front door opening gets his attention. He looks up and wonders who has just come into his house without knocking. It's Rulef, and the gray furred wolf is smiling.

"We've got him back! The GBI found Vulpie!" The Blacktail commander declares and Polar blinks in shock. He's been crying for so long that he can't believe what he's hearing.

"Where?" The arctic wolf breathes.

"He just called me and told me to tell you to bring one of his white t shirts! He's riding to the hospital where Tiala is right now!" Polar leaps up from the couch and isn't sure whether he laughs or grins, but he lets out a very happy sound. "Go get his clothes and I'll take you to him!"

"He's really okay?" Polar asks with wide blue eyes.

"He's okay! The GBI is guarding him until we can pick him up at the hospital!"

"Thank you Goddess Khalan!" Polar shouts.

"There they are." Rulef says as he drives the SUV towards two brown sedans. Blacktail is meeting up with the agents that have protected Vulpie in their absence. They're in the parking lot of the hospital where Tiala is being treated, and Blacktail pulls in just when the lights come on. The sun is going down and crickets chirp from their hidden places. The agents open their car doors and get out and Rulef parks the SUV next to them. Polar opens the side door and gets out in a hurry. His heart speeds up when he sees Vulpie get out of the back left seat of agent Rotick's car. The orange furred fox is still wearing his dress slacks, but he's shirtless. Rotick waits for Vulpie to scamper around his left towards Polar and the white furred wolf intercepts him with a big hug. He picks Vulpie up off of the ground and holds him against his chest.

"VULPIE! OH THANK THE GODDESSES YOU'RE OKAY!"

"I'm okay! I'm fine!" Vulpie breathes with a smile and returns Polar's mighty embrace as best as he can. "Ugh! You're gonna crush me!"

"Sorry!" Polar says and lessens his hold on his fox husband. Vulpie laughs as Polar sets him back on his feet, but doesn't let him out of his arms.

"I made it back to you baby!"

"Are you hurt?" Polar asks. "Rulef told me on the way here that all of the foxes that kidnapped you are dead!"

"Yeah, Karl Vulches and Nathan Fenrir are both history..." Vulpie answers while shaking his head as if disappointed.

"Those two really had no idea what they set into motion."
Agent Rotick comments and Polar and Vulpie look to him. "That gray
fox that they had leading the Vuldrofein was a Vixil. And foxes from
that family have a long history of murder, robbery, and rape... So
letting him take charge was a bad move. Plus his family owed Karl
Vulches money. So he turned on him and Fenrir. Isn't that right?"
The brown and white furred wolf asks Vulpie.

"Yeah, he just shot them both! It was horrible!" Vulpie
answers. "And then down in the bunker behind that house, Zorpiv
got into an argument with another one of them. And he just fucking
shot him too! He was insane! If Druward hadn't shown up I'd be
dead!"

"Druward..." Polar growls and Vulpie looks up at the white
furred wolf that is still holding him tightly.

"I heard you got into a fight with him!" Vulpie says
mischievously.

"I didn't know how it was going to end, but Polar finished
it. He took Druward down." Rulef comments and Vulpie looks at the
Blacktail commander. He sees that the gray wolf has a little smile.

"He actually told me about it himself... But we won't have
time for all of that now. I want to see Tiala and find out if she's
okay." Vulpie hurriedly says and Polar squeezes him protectively.

"I thought you were gone forever... I can't tell you how
happy I am!" The white furred wolf says to his husband and Vulpie
affectionately paws his sides.

"Me too! But let's go see Tiala before we... Share our
feelings..." Polar recognizes the look in Vulpie's pretty blue eyes. He
has the submissive and adoring expression that means he really
needs to be taken. After the day's terrible events, they both want
reassurance, and nothing more needs to be said. They smile at each

other and Polar releases him. He turns to the side and offers Vulpie his big right paw. Vulpie gladly takes it with his left and they hold hands as they start walking towards the hospital entrance.

Deepwolf and Rulef spread out to ensure Vulpie and Polar don't have any other adventures today. There's nothing going on at the hospital, but their job is to plan for the unfortunate and the unforeseen. Who knows when an animal on pain medication might slip up on the wheel and hit a bystander. But their entry to the hospital is easy and the lobby plays enjoyable music, and there is a middle aged female panther at the desk that Rulef speaks with. He finds Tiala's room and then leads the group upstairs to the third floor.

The doctor that is handling Tiala's treatment is more than happy to guide the group when he sees Vulpie. The man talks a lot about this and that, and mentions the attack in the news, but everyone ignores him for the most part. He stays outside the room with Blacktail, and Rulef closes the door after Polar and Vulpie go into Tiala's room, deciding to give them privacy.

Tiala's parents are with her. They both look very old, but may not necessarily be so. They just have ancient features that are a telltale sign of hard work and desperate conditions. They probably have been poor most of their lives, and Vulpie suspects this is why Tiala chose her career with the military, and then, with Blacktail. The fox is very right, because the two older tigers had to worry about gas prices on the way over to the hospital. Tiala looks beaten but she is very alert, and she blinks in surprise, seeing Vulpie alive and well. Her right arm is bandaged extensively, as well as her right shoulder. The doctors had to remove three bullets from her arm and three from her shoulder.

"Are you okay Tiala?" Vulpie asks with a friendly voice and smiles at her and her family.

"You're alright! I thought that they... You know... Were going to kill you." Tiala answers with a perky voice. She's a little high on pain medication and Vulpie knows the feeling.

"It's a long scary story, but I owe everything to you!" The gay fox replies. The tigress looks to her mother and father.

"Mom, Dad, this is Vulpie Vivixen." Tiala says, introducing her boss. Everyone knows who Vulpie is, and they look happy enough to meet a celebrity. They nod and smile back.

"She saved my life... Twice..." Vulpie tells the old tigers. "I owe so much to her, and I promise I'm going to make it right. She didn't accept money last time, but this time I'm going to force her!"

"They still kidnapped you. I didn't stop them." Tiala says.

"You took two of them down and then got shot for me. You've taken bullets for me two times now, and I'm not going to let you work for me anymore unless you accept more money. You got it?" Vulpie mischievously responds.

"Okay, thanks, but how much?" Tiala inquires.

"You're getting a million, and I'm not taking no for an answer!" Vulpie quickly replies.

"Vulpie... I can't accept that."

"A million dollars?" Tiala's father asks and starts laughing in disbelief. The old man clearly looks excited at the prospect. It's more than the idea of his daughter being rich. Vulpie can see that they need the money for the family.

"Absolutely! I'm gonna pay your daughter one million dollars for saving my life again!" Vulpie declares. It would be an unfair statement to say that big cats don't understand or care for foxes, because foxes are canines and are little canines at that, but there certainly is a bit of a disconnect in their cultures. However, Vulpie bridges that disconnect and smashes it completely into dust with his offer. Tiala's mother and father look at the orange furred fox boy as if he is an angel.

"Are you sure?" Tiala's mom asks.

"I sure am! I know she means more to you than you can tell me, and now she'll be able to get everything she ever wanted out of life! Maybe she can even get out of working with guns and just go play!"

"Vulpie, this is what I do!" Tiala laughs.

"Aw, shush! Don't tell me you never wanted to do anything else!" Vulpie giggles.

"Well, I wanted to visit other countries. And mom and dad have never been to the places Blacktail has taken me, even though we were always working."

"Then that's it! You just go on vacation for as long as you want! Your job will be safe at Vulpie Industries if you want to come back and if you don't, that's cool too!" Vulpie offers with his friendliest voice. When he turns on the charm, he's truly hard to resist. Tiala finds herself fantasizing about that kind of freedom already.

"Take it!" Tiala's father suggests, and everyone laughs a little.

"Okay! Thank you so very much Vulpie. You're a good man to work for." Tiala says with a moved voice. Polar puts his paws around Vulpie's shoulders from behind and embraces him with a loving face. Vulpie coos and looks back to his left to smile in return.

Once Polar and Vulpie are finished visiting with Tiala, Blacktail takes Vulpie back into their care. The GBI agents left much earlier, having other matters to attend to.

"So how did it all go down after they kidnapped you?" Deepwolf inquires as the SUV drives out of the hospital parking lot. Rulef looks to Vulpie in a respectful manner, because he has already heard about what the fox boy had to do to survive. However, Polar has yet to hear the story and Vulpie looks to his left at him before answering.

"They had me in the trunk and pulled me out in front of Nathan and Karl. To tell the truth, I wasn't that surprised. I mean, I was shocked that they hated me enough to have me killed, but I already knew both of them were really bad guys." Vulpie answers. "I had history with Nathan, because he said some nasty things to me after I turned myself in to the government."

"You mean the time you REALLY turned yourself in." Polar smirks.

"Yeah, not when I was still messing around, sending them a robot instead. The second time when I really gave up, because of you." Vulpie smirks back.

"Did you really bite his face? I heard that from Rulef." Deepwolf grins.

"Yep! Can't say I liked the taste though." Vulpie mischievously answers. "And then there's Karl. We played the stock market together and I had another fifty million all guaranteed for Vulpie Industries to earn through the deal, but then the story got out about him killing the competition. Literally! He poisoned wolf businessmen that he dealt with."

"How did he do it again?" Rulef inquires.

"He put something in the bottled water and the coffee whenever we had meetings with wolves, and they became ill very quickly. But the stuff didn't make them puke, so they couldn't figure out what was happening to them, and Karl used it to his advantage. He got them to sign deals when they were under the influence of whatever drug he was using."

"Wow, it's a good thing he's dead. I'm gonna be honest." Deepwolf comments.

"Yeah, he was a terrible guy." Vulpie replies. "So that psycho gray fox pulled me out of the trunk and held my arm while they gave me a little speech about how I shouldn't have disrespected their awesome fox families. Guys, you've never seen such a bunch of little arrogant cowards."

"What else did they say?" Polar asks his fox husband.

"They said I was going to die. And I told them that I've loved my life with you, and would do it all over again. So Karl's response was that it didn't matter, because they were gonna film torturing me to death and that's all animals would remember me for." Vulpie answers.

"God, I'm so glad you're alright! I wouldn't be able to survive that." Polar admits. The emotional dependency he has for Vulpie is obvious to everyone. The white furred wolf's voice is a little weak, still terribly shaken up from the possibility of losing him.

"I couldn't live without you either. I know I need you more than you need me." The fox boy affectionately replies.

"So when did this Zorpiv guy turn on them?" Rulef interrupts. The Blacktail commander is very interested in getting more details before Polar and Vulpie get lost in each other's eyes.

"Well, it happened like this." Vulpie answers, holding onto Polar's right knee with his left paw when the SUV hits a bump in the road. "I told them a little story about what would happen if I died. I lied and said that I had Vulpie.net programmed to take over the moment that I'm gone. That's not really true, but when I suggested Evil Vulpie might pay them a visit, Nathan Fenrir got scared."

"The Vulpocalypse." Rulef says, referring to what Evil Vulpie told Vulpie in the Sufias Heritage Museum years ago.

"Yeah, but it's not true. If I die, there's no command in Arctic.net to let Vulpie.net run wild. Karl thought I was lying, but Nathan believed me. I think I came off pretty convincing too. But what really sold the story, was when I told Fenrir what his home address was. I've been watching him for years, ever since I recovered from Evil Vulpie almost killing me, and I knew it. I couldn't remember all of the zip code but I knew the street address and everything else. Four one two seven, Old Carrollstead Road, Duwalk, VS... I still can't remember the zip, but I know it ends with four five seven."

"Nice..." Rulef says and smirks with an impressed look. "So that was enough to create trouble in paradise?"

"More than enough." Vulpie responds and licks his lips. "Nathan and Karl started going back and forth about it. Nathan suggested that they could just let me go, but Karl didn't want to. And that was when Zorpiv just walked over and shot Nathan to death. He hit him with that terrible gun he shot Tiala with... And then he died in the grass a few moments later... It was just awful. I feel bad for him just thinking about it."

"No big loss." Deepwolf comments and Rulef nods in agreement.

"I've never been so scared of another fox... Evil Vulpie doesn't count because it's a machine." Vulpie replies.

"What did Karl do when he shot Nathan?" Rulef asks.

"He freaked. He started screaming and was just as shocked as I was. You're right about him and Nathan. They had no idea what they were doing putting that kid in charge."

"I bet he was supposed to be the fall guy. I figure if things went wrong, Karl and Nathan planned to blame the Vixil foxes for everything." The Blacktail commander pauses for a moment. He considers how to frame his next questions. "So Zorpiv took over and had you taken down to the bunker anyway?"

"Yeah."

"Did they... Well..."

"What did they do to me?" Vulpie answers with a distraught look. Polar notices the nervous twinge in his lover's voice and wraps his right arm around him. Vulpie reciprocates, squeezing the white furred wolf's leg with his left paw.

"Maybe we should wait until later?" Polar suggests.

"It's okay..." Vulpie meekly says.

"The GBI mentioned that they were distracted when Druward walked in." Rulef comments.

"They didn't rape me if that's what you're wondering. But they got pretty close." Vulpie says, cutting to the chase. "If Druward was a few minutes late it would have happened."

"Sick fuckers..." Polar growls.

"It was that gray fox's idea. He had issues." Vulpie responds.

"I'm guessing that Druward killed all of them but missed Zorpiv. And that's when Zorpiv shot him?" Rulef inquires. "Was Druward out of bullets?"

"It happened so fast I could barely see it all, but to me it looked like Zorpiv dodged before Druward shot at him. Druward shot everyone else and then Zorpiv shot him, but he ran out of bullets. That's when I grabbed the knife and chased after him." Vulpie answers.

"Up the cliff behind the house?"

"There was a path that led down to the bunker and I chased him all the way up it. He managed to knock the knife out of my paws with his gun even though it was empty. I knew if he got to their cars he would get another gun and kill me."

"And that's when you killed him." Rulef says with a nod and Polar blinks. Vulpie slowly looks to his left at him and sighs.

"I had to throw him off of the cliff." The orange furred fox boy admits.

"You did?" Polar responds in shock but takes a moment to think things through.

"There was no way to avoid it. He was going to kill you." Rulef says.

"But it's still going to haunt me... Now I'm a murderer..." Vulpie whispers. Polar imagines what his husband must have went through.

"Rulef's right. You did what you had to do." The white furred wolf agrees. His voice is compassionate and he rubs Vulpie's right shoulder.

Polar's Love

Vulpie and Polar arrive home around seven in the evening. The orange furred fox goes upstairs and cleans up, taking a shower. He has to wash off all of the dirt and dust from his pretty fur. When Vulpie's done he comes back downstairs and sees Polar standing behind the couch. His husband looks ready to help with whatever Vulpie may be feeling. He smiles and walks over to Vulpie, and they share a hug. Vulpie caresses Polar's strong sides and Polar rubs Vulpie's soft back.

"How are you feeling?" The white furred wolf tenderly inquires.

"Better, now that you're here to protect me." Vulpie answers.

"I should have gone with you." Polar says with a regretful voice. "I should have known something was wrong with Druward."

"If it wasn't for you I'd be dead." Vulpie affectionately responds. "Druward told me that you were the reason he changed his mind."

"It wasn't easy. You wouldn't believe how that guy can fight. I knew he would be tough but it took everything I had just to keep up with him." The white furred wolf admits.

"But you got him down and beat the shit out of him..." Vulpie replies and shows Polar a mischievous smile. "I can believe it. I know how strong you are... Yeah he's some kind of trained killer, but I would always put my money on you."

"Thanks, but I got lucky." Polar smiles back.

"You're really a thing of beauty, Mr. Polar." Vulpie says while looking the arctic wolf over and smiles even more. "You know that don't you?"

"Well, it's true." Polar playfully taunts and winks at his husband.

"Can I get you anything for your nose? Where do you hurt? I'll go get some painkillers for you." The orange furred fox offers.

"I'm fine. You're the one that needs to be taken care of. Are you okay?"

"Yeah. I'm just..." Vulpie says and looks at the couch. He walks around Polar's left side and finds a spot on the left end of the expensive piece of furniture. Polar turns and walks to the right, going around the right side of the couch so he can sit with his husband. He drops down next to Vulpie and stretches his left arm around the fox boy for a hug. Vulpie returns it, sending his little right arm around Polar's torso.

"Do you want to talk about it?" Polar asks, rubbing Vulpie with his big paw.

"Not right now... I just... I can't... I don't know why..." Vulpie answers with a distant expression.

"I know that face, Vulpie..." Polar gently tells his husband. "I know what you're thinking. You're blaming yourself for having to kill that gray fox. But it wasn't your fault."

"But it was." Vulpie whispers and looks up into Polar's handsome blue eyes. "Sure I can rationalize it. And everybody will say I was right to kill him, but I still murdered an animal today. I'm a killer."

"Oh please, You're the furthest thing from a killer, you little softy..." Polar teases. "You're too sweet."

"I'm serious." Vulpie replies.

"I know you are. And I am too." The white furred wolf leans down and kisses the side of Vulpie's head. "I'm also pretty wound up from today... So why don't we go upstairs? I'll help you relax..."

"Polar, I'm not really in the mood. I was almost raped today." Vulpie answers and frowns.

"And that's why I want to make love. You need it. Otherwise, you're going to think about this day over and over again, and all you'll remember is what you had to do to survive... Let me take your mind off of it..."

"Thanks, but I just don't have the energy right now. Later, okay?" The fox boy answers.

"You don't have to do a thing... I'll take care of you..." Polar coos and strokes Vulpie with his left paw.

"You're persistent aren't you?" Vulpie shyly responds.

"Say yes... I promise you won't care about any of this..." The white furred wolf breathes and tenderly strokes Vulpie with his left paw.

"Alright, I guess..." Vulpie sighs and smiles at Polar as best as he can. The fox boy is uncharacteristically lethargic.

"Come on." Polar says with a smile, and pulls Vulpie up from the couch as he stands. The white furred wolf reaches for and grabs ahold of the fox's paw with his left, and proceeds to lead him out of the den and upstairs. When they reach the top of the steps on the second floor, Polar heads towards the bedroom, pulling Vulpie along. Vulpie keeps up, but just can't get excited with the terrible memories of the day tormenting him.

Polar lets go of Vulpie's paw and heads towards the desk near their bed where they keep sex lubrication In a drawer. Vulpie undoes the khaki shorts he's been wearing since he showered, and slides them down. He reaches into his white t shirt and pulls it off as well, tossing it aside. Vulpie slides down his underwear just as Polar starts undressing himself. The white furred wolf drops the tube of lubricant onto the ground while he takes off his clothing. He hungrily looks over Vulpie's beautiful naked body, while the fox boy gets onto the bed. Polar quickly tosses his turquoise shirt aside and slides down his pants. He slides down his boxers as well, and steps out of them both.

The white furred wolf already has a big erection and it bounces as he walks to and gets onto the bed with Vulpie. They meet in a kiss, and Polar reaches behind the fox boy's head to cradle it while they enjoy the tender moment. Afterwards, Vulpie lies on his back and pulls his knees up towards his chest. He uses his black tipped fox paws to spread his legs for Polar, and reaches up to grab his ankles, assuming a slave sexual position. Polar smiles at Vulpie and reaches out with his left paw to knock the fox's right hand off of his ankle. Vulpie blinks in surprise, and releases his left paws hold on his left ankle, and just keeps his legs spread instead.

"What do you want me to do?" Vulpie asks.

"Nothing." Polar answers and grabs Vulpie's left leg. Vulpie can see what his husband is going to do, so he raises and slightly twists his pelvis upwards towards his chest, exposing his butt, as Polar aims the fox's left leg onto his right shoulder. Vulpie's left leg is supported by Polar's position, and Vulpie slides his right leg between Polar's as Polar positions himself on his knees against Vulpie's ass. Polar reaches down and finds the sex lubricant nearby, popping it open. He then squirts a plentiful amount of fluid in his right paw and masturbates it onto his big erection while Vulpie waits. When it's nice and slick, he aims the head of his wolf dick against Vulpie's fox anus.

Vulpie tenses up when Polar starts penetrating him, but his vast experience as a gay bottom helps the white furred wolf slide inside him. The wolf grunts, pushing more and more inside, until he's deep into Vulpie's ass.

"Oh…" Vulpie moans in relief. It already feels good, and when he locks eyes with Polar, he starts to become very excited. The white furred wolf begins fucking Vulpie and it feels phenomenal. With one leg raised, Polar's big cock rubs into and pushes against the fox boy's prostate perfectly. Polar doesn't have to try very hard to get his husband excited. The position allows Vulpie to masturbate with his right paw very easily. Polar fucks him slowly and intimately, and the pleasure Vulpie experiences makes him wince with a happy face in no time.

"There you go…" Polar breathes in pride. "That's hitting the spot isn't it?"

"Oh god, Polar, you are too good…" Vulpie shyly moans in response.

"I told you this was a good idea!" The white furred wolf replies with a big grin. He watches the gay fox's masturbation increase in enthusiasm. At first Vulpie just started pawing because it felt good to do while adjusting to the wolf's big cock squeezing him open, but now he's doing it because he needs more. Polar recognizes the expressions Vulpie makes all too well. The fox boy's shyness over the day's tragic events is starting to fade away.

"So you're not just doing your husbandly duty? You're saying you like this?" Polar breathes and Vulpie grins at the question.

"Well it's not like I could stop you, is it? Uh…" Vulpie moans, wincing from the amazing warmth of his prostate being stimulated all over.

"No you can't... I'm just a little too strong for you..." Polar answers and grins as well, showing his sharp teeth. Vulpie starts masturbating faster, and breathes quicker.

"Mneah! God it's so amazing to get fucked by a real man! You're so handsome and strong!" Vulpie whimpers. The white furred wolf can see that the fox boy's words are heart felt. Vulpie gives him the most beautiful look of adoration and clutches the left side of his furry butt with his little paw, holding it while getting fucked and masturbating with his right paw.

Polar decides to intensify the sex, and leans back just a bit, so he can reach up with his right paw to grab Vulpie's ankle. The strong wolf continues to fuck Vulpie just like before, with only the fox's left leg raised, but now he keeps that leg in his grasp instead of resting on his right shoulder. Polar moves Vulpie's left leg around a little bit, showing off his hold on his husband's little ankle and foot, and Vulpie opens his mouth to breathe in excitement.

"Ohhhhh that's so good!" Vulpie gasps while playing with his hard little cock.

"What's my name, Vulpie?" Polar asks, and the gay fox loses himself in the arctic wolf's blue eyes.

"Polar!" The fox boy moans.

"And who do you belong to?" The arctic wolf demands while enjoying himself.

"You! You own me!" Vulpie quickly answers.

"You're not worrying about anything now, are you?" Polar laughs with a very smug look. "Huh?"

"Just keep fucking me! Don't stop! Feels so good!" Vulpie replies with his eyes half open. The pleasure has consumed him. He plays with his cock feverishly, masturbating this way and that while staring up at Polar with adoration.

"I love you..." Polar breathes with a tender but hungry look, and thrusts harder and deeper than he has so far.

"I love you too!" Vulpie whines with tears brimming in his eyes. He's getting close to orgasm. The white furred wolf sees it on his adorable face.

"Now when you cum, you think about how I took punches for you. You think about me fighting Druward and bloodying his face, you think about that, and just how much I care about you." Polar advises. His intense loving words make Vulpie return the most vulnerable and excited smile. The gay fox boy whines louder and louder, and trembles while getting it from the white furred wolf. Polar's words turn Vulpie on so much that he feels his orgasm coming on way sooner than it would have before. The wolf's intense statements make Vulpie's body convulse, and he feels pleasure so deep inside him that a tear runs down his right cheek when he squints. Polar's blue eyes widen when he sees it.

"Fucking you so good that you're crying now?!" Polar laughs while relishing the feeling of Vulpie's tight asshole on his big cock.

"NNEEEAAHHEEHH!!!" Vulpie cries out, his fox mouth flying open. His tongue hangs out and his entire body spasms, making Polar clench his iron grip on Vulpie's left ankle. "UUHH! AAHHH! AHHH! AHH! AHHH! AH!! AAAH!" Vulpie whines each time as he ejaculates, squirting out copious amounts of semen from his hard little cock. It splatters onto the white bed sheets everywhere. His prostate is so excited that he keeps on cumming, over and over, and then continues to come a little more, until Vulpie is trembling, and kicks his left leg. Polar holds it tightly in the air, keeping the pressure of his fat cock right on Vulpie's prostate to make sure that it has as much stimulation as possible.

"Oh that must feel so good!" Polar taunts while enjoying Vulpie's super tight asshole on his hard penis. The white furred wolf stopped fucking him when the fox boy started climaxing, and he lovingly waits while Vulpie reels from the release.

"OH GOD POLAR! POLAR! OH MY GOD!" Vulpie exclaims with an incredibly satisfied wail.

"And you said you weren't in the mood!" Polar laughs while holding his position in his husband's ass.

"OW! Ow! Ow!" Vulpie suddenly whimpers, and he doesn't need to say anything else. Polar sets his own needs aside, and slowly starts pulling out of Vulpie. Now that Vulpie's prostate has sent him through such a gigantic ejaculation, it's very sensitive, and just the presence of Polar's fat cock touching the anal wall beside it is very painful for the fox boy. Polar smiles and pulls more of his dick out, until it finally pops free, and when it does, Vulpie starts kicking his left leg.

Polar releases it and Vulpie immediately rolls onto his right side, his orange fur squishing in his own cum on the bed sheets. He curls up into a fetal position. The fox boy reaches down and strokes his tender perineum and balls, and pants in exhaustion. His ass burns, but his most intimate places all throb with a wonderful glowing wave of pleasure and release.

The white furred wolf starts masturbating while he watches his fox husband recover. Vulpie trembles a bit more but eventually opens his eyes, and slowly leans up on his right paw. He gives Polar a purely gracious smile.

"Oh I love you Polar! THAT WAS INCREDIBLE!" Vulpie moans.

"Tell me when you're ready... So I can finish up." Polar smiles in response, continuing to masturbate and Vulpie bites his lip.

"I'm ready! Come get me!" The fox boy offers.

"You're sure?" Polar asks.

"Yeah!" Vulpie answers and crawls around on all fours, showing Polar his tail end. Polar crawls against him and gladly mounts the fox boy. The white furred wolf is very excited after the performance he's just given, and is going to enjoy cumming inside the gay fox. Polar puts the head of his wolf cock against Vulpie's anus and pushes it in. It slides inside easily, because Vulpie stays as relaxed as he can, and the white furred wolf clutches the fox's hips. He starts fucking his husband and Vulpie leans forward and raises his rear more, putting his face down on the bed and tucking his little arms under his chest submissively.

Polar accepts the position without hesitation and gets to fuck Vulpie as deep and hard as he wants. Vulpie winces from the pain on his prostate but he doesn't dare let a single whimper escape while he takes it from his husband. Polar's made Vulpie feel so incredibly good that he'll suffer through any discomfort to at least let his lover enjoy the sex as much as possible.

And the white furred wolf does. Vulpie's ass is incredibly tight, feeling magnificent on his throbbing cock. He pumps and pumps and pumps the fox boy, savagely, and throws his head back in delight. He relishes the feeling of having overwhelmed his partner to such a degree. Without a doubt, Polar has dominated Vulpie to the fullest sense of the word. Vulpie is helpless against him, a willing slave, having just been shown what a stronger and bigger man can do.

But there is more to a gay man than just the size of his cock and the strength he possesses. Polar frequently excites himself by thinking about how much smarter Vulpie is while fucking him. The fox boy is so intelligent there is no way Polar could ever hope to understand the ideas or vision he has, whether it be in the realm of math, innovation or artistic quality. Polar admires Vulpie's genius and his beauty, because Vulpie has prettier fur and features. Polar is an intimidating handsome wolf, but Vulpie is a sweet and adorable fox genius.

The white furred wolf believes that they were meant for each other, and he thrusts hard, making Vulpie whimper despite the fox boy's efforts not to. Polar is close to cumming and he tenses up, gritting his sharp teeth.

"FUCK!" Polar growls and then thrusts and thrusts and thrusts while he starts cumming. He clutches Vulpie's hips powerfully, and makes sure he cums all of his massive load inside his submissive partner.

"Oh baby! Yeah!" Vulpie moans with his face against the bed.

"OH MY GOD VULPIE!" Polar exhales in delight, and gasps in release. He's finished ejaculating, and holds still while coming down from his orgasm. Vulpie slowly moves his little arms out from underneath his chest and sits up on all fours again, looking back over his left shoulder at Polar. He grins and Polar grins back. Vulpie touches Polar's left leg while the wolf starts pulling his cock out, and the fox boy yelps a little when it pops free. A bit of Polar's wolf semen squirts out of Vulpie's asshole, and he turns around to meet the white furred wolf in an embrace.

Polar and Vulpie hug each other as hard as they can, Vulpie getting a little smothered from Polar's strength. The white furred wolf notices and lessens his loving hold on his husband to accommodate him, and Vulpie affectionately snuggles up to Polar, swishing his pretty tail. Polar pulls Vulpie down on to the bed, Polar on his right side and Vulpie on his left, both of them still in each other's arms.

"If I ever lost you, I would die Polar. I would just die!" Vulpie lovingly breathes.

"You should have seen me today after they took you! I was crying my eyes out!" Polar breathes back with an equally devoted expression.

"I love you so much! And I don't care who or what tries to stand in our way! I'll never give you up for anything!" Vulpie promises.

"You don't know how much that means to me to hear you say that..." Polar says with a moved voice and the wolf and fox share tender smiles.

"Your name's Polar, and you own me!" Vulpie mischievously whispers.

"You better believe it!" Polar laughs.

Friends in Powerful Places

Druward lies awake in his hospital bed, but he seems like he is somewhere else. He doesn't move despite being able to. He's had a steady flow of blood given to him to make up for what he lost as a result of the shootout, so he's healthy enough, but mentally he is detached. He has had several hours to think since waking up, with only a visit from agent Rotick to hold his attention. There is a TV mounted in the top right corner of the room but he turned it off using the remote provided on a desk near his bed. The major news story has been about Vulpie's short kidnapping and the mystery surrounding it.

There is a knock at the door and his attention goes to a she-wolf nurse. She's the same one that has been looking after him and she holds a clipboard in her paws.

"Mr. Druward?"

"Yes?"

"You have some visitors here to see you." She says and gestures behind her. Vulpie leans around the corner and smiles. The orange furred fox is sporting his full business attire and looks to have come from his company or is heading there. His jet black suit with a white undershirt tightly hugs around his little body, and the neon pink tie he has on accents the beauty of the ensemble. The fox boy also seems to be holding a gift wrapped present in his paws that is about seven and a half inches tall and four and a half inches wide.

Polar steps up behind Vulpie, also wearing a matching black suit but with a neon blue tie. Druward's yellow eyes go to Polar and he can see that the white furred wolf is on edge. Polar is very controlled, and Druward expects he will not say anything or do anything to start a fight, but he also knows he had better not say anything hateful to Vulpie anymore. But Druward doesn't see any reason to insult Vulpie. He's happy to see him, but has trouble smiling because he isn't used to it.

"Let them in." Druward answers and the nurse nods and backs out of the room. She gently closes the door behind Vulpie and Polar and Vulpie walks over to Druward's bed. Polar follows but keeps his distance.

"How are you feeling Druward?" Vulpie asks with a friendly voice.

"I'm going to be fine. They treated me all last night and were able to remove the bullets and they say I'm healthy enough to make a full recovery." The black furred wolf answers.

"I'm so glad to hear it! I was worried about you." Vulpie replies and the statement makes Druward squint in surprise. The fox boy looks to be telling the truth, but also has a twinkle in his eyes.

"Vulpie... Thank you for not... Telling them everything... The GBI is my life and it would be over if they knew." The black furred wolf admits.

"It's okay. I know your sorry better than anyone." Vulpie responds, referring to the moments they shared when Druward almost bled to death. "But Mr. Polar is going to take a while to convince!"

"I'm sure." Druward answers and glances at the white furred wolf.

"I want us to be friends now. I hope we can be... So I brought you a present!" Vulpie says and shows Druward the gift in his paws. It's wrapped in an expensive looking white and golden design and the black furred wolf accepts it when the fox boy hands it over. There is a pretty white bow attached to its top and Druward almost feels bad for tearing it open. When he does, he finds that there is an electronic device inside it. Druward removes the packaging and Vulpie helps him collect the pieces and put them on the table near the bed. Druward moves the slick orange device in his paws and smirks. He recognizes Vulpie Industries' product.

"It's the latest model V-Screen!" Vulpie tells the GBI director in excitement. And It has fast wireless internet so you can browse the web without having to leave your bed here. Isn't that awesome?"

"Yeah." Druward responds while feeling of the sturdy toy.

"You can send emails and work from here if you need to. Or you can watch TV or whatever else you might want. I thought you'd get bored sitting here all day! You don't seem like the kind of guy that likes to lay around!" Vulpie giggles.

"Well thank you. I can't believe you would give me this after what happened..." Druward answers, and finds that he could become emotional. He quickly kills the possibility, but Vulpie notices.

"I think you're a good man at heart, Druward... You just forgot..." Vulpie warmly responds.

"I'd like to believe that..." Druward replies.

"You are. I know it." Vulpie confidently responds and then licks his lips. "But when you get better, I have a feeling that I'm going to need your help... Do you think you could be there for me?"

"What do you mean?" The GBI director inquires but quickly figures out the answer for himself. "The robot..."

"I need to find out where they're coming from and put an end to it..." Vulpie says and sighs. "I thought I had left Vulpie.net behind me... But now I'm afraid that I've ignored it for far too long."

"I know more than I've told you." Druward admits and this gets Polar's attention as well as Vulpie's. The statement creates a short silent moment.

"Like what? What do you know?"

"The GBI has been tracking a ship in orbit around a planet called Zeravyn..." Druward answers and Vulpie perks up, indicating that he is aware of what the black furred wolf is referring to. "You know about Sevrif Industries already. They're your biggest competitor... But the ship they operate out of is the largest ever built and they keep expanding it. We've had our eye on them and we still don't know where their funding is coming from."

"From Sevrif. What do you know about him in particular?" Vulpie asks.

"Only that the entire company is registered in his name and it was registered on Zeravyn... We haven't fully investigated him or the Sevrif ship but... I think you might find answers there." Druward explains.

"Will you help me find them? Can the GBI help me?" The orange furred fox inquires with a determined voice.

"Not legally. They haven't done anything criminal and they are registered under a foreign planet... But technically, the Sufias world government has jurisdiction over the entire solar system."

"I'm sure a courageous man like yourself is not afraid to use his authority..." Vulpie playfully says and gives Druward a sly look. "To do something good."

"I felt that we needed to investigate them years ago." The GBI director thinks out loud.

"So you'll back me up?"

"I'll back you up." Druward promises. "I can get you to the Sevrif and Zeravyn so you can help us find answers as well. Maybe you'll see something that we can't."

"Thank you Druward..." Vulpie whispers and gives him a warm smile. Polar watches the black furred wolf carefully. The white furred wolf has been very suspicious while watching him speak with Vulpie, but now he too can see that Druward has changed. He still doesn't trust the black furred wolf, but is very happy to see Vulpie win him over.

VulGrid

Vulpie stands at attention while the audience of the Fort WintersBank observation booth fills up. The fort is the main training facility for animals that have chosen to serve in the military in the snowy and mountainous area of Winter's Dale, where Polar is from. Polar is here with Vulpie today to demonstrate what VulGrid can do, but is mostly around for emotional support, as the fox boy will be doing all of the talking. The retired colonels and generals filling up the seats of the observation booth are all expecting excellence from Vulpie Industries.

And they will have it. Vulpie has no doubt that his star product this year, the VulGrid, will astound them in ways they never thought possible. But it's the way in which this amazing piece of equipment will be portrayed that concerns the orange furred fox boy. Though he doesn't show it, he intends to draw the focus of VulGrid away from strict warfare and offer passive approaches.

Polar sits with his parents, who have been kind enough to attend the ceremony. Vulpie smiles at them, seeing them in the front row to his right, and Kimberly winks at him. The fox boy loves Polar's mom. She's the sweetest thing and always supports him when he needs it the most. Vulpie can see how Polar turned out to be such a good man by observing the white furred wolf's wonderful family. It's been quite nice to have Victor and Kimberly here because they have spent some time talking to the fellow white furred wolves that have arrived.

Arctic wolves make up half of the audience because WintersBank has a long history of preparing white furred wolves for battle. Vulpie brushed up on a little history before the presentation today and is aware that soldiers from WintersBank have fought for and have held every major territory north of Sufias City for the world government over the last four centuries. The white furred wolves are renown for not only their strength but their cunning, as many of their battles enabled them to blend in with the snow in order to confuse and eliminate the enemy.

It's an interesting sight for Vulpie to see so many strong white furred wolves like Polar. Many are the same height and weight, and some even look like him out of their eyes. A naughty thought pops into the fox boy's head, and he secretly wonders how delicious it would be to be taken by an entire room full of Polars, but he keeps this little fantasy to himself.

Polar knows how Vulpie thinks and sends his husband a playful look, and glances around the room with wide blue eyes and a smirk. Vulpie fans his little black furred paw near his face in response, acting as if things are just getting too hot in the room despite the fact that it's actually rather cold. Victor and Kimberly notice and seem to be somewhat amused.

"I can't wait to finally see this thing in action." Colonel Worhel tells Vulpie. The fox boy looks to his left and sees the retired brown furred wolf and smiles. They had a long discussion about VulGrid during the brief vacation in Casillfori.

"I think you'll like what you see." Vulpie replies, and Worhel chuckles. The wolf takes a seat with the rest of the audience In the comfortable bleachers, facing Vulpie and the wall with a window behind him. Outside, behind Vulpie, there is a large empty space, a training ground where VulGrid currently sits by itself. Snow covers the ground and there are forests nearby WintersBank that make anywhere outside seem beautiful.

VulGrid draws attention when every member of the audience sees it outside. The model Vulpie will be demonstrating is the largest current design, and is slightly bigger than a tall refrigerator. It is much more dense, with a thick middle that weighs in VulGrid's premiere model at one ton.

The machine is eye catching at first glance alone. It's simplistic yet efficient engineering shouts perfection. VulGrid's design is cylindrical in shape. It is rounded on both the top and the bottom parts, making it pleasant to look at. It's well known that animals like to look at symmetrical objects. Psychologically there is a draw to the beauty of something that has been crafted or is naturally balanced in all dimensions, and VulGrid is exactly that. The machine is composed of two parts, an upper and a lower, that are separated by a thinner area. The divide is balanced perfectly, rounded above and below, giving the piece of equipment a projective like appearance. It can be assumed that the lower portion houses the main power unit for the machine while the upper portion is the part that projects the magnetic and visual fields that the machine uses.

VulGrid's solid black design has also been recently waxed and it shines in the snowy cloud hidden sunlight. Whenever the machine is deactivated, its upper portion lowers against the bottom portion and snugly locks into place, making two perfectly identical rounded cylinder shaped segments that allow it to be transported. The machine is currently on, and its heat melts the light snow that lands on it. Thus, some snow has accumulated in the area around the machine, but it itself remains with a slightly wet exterior. Weather is not an issue. VulGrid is completely self-contained and could operate just as well if it were sitting at the bottom of a lake. It took Vulpie a long time to invent a mathematical solution that could allow the machine to imitate water and its movements in real time. But the orange furred fox solved that challenge over a month ago, and declared VulGrid field ready as soon as it could imitate every conceivable environment.

Before long all of the bleachers are filled with animals, and a military attendee closes the entrance to the chamber. The soldier, a red fox, gives Vulpie a signal that everyone who will be with them has arrived.

"Good afternoon, everyone. It's truly an honor to visit WintersBank and I would like to thank the armed forces for allowing me this opportunity." Vulpie begins. His effeminate voice fills the room full of wolves, amusing many of them, but they show respect to the gay fox. Most of them honor the military code and if Vulpie has been contracted to work for the armed forces, than he is someone to be listened to. Everyone already knows he's a super genius, but this is the first time Vulpie has been in a situation like this. He's dealing with men that are used to working with military contractors. Military contractors who dream up bigger and deadlier guns, but in no way does Vulpie want to make weapons. His product will be something quite different.

"Many fine soldiers have come from this base and I am proud to see a part of my husband's lineage right here in Winters Dale. The arctic wolves have always prized stealth as well as combat. In the War of 2059, white wolves out maneuvered the southern invasion of the Kossdam timber wolves by using superior camouflage. The lives lost in that conflict were so few that the world government awarded Winters Dale's military twice the resources it had already earned for its defense.

During the West Snow Leopard War of 1847, the arctic wolves had already shown their courage for taking the majority of the enemy forces captive instead of killing them. In the midst of the War of 1641, when the world government was just forming, Winters

Dale was crucial to holding the northern lands against threats from every species that resisted. Truly, the heritage of Winters Dale as a city and Winters Dale as a beacon for hope, has inspired much of the world government's continuing honor during military conflicts and is a standard by which all division of the armed forces look to for guidance." Vulpie continues, and licks his lips before looking to Polar and smiling at him.

"I can see the honor of this land in my husband, who comes from a long line of arctic wolves, many of whom served in the armed forces." Polar smiles in embarrassment at being included in Vulpie's speech, but he does appreciate it. "So when I considered demonstrating VulGrid for the military, I thought, what better place than Winters Dale to share an intelligent solution to warfare?" The orange furred fox boy asks and he pauses for a moment when he receives clapping from the audience.

"My hope for VulGrid, is an end to the death and bloodshed caused by full scale wars, and a beginning of selective strikes that will end the battles before they have a chance to begin. The arctic wolves, of all species, can appreciate the value of proper camouflage. Whenever I come up here with Polar, I'll lose him the minute he goes outside! It must be nice to just disappear!" Vulpie notes and the audience chuckles. The white furred wolves take pride in their snowy home and they enjoy the way the gay fox seems to appreciate their matching fur. Polar gets a few glances to see his reaction, but he just watches Vulpie with a proud smile.

"What I am going to share with you today is a tool, not a weapon. I still firmly hold to the belief that Vulpie Industries should never be involved with the production of weapons. So I'll leave the guns and the bombs to you guys." Vulpie says and smirks, holding up his right index finger to make his point. "But you just might have an advantage over the enemy if they are unable to see you..." The statement draws a few surprised looks. Most members of the audience are aware that VulGrid has something to do with magnetic fields, but that's about it.

"It's too bad with all of the technological achievements animal kind has made that we still can't really use force fields on our space ships." Vulpie continues. "That's just a fantasy you see in movies or read about in a book, like cloaking devices, right?" The fox boy asks and then slyly looks around the room. "WRONG..." Vulpie deviously whispers. "Vulpie Industries has found a way... VulGrid is the first piece of machinery ever built that can actually project virtual reality. Going invisible? That's the easy part! How about projecting a false image instead?"

There is disbelief but fascination in the audience and Vulpie looks at a brown furred she-wolf. He takes a step towards her and smiles politely.

"Miss, would you be kind enough lend me your purse?" The fox boy asks, referring to the white leather pocketbook she has.

"Sure, I guess." The woman politely responds and hands it over.

"Thank you." Vulpie respectfully responds and holds it up for everyone to see. "What would you say if I told you that I could make a virtual copy of your pocketbook? With all of its finest details, all of the little cracks and tears, and the coloring imperfections that makes it look so complete and real?"

"I would have said that was impossible." The woman smiles and Vulpie smiles at her choice of words.

"We're going to start off small, ladies and gentlemen. I think that's the best way to demonstrate how multi-functional

VulGrid is." Vulpie explains. "Would you mind if I had VulGrid scan your pocket book?"

"Sure, you can." The woman answers and Vulpie holds the pocket book up to the side of himself. He remains still for a moment and then leans down and hands it back to the she-wolf. Afterwards, he walks over to a small table where his personal V-Screen is. Vulpie picks it up and manipulates it. He accesses the route he assigned for VulGrid and finds the machine communicating as desired.

"Before I send the command to VulGrid I want to assure everyone with us today that it is perfectly safe." Vulpie says as he finishes prepping the device. He looks around the room and shows the animals a clever smile. "What's the point of a billion dollar machine if it causes you harm? VulGrid uses powerful magnetic waves, plus other company secret techniques that allow it to project the visuals you'll enjoy. But don't be afraid of exposure. I can go outside and stand right next to it if anyone doesn't feel comfortable."

"Are you saying there's a danger of radiation?" An old brown wolf inquires. He appears to be a highly decorated colonel.

"There is no danger of radiation, and I'm glad you mentioned it because that's what I'm referring to. When you see what VulGrid can do, you might start to worry about what it does to you. But what it does to living animals, is simply, nothing at all. It's completely safe, but it will fool your eyes one hundred percent." Vulpie explains with a mischievous smirk. "Even though VulGrid is outside, it can project visuals into this room, and well beyond.

"What's the effective range, then?" The colonel inquires.

"Oh... I shouldn't spoil the surprise just yet!" Vulpie teases.

"Two hundred meters? Five hundred meters?" The colonel guesses.

"Easily! But that wouldn't give the boys defending us much to work with... Think bigger, and we'll get back to that question."

VulGrid starts to hum as it cycles into action. The magnetic fields are generated internally in about a second, so it doesn't require a warm up period. The animals listen and shift in their seats in interest. The hum is just barely loud enough for them to hear it from inside the observation chamber. Vulpie aims VulGrid at a spot nearby himself and then sends a request for the machine to project the pocketbook.

"Miss, I think you might have dropped your purse!" Vulpie says and points to the middle of the room where there is a small walkway between the bleachers. Some of the animals in the back row noticed the pocketbook as soon as it appeared, but most of them notice it only after Vulpie's statement. Surprised and amazed sounds fill the room and some of the audience stands so they can look over the ones that are close to the item in question. The white pocketbook sits on the floor as if it has been there the entire time. Its handle seemingly droops from gravity, thus giving it a completely realistic appearance.

"It looks just like it!" The she-wolf says and raises the real pocketbook a bit so the rest of the animals can judge the two. Vulpie types something into his V-Screen and the false purse rises. The audience watches it float over to Vulpie, and all of those that were standing take their seats once more. Vulpie outstretches his left paw and the pocketbook floats right on top of his palm. It seemingly rests there, creating whispers of amazement once again.

"VulGrid projects a physics friendly object, so this happens when I pull my hand back." The fox boy says and drops his left arm, seemingly removing his support for the pocketbook, and it falls. The imitation purse plops onto the cement floor, but doesn't make a sound. "But as you can see, there is no sound. Projecting a magnetic field to distort visuals, and creating perfectly realistic sound effects are two different things entirely. Though it would be nice to have a completely perfect space of virtual reality, Sound carries and dissipates, and speakers are not currently capable of fooling the ear from any distance while also simultaneously generating thousands of sound effects." Vulpie explains and then kicks the image of the pocket book with his left foot and it falls over on its side. "But it will react to stimuli."

"That is incredible, Vulpie." Colonel Worhel says.

"Thank you."

"Are you saying that this thing could imitate tanks and soldiers?"

"As many as you want." Vulpie smiles.

"But do they move?"

"Absolutely. Once VulGrid has observed an object in the real world, it can project an accurate depiction of it. It will see the weight of the tank and how the dirt spreads out from underneath it, and then apply that information to its own projections.

"What about soldiers? How realistic can it make a living animal?" Worhel asks and Vulpie types something into his V-Screen. He smirks when he sends the command to VulGrid and Colonel Worhel appears outside. The audience gasps and they move in their seats while the second Worhel starts walking around.

"How accurate is that?" Vulpie smirks and Worhel watches with an open mouth. The second Worhel is walking around in the snowy test area outside, but is right next to the wall between it and the outside area. Everyone can see the new visitor through the glass and Vulpie types something else in. The second Worhel begins to look at the audience. At first it seemed to be lost, but now it walks near the barrier and peers inside with an emotionless expression. Even though the audience is awestruck, they focus their attention on looking over the second Worhel instead of asking questions.

"VulGrid has several modes that it uses to display behavior. What you're watching now is a script I wrote that tells it to recognize faces. VulGrid is watching from outside and can see all of you wonderful animals, so its projecting our friend to look back at you." Vulpie says.

"This is impossible!" Someone comments. The statement gets everyone's attention.

"Thank you." Vulpie grins, and the audience laughs. Victor and Kimberly watch along with all of the other amazed spectators while Polar happily shares a smile with Vulpie. He knew what his fox husband would be unveiling here today and was sure things would go well. How could it not, when the fox boy discovered a way to project virtual reality. The white furred wolf thinks to himself and wonders whether there truly is no limit to Vulpie's genius.

"That's amazing! How long can your machine imitate a real animal?" One of the audience members inquires. This one is a gray fox, but obviously much more of a better animal than Zorpiv was.

"VulGrid has a battery life of five days if running at full capacity." Vulpie answers. "That has been a key concern to us. We know that in several situations VulGrid will be alone and projecting scenery to confuse the enemy. So without someone to charge it back up, we knew it needed a reliable power supply."

"What else can it imitate?" Worhel asks while watching himself walk around outside.

"Anything it has an opportunity to scan, including vehicles, terrain and even weather." Vulpie smirks.

"Are you actually saying that this machine can project an entirely false landscape?"

"Goody! I'm glad we're to that point now!" Vulpie gleefully responds. "Yep! And I have a few already chosen for all of you to enjoy. But I'll have to lower the range so I won't confuse everyone else at the fort."

"Wait, what?" Another decorated male wolf asks.

"When VulGrid changes everything around you, I plan to keep its range just so all of you can watch it. Otherwise the entire base will disappear and become whatever VulGrid projects."

"So what is the range?" Worhel asks, taking up the other colonel's previous question.

"Well, he asked me about five hundred meters." Vulpie replies while giving a nod to the other colonel. "VulGrid can do just a little bit more. It starts losing its signal at four thousand eight hundred and twenty eight meters." The statement makes Worhel sit back in surprise.

"Three miles? More or less?" The first colonel asks.

"That's right." Vulpie smiles and raises his eyebrows.

"That's impossible. How could it be possible for a machine to send an image that far with such a strong signal?"

"Don't say it isn't so and fret! I haven't even scared you yet!" Vulpie giggles and looks around the room. "Alright everybody? Are we ready to see what VulGrid can really do?"

"Yeah!" Victor cheers and Vulpie smiles over at Polar's father. After the white furred wolf shows his support there is more of a response from the rest of the stunned animals. They realize that what they're seeing today is something that will quickly become the talk of the universe, and start to clap and cheer.

"Yeah? Okay then! Let's take a vote!" Vulpie mischievously announces. "Do we wanna visit a lush rainforest? Or how about the top of an icy mountain? Oooo! Chilly! brr! Or a trip to the desert to get a lemon smoothie at a dig site? Yummy!" The audience starts to get worked up with Vulpie, sharing in his excitement. Polar grins, seeing them react the say way he does every day. The orange furred fox boy brings excitement into his life from morning to evening.

"The desert!" A she-wolf suggests and a man agrees, followed by another woman that interrupts. "The jungle!"

"Two for the desert one for the jungle!" Vulpie enthusiastically counts.

"The ocean." The same wolf colonel that first questioned Vulpie about VulGrid's range suggests and Vulpie quickly points his left index finger at him.

"Ah hah! This guy knows where to look for a weakness! Imitating water in real time is the most difficult thing to do, but VulGrid's up to the challenge!" The fox boy explains and smirks at him. "You're just lucky I haven't had VulGrid scan a shark yet!" Vulpie's teasing makes a great deal of the audience start voting. The room is filled with shouts for the ocean, jungle and the desert until Vulpie counts the jungle ahead of the desert. "Okay, Jungle wins but I've gotta start with the ocean since our friend here wants to see how I can turn an arctic paradise into a day at the beach!" Vulpie teases. Once again the fox boy manipulates his V-Screen and communicates with VulGrid. He sets up the parameters he wants, selecting the ocean scene, and then raises his left paw to share a cautious gesture with all of the viewers.

"Everyone stay in your seats for the entire ride and please do not leave the car!" Vulpie says as if running a ride at an amusement park. And looks around. He sees that all of the animals are fairly intelligent and surely none of them will freak out once he activates the program. At least, none of them will lose it in a bad way. If what Vulpie says is true, they all know they are going to be freaked by the awesome power VulGrid possesses.

Without further ado, the orange furred fox sends his command and VulGrid complies. There is no sound for the transition, and it is indeed a bizarre sight to suddenly see water all around the seated animals. Everything that is real has disappeared except for all of the animals themselves, their clothing and anything that they are holding, such as Vulpie and his V-Screen.

"Please don't move! We're still at fort WintersBank and you could trip on the bleachers if you try to get up." Vulpie advises while everyone gazes about with wide eyes. Even though Polar has seen the miraculous effect of VulGrid already, he is still fascinated by the level of detail in the false ocean water. It is a dark murky blue with a bit of green, the same color one would see off the coast of any temperate continent. Many members of the audience start reaching out to touch the water as it sloshes up against their middle torsos with absolutely no feeling or sound.

"This is incredible..." Colonel Worhel says and looks around in astonishment. He tries to touch what he sees but it is entirely an illusion. It's a deception to the eyes. "Vulpie, are you telling the truth about its range and how long it lasts? Can it really do this for five days at a time?"

"Of course." Vulpie answers and swishes his tail, his orange fur tickling just above the false water.

"For three miles? It can cover three miles with this kind of a distraction for five days at a time?"

"I told you it was a billion dollar piece of equipment. Actually kind of cheap isn't it? I bet you pay more for fighter jets than you would for one of these babies." Vulpie smiles.

"Oh, we'll need more than one. The navy is ready to buy as many as they can as long as I bring them good news." Worhel smiles back.

"If you want three I have them ready to go." Vulpie offers and winks at him.

"I think that would work."

"Sweet." Vulpie grins and plays with his V-Screen again. Suddenly the room changes into a tropical rain forest. Astounded gasps fill the room and all of the animals excitedly observe the new surroundings.

"The detail... How does it project so much detail on the dirt, and little water droplets on the leaves?" Another she-wolf asks while eyeing a false red tipped plant next to her muzzle.

"VulGrid has to scan them. VulGrid is very good at creating new generic objects, but when it comes to plants and such, it needs a base file. So I created an expansive location file for all VulGrids to start with. Most of the plants and wildlife like these little bugs." Vulpie says while watching a dragonfly buzz past his face. "Are from a real rainforest in lower Ceon. I flew the VulGrid prototypes to actual locations, so they could scan real terrain. So everything you see is authentic animal and plant life representations." Vulpie explains while the woman stares in amazement.

"So every VulGrid will be able to do what this one does right from the start?" Worhel inquires.

"That's right. You won't get any dumb ones. Every one that Vulpie Industries ships out will have similar location files. I plan to release updates so you boys can have ever expanding weather and terrain information, and you could make your own database so we could share information."

"I can't think of a single reason why the navy wouldn't want to install as many of these VulGrids as they can. Unless there are any drawbacks?"

"The only drawback is the price. They are a billion a piece and Vulpie Industries can't go lower than that. Half of my company's research goes into the VulGrid project."

"That won't be a problem. Nicely done Vulpie." Worhel says with a very impressed expression.

"What, did you think I couldn't deliver? It's me you're talking to!" Vulpie teases.

"Can you make an army invisible on a real battlefield?"

"It can hide friendly forces, or even make the enemy invisible so they have no clue what is going on and they run their tanks into each other... Whatever you want."

"And this projection technology could be used as a weapon could it not? I assume these powerful magnetic waves could easily be made on a lethal frequency?"

"Yes they could, but not easily. I've designed several little traps inside the VulGrid model so that doesn't happen..." Vulpie says and licks his lips with a serious face while the rest of the audience watches the conversation between the orange fox and brown wolf. "And let me warn the navy, that VulGrid is never to be used as a weapon. If that's going to be a problem, the deal is off. And if we go ahead and I find out down the line that my VulGrids have been re-engineered into weapons, I have ways to destroy them. Arctic.net is everyone's but you know it's really mine... And the navy needs to know that as well."

"I'm sure they will agree, Vulpie." Worhel smiles. He likes how this little fox boy can be just as firm as he is charming.

"No weapons. Period." Vulpie tells Worhel.

"And out of sheer morbid curiosity, exactly how would you stop an organization from altering a VulGrid?" The retired colonel inquires. "The navy has moral principles that would keep them from doing it, but what if one of these machines were captured by the enemy?"

"Simple... Every VulGrid has to communicate with my company as it stands right now. And if they don't... They self-destruct..." Vulpie admits with a wild expression.

"These things are bombs?"

"Not if they check in with my company every four months..." Vulpie answers. "And they're not going to kill anyone when they go boom, but they will definitely stop working..." Worhel looks around the room and smiles at other animals that are watching and Vulpie touches his V-Screen to deactivate the jungle projection. Instantly, they are back inside the room and nothing has changed. VulGrid is still outside and it still appears to be snowing a little bit.

"No disrespect, Vulpie, but a finished product with an implied threat?" Worhel asks.

"It's not a threat. I would say it's a promise but that's overused and doesn't explain how I feel about the matter. So let me elaborate... I've worked long and hard to build Vulpie Industries after what I did with Vulpie.net and I've done enough awful things to last me a lifetime. If one of my machines was used to kill animals, I wouldn't be able to go to work anymore. It would threaten who I am both as a professional and as a converted hacker."

"Fair enough." Worhel answers and nods respectfully. "I will stress it to the navy and the air force when I meet with them next month."

"Please do. VulGrid can help save lives by making killing unnecessary... Using it to do the opposite is something I will never tolerate." Vulpie says, and uses a friendly voice. "But I promise VulGrid will belong completely to the armed forces once purchased. The only requirement is that I can see if any modifications are done to them."

"Understood." Worhel responds and Vulpie looks around at the audience.

"I'm sorry for getting all captain serious just now, but it had to be said!" Vulpie laughs and most of the animals chuckle with him.

Vulpie's Trepidation

Druward feels like a new man. He's on his feet after a week in the hospital but is still bandaged up where he was shot. The skill doctors have astounds him, as he thought if he was ever shot in the gut he would suffer gunshot sepsis and die, but medicine seems to have advanced a long way. Though he isn't aware of it, the doctors used potent immunoresistance drugs to secure his recovery.

He looks to his left and sees Polar coming much earlier than the first time the white furred wolf visited the Ashcrest facility. Vulpie, Polar and Blacktail have all been invited by the GBI to venture towards planet Zeravyn, and Druward is here to see them off. They will be launching in a STF/A-17 Breaker, just like GBI agents who head out on missions beyond planet Sufias. Vulpie and Polar are both wearing casual clothing for the trip. Polar is dressed in a stylish blue t shirt that matches the color of his eyes, and has sturdy gray pants. Vulpie is sporting one of his favorite pink shirts and khaki pants.

"You look like you're going on a vacation." Druward tells the fox boy.

"I don't know how you stand that black trench coat all of the time. It makes you look intimidating but must be really uncomfortable. You could learn a thing or two from us!" Vulpie replies with a smile.

"I suppose I could." Druward says, and Polar raises an eyebrow. The black furred wolf actually looks happy to see them. "Thank you for the V-Screen by the way. Now that I have one I don't know how I ever got along without it."

"Mmhmm! You can fill out forms stored on the device instead of having to write on a clipboard!" Vulpie responds with a friendly voice.

"Load their luggage." Druward orders to a GBI agent nearby. The man looks over Vulpie and Polar, amazed that they really will be leading the trip to Sevrif Industries. The agents received their orders two days ago, but seeing the famous orange furred fox and white furred wolf in person is surreal. Druward looks to Rulef and speaks. "We're bringing additional firepower if needed. There will be four ships leaving with you. Make sure you secure the docking area of the Sevrif when you land and do not allow anything to endanger it. Capture that part of the ship and monitor it."

"Yes sir." Rulef responds.

"Four ships? How many GBI agents are you sending with us?" Vulpie asks.

"Fifty." Druward answers and Polar and Vulpie both blink in surprise.

"That much? Wow!"

"I don't play around when it comes to matters like this..." Druward tells the gay fox and allows a little smirk to creep on his face.

"Thank you. I don't want anything to happen to him." Polar tells the GBI director and Druward looks at the white furred wolf. Most of the nearby agents and Rulef think back to the fight the two had and they wonder what Druward will say to the gay wolf that beat him.

"You're welcome. I promise he'll be safe, but only if you two listen to me. Do not go against my or Rulef's commands. We're sending you out there to commandeer that ship against Sevrif's will and things could get ugly. Don't go anywhere without Blacktail or several GBI agents to guard you. Understood?" Druward informs Polar.

"Understood." Polar responds.

"I just want to talk to him and look over his ship. We don't need to start a war." Vulpie comments.

"They might start one first. Most likely they won't resist when we arrive with overwhelming force. But you never know." The coal furred wolf explains. "We've sent a few agents to planet Zeravyn, and we've had one there for over a year, but he still hasn't been able to find hard evidence of where Sevrif's wealth came from. And the reports he's sent us are... Concerning..."

"What did he say?" Vulpie asks.

"You wouldn't believe me if I told you."

"Sure I would! What did he find out?"

"No, you really would not believe me Vulpie..." Druward repeats and shakes his head. "It's fairly embarrassing for an agent to send the sort of reports he has. I think maybe the high oxygen on Zeravyn has gotten to his brain."

"Just tell me. I want to know before we leave." The fox boy stresses. Druward looks to Polar and can tell that the white furred wolf wants to know as well. The GBI director then glances at Rulef, and finally back to the fox boy and snow wolf.

"The man has sent messages claiming that he was visited by the goddesses... Goddess Cyrilla, Sherrie and Khalan..." Druward explains and everyone nearby is confused at the answer.

"What?" Polar asks and squints.

"I told you he might have lost it. He's had a long stable career but I was planning on having him replaced." Druward elaborates.

"You mean this guy says the actual goddesses are on planet Zeravyn?" Rulef inquires. Even the Blacktail commander is shocked.

"That's right. Well, actually he said they appeared there first but now have ended up on... I'm sure you can guess where they are now..."

"That's insane. That's completely insane." Rulef thinks out loud but Vulpie stares at Druward and contemplates the possibility.

"I don't think you are going to run into goddesses out there. Just stay alert. And Vulpie..." Druward says and gives the fox boy a concerned look. "Don't try to be a hero, okay? Let the GBI do its job." Vulpie is surprised at the statement and he smiles at the GBI director thankfully. "Sevrif may be the leader of a deep space crime ring, or possibly a terrorist. Don't give him the benefit of the doubt."

"I'll be careful." Vulpie promises. Polar can't believe Druward is being so kind. Even more amazing is the fact that the black furred wolf is not faking his concern. He's not the kind of man that holds back. When he says something he means it.

"There's something else you need to know." Druward says and steps aside when an agent comes near him with a hand truck, carrying equipment for the trip. "Someone working at the CTGD leaked what they knew about our friend, Ivo Lorcan. The news got out onto the internet long enough for it to get some attention. But the strange thing is, Ivo died the next day."

"He's dead? How?" Vulpie inquires with wide blue eyes.

"Howlstead said all of his inner parts stopped responding, and his organic pieces are breaking down, the same way Chris Cefil's did. He just died."

"Right after the news got out?"

"Yes."

"That's no accident..." Vulpie whispers.

"Do you have that device with you that you used to read Ivo's body temperature?" The GBI director asks.

"Yeah. I brought a newer model." The fox boy answers.

"If I were you I'd take a look at Sevrif... That's just a suggestion."

"I definitely will."

"Alright then. You'll dock with a military carrier and that ship will fly you to Zeravyn by nightfall."

"I've had longer plane trips." Polar pleasantly muses.

"Yeah, it's pretty quick." Druward comments. "I'll monitor the situation from headquarters." The coal furred wolf looks to Rulef. "The agents will follow their standard chain of command, but I've given them instructions to take orders from you as well, second only to Rotick. "If there's an emergency don't hesitate to commandeer more agents."

"Yes sir." Rulef responds and Druward sends his attention to Polar and Vulpie.

"If your investigations takes you to Zeravyn you should know that the oxygen in the atmosphere is slightly higher than Sufias. Some animals are allergic to that kind of condition. Are you sensitive to that kind of environment?"

"Winters Dale has a pretty high elevation, so it won't be a problem for me." Polar answers.

"I don't think it'll bother me either." Vulpie replies.

"Alright then. Launch will commence in fifteen minutes. The breaker will take you to the SWG "Endeavor," the military's quickest deep space vessel. It will have you to the Sevrif and Zeravyn in two hours. When you arrive the breaker will launch from the Endeavor and shuttle you back and forth to the Sevrif." Druward explains. "I'm sure I don't need to say this, but don't sleep on the Sevrif even though there are fancy hotels inside the ship. If Sevrif offers you accommodations decline them respectfully and go back to the Endeavor."

"You got it." Vulpie smiles.

"Good luck." The GBI director says and steps aside. Several GBI agents come over to assist the group and Rulef, Polar and Vulpie follow them. The agents lead them to an entrance on the side of the ship. The white docking bay of the Ashcrest launch pad dips down on the edges a slight bit where the breakers have an access port. Thirteen animals enter the STF/A-17 Breaker, all eight members of Blacktail that are taking the trip and three GBI agents.

All of them are wolves and Vulpie feels a little inadequate. Being the only little fox makes him feel out of place around so many strong men, but he does feel safer. There are rows of seats against the left side of the interior chamber and the right side, with an additional two rows in the middle sitting back to back. Polar chooses one of the middle seats, on the left side that faces the seats on the left wall of the vessel and Vulpie takes one to his right.

"I'm actually kind of excited. Blasting off into deep space on an important mission!" Polar tells Vulpie with a playful smile.

"Yeah like the time we flew into the Lupus Canis Mountains!" Vulpie smiles back. "With my robots looking after everything so we could have a little adventure."

"Oh yeah..." Polar says with a smirk while he remembers the event. "Except this time I'm not afraid for my life!"

"Were you really that scared? You seemed pretty steady the whole time." Vulpie replies.

"You knew I was terrified!" Polar laughs and lowers his voice when some of the seats are taken around them. Mechanical and hissing noises fill the chamber as the breaker is prepared for launch. "You brought up the ten million dollars that Vargas promised me if I killed you. Don't even act like you weren't screwing with me. I know you better."

"You got me. I was screwing with ya." Vulpie responds and bites his lip. "But we still had fun didn't we?"

"Well chasing you down and pounding you was pretty delicious." Polar whispers.

"While my hollow wolves watched..." Vulpie whispers back.

"Yes, I remember that Vulpie." Polar smirks and watches Vulpie fidget. The orange furred fox looks like he's trying to keep his usual playful demeanor up but something is bothering him. The white furred wolf notices how his tail twitches a little bit and he squints every now and then. "Hey... Relax..." Polar says and leans to his right to nudge Vulpie with his head. Vulpie gladly nudges back, but they keep the intimacy to a minimum when the other wolves start averting their eyes. Polar usually makes a point not to overdo public affection because he knows it annoys him when he sees two animals making out in an exhibitionist manner. The ship shakes as a few of the docking mechanisms are released and one of the agents shuts the door to the ship. Vulpie tenses up and tries to relax but he can't. Polar thinks about what the fox boy must be thinking and comes to a quick conclusion. "You're really worried aren't you?" Polar asks.

"Yeah." Vulpie admits and looks to Polar with a frightened expression. "I just have a feeling... It's like, here we go again, you know?"

"With Vulpie.net?" Polar whispers.

"You always know what I'm thinking." Vulpie affectionately answers.

"Well it could only be one thing that has you this worked up." The white furred wolf responds.

"I know it's there..."

"But how could it be? Evil Vulpie is still locked up in the Sufias Heritage Museum."

"That robot is." Vulpie quietly replies.

"I have no idea where those Ivo and Cefil guys came from, but maybe it's not Vulpie.net. " Polar responds. "Maybe this Sevrif person really is behind it."

"Could be... I'm just really worried..."

"Whatever we find, we'll face it together." Polar promises.

"That's kind of what I'm concerned about. Maybe I should be doing this by myself."

"Let you go into deep space towards a mysterious ship by yourself? After the association of fox rights tried to have you killed? You're crazy if you think I'd let you."

"Nathan and Karl. The AFR's not that bad actually now that they're gone." Vulpie responds.

"Well whatever. You don't have my permission to go it alone." Polar informs the fox boy with a smirk.

"Your permission huh?" Vulpie grins.

"That's right. I own you, remember?"

"Yes you do..." Vulpie breathes, thinking about the last time they made beautiful love together. He plays on Polar's commanding look and puts his left paw on the white furred wolf's leg with a submissive expression. Polar doesn't need to say anything. The stare he returns indicates his approval of Vulpie's worship. The breaker rumbles as all of its landing mechanisms retract and pull up into the ship. The engine comes on and fills the chamber with a loud hum.

"Takeoff in sixty seconds! Everyone lock down your gear and take your seats." Rulef orders as he walks to the front of the ship. A specially trained GBI agent takes the pilot chair and Rulef locks himself into the passenger seat. The pilot checks all of the gauges to make sure everything is within acceptable ranges even though the GBI has done a pre-flight.

Everyone is quiet until the launch, and the ship suddenly lurches. It blasts off from the Ashcrest Facility near Evenwater Village with a loud air sucking whoosh, that is followed by the other three STF/A-17s in succession. The tactical ships rocket up through the sky and burn as they pass through the atmosphere. All of the animals brace in their chairs against the heavy G forces. Exiting planet Sufias requires the GBI pilot to hold onto the flight control stick for some time, but as soon as they go into the great beyond, all of the stresses disappear and they feel zero gravity.

When this happens, the pilot activates the ship's artificial gravity drive which is even louder than the engines. The gravity drive roars with a wind like gushing sound, but dissipates over the next few minutes after warming up. The artificial gravity itself is perfect, as is the case with most Sufias Space Administration certified space ships. In years past the process of going into space was quite laborious but as it stands now, if a ship is capable of space travel, it can at least handle launches and planet re-entries with ease.

The pilot engages the breaker's fastest speed and it starts roaring forward even quicker. The four STF/A-17s come up on the Endeavor very fast, as the large ship is meeting them in orbit. Vulpie and Polar both lean out from their chairs a little so they can see the gigantic vessel they are coming up on. It's difficult to get a full view of it, but it appears to have a long rectangular design, with command decks at the top of the structure. As they get close, rows of windows and beacon lights can be seen.

The Endeavor is a solid gray vessel. It has one very large engine at the rear of the ship with supplemental drives to the right and the left. They round off next to the main engine and provide the steering capabilities the ship requires. Its hull is very thick. Without a doubt, the Endeavor is designed as a warship, because it is armed from back to front with gigantic guns. There are smaller guns as well, for fending off quicker threats such as the enemy equivalent of the STF/A-17s, but Polar doubts anything has taken down a ship like the Endeavor before. He remembers being taught about the overwhelmingly efficient ships the Sufias world government uses and the fact that there is little resistance to them. A fuzzy voice crackles into the ship as they are hailed by the Endeavor and the pilot looks over the information he has on the computer.

"Approaching vessels please state your registration and cargo." The military ship orders.

"Breaker 74, registration 294233, cargo is Vulpie Vivixen, Polar Arctic and Blacktail support, over."

"Received breaker 74, proceed to docking bay L7"

"Orders confirmed. Over and out." The pilot says and checks the computer's suggestion for a route to the L7 docking bay. He steers the breaker towards the open area to the back right of the Endeavor where there is a space for a ship the size of a STF/A-17. The pilot aims the ship inside the opening and then activates magnetic landing gear to find the steel interior while the outer doors close behind. When the chamber is shut, it re-pressurizes for about thirty seconds until it is safe to open the interior doors.

But even the large ship sized interior doors don't open to the entirety of the Endeavor, as it wouldn't do to jeopardize the crew if an enemy vessel attacked the launching bays. Instead, there is a smaller door the slides open to the bottom right of the bay chamber, and that leads into a long hallway. A security attendant steps inside the bay, signaling the all clear for the STF/A-17 to open its doors as well.

Everyone gets out of their seats inside the breaker and they gather their belongings. Polar and Vulpie wait a bit to let the GBI agents and most of Blacktail leave the ship first so they don't get in the way. Probably all of the GBI members have been to the Endeavor before, as they are a paw selected group of agents that handle inter space missions. And all of the Blacktail mercenaries seem right at home as well. Vulpie walks in front of Polar and Polar puts his big paws on the fox boy's shoulders affectionately. He guides his husband out of the ship and the one agent left on the ship attends to it.

"We need to get them to their room as soon as possible." Rulef says to the docking bay attendant, gesturing towards Polar and Vulpie in the distance.

"The captain thinks so as well. He'd rather them not wander around the ship during the flight." The attendant wolf responds. "Follow me." The attendant leaves the chamber and the GBI agents and Blacktail follow him. Deepwolf makes sure to walk behind Polar and Vulpie in the rare chance that there might be a disgruntled soldier lurking somewhere on the vessel. The Endeavor is a tightly run ship, but he isn't about to take any chances. Vulpie pays him very well and he would like it to stay that way.

The group walks down the long and well lit docking bay corridor. It's ceiling is rather high, and it looks as though the design follows the overall structure of the large ship. Though the hallway has only a short width, the area is built into one section of the ship where ships can dock at the "L Level," where they have docked their breaker. The other STF/A-17s are most likely docked on nearby spaces, and Rulef expects to see other GBI agents joining them soon.

The Blacktail commander's assumption is proven correct when he looks back and sees one of the doors on the long hallway allowing several agents to follow behind them. Rulef observes that if the Endeavor follows the alphabet, it must house an enormous number of bays, and maintenance ports.

It takes the group about a minute and a half to transverse the very long corridor. On the left there is a stunning view of the exterior of the ship and the stars beyond, courtesy of a multi layered ceramic glass window. The door that grants access to the inner areas of the Endeavor is not very grand. It's just another sliding entranceway that moves when they approach it.

The group walks into the main chamber of the Endeavor and its sight is fairly more impressive than the corridor. The Endeavor is a planet class star ship, meaning that on top of its impressive speed, it can house enough animals and vessels to attend to a planet wide crisis. To say the least, the sight of the half mile wide and three mile long interior is a jaw dropping experience. There are hundreds of animals going here and there, either members of the armed forces or civilians on special assignments.

"Oh wow..." Polar whispers and his blue eyes widen.

"Really cool!" Vulpie smiles and looks around with similar excitement.

"I served on a ship this size once. My jaw was on the floor too the first time I walked in." Deepwolf comments from behind the white furred wolf and orange furred fox.

"So this is where all of my taxes have been going to over the years..." Polar smirks.

"I should have hijacked this baby six years ago!" Vulpie teases, referring to the earlier conversation he and Polar had about their experience in the Lupus Canis Mountains.

"I don't think even your robots could have taken a ship like this."

"Would have been fun to find out." Vulpie slyly answers while looking about.

"And remember, the Sevrif is supposed to be even bigger." Polar notes.

"Yeah. Really seems possible for one guy to pull that off, huh?" Vulpie snorts and Polar nods in agreement even though he's behind Vulpie and his husband can't see him. Vulpie's blue eyes suddenly lurch to the left when he notices something very familiar. About a few hundred feet away, there is a gigantic thirteen foot wolf lifting a very heavy crate. Except it's not a wolf at all. It's a Delanson anti-tank robot, and there are three of them being directed to load and unload different parts of a large treaded vehicle.

"Hey look Polar! It's Mr. Big Teeth!" Vulpie gleefully declares while pointing and the white furred wolf laughs in surprise.

"Yeah! They sure are, aren't they?"

"They need some flare! No orange paint? Aw! Jeez they're so BORING with just plain old gray!"

"Whatever happened to that one that you had?" Polar asks his fox husband.

"Howlstead told me that the GBI sent it back to Delanson. Hey! Maybe one of them is my old robot!" Vulpie suggests.

"Those things are scary... Ugh, I have to admit, Vulpie. I never liked it very much." Polar says while the group continues to transverse the interior of the Endeavor. The three anti-tank robots grow smaller and smaller as they pass them by, but even at a distance they are easy to see.

"If you think those are impressive just wait until you see a Mange Devastator." Deepwolf comments and Vulpie perks up his left ear. Polar still has his paws on the orange furred fox's shoulders, pushing him along.

"Mange? Sounds yucky!" Vulpie responds.

"They're full scale assault mechs and they call them that because the first one they built was used hundreds of times without tanks being able to stop it. It lost all of its paint and had fucking holes and shit in it before it finally fell to pieces. Those babies are the future!" Deepwolf chortles.

"I bet Mr. Big tooth would still give it a run for its money! Especially in a dance contest! At least Mr. tooth could be taught a little bit of humor!"

"What's the difference between a steak and great sex?" Polar asks, referring to a joke that they both remember.

"They're both rare!" Vulpie giggles and the white furred wolf laughs with him. A tram goes rushing by, carrying passengers, driving between crates and equipment. There are many different species of animals around, and those that see Blacktail leading Polar and Vulpie, as well as a group of fifty GBI agents naturally stare or forget what they are doing.

Rulef notices and is glad when the attendant sent by the ship's captain leads them to the right into a different section. They enter a curved hallway that then straightens back to the left in the direction of the main chamber. There are rows of rooms for animals to use while staying on the vessel and Rulef turns back to motion towards Deepwolf. He acts as though he is cutting his own throat with his right paw, signaling that Deepwolf needs to halt the GBI agents where they are. Vulpie and Polar's quarters are up ahead, and Rulef prefers for the exact room number to be a secret rather than let fifty animals know for sure... GBI agents or not.

Polar sees what Rulef does, but Vulpie doesn't notice, being too short and preoccupied to see the gesture in time. The white furred wolf is very happy that the commander of the Blacktail mercenaries is so good at what he does. Keeping their room number a secret is not something Polar would have thought of, on an army ship, but Rulef clearly doesn't trust anyone but himself and his own men. And if he has to work with the GBI, he's going to use them in an intelligent manner, not leave them with wide open opportunities to question their loyalty.

"This is it." The attendant says and Rulef nods when the man passes over a set of keys for the room. They are both electronic and Vulpie wonders what Rulef is doing when he stands in front of him while looking back. He makes sure that Deepwolf has directed the men back a little and then hands a key card down to Vulpie. The fox boy accepts and Rulef gives the other to Polar.

"The captain wants both of you to stay in your room while you're on the ship. There are just too many animals serving on the Endeavor for him to guarantee complete safety." Rulef tells the orange furred fox and white furred wolf.

"I think that's a good idea." Polar responds.

"How are we going to get food or something to drink besides water?" Vulpie asks.

"Knock on the door and ask one of us to do it for you." Rulef answers, referring to Blacktail.

"Alright." Vulpie agrees and looks back and up at Polar.

"How long until we get there?" Polar asks.

"Should be about two hours. They just took off towards Zeravyn."

"Didn't feel a thing." The white furred wolf observes. "Must have stealth runners I guess."

"They do." Rulef responds and nods. "Some of us will bring your luggage in a few minutes and I'll be back when we're ready to board the Sevrif."

"Thanks Rulef." Vulpie says and Polar gently directs his husband inside. Rulef walks off and Polar shuts the door behind him. He locks it and the white furred wolf and orange furred fox look over the room. It's not much, but it doesn't need to be a palace. They're going to spend their time on the Endeavor like normal crew members, and the room is rather bland. It's an eggshell white with a small refrigerator, a sink, and a small bathroom. There is only one bed, but it looks just big enough for both of them.

"Well!" Vulpie says and runs over to the bed. He leaps onto it and rolls over playfully. "Just WHAT are we gonna DO for the next two hours?" The fox boy asks with a delicious grin.

"Nothing until they bring in our luggage." Polar chuckles and takes off his shoes. Vulpie does the same and kicks his sneakers onto the ground. Polar walks around a little bit, eying the bland surroundings and Vulpie stretches out on the bed. Polar walks over and takes a seat on the bed next to Vulpie and lies down for a little bit as well. They wait for about ten minutes until someone knocks on their door.

Polar gets up and walks over to it. He unlocks the door and sees one of the Blacktail wolves he and Vulpie stay with on a daily basis.

"Thanks." Polar says and the man hands over their belongings. Polar takes them and then slowly shuts the door again.

He locks it afterwards and rolls his suitcase and Vulpie's suitcase over towards the sink, a little ways from the bed.

"Going new places! Seeing new faces!" Vulpie says while swishing his tail on the bed.

"I can't imagine what I'd be doing if I never said hi to you in the bar that night." Polar responds with a smirk, referring to the first time they met.

"Probably rich and famous and on your way to becoming president!" Vulpie playfully answers.

"Yeah. Try bitter and depressed..." Polar responds with a thankful expression. Vulpie reads the satisfaction on his wolf husband's face.

"I don't think so."

"I do. God I would have been nobody if you hadn't come along and got me into trouble!" Polar grins.

"I'm still getting you into trouble! Just look where we are! On a deep space army mother ship, going to start a fight on an even bigger ship, with a whole bunch of GBI agents backing us up! I'm aiming higher and higher!"

"I'm having the time of my life..." Polar says and shakes his head with absolutely no regret. "I was a goddamn finance manager at a software company and look at me now..."

"Vice president of your own company!" Vulpie adds.

"Of your company..." Polar corrects and walks around a bit more before leaning on the wall nearby the bed and looking down at the fox boy. "I still want to have children. We've been so busy with Vulpie Industries, but we still should do it. The science exists right now. Other gay animals are using the procedure to have it done."

"I know. And I want to do it too... But..." Vulpie says and thinks for a moment. "I have a feeling that I can't settle down just yet. There's just too much going on here for us to turn our attention on raising our little fox wolf hybrids."

"I want tons of little fox wolf hybrids." Polar declares with amusement.

"I promise we'll do it. And when we do, I'll stay at home with our babies and raise them. But I can't leave Vulpie Industries now." Vulpie responds.

"You can't leave your company. I was thinking that I'd be the one to stay home with them." Polar replies.

"While I go out and party every day? Polar, I can't ask you to do that." Vulpie says with love.

"You wouldn't be partying!" Polar laughs. "You would just go to work like always while I take care of the family.

"But you know me..." Vulpie says with a small voice. "If I don't have you around to keep me in line, I'll get out of control... I'll be at the top of the tower thinking, HEY! Why not spy on some more animals for old time's sake! And then you won't be there to tell me that I shouldn't."

"I wasn't there any of the times you've already done that." Polar reminds Vulpie with a sly look. "You hid it from me pretty well I'd say."

"I guess so." Vulpie admits with a halfway innocent and half naughty look.

"But you don't give yourself enough credit, Vulpie. I know you spied on those people for a reason. Hell, my brother would still be talking to a robot every day if you didn't sneak into his emails and figure out something was wrong."

"I've been looking up tons of gay porn too. Since we're being honest." Vulpie says and winks.

"Of course." Polar smirks in response. "Find any good stuff?"

"Meh. Not really. No men as sexy as you..." Vulpie confesses and bites his lip.

"So I'm guessing you want me to fuck you, right? Since you keep dropping hints as often as possible." Polar taunts.

"Oh how romantic..." Vulpie pouts. "Don't you want to?"

"Maybe I have a headache. Or I'm too tense to do it right now." Polar teases.

"I'll fix that problem! Let me play with your prostate!" The fox boy offers. "You want me to give you a massage or do you? My big wolfy?"

"Not really in the mood..."

"Then come lie down and I'll ride that wolf cock! How about that?"

"I'm just playing with you. I'll give you a pounding..." Polar promises with a big smile.

"Slam me hard! I'm just so confused after seeing all of those handsome white wolves up in Winters Dale! I forgot which one I belong to!" Vulpie grins. Polar stops leaning on the wall and puts his right paw out so he can turn around and get onto the bed with Vulpie. Vulpie crawls to his right and Polar leans back, with his feet still on the floor in front of the bed. The white furred wolf pulls his arms behind his head and smiles to his right at the orange furred fox.

"Well, get to it. Suck me until I tell you to stop." Polar orders.

"Yes sir!" Vulpie grins and leans over the white furred wolf's crotch. The fox boy goes to undoing and unzipping the wolf's pants and has them down in no time. Polar moves a bit, helping his husband, and Vulpie has the white furred wolf's underwear down as well. Polar kicks his pants and underwear away, and happily watches Vulpie grab his half erect penis with his little right paw. Vulpie bends forward and opens his mouth. He slurps his lips around the snow wolf's fat cock, making Polar groan in satisfaction.

"Take your time. We've got two hours now..." Polar instructs and Vulpie makes a cute noise of approval while he starts sucking. The white furred wolf closes his eyes and relaxes. Vulpie starts off slowly, bobbing his head up and down and fondling the wolf's big testicles with his little fingers. Vulpie's spit runs down Polar's hard penis, making it feel oh so good for his husband. "Good boy..." Polar breathes. "Don't forget to deep throat it..."

Sevrif

Polar and Vulpie's ship launches around one in the afternoon, though in deep space day and night is difficult to judge. Their breaker rockets out towards a massive ship in front of the SWG Endeavor. The Sevrif is indeed larger than the Endeavor, but it doesn't seem to be by much. Instead of a long sleek design, the all black starship favors a giant rounded build over a sharp one. Upon first glance it is fairly obvious that the Sevrif is a commercial vessel.

Vulpie wiggles in his seat, rocking back and forth while he stretches to see it. Deepwolf is sitting to his right so his view is blocked by the muscular gray wolf. Polar doesn't have a problem, and sends his handsome blue eyes over the Vessel. Deepwolf notices Vulpie straining to get a view and courteously leans back for his little boss.

"Wow, you can barely see it out there with that black exterior." Vulpie observes. Zeravyn is below the Sevrif as they approach the ship. The planet has a bright white atmosphere because of its naturally cloudy weather. It's difficult to see any major landmarks from space, just a few glimpses of a mountain peak here and there.

"There's that ship again." The GBI pilot comments and Rulef moves his head towards the direction indicated. A small white spacecraft, a bit smaller than a Breaker, is launching from the Sevrif. It silently engages its thrusters and rockets away towards the planet below.

"I see it." Rulef responds while focusing on the space craft. It burns while passing through the atmosphere and then disappears into the clouds. "Looks like the same size and description Captain Ristau gave us, Rulef replies, referring to the commander of the Endeavor. Ristau is a brown fox, and has years of experience leading military vessels. Rulef feels confident that the captain will send help if something unpleasant were to develop on the Sevrif. "I wouldn't be surprised if it was Sevrif's personal transport. He probably fled the ship as soon as he detected us."

"Should I message the other three breakers to follow it?" The pilot asks.

"Not yet. Let's secure the Sevrif first." Rulef answers. The four STF/A-17s move in an arrowhead formation as they approach the Sevrif, with Polar and Vulpie's ship at the front left of the group. The Sevrif hails the breakers quickly.

"*Incoming vessels please state your registration, cargo and destination.*" Someone from the Sevrif orders.

"Registration 423242." The pilot responds and slows the STF/A-17 near the front of the Sevrif.

"*That number is not in our system. I will have to ask you to halt your present course.*"

"The registration is directly from the SWG Endeavor. Check your communication feed again." The GBI pilot replies.

"*We have received the Endeavor's communication but we do not accept blanket requests to enter the Sevrif without further explanation.*" The voice responds and another party enters in the conversation.

"*This is Captain Ristau of the SWG Endeavor. You will open your doors to the GBI operatives that wish to board your ship. Under direct command of the governmental bureau of investigations, you must comply.*" Ristau's voice is very firm, and Vulpie smiles at hearing another fox bark orders for once.

"*This is not planet Sufias. Are you really intending to fire upon a civilian vessel for not immediately jeopardizing its crew?*"

"There is no jeopardy facing the Sevrif. You know very well that the Sufias World Government holds jurisdiction over this region of space and well beyond." Captain Ristau responds, and static enters the conversation once again as yet another party joins the communication feed.

"This is Sevrif Vosuf. I apologize for the confusion regarding your request Captain Ristau. We will receive your agents immediately."

"There you are..." Vulpie whispers while focusing with his fox ears. He listens to the tone of Sevrif's voice and can already discern intelligence and a methodical personality.

"We appreciate your compliance. Thank you Mr. Vosuf." Captain Ristau replies and leaves the conversation.

"Breaker 74 please mind the satellite equipment in your area and proceed to docking bay 14." The Sevrif's flight controller requests, apparently having received new instructions from Sevrif himself.

"Confirmed. Over and out." The GBI pilot responds while noticing that there are quite a few antennas in the area around the docking bay. He engages the thrusters and directs the ship towards the 14 location suggested by his computer screen. "I can't believe they tried to turn the GBI away." The pilot says to Rulef while steering.

"It surprises me too." Rulef snorts. "You'd think they would avoid being harassed by the government. Druward is going to be on their asses like Polar on Vulpie." The Blacktail commander responds, making the pilot laugh loudly, and the amusement spreads through the ship. Vulpie just barely heard what Rulef said and looks around with a grin.

"What's that?"

"Nothing." Rulef says from the front of the ship.

"Good analogy." Deepwolf smirks.

"You guys are mean." The fox boy says with a wry expression. The ship is directed into the 14 docking bay and the pilot engages its magnetic landing gear. Everyone is a bit on edge, even with backup from the Endeavor. They are, after all, landing on a foreign spaceship under less than pleasant circumstances. It would have been great for the Sevrif to just open its doors to the GBI, but that would have been an unlikely development. If they refused to grant entry at first, even with the Endeavor's initial order, there's no way they would have simply had a change of heart.

Polar thinks about these things while the ship locks onto the interior of the Sevrif and the exterior doors shut behind the ship. Their breaker has landed in a bay similar to the ones found on the Endeavor, but when the smaller interior door opens and an attendant comes into the bay, he doesn't appear quite as inviting. He's a black furred wolf and looks positively unhappy at what he's dealing with. He signals that it's okay to exit the breaker, but the GBI pilot runs a scan on the exterior atmosphere regardless. Oxygen levels appear satisfactory and there is no sign of potential contaminants, so he opens engages the outer doors.

The GBI agents inside the ship gladly start to exit, followed by a few enthusiastic members of Blacktail. They enjoy the opportunity to use their weapons as bargaining chips. If there ever was a time to appear threatening, this is it. No one knows what to expect once they enter the main interior of the Sevrif.

Polar stands up along with everyone else, and turns, watching the others around him leave the ship. He almost jumps out of his shoes when he feels someone touching his butt, but quickly recognizes the sensation of Vulpie's little claws. He holds still so he won't draw attention and Vulpie gropes him.

"The hell are you doing?" Polar growls back at the orange furred fox with a shocked grin.

"Watch out for this in there, okay?" Vulpie asks with a funny face and squeezes the white furred wolf's ass a little more before letting go. Polar considers reprimanding his cute husband for embarrassing him, as some of the other wolves notice, but he sees that the fox boy has definitely made his point. There's no way Polar could ignore being grabbed, and the real goal was to affectionately warn Polar that he too could be in danger.

"Come on." Polar smiles and sends back his left paw. Vulpie takes it with his little right paw and follows his husband's lead. Polar directs Vulpie off of the ship and in the middle of the intense wolves, all of them looking around for potential threats. Rulef is already speaking with the attendant by the time the white furred wolf and orange furred fox walk off of the ships' exit ramp.

"Is that Vulpie Vivixen?" The black wolf attendant asks.

"Yes. He would like to speak with the owner of this ship, and so would the GBI." Rulef answers.

"Follow me." The man snorts in irritation. Even though he doesn't know Rulef, he isn't appreciative of the lack of respect. Rulef doesn't feel that they are handling the situation badly. Within a matter of moments, all but three of the wolf men leave the docking bay and enter the main interior of the Sevrif. This time three GBI agents stay behind with the ship, as is common procedure in potentially adverse situations.

Polar takes a deep breath of the space vessel's atmosphere. The air smells very fresh, like the sort you would find on top of a mountain, but regulates down to a normal taste as one goes through the white chamber leading into the rest of the Sevrif. The white chamber is the docking station, one of many, and only needs to be about twelve feet wide. It's empty of ship personnel, monitored by engineers just inside the Sevrif around the entrance. The Sevrif staff that is trained to work the airlocks are behind gray chambers along the wall near the entrance. They don't look at visitors much, as they can see them on cameras in the airlocks. Once inside the Sevrif, an animal's senses are bombarded by utterly unique flavors both of sight, smell and feeling. The circulated air conditioning flows through the ship at a brisk pace, maintaining a very comfortable experience.

The sounds of the Sevrif at the docking bay are quite jovial. It's a civilian docking bay, but Vulpie didn't expect to see what looks like a mall just inside the ship. As a matter of fact, there are shops of all sorts, everywhere. Polar blinks and looks around in surprise as well. It's like walking straight into an amusement park where unique memorabilia can be spotted in every direction. There are cookie shops, sandwich shops, bakeries, clothing stores, general retail stores and more.

"Didn't know we were visiting an amusement park today!" Vulpie giggles.

"I know, right?" Polar laughs as well and pats the fox boy on the shoulder.

"Wanna buy some kitten sticks?" A snow furred cat quickly asks and Vulpie jumps at how close he comes. "Whoa!" Vulpie yelps and recoils a little.

"Back the fuck up!" One of the Blacktail wolves growls while quickly pushing the odd cat backwards. Polar is glad that the mercenary saw him coming and so is Rulef. He seems pleased at his man's performance as well as irritated by the development. The cat is a little odd, wearing red jeans and a white t shirt with "Kittens" written across it.

"Kitten sticks?" Rulef asks with an unflattering voice while simultaneously eyeing the bucket that the feline has under his left arm. The cat reaches inside with his right paw and retrieves some candied treats, holding them up for display. They are white with pink speckles throughout their sugary texture.

"Ninety nine cent!" The man declares and shows them off. "Not right now, but thanks!" Vulpie says with a "nod and grin" expression. The orange furred fox perks up as he sees a gray wolf approaching them, wearing a dark green suit.

"My apologies, gentlemen. Mr. Sevrif is on another deck but he would be happy to meet with you." The courteous attendant declares. "My name is Sapher, and I handle Sevrif's responsibilities in his absence."

"That's very good. We need to meet with him as soon as possible." Rulef replies without hesitation. Vulpie watches him continue to take charge and has no intention of getting in the gray furred wolf's way. The fox boy is aware that this is a time for him to follow, at least until he and Polar are in a relatively safe place. Sapher shifts on his feet in response to Rulef's aggression but remains polite.

"Mr. Vosuf is preoccupied, but he will be with us very soon. There are matters on the upper decks that require his attention. There is a pressure leak and if not attended to, it could endanger animals on the ship."

"We certainly can't have that." Rulef responds and looks to his left as some wolves walk by.

"Follow me." Sapher replies and glances at the full complement of animals that have finally gathered into Vulpie's group. Seven GBI agents join the Blacktail contingent and in the distance agent Rotick appears to be directing the other forty three. Two of them are giving a quick interrogation to the cat that tried peddling his treats to Vulpie.

Sapher heads off to the right, leading Polar and Vulpie's group into a wide corridor. The hallway has new age bathrooms with neon blue designs to the left and retail shops adorned with neon white signs to the right. They walk a ways, and come to a very interesting part of the ship, a short sky bridge. Part of the hallway floor is transparent, drawing eyes downwards to the open space beneath the ship and Planet Zeravyn below. It is a very cool spectacle, something obviously designed to engage visitors on this lower deck of the ship. The group goes down the full length of the corridor and are greeted with two very large doors that open automatically.

"This way." Sapher says and gestures straight ahead as they walk into another corridor. The gray furred wolf leads them into a moderately sized room ahead, where Sevrif is waiting for them. Vulpie thinks he sees a red fox when going in, but as he steps to the left and gets a better look, he observes something quite different. The man waiting on them has his arms clasped behind him, and has the colors of a red fox... But the body of a wolf. He is quite large and slender, and sets his brown eyes on Vulpie.

"Mr. Sevrif, these are the GBI agents that wished to speak with you... And Vulpie..." Sapher introduces and Sevrif takes his brown eyes off Vulpie to put them on Rulef.

"Welcome..." Sevrif says with an unimpressed voice. "Such a spectacle is hardly necessary. I'm glad to finally meet Mr. Vivixen."

"I'm sure you are, but the GBI has decided to inspect your ship. Do you think you could have your employees comply?" Rulef asks.

"Of course." Sevrif answers and looks to his left at Sapher who nods, signaling that he will go spread the word. The gray furred wolf leaves the room and Sevrif looks over the seven GBI agents, and eight Blacktail mercenaries. "So what's the reason for all of this? Do you think you've brought enough guns?"

"There's a very good reason." Rulef answers while Vulpie whispers up to Polar.

"What kind of animal is he? Is he a wolf?" The fox boy asks.

"He's a maned wolf. They're very rare." Polar whispers in response.

"Ohhhh…" Vulpie answers and licks his lips.

"They call us red foxes on stilts, but we're hardly vulpine." Sevrif says, and both Polar and Vulpie's blue eyes widen.

"I can certainly see why!" Vulpie answers with a coy smile. "But you do seem to have fox ears!"

"Oh, I get that all the time." Sevrif responds with a patronizing voice. "Your company is much larger than mine, Vulpie. And your products out sell Sevrif Industries two to one, so is barging onto my ship really necessary? I find it rude if not threatening."

"Well ya gotta forgive us!" Vulpie mischievously answers. "We just didn't know what to do when strange robots kept on showing up. You know, like that one the GBI captured six years ago, or Ivo, hanging out with Polar's brother! The suckers are everywhere!"

"Who, why, what, are you talking about?" Sevrif responds.

318

"I gotta admit Sevrif, I am impressed! Not at how clever Vulpie.net is being, but by how ballsy it's gotten! I mean, I just haven't been paying attention!" Vulpie giggles. "It's been practically begging me to come out here, hasn't it? I should have made a trip the first time I suspected something. Just look at you! A MANED WOLF! Man I've never heard of that before! Vulpie.net is really getting creative!"

"First time meeting you, and you accuse me of being made by your artificial intelligence? I knew you were bizarre, but that surprises me." Sevrif replies and cocks his head. "But I'm used to it. Maned wolves were pushed to the brink of extinction by our lovely cousins. And remote planets like Zeravyn were the only places we felt safe."

"Oh so you're a native!" Vulpie asks and bites his lip in excitement. "I read that Zeravyn is mostly a tourist destination for rich animals. Do they have nice schools down there?"

"Must I give you my life story? I don't appreciate any of this." Sevrif answers.

"You don't? Oh Phooey! I thought the whole point was to fuck with me!" Vulpie grins and Sevrif shakes his head.

"So you do act just like a child. I had hoped otherwise." The maned wolf snorts.

"Nu uh! I'm for serious here!" Vulpie protests and swishes his tail playfully.

"Am I really supposed to put up with this?" Sevrif asks Rulef.

"Director Druward thinks so." Rulef responds.

"I will be reporting this to other authorities. Maybe the GBI is too corrupt to care, but I'll file a formal complaint with congress. Druward doesn't own the Sufias World Government."

"You say that like you know the guy. Been spying on him too?" Vulpie taunts.

"There's no need for that. You do enough spying for everyone, Vulpie." Sevrif retorts. "Yes, I'm aware that you've been rifling through Sevrif Industries on a monthly basis looking to steal company secrets."

"You big meanie! You're telling stories!" Vulpie pouts.

"Alright, that's enough. I'm not putting up with this crap." Sevrif groans as he holds up his left paw. "Shoot me if you must, but I'm leaving."

"You're not going anywhere Sevrif." Rulef quickly replies. "The GBI is searching this ship and I and my men are under strict orders to help Vulpie investigate."

"Investigate what?" Sevrif growls.

"The robots! And I have to hand it to ya! Ivo was really impressive!" Vulpie interrupts as he walks towards Sevrif. The maned wolf looks down at Vulpie and sends him a condescending smile.

"The robots?" Sevrif mocks, using a childish voice.

"The bots!" Vulpie eagerly chimes back. "Ivo was REALLY believable! My goodness! Richard didn't have a clue!"

"Who?"

"My brother." Polar answers. The white furred wolf has faith in Vulpie unlike some of the men, and watches Sevrif closely.

"And then when you found out the GBI captured him you made him die! Was it like a time release thing where he automatically stopped working after a while, or did you send a command for it?" Vulpie innocently inquires.

"You might as well be asking me what the weather is in Sufias City. I have no clue, at all, what you are talking about." The maned wolf answers.

"THAT IS nice fur. I mean it's kind of matted and it's not silky, but the coloring is great. Did you ask Evil Vulpie for it or did it want you to be a maned wolf look alike?"

"It just so happens that I'm a real living animal! Crazy! I know!" Sevrif says with wide brown eyes.

"Yeah?" Vulpie asks with a little smile. "Mind if I take a picture?"

"Please do. I can pose if you like." Sevrif sighs. Vulpie reaches into the left side pocket of his khaki pants and pulls out a device much smaller than the one he used in the Lupiv Museum. Polar sees that the black device is about half the size, but it opens and activates the same way. It's input panel can be opened by a downward twist of the paws, and Vulpie slides open its user interface. He activates the device by hitting its small black power button and it lights up with a white ring around its exterior, showing Vulpie an image of what it is recording from the camera on the other side.

"Recognize this?" Vulpie asks and holds it so he can film Sevrif.

"Should I?"

"Interesting." Vulpie says while looking at the maned wolf's heat signature. "Your body temperature is normal."

"And after all of that build up. Sorry for disappoint you." The maned wolf smiles.

"He's real after all?" Rulef asks the orange furred fox.

"I... I guess so..." Vulpie whispers and lowers his fox ears, looking rather embarrassed. He glances around and sees the GBI agents giving him unimpressed expressions.

"When you make large assumptions all of the time you're bound to screw up. And then you look pretty foolish because you built up so much anticipation." Sevrif says with a smirk.

"What if Vulpie.net made you with a normal heat signature?" Vulpie meekly inquires.

"If you were really basing your ridiculous accusations on my body heat being higher or lower than normal, I'm afraid I'm quite disappointed. I thought you were smarter than that. You're supposed to be a super genius."

"Shut up!" Vulpie snaps.

"You're really upset aren't you?" The maned wolf asks while raising an eyebrow.

"Hey, just take it easy. This doesn't mean he's not in on it." Polar whispers down to his husband. Vulpie nods and shifts on his feet, looking humiliated.

"Well, we should report it to Rotick at least. He needs to know." Rulef comments.

"OH WAIT!" Vulpie suddenly says with wide eyes. "I forgot! My new prototype does more than just read body heat!" The fox boy adjusts its settings and aims it up at Sevrif again. Polar leans down to see what Vulpie is seeing and his blue eyes widen. "There we go! Oh... Uh... Well that's not normal..."

"I guess I'm supposed to ask you what you've discovered?" Sevrif inquires.

"Oh, nothing important..." Vulpie mischievously responds and then smirks around at the GBI agents.

"What is it?" Rulef asks, and Vulpie holds the device out for him. Rulef takes a hold of it and turns it so he can look into the viewing screen. The gray furred wolf doesn't know much about technology, but he instantly sees what Vulpie found.

"How come your bones don't look normal?" Vulpie asks Sevrif while swishing his tail. Most of the GBI agents change their opinion about the orange furred fox after hearing this, and set their eyes on Sevrif.

"Are you a doctor?" I don't know. Sevrif responds.

"Goddesses... He's... He has to be a machine. I've never seen anything like this." Rulef thinks out loud, and Blacktail spreads out a bit to cover the maned wolf. Sevrif watches and listens with no visible reaction.

"Come on, did you think I wouldn't bring my A-Game? Vulpie.net isn't dumb enough to make my biggest competitor an obvious fake! I wasn't sure if an X-Ray would find anything! I even had another little test planned but I got ya already!"

"You expect me to believe that tiny machine could do that?" Sevrif asks. "That you were carrying a radioactive device in your pocket just in case you needed it?"

"You make it sound so farfetched, but you should see what I can do with a VulGrid!" Vulpie taunts.

"So what about you? You're really going to believe him because he showed you a picture on his toy?" Sevrif asks Rulef.

"I've never seen Vulpie aim this high and miss." Rulef answers while staring at the image. He looks to his left and hands the prototype back to Vulpie after a moment. And this time, he considers Sevrif a very serious threat. "You're not an animal, and this is exactly why he came to this ship looking for answers."

"So Vulpie is judge, jury and executioner, I take it?" The maned wolf growls.

Fur On End

"Son of a bitch..." Druward whispers while reading the email that he's just received. He was checking the initial reports sent back by agent Rotick when the new message popped up.

From: "Milthorpe, Rotick" <Rotick.milthorpe@gbi.gov>
To: "Druward, Wraulgh" <Druward.wraulgh@gbi.gov>
Date: Mon, 5 Oct 2109 14:03:05
Subject: Trouble on the Sevrif

Vulpie was right,

Sevrif is not a real animal. His bones are mechanical. We need reinforcements, ASAP. Taking control of the ship now.

"That was fast." The black furred wolf thinks out loud. His fur stands on end but there is a certain satisfaction that comes with it. His decision to help Vulpie is going to make him look like a hero. Without a doubt, the Sevrif will have to be commandeered and investigated, and Druward is happy to take the credit. He smiles to himself despite the worrisome development.

"You're making a big mistake..." Sevrif sighs while being paw cuffed by GBI agents.

"Watch yourself. He might be strong enough to break out of those." Rulef warns while supervising. Polar and Vulpie are on the other side of the room because the white furred wolf pulled his husband away from danger. They watch Sevrif's every move, and Blacktail is ready to shoot if need be.

"And what do you mean by that?" Rotick inquires.

"This isn't going to end well." Sevrif cryptically answers. "You have no idea."

"Well why don't you tell us?" Vulpie suggests from across the room.

"There's no point. You fools don't have a chance." The Maned wolf replies. "You've already made too many mistakes."

"So you admit it, then?" Vulpie quickly asks in determination. "Vulpie.net did make you, didn't it?"

"I feel sorry for you most of all... It must be hard to have come so far on false hope." Sevrif answers while showing the fox boy a seemingly concerned expression.

"Where have you been making the robots? On this ship or Zeravyn?" Rotick asks the maned wolf.

"Please be gentle with my ship. I've put my heart and soul into it." Sevrif responds.

"I've contacted GBI headquarters and we have the authority to take charge of the Sevrif. Resist us and I can't guarantee that your ship will stay in good condition." The brown and white furred wolf warns.

"I'd be happy to..." Sevrif answers while yawning at the same time.

"You can start by admitting who made you!" Vulpie suggests. Rotick looks to the fox boy and sees Polar protecting him.

"Vulpie, do you have any more of those scanning devices?" The agent inquires.

"This is the only one I could bring. They're still prototypes."

"Then leave it with me. There are hundreds of animals on this ship and we'll have to collect them for a ship wide census. We need to make sure this vessel is safe to stay on while we conduct our investigation. In the mean time I suggest that you go back to the Endeavor."

"Go back? We've only been here for an hour." Polar comments. "How's Vulpie supposed to investigate from there?"

"Just until we conduct a ship wide census. You don't want to be here if something goes wrong do you?" Rotick asks. "We didn't expect to find something this quick, but now that we know the CEO of this company isn't a living animal it's time to lock this place down."

"What about Zeravyn? Can I go down to the planet and take a look around?" Vulpie inquires.

"A world is a little harder to search than a ship but I guess so. The main concern for now is the ship. Since Sevrif's not talking we have to assume that there might be more like him."

"No, I'm the only maned wolf." Sevrif comments and draws the attention of everyone. His smart ass statement makes Rotick give him a glare. The wolf with patchwork brown and white fur has already seen the scan copied by Vulpie's device. He even made sure to see it in real time before emailing Druward. So he has no doubt about Sevrif's inauthenticity.

"The GBI is prepared this time, Mr. Sevrif." Rotick replies. "When Vulpie.net attacked Sufias the first time we didn't have weaponry to stop it. Now we do."

"Perhaps you're referring to those rail guns made by Blanaire Corporation and licensed by Delanson." Sevrif replies with a very coy look. His statement causes Rotick to stare back at him in silence.

"Blow up the ship!" Vulpie tells Rotick from across the room. The orange furred fox's suggestion even makes Sevrif blink in shock.

"What?" Rotick frowns.

"He probably has this place full of nasty surprises, so let's not give him the satisfaction! Scan all of the animals on this ship to make sure they're real, and then evacuate them to the Endeavor. Hold them there and then blow this place to bits!" Vulpie elaborates.

"There are hundreds of families onboard the Sevrif. You can't do that! All of their belongings will be destroyed not to mention the chance that someone is left behind and killed!" Sevrif argues. "And every asset my company has will be gone, meaning that all of my workers will lose everything they have!"

"I see something scares you after all, huh? Don't like me ruining your fun? Well too bad Vulpie.net!" Vulpie responds. "I'll deal with the fallout! Hell, I'll even pay your employees on a case by case basis if they are innocent, but this is going to end right now!" Vulpie snaps in determination.

"We can't do that Vulpie. It's too dangerous. Sevrif might just be covering for himself, but we can't take that kind of risk." Rotick says.

"Listen to me... I know what's coming..." Vulpie stresses. "We can't wait for whatever Vulpie.net has planned. It's fucking with us. If we play it's game we're gonna lose."

"Have you found evidence that Vulpie.net is actually doing this? All we know so far is that Sevrif and the others are artificial."

"He IS VULPIE.NET!" Vulpie growls while glancing at the mancd wolf. "Look at him! He's a sick joke! A red fox on stilts? Give me a break! If that's not a twisted sense of humor I don't know what is!"

"So you're saying Vulpie.net made Sevrif to look like you? Except he has the fur coloring of a red fox. His fur isn't orange like yours." Rotick responds.

"Dude, close enough... Vulpie.net left it the way it is because a maned wolf is strange enough but they're also real. So you can see what it's doing. It's screwing with me!"

"I never knew my father was a toaster." Sevrif smirks.

"Oh shut up." Vulpie says and rolls his eyes.

"Is destroying the ship really not an option? I came face to face with Evil Vulpie too and I remember how easily it took me out of commission." Rulef tells Rotick. "Sevrif might not have done anything yet because he knows about our rail guns. But when we're distracted he might make his move."

"We'll conduct a ship wide census." Rotick repeats. "That way we'll know what we're dealing with."

"Where are you going to keep him? He's too dangerous to stay on this ship." Rulef argues.

"I'm not sending him back to the Endeavor. He'll stay here for interrogation. I'll assign twenty men to watch him and they'll have the necessary firepower."

"We have to get every real animal off of this ship!" Vulpie says while looking between Rotick and Rulef. "Are you going to send them back to the Endeavor?"

"We'll collect as many as possible." Rotick responds.

"But you can't leave them here! Vulpie.net is planning on you staying on this ship! I told you we can't play its game or we're going to lose!"

"Just go down to Zeravyn with Blacktail and stay there for now. The GBI has a small operation there so you can meet up with it."

"Okay... I tried..." Vulpie says while looking at Sevrif. He isn't sure if the maned wolf is amused or just merely paying strict attention, but it watches him nonetheless.

"Not much of an operation. They have one GBI agent listed down here." Rulef mentions while the breaker enters Zeravyn's atmosphere. He used a voice loud for Vulpie to hear, sitting in his usual seat.

"One guy? Grrrrreeeeeaatt!" Vulpie replies while perking up his fox ears.

"We're landing in Lower Richview. It's the largest town down here but there aren't a lot of animals on this planet. It is just a tourist stop." Rulef adds.

"Fitting name." Polar comments and Vulpie laughs a little.

"The agent's name is Jesse Clawson... Wow... Prescription drug abuse charges. And this guy is still an agent." The Blacktail commander elaborates while using the STF/A-17's computer system.

"It happens a lot on Zeravyn. They say everyone has at least one." The GBI pilot comments.

"What kind of drugs?"

"Mostly opiates. I know a guy that's flown out here twice on supply missions. He said the cops know but are taking the stuff too."

"I would too. I'd hate to be stuck out here watching a bunch of rich dilettantes." Rulef replies.

"Nice one Rulef! That's a big word for you!" Vulpie taunts and Polar grins. He enjoys seeing his fox husband get a little payback for the Blacktail commander's teasing during their last flight. Rulef turns and looks back at him with a smirk.

"Thank you." He simply responds.

"Funny that they've never confiscated any drugs I hear." The pilot mentions. "They've busted a lot of animals for being intoxicated but rarely find the pills."

"I'm sure they found them." Rulef snorts. "The cops are just re-selling them on the side. I bet you can pull anything way out here."

The ship lurches while encountering turbulence, causing the pilot to quickly counterbalance his trajectory. The breaker roars down through endless clouds for what seems like forever, until the clouds become a heavy fog. The only thing that can be seen out of the front windshield is white everywhere. The pilot is guided by flashing green beacon lights and finds his way to the GBI airport in Lower Richview.

Vulpie holds onto his seat when they touch down but the transition from flying to sitting is very comfortable. STF/A-17s seem to touch down on a planet just as easily as they dock in a spaceport. The breaker's landing gear sucked to the pavement upon landing just as gracefully as it grabbed the metallic insides of the Sevrif.

"How's the gravity out there?" Vulpie asks while he undoes his seat belt.

"The same as Sufias. It's slightly more, but not enough to notice." The pilot answers. "It's about fifty degrees out there, so you might get cold."

"That's not cold." Polar chuckles while undoing his seatbelt and Vulpie grins at him.

"There they are." Rulef observes while looking out the windshield at a few GBI staff members waiting at the edge of the landing zone.

"The local field office knows we've landed. They've sent out communiqué to the police as well." The pilot notes.

"Alright then, listen up." Rulef says while unbuckling from his chair. He turns and addresses the men that will be under his command. There are four GBI agents on the ship, including the pilot.

"I think we'll only need one outside of the ship, so two of you stay here and guard it with the pilot. We don't know if Sevrif has people in the area so best not to take any chances. The seven members I have in Blacktail should be more than enough to handle whatever we come across." Rulef looks to the pilot. "This is simply a field office isn't it? There's no active agents?"

"None but Jesse. And he's not here." The pilot responds.

"Okay, well we can't completely trust the animals here at the launch site. Some of them may be civilians contracted to maintain the airport, so we can't take any chances."

"So if someone approaches the ship without clearance?" The pilot inquires.

"If that happens radio us immediately so we know about it. I don't care if they are training to become GBI agents or whatever they tell you."

"We have jurisdiction." The pilot says and nods.

"Right. We don't have to explain ourselves. They've received Rotick's orders. I suggest two of you patrol the area while the other two stay inside." Rulef says and cracks his knuckles. "This planet is covered in fog that never lifts so this time I do want you to bunch up. Stay close to Polar and Vulpie both, and if an animal comes too close too quickly... Shoot..."

"Just like that?" One of the GBI agents inquires.

"Vulpie pays me to protect him and this is what it means. He's recognized everywhere he goes and it wouldn't take much to kill him. He's pretty helpless." Rulef responds and looks to Vulpie with a smirk. "No offense."

"None taken!" Vulpie mischievously declares while flipping off the gray wolf.

"Questions?" Rulef asks and looks around. No one says anything, and he goes over to the ship's side door. He activates it and it slides up, letting in Zeravyn's cool air. The breaker's retractable landing bridge slides down to the pavement and stops when making contact. Everyone unbuckles and gathers their belongings. The foggy world smells very nice. The high oxygen quickly has an effect on all of the animals. Polar takes a deep breath and enjoys the memory he has. His Olfactory memory makes him think about going camping in the high mountains of Winters Dale. His family has taken several trips over the years.

The animals exit the ship and move into the wispy surroundings. Visibility is very low. Though not bad enough for the government to issue a dense fog advisory notice, it's hard to see anything more than four hundred and fifty feet away. A brown furred timber wolf walks up to the group and nods.

"Rulef?" He inquires.

"Yes. Hello." Rulef answers and they shake paws.

"Nick Hutchinson. I'm in charge of this site." The man explains. "I'm not an agent, but I have handled the GBI's logistics on Zeravyn for twenty years. How can I help you?"

"We'll need three cars and someone that knows Lower Richview. " Rulef replies.

"Not a problem." Nick responds and glances at Vulpie. He takes a moment to look over the famous ex hacker. The orange furred fox is cuter than he expected, almost like a vixen, but still definitely male at the same time. He tries to make a mental note but classifying him is difficult. He looks to Polar as well. The arctic wolf looks strong, but clearly has a kind personality. He turns back to Rulef and continues speaking. "I can take you anywhere you need to go. There's only three towns on Zeravyn."

"No other colonies?" Rulef asks.

"Nope. Lower Richview is the largest community with the biggest tourist shops." Nick says and notices the other GBI agents beginning a patrol around the ship. "Are you here to talk to Jesse? He's the only agent we have."

"Yeah, I'd like to see what he has to say. Druward told me some crazy stuff about him." Vulpie comments and Nick turns his attention to the fox boy.

"The bureau plans to replace him as soon as possible, but right now, there's no one else down here." Nick replies and licks his lips. "I feel like he's still doing his job but I've seen the reports he's sent back to Sufias... And they're pretty bizarre."

"Yeah, something about goddesses, right?" Vulpie asks while carefully watching the timber wolf.

"That's some of it." Nick admits. "I still send them to the bureau, but I've considered having a talk with him."

"I'll handle that." Vulpie says.

"I saw that the Sevrif's been taken over by the GBI. I'm not sure what you're looking for down here, but I'll be happy to help." The timber wolf responds and then looks to Rulef. "Need anything else besides transportation?"

"This is his show. We're just here to protect him." Rulef answers.

"Alright then."

"Hey Nick, one more question." Vulpie interjects. "Does Zeravyn have any large industries, like mining or steel plants?"

"Nothing too big." Nick answers. "There were a few construction companies that made robotics, but they went under years ago."

"Is that so? Robotics huh?" Vulpie replies. "What kind were they?"

"Machines that helped load and unload equipment." Nick elaborates. "There were three of them... Duric, Zeraite, and SilverLeaf. Though I think SilverLeaf is still around somewhere. They restructured or something. I just saw a lot of animals lose their jobs seven years ago."

"Seven years? That's good to know." Vulpie cryptically responds.

"What do you mean by that?" Nick asks and blinks.

"Why did they go out of business?" The fox presses.

"Accounting problems I think."

"Do you know where the buildings were? Could you take us to them?"

"Uh, I believe they're all abandoned or demolished. But I know where they are."

Riding down Zeravyn's streets feels like spinning your wheels. Even though Polar, Vulpie and the others have been at it for two hours, having visited both the Duric and SilverLeaf sites, it seems like they haven't gone anywhere. The fog is all around them everywhere they go. The GBI field office lent them three brown sedans to travel about the misty planet, and they've certainly used the cars. They've been driving nonstop with only short breaks at Duric and SilverLeaf to investigate. So far, no one has found anything unusual. Both of the factory buildings were still around, but they were in a terribly dilapidated state.

"This is it. Pull in there." Nick says, directing Rulef who is driving Vulpie and Polar's car. The gray furred wolf slows down and makes a right into a grassy and somewhat sloshy terrain. It's

October and there is a lot of brown. The grass is tan and brittle, but the autumn red trees of planet Zeravyn are not a seasonal sight. Their leaves are not dying off. They are evergreens, or "everreds," as one might say. Amidst all of the haunting mist they are a stark comparison to naturally green flora. Traditional looking trees look to be going through their fall cycles, their leaves crumpling and falling in yellow, and brown shades. But the everreds are constant. Polar asked Nick about them earlier and the timber wolf confirmed that they are indeed, always red. The three cars come to a stop and everyone gets out. Polar stretches and Vulpie does as well, swishing his pretty orange tail.

"So this is Zeraite?" Vulpie asks Nick and steps around to the wolf's right side.

"This is where it was." He replies while looking at the large empty building ahead of them. The lot where the factory once operated is quite big, but not any bigger than Duric or SilverLeaf were. All of them share similar decorations. Open, gaping entryways where doors have fallen down with time or have been pulled down for safety reasons. The government has taken time to discourage the homeless from visiting these places. They demolished most of the things that might attract an animal wishing to do illegal drugs or avoid law enforcement. There are no exterior doors, and many have been removed from the inside as well. But Graffiti is everywhere, indicating that some animals have used the building in the past. "About four hundred animals used to work here."

"Why didn't they just flatten the place?" Polar asks while considering the dangers of the empty building.

"The mayor thinks they could be attractive to off world colonists, but that's a joke." Nick answers. "The only animals that come to Zeravyn are rich settlers. They're looking to finish their days in a mystical place and build several houses, but none of it this far off from Lower Richview. That's where all of the good real estate is. The weather is worse out here too because the fog can get extremely thick."

"So why did they build the plant here to begin with?" Vulpie inquires. "Something to do with pollution?"

"Most likely. They could dump chemicals out here I suppose. I never heard any stories about that, but the further away from the tourist hot spots the better." Nick responds and looks down at the orange furred fox. "Why did you want to see these places anyway?"

"You wouldn't believe me if I told you." Vulpie answers and looks to Rulef. "Gonna take a look around." The gray wolf nods and follows the fox when he starts off towards the dilapidated building. There are several large rusted barrels around the property, yet they don't appear to have been used by the homeless. There is no trash stuffed in them when Vulpie looks, and he sends his blue eyes over the outskirts of the area. There are broken vehicle parts here and there, and a few gigantic tires that were presumably used on construction equipment. Vulpie and the rest of the group visited the interior of the Duric and SilverLeaf plants, but nonetheless, Rulef still warns the fox boy of his surroundings.

"Careful." Rulef says while eying a few good sized aluminum shingles above. Vulpie walks up in front of a large entranceway that used to have very sturdy doors. They're lying on the ground underneath his sneakers now. Something catches his pretty blue eyes and he blinks. He sees a smeared metallic plaque on the wall next to the doorway and can still make out what it says after straining a bit.

"Zeraite…" He whispers. The words bleakly roll off of his tongue. "Why does that sound so familiar?"

"You recognize it?" Polar asks his husband and walks up behind him. He looks down at the plaque as well.

"It just… I know that word from somewhere but I can't remember…"

"Named after Zeravyn. They did some mining somewhere out here for Kinstenite as well, so they just put the two together. Kind of catchy." Nick muses.

"Zeraite did the mining?" Vulpie inquires without turning around.

"No, there was another company here a hundred years ago when they first colonized the planet. I don't remember what it was called but the same one handled all of this territory. There are abandoned mines all over Zeravyn. Kinstenite was one of the first things they extracted. There's not a whole lot else underneath the ground that's very useful." The timber wolf elaborates. Vulpie turns back for a moment as if thinking something. The orange furred fox looks at the red leafed trees on the outskirts of the misty property and runs his tongue over his teeth.

"So why did they stop mining? Did they get all of the Kinstenite?"

"Yeah. The mining companies dug up all they calculated was there and then left this part of the planet. I believe there's still some mining going on way down south but I'm not sure."

"Was there ever a mine under this building?" Vulpie asks and turns to his right to look at Nick. Polar sees that something is worrying his husband immensely. Blacktail has nothing else to do but watch as well, so many of them look for his reactions too.

"Well I don't know, Vulpie." The timber wolf responds.

"Could you find out?"

"Sure." Nick replies and digs into his pocket for his cell phone. "I'll call the office and get Macy on the line. She was a teacher before she joined the bureau." Vulpie steps inside the building and peers around while waiting for Nick to connect. He sees rusty floors, holes in the ceiling far above, nails jutting up from discarded wooden pieces, all the things one would expect. There is more blue graffiti on the walls as well. The stylistic artwork looks similar to those drawn on the exterior of the building.

"Remember what he said about particulates in the air and stuff." Polar reminds his fox husband while walking up behind him.

"Yeah I know." Vulpie softly responds.

"So what are you thinking?

"I don't know… But something about that name bothers me… Goddess, what was it?" The fox boy asks himself with a frown. "Zeraite… Zeraite…"

"Hi, Macy? Yeah." Nick says. Both Polar and Vulpie turn around and head back out of the abandoned building. They reach the timber wolf before he speaks again. "I'm here at Zeraite with Vulpie and he wants to know if there was ever an underground mind in the area?" Nick looks from side to side, contemplating what he's hearing. "Yeah, mining for Kinstenite… There was? No, underneath the building. He wants to know if there's a mine underneath Zeraite… Uh huh… Oh really? You're sure?" Vulpie squints, watching Nick's reactions very carefully. Everyone is quiet while he finishes his conversation. "Thank you. Goodbye." The timber wolf says and closes his phone. He stashes it back into his pants pocket and looks to Vulpie.

"So?" The fox boy inquires.

"There was a mine under this lot but it's very old. It's one of the first places that was mined."

"I knew it..." Vulpie whispers.

"Knew what? ... Look, I don't know what's going on here. Could you explain some of it to me? I know you found out that Sevrif isn't a real animal, and that's why you're here, right?"

"That's right."

"So what, you came down here looking for... More of them? Why are you interested in the mines?"

"Because something's wrong with Sevrif. He gave up control of his ship WAY too easily..." Vulpie tells the wolf and glances at Rulef.

"Something is wrong with him. He's a robot." Nick replies.

"Besides that."

"You think they're being made down here..." Polar concludes and Vulpie nods. He looks to his right at the arctic wolf and shows a worried face.

"Yeah. I do Polar."

"So why bother with the ship?" Rulef asks and clasps his paws together in thought, his assault rifle rattling under his big furry arms.

"The ship is just a front. Sevrif might be making the other robots but he's not doing it up there. I don't think Rotick's going to find anything." Vulpie explains. "Whoever or whatever is making these sick jokes has to be doing it with lots of privacy. It would take a whole factory plus a ton of other equipment to build the sorts of things we've seen. Artificial fur and blood? Eyes? I mean, there's no way a company could have hundreds of employees working on that sort of stuff and no one finds out! Sevrif Industries has just been imitating my company's products. I haven't heard about advanced robotics like that."

"So maybe Sevrif doesn't know anything after all. Maybe he's just like Ivo was. Didn't even known he was a machine." Rulef suggests.

"Nah, he knows... He knows..." Vulpie responds while shaking his head back and forth. "I can feel it. I know what the score is. Now it all makes sense... Sevrif is up there running his company to bring in resources and make money. It's legitimate... But what he's REALLY doing, is using that money to gather equipment and bring all of it down here to Zeravyn... For Evil Vulpie to play with..."

"That's a bit of an assumption. You don't have any evidence to support it." Rulef notes.

"It just seems too perfect to me. You know, like something I would dream up if I had dreams of controlling the universe... Catch my drift?" Vulpie asks the gray wolf while bowing his head, giving him a suggestive face.

"Well I suppose it would think like you. It does." Rulef responds.

"There's no way in hell, that somebody could design all of these fake animals, come up with new ideas to counter balance the ones that failed. I mean, you would need like a place to toss the rejects." Vulpie elaborates while waving his left paw. For a moment he sounds like Evil Vulpie dreaming something up. He seems a little too excited about it all. "And when you make em, you gotta test em right? You can't just send them out there and expect em to give a hundred percent! No, no, no, no, no! And on top of everything else, you'd need a massive power supply! Where would you get it? And more importantly, how would you keep it a secret? It's not like the power companies are gonna ya free juice!"

"So you're saying it's hidden. Fair enough. What has that got to do with this place?"

"I wanna go inside and look around." Vulpie answers, dodging the question.

"That wouldn't be safe Vulpie." Rulef advises. "It's a condemned building. There's probably a lot of cancer causing shit floating around in the air." Vulpie listens to the Blacktail commander but doesn't change his opinion. He looks around and runs his tongue over his sharp little fox teeth.

Second Chance

Rotick drops his file folders on the desk in front of Sevrif. The maned wolf is restrained with three handcuffs. His arms are behind his back and he watches the brown and white furred wolf look over a few short reports that have been pulled from the Sevrif ship's log.

"Balance sheets, tax reporting, medical plans for your employees... All checks out. You avoided disclosing some of it by registering yourself as a citizen of Zeravyn, but it all looks legal." Rotick says.

"I am a citizen of Zeravyn." Sevrif simply replies.

"Were your parents a couple of hollow wolves? Because that bone structure you have is anything but normal. I don't even know why you're still lying about it. We know you're not alive."

"All because of Vulpie's word? You have that much faith in him and his toys?" Sevrif sneers.

"Alright..." Rotick mutters and turns his attention on some of the papers again. Sevrif is still on his ship, but the GBI have taken over the security wing of the vessel and have him behind several locked gates. They're keeping him in the only interrogation room on the ship, a small gray chamber with not much to look at. There are five GBI agents in the room, all armed with rail guns, so they don't consider killing Sevrif to be an issue. Rotick's right ear twitches. He hears the door behind him open and Druward walks in.

"Welcome boss. Good to have you here to blame if this blows up in our face." Rotick declares and Druward smirks. Sevrif watches the black furred wolf with interest, as the man seems to be happier than anyone he's met in the GBI so far. Druward takes a look at the maned wolf and nods his head.

"Hello Sevrif." Druward simply says.

"Greetings..." Sevrif yawns.

"I'm sorry we barged on your ship and locked you up, but you can understand our concern... Right?"

"The governmental bureau of investigations abuses its authority universe wide. Yes, I know that." The maned wolf answers.

"Not really in this case. Don't you think all of this is pretty strange?" Druward inquires with a friendly voice and Rotick frowns in confusion. He almost looks backwards to check if Druward is an imposter. He's never friendly.

"Vulpie's the one that should be in prison I think. But he's lied his way out of every crime he's committed. You should be focusing on him instead of men like me."

"Yeah, I thought that for a long time myself." Druward says and takes a seat next to Rotick. Rotick peers at the GBI director with a bewildered look. "But I think he's contributed more to animal kind than he's hurt it. Computers everywhere run much faster because of him. His company has made technology affordable for everyone. Heck, he's even come up with a machine that can make you go invisible. He's pretty amazing I think.

"You feeling okay, Boss?" Rotick asks.

"Fine." Druward chuckles.

"Well I never would have expected you to take up for Vulpie." Sevrif comments.

"Why, do you know me? Did Vulpie.net give you memories about me? I was there the night it almost killed Vulpie. It was horrible." Druward replies.

"Just because you keep on accusing me of being a toaster, that doesn't mean I am." The maned wolf growls.

"I'm not accusing you. I just don't know another way to wrap my head around the situation. You're a maned wolf, which is fairly rare already, and they tell me x-rays of your body look abnormal... So what else could you be?"

"He also threatened us. Said we'd be sorry and HE wasn't going to like any of this. But never admitted who HE was." Rotick notes.

"So does Vulpie.net let you do what you want? Are you in complete control up here? I have to say, your company ship is very nice. All of the other animals working here seem to be real. Their scans turned out just fine, so you must be intelligent to juggle all of this and hide who you are. It must be hard to do that."

"Stop patronizing me." Sevrif growls.

"I'm not. It just seems pretty impressive. I've worked with double agents and they always told me that the guilt gets to you after a while. Even though you're working with the enemy and are supposed to be doing them harm, you start to like the animals you see every day... Ever feel the same way?"

"Oh all the time. I feel so guilty right now, I can barely contain myself."

"Well, you do seem to have emotions. You hate Vulpie but is there a reason why?" Druward inquires?

"YOU are asking me if there's a reason to hate Vulpie?" Sevrif snorts. "That is rich."

"There you go again. You talk as if you were there when I picked on him."

"I could care less about gay boy Vulpie's feelings." The maned wolf retorts.

"You know..." Druward says and gently puts his big paws on the table. "Some foxes paid me to help them kill Vulpie." Rotick's ears twinge when he hears the director's statement. He sits up in surprise and the other GBI agents in the room have wide eyes. "I could have gotten away with all of it. And in fact, I planned to."

"Okay..." Sevrif whispers.

"Yeah, the little scumbags that wanted me to conspire with them were fairly pathetic. They were AFR foxes, a fringe group of them, and they just hated Vulpie so much it went beyond words. Their seething anger was so nasty that it even made me hesitate a few times..." Druward elaborates. Everyone except for Sevrif watches him in shock while he incriminates himself. It's obvious that the GBI director believes no one can touch him. And considering his company, he's right. None of the agents would dare report Druward unless they desired a swift end to their career. "But I decided to help them anyway. They offered me several million for the job and I thought, why not?"

"What changed your mind then?" Sevrif asks.

"Losing a fist fight to Vulpie's arctic wolf." Druward answers and leisurely leans back in his chair. "I thought I ended him a few times but he just kept coming. His determination was really surprising."

"So that's it? You changed your mind about a conspiracy to kill Vulpie because you lost a fight?"

"No. I changed my mind when the guilt ate me alive afterwards." Druward admits. "I started wondering who I was, and why I would help those other foxes kill him. I just couldn't find a reason. And the more I thought about it, the clearer it became. I actually like the kid. I like him!" Druward chuckles. "He's a pain in the ass but you have to hand it to him. No one can do what he does. He's a genius."

"A genius that ruined the entire universe with his computer virus." Sevrif reminds the black furred wolf.

"But that's how you got here, isn't it?" Druward politely asks. Sevrif doesn't answer. The maned wolf looks at Rotick and then back to the GBI director.

"Is this a new interrogation technique for the bureau? A better version of good cop bad cop. I see. I've got to hand it to you. It actually was believable for a moment."

"You still believe me." Druward replies. "I'm telling the truth."

"You have my ship. You have me locked up. So go ahead and do whatever it is that you want to do. Search the ship all you like."

"We've been to every deck now." Rotick says and looks over the reports again. "Engineering is full of felines. Mostly lions and panthers are handling ship maintenance but you do have several wolves down there as well. The medical deck is completely normal. On hydroponics it looks like you're working on some kind of sustainable food supply for herbivores?"

"That's right. Sevrif Industries plans to produce synthetic food in the next six years." Sevrif replies.

"Fascinating. That was probably your idea, wasn't it? I don't see Evil Vulpie caring much about charity." Druward comments. Sevrif doesn't reply. He only looks away and sighs a little bit.

"Operations and command decks are fine as well. No indication of smuggled arms or drugs. Your ship seems to be quite bland actually, Mr. Sevrif. The biggest thing you have going here are the small business owners that sell food, retail items and lodging."

"Anyone can apply to run a shop inside the Sevrif if they are willing to pay rent." The maned wolf responds.

"So where do you build all of your products then?" Rotick inquires. "It looks like you have a large mining operation with Zeravyn. Half of deck three is devoted to storing Kinstenite, so you have industrial loaders there, but we haven't found a lot of high end technology besides the ship itself. So how do you manufacture the products that compete with Vulpie Industries? Like your SFX 23. It's almost an identical copy of Vulpie's V-Screen."

"We build all of our products right here on the Sevrif." The maned wolf replies.

"Then why can't we find any evidence of it?" Rotick retorts. "Vulpie Industries has several factories."

"Well they're bigger than our operation. Does that make what we do a crime?" Sevrif asks.

"Alright, enough of this..." Druward chuckles and cracks his knuckles. "The fact is, you're not a real wolf. Tell us who made you."

"I don't know what you're talking about. I've told you people over and over."

"I saw the pictures Vulpie took. I know he wouldn't lie. Not to me. Not to the GBI. I authorized him to come out here and investigate your ship."

"I didn't know Vulpie was a detective." Sevrif snorts. "Joke."

"His IQ is two thirty. I don't have agents that smart. Plus he has a reason to look into what's happening out here. So I'm going to take his word on you not being a real maned wolf."

"That's obvious." Sevrif replies and rattles his paw cuffs.

"So just listen to me for a moment..." Druward says and the black furred wolf licks his lips. He uses a careful voice. "I asked you if Evil Vulpie lets you call the shots up here because of what you've accomplished. This is a well-run ship. It's clean and the oxygen standards are perfect."

"Just wait..." Sevrif mutters.

"What's that?" Rotick inquires but the maned wolf says nothing else.

"The small business owners you talked about wouldn't have risked staying on this ship if it wasn't a good opportunity for them." Druward continues. "So I just have to wonder if you're different from the rest of Vulpie.net. You don't act like the insane monstrosity I saw. You're something else. But even so, Evil Vulpie still calls the shots doesn't it? And it wouldn't hesitate to ruin everything you've built if it needed to... Do you agree?" Sevrif says nothing. He stares to the right with an expression that is difficult to read.

"This place must have taken a lot of effort to build." Rotick comments.

"Oh, without a doubt!" Druward acknowledges with a friendly voice.

"You have no clue..." Sevrif says while staring at the table.

"I'm sure we don't." Druward replies. "I can only imagine how much planning and hard work was involved..." The black furred wolf watches Sevrif carefully. Since he's not a living animal he's unsure whether he's reading him correctly, but he thinks he sees his defenses weakening. Apparently the ship does mean a lot to the maned wolf because he hesitates to look at either Rotick or Druward. "As bad as it seems, we don't have to be enemies..." Druward offers and Sevrif blinks.

"What are you talking about?"

"If we take you back to Sufias as you are, I have no clue what the government will do with you. Maybe they'll give you to

Howlstead at the CTGD or they might divide you among the military industrial complex. But if you refuse to cooperate, I'll simply have to tell them that you're dangerous. And that will be the end of the discussion. They'll look at you as a robot... But things could go differently."

"How so?"

"This is how you take down a crime lord. You find the animals that work under him and get them to talk. But in order for them to help, we have to honor our end of the agreement. We have to grant them amnesty..."

"Amnesty? A full pardon huh? So you're actually saying that you're willing to let me go?" Sevrif asks in disbelief.

"We'll let you go and I'll try to leave you the ship as well. I don't see any reason for us to destroy it if you help us stop Vulpie.net. Well, stop Evil Vulpie I should say. You are part of Vulpie.net, but seem to be different. You're one of its creations." Druward elaborates.

"You don't make deals with it..." Sevrif growls and Rotick's ears perk up.

"So you're finally coming clean?" The brown and white furred wolf asks.

"Let him speak." Druward tells his friend. "Go on Sevrif."

The Goddesses

"Maybe we'll find something here. I bet this guy knows Zeravyn pretty well since he's the only agent." Polar tells his fox husband while they ride down Zeravyn's highways. The orange furred fox has been very withdrawn since they left the abandoned Zeraite building.

"I guess so." Vulpie whispers. He stares out of the side window at nothing. The heavy fog never lifts so even though they pass all sorts of landmarks it still feels like they aren't going anywhere from one mile to the next. Polar puts his big right arm around Vulpie in the back seat. Vulpie looks to his left and smiles at the white furred wolf lovingly, but can't muster a lot of optimism.

"We'll find out what's been going on. The GBI has the Sevrif and they know we're looking down here. If there is anything to worry about, we'll find it."

"I feel embarrassed... Driving around all day looking at abandoned buildings..." Vulpie admits.

"I guess that's what investigating is all about." Polar responds.

"Pull in on the right side. He lives in the last one on the end." Nick tells Rulef while the Blacktail commander drives. The convoy of three brown cars ride into a decent looking apartment complex. The real estate is covered in mist like the rest of Zeravyn, so the lot's gray and white design is fairly nice looking.

The three cars pull into whatever parking spaces they can and kill their engines. Everyone gets out but the Blacktail mercs not riding with Polar and Vulpie just linger near their vehicles. There's not enough room for them to go inside Jesse Clawson's apartment as well. Nick leads the way, walking up a small set of stairs, and knocks on the door with Rulef, Polar and Vulpie following. Polar tries to peer inside the GBI agent's window but it looks like there is a lot of junk blocking the view.

"Jesse? It's Nick from the field office. Are you home?" The timber wolf says to the door. There is a brief pause but the doorknob turns in a reasonable amount of time. A gray wolf wearing blue pajamas answers the door, making Vulpie blink and smirk in amusement. Jesse's fur is frazzled looking, as if he's been around sun lamps all day. He looks like he's half asleep and holds a bowl of sugary cereal in his left paw. He sends his yellow eyes over all of the animals outside and looks back to Nick.

"I don't have enough for all of you..."

"What?" Nick asks.

"Cereal... Low on milk..." Jesse mutters and squints when he notices Vulpie.

"Okay..." Nick responds with wide concerned eyes. "Well, I have some people here that would like to speak with you if you have the time. Vulpie Vivixen is working with the GBI to investigate Sevrif Industries on Zeravyn. Do you have time for us to come in?"

"Make it quick. I've gotta log on for a clan match later..." Jesse mumbles and walks back inside his apartment.

"Uh, what?" Nick asks in confusion.

"He must be a gamer! Cool!" Vulpie giggles as he walks by the timber wolf. Rulet quickly follows. Polar comes inside after Nick and the four of them look over Jesse's place while the gray wolf plops back down on his gray sofa. He spills a little of his cereal's milk and growls in irritation, but doesn't bother to clean up. He retrieves the spoon resting in his cereal and begins eating while watching television. His TV is nice enough but it has clutter all around it. His entire apartment is full of empty boxes, plastic wrapping. It isn't filthy, but he seems not to place much value on appearances.

"What happened to you Jesse?" Nick asks while frowning in concern.

"Huh?" Jesse replies without taking his eyes off of the TV. He doesn't check to see what any of them are doing in his home.

"Are you even going to work anymore? I haven't seen you at the office in a long time."

"Uh, I've been busy." Jesse mumbles. He munches on some more cereal.

"Busy doing what? Don't you care about your job? The bureau is going to let you go if you keep this up."

"Keep what up?"

"Not coming into work… Sending bizarre reports back to Sufias… Hello? Are you even in there?" The timber wolf asks and Jesse starts laughing. The gray wolf chortles quite a bit about something.

"Kay bro…" Jesse smirks.

"Hey, uh, Jesse?" Vulpie asks while coming forward with a friendly smile. "I'm Vulpie. I wanted to come down here and see what's up. Nice to meet you." At this, Jesse looks to the orange furred fox and blinks in surprise. He returns a face that suggests he has completely forgotten about seeing Vulpie earlier.

"Oh wow man, hey! Nice to meet you!" Jesse mumbles and offers his left paw for a shake, that the fox boy accepts.

"Nice to meet you too!" Vulpie smiles and swishes his pretty tail. "Um, so whatcha doin today?"

"Gamin… Got a clan match at three… You play Formation Seven?"

"Actually yeah! I played with someone at my company last month!"

"Dude you gotta send me your gamer tag so we can play! I bet you're better than everybody since you're a big hacker." Jesse responds in slow excitement.

"Definitely! But, um! So like, did you quit the GBI?"

"Just don't care about those assholes anymore..." Jesse admits and glances at Nick. "I did my job but they didn't like my reports. Oh well. I did what I was supposed to do."

"Yeah that sucks if they didn't believe you." Vulpie replies while nodding as if they are longtime friends. "But what kind of stuff didn't they like?"

"Are you religious?" Jesse asks and does notice Rulef walking behind the couch. The Blacktail commander doesn't approve of the way Vulpie is standing so close to Jesse but doesn't do anything about it.

"Not really dood." Vulpie laughs. "Don't believe in fairy tales."

"Man I didn't either until I met the goddesses... They're right here on Zeravyn..." The gray wolf's statement makes everyone hold still in shock. Jesse appears serious.

"You're kidding me?" Vulpie smirks.

"Nah man. They're here. And I've been hanging out with them like a lot of other guys around here... Kind of makes everything else seem pointless..." Nick can't believe what he's hearing. His mouth hangs open. He knew Jesse was out of it, but the GBI agent seems to have completely gone off of the deep end. Jesse grins when he talks and swoons occasionally. He appears to be heavily intoxicated by something.

"Are you taking any good drugs? You look super high dude!" Vulpie giggles.

"Nah man..." Jesse responds and frowns in confusion. He looks surprised. "Not high right now..."

"Jesse, what are you talking about?" Nick asks. "We don't understand. What do you mean you've been hanging out with the goddesses? Have you completely lost your mind?"

"Man assholes like you don't deserve to be around THEM anyway... They wouldn't want you around... Not around em at all..." Jesse says while swooning. He looks as if he could go to sleep at any moment.

"He's wasted on something. This must be the opiate problem you were telling me about." Rulef comments while looking at Nick.

"Not taking any fucking drugs you dickhead... Get out of my place..." Jesse mumbles and slouches some more.

"Jesse I know we just met, but can you show me the goddesses? I believe in the Velora sometimes and I'd be respectful." Vulpie tells the GBI agent.

"But dude you're the anti-Khalan... Heh." Jesse chuckles.

"What?"

"They say that about you... But he is supposed to be Goddess Khalan's son... Are you?"

"Not last time I checked. Don't have any evil powers I'm afraid. Just overwhelming sexiness!" Vulpie grins.

"Well I can TAAAKKKE... You...." Jesse groans as if struggling with the thought. "But they might not like it... I don't want to make them mad at me..."

"I'll go away if they want me to. But I bet they won't. I bet they want me to find them." Vulpie grimly responds.

"Okay, but they're not going to like some of these other guys... They're goddesses and they don't have to answer to anyone..." Jesse drunkenly stipulates.

"I'll make them be quiet. I promise." Jesse looks back over his left shoulder at Rulef as if he wants to do something. Rulef returns the glare, causing Jesse to curl his right paw into a fist at him.

"And don't make me start swinging!" The frazzled gray wolf warns. Rulef rolls his eyes and both Vulpie and Polar snicker. Jesse struggles to stand up gracefully. He has decent balance but looks to suffer from a delayed reaction time. Some of the milk from the cereal bowl seeps onto his left paw and he mumbles a profanity. Jesse goes over to his cluttered kitchen sink. He tosses the bowl in without regard to it cracking, and turns on the water faucet. He washes his paws for a bit and then turns the faucet back off.

"We'll meet you outside, okay?" Vulpie offers and tip toes through the agent's apartment. He makes an effort not to step on anything valuable.

"Huh?" Jesse responds and then blinks. "Oh... Yeah, be out in a minute." Rulef looks to Nick and both of them shake their heads silently. Everyone vacates the apartment and Vulpie gently closes the outer door halfway. He leaves it open just a little bit so they can get back inside if they have to.

"Let's hope he doesn't pass out while changing clothes." Rulef mutters, making a few of the Blacktail mercs laugh.

"Unbelievable... He's long gone." Nick whispers. Vulpie's fox ears detect the sound of footsteps coming from inside. Jesse comes to the door dressed rather well considering his earlier appearance. He has a black t shirt on, and blue jeans, and shuts the front door behind him. He locks it and then blinks when a thought pops into his head.

"Hey, are any of you guys hungry? You want to pick up some burgers on the way?"

"We probably should get going. I wouldn't want to miss them! Do you know where they're gonna be for sure?" Vulpie asks while walking down the apartment steps.

"Yeah. They're over at Cherryview Park every day." Jesse answers and notices that there are seven armed mercs and another GBI agent protecting Vulpie. "Don't shoot anybody though. Damn, you have enough guns?"

Jesse drives a fairly nice looking car. It's a blue luxury vehicle, and gets up to a decent top speed. The sedans lent by the GBI field office have a little trouble keeping up with it, but the heavy mist on Zeravyn antagonizes any serious speeding anyway. If you came up on someone crossing the road doing over sixty five miles an hour it would be difficult to stop in time. Jesse is leading them into Cherryview Park. It's just beyond downtown Lower Richview, past all of the old stately buildings is a flat terrain with well-manicured grass. It's trimmed to golf course standards. And everyone can see that there are a lot of animals inside the park. Jesse stops his car in an open space next to the grounds. The three brown sedans find equally close places to pull into, and get out quickly.

Blacktail acts quite nervous about the surroundings. Every one of the private security members looks for potential threats. The heavy mist makes it difficult if not impossible to prevent someone from getting close.

"Here we are!" Jesse says while hanging on the driver's side door of his car. He taps his keys on the car and looks to the left, noticing there are more foxes around than usual.

"This is dangerous. We can't stay here long." Rulef warns Polar and the white furred wolf nods. Vulpie also heard the statement.

"Aren't you going to lead the way?" Polar asks Jesse.

"Of course I am." Jesse responds and gets off of his car. He shuts the driver's side door and doesn't bother to lock it. "Get ready to be amazed!" The gray wolf grins.

"Should we follow him? Is this a good idea?" Vulpie quietly asks Rulef.

"If you want to find out what he's talking about." Rulef answers. "But make your mind up either way. I don't like being exposed like this. The visibility is shit." The Blacktail commander looks back at his men. He doesn't need to tell them to ready their weapons. Four of them are armed with rail guns.

"Don't shoot any innocent animals! What are you gonna do if someone gets close?" Vulpie quickly asks in concern.

"You should have thought about that earlier!" Rulef growls in response. "We're not going to shoot civilians but if they try something, they're not civilians."

"Hey? Are you people coming or what?" Jesse asks while half covered in mist. He's walked onto the park grass a good ways and is waiting for everyone else.

"Don't! I couldn't take it if someone was shot because of me!" Vulpie says and Rulef groans.

"Vulpie, what do you want us to do if we really see these women?" Rulef demands. "Because I plan to fire."

"Run, but if we can't get away, shoot them!" Vulpie answers.

"Let's go." Rulef says and signals for the men to follow. Polar gently pushes Vulpie into walking, and then follows the fox boy. A few animals have decided to camp out on the well-manicured grass. Fox, wolf, panther, tiger and lion families sit throughout Cherryview Park. The group passes them by and the residents look to them curiously. None of them seem particularly energetic. No one moves. The Blacktail wolves walk by several of them and only receive looks.

"Where are you leading us Jesse?" Vulpie asks.

"To the park gazebo. They like to give their sermons up here." Jesse replies and gestures with his right paw towards a building in the distance. The mist makes it hard to observe, but visibility improves as the group approaches it. Female voices can be heard. There are others as well, including men and children. A very large white gazebo with a gray roof sits in the middle of Cherryview Park. Two potted plants sit at the bottom of its steps. The Gazebo is very elegant, decorated with small bushes around its outer edges. Its steps lead three feet up into a spacious interior, where the animals heard earlier have congregated. Jesse climbs them after glancing back over his shoulder to make sure Vulpie and his group are still behind him.

What Polar and Vulpie's group witnesses next is beyond words. Amidst the eerie mystical surroundings, there are three jaw dropping women standing in the middle of the Gazebo. Every animal recognizes them at first sight, not because they know the animals personally, but have heard of them their entire lives. Deivaism is the most popular religion throughout the universe, and its three main deities are Goddesses Cyrilla, Sherrie and Khalan, a rabbit, a cat, and a hound. Dig sites like the one in Ninvia have yielded countless artifacts depicting them. Children are taught about the Deivaism religion in history class, if not at a Deivaist Church itself, so it's impossible not to recognize these iconic creatures. Everyone stops moving. Vulpie stops walking. Polar stops, Rulef stops... All of them are stunned.

It looks like the goddesses were giving a sermon, but when they turn and stare at Polar and Vulpie's group, it's something out of a horror movie. They go completely silent. They don't smile and they don't move. They hold still as if contemplating what they wish to do, and Vulpie's orange fur goes on end. They focus on him, all three of them, and then finally smile.

They are gorgeous beyond words. These women have inspired prophets and poets since the beginning of recorded civilization. The goddesses' beauty is supposed to be unrivaled. And as far as anyone can tell, these women seem to be perfect. They're flawless. Not even their furs have the slightest hint of imperfection, thus giving them the unnerving appearance that Vulpie recognizes. It's too perfect... Just like Evil Vulpie's fur...Vulpie recognizes the joke right away... The goddesses are supposed to be perfect, and here are three freakishly flawless creatures.

They all seem to be wearing similar clothing. If the situation weren't so dire they would be a comical site with their tight blue shorts and flamboyant shirts. Cyrilla, the rabbit, is just as tall as she has been depicted over millennia. Rabbits are very short creatures, but their mother is five foot three inches tall, the average height of a female fox or small she-wolf. This one quickly draws the most attention because rabbits are generally second class citizens and quite little. Seeing one Cyrilla's size is already bizarre. But it follows the mythology of her being the mother of all herbivores.

According to the bible of the Deiva religion, the Velora, she was the first goddess that set life into motion. She created all plant life for herbivores to consume and her offspring provided food for the carnivores that were to come.

Cyrilla's fur is completely snow white, but has black hair combed forward into a cute tuft. She has very large lopping bunny ears, and their fur is black tipped towards the bottom. Her ears are so long that they hang down to her backside when she stands tall. Her rabbit tail is a puffy white, and is almost the size of her head. Thus, she has a very adorable appearance, as her shoulders are quite narrow and her head larger in ratio, like a child. She has another cute tuft of fur that covers her neck and throat like a permanent scarf, and her eyes are an eerie turquoise. The color seems unnatural but is quite lovely nonetheless. She has a nice looking yellow t shirt on that is way too tight against her flawless body. This doesn't look accidental. One would deduce that the skimpy clothing is having its intended effect. Her large breasts look ready to pop out from underneath the shirt at any moment, making it hard for straight men to focus on anything else.

To her right, is what appears to be Goddess Sherrie, an entirely different creature altogether. All three of them seem to share the same height, but Sherrie has wider arms and legs than Cyrilla. She is still lean and sexy like her rabbit sister, but has the natural build of a predator, like Khalan as well. Sherrie's fur is taupe colored, a gray brown, and brings out the full intensity of her green eyes. She looks to have panther, cheetah and leopard characteristics. Black splotches adorns her fur across her arms and her sides. She has the same cheetah/leopard markings on the base of her tail stem in addition to the sides of her face. A streak of brownish white fur runs up her front.

Goddess Sherrie has been accused of being evil by canines, because of her mystical fur splotches. The accusation is baseless, but Sherrie does seem thoroughly disinterested in the affairs of mortals. In keeping with the feline life cycle, she enjoys sleeping for hours on end. Over the centuries Goddess Sherrie has been referred to as "The absentee land lady," because of her seemingly disinterested take on her children. This has caused felines some grief thanks to canine harassment, but true scholars of the Velora are aware that Sherrie is not disinterested in the universe she helped create. She is contemplative, and any argument against her fur markings is usually just an excuse some canines use to lessen feline influence in Deivaism. It would have been helpful if Sherrie discussed her fur patterns in the Velora, but the goddess rarely speaks.

Sherrie's shirt is a bright green and has the same pretty floral pattern on it as Cyrilla's and Khalan's. The green matches her eyes perfectly, enhanced by heavy eyeliner. Her tight blue shorts are just as snug on her wide hips as Cyrilla's. And lastly, but certainly not least, to Sherrie's right stands Goddess Khalan, the mother of all canines.

Goddess Khalan is a stunning beauty like her sisters, but is difficult to clarify species wise. None of them truly have a species because they are supposed to be all powerful fertility goddesses, but Sherrie looks like a cat and Cyrilla a rabbit. Khalan on the other hand, is a bit of a folf. She has both vulpine and lupine characteristics, giving her a foxy and wolfish appearance. This, of course, also makes her quite gorgeous to both species and all cousins in between.

Khalan's fur is a delicious caramel color. Her eyes match the color so perfectly that it truly looks divine. Vulpie has a different opinion upon seeing it, but the effect is still quite powerful. Khalan has even wider hips than Sherrie and possesses the same predator build. Khalan's long bushy tail is quite silky like the rest of her, and is used gracefully when she moves for balance purposes. Both wolves and foxes are taught to worship goddess Khalan as their true mother if they are born into Deivaist families. But there are no pleasant memories coming back to Vulpie. The religious experiences he's had have not been very good. Vander Clishaw was an assistant pastor at a Deivaist church, and seeing these women sends a chill up his little spine. All of this is especially creepy for him, and he assumes that is the idea.

Vulpie has never believed in Deivaism for obvious reasons, and the Deivas are used as an excuse to bash gay animals as well. The bigots argue that homosexuals don't follow the natural order set up by the fertility goddesses. The logic is rather simplistic, but is a major reason why gay animals still suffer from discrimination. That's why Vulpie also could never figure out why Polar believes in the goddesses. Their religion is used against the love he and Vulpie share, but there is an answer. Polar has read the Velora and is of the opinion, like many others, that the Deivas would not condemn gay love, but cherish any love that thrives. But all of these considerations are secondary at the moment, as the real question now is, are these creatures going to attack Vulpie or Polar? The sight is beyond bizarre.

"Here they are!" Jesse smirks over his shoulder while climbing the gazebo's steps. The frazzled looking gray wolf walks up to Khalan and touches her side intimately. Khalan acknowledges him with a little glance but keeps her attention on the orange furred fox.

"The anti-Khalan!" A brown fox declares from behind Cyrilla. He peers over the railing at Vulpie. "Jesse, you brought HIM here? Why?"

"He wanted to meet the goddesses..." Jesse answers while walking behind Khalan. He clearly likes to be as close to her as possible, and isn't the only male wolf that's infatuated with her. There are two timber wolves and three additional gray wolves sitting on the right side of the gazebo near Khalan. Most likely she was speaking to them before Vulpie's group arrived. Vulpie turns and faces Rulef with a petrified look on his face.

"Okay... Time to go..." The orange furred fox urgently whispers. "I've seen enough..."

"What is this?" Deep wolf asks while squinting up at the three women. The Blacktail merc forgets where he is for a moment and thinks about going to church as a child. Polar's family isn't too religious. They accepted him for being gay, but did send him to church when he was young, so he experiences the same thing. His mind races through memories of learning about the Deivas on Sunday morning and specifically, Goddess Khalan. What all of them see is that concept in physical form. It's difficult to process Khalan the goddess with the Khalan they see now. Yes, she looks identical, but no one has ever laid eyes on her before. Now this deity, this ever present idea, has come to life.

"Get me out of here! Now!" Vulpie pleads and Rulef nods.

"I think you're right..." He says and starts backing up. Blacktail spreads out a bit to watch the animals camping on the park grass, but stay around Polar and Vulpie.

"Where are you going? Do you not wish to speak with your goddess?" Khalan asks from the gazebo. Her voice is flawless in every way. The words roll off of her tongue as if spoken by an English professor, beautiful, but demanding as well.

"Ready up!" Rulef shouts to his men. They already have their paws on their guns, but the yell lets them know they have permission to fire if threatened. The one GBI agent with them, another gray wolf, pulls out his semi-automatic pistol and holds it firmly in his grip. The Blacktail members with rail guns move to the front to join Rulef, and Vulpie pushes behind them towards Polar. "Stay where you are! We're leaving!" Rulef shouts at the goddesses.

"You interrupt our sermon and then have the audacity to threaten us?" Goddess Cyrilla inquires. Her voice is similarly perfect, but is a bit perkier than Khalan's.

"Canine mortals with no respect." Sherrie says. She speaks just as clearly and beautifully as Khalan, and Cyrilla, but has a distinct voice of her own. Somehow it's possible for perfect to be presented in three separate ways.

"They don't but I do..." Jesse breathes and wraps his arms around Goddess Khalan from behind. He puts his big paws on her hips and rubs them, groping her delicious caramel colored fur. She doesn't seem to mind. If anything she appreciates the lust and allows him to press up against her from behind and breathe on her neck. "They don't know you like we do, but you could teach them..."

"Quite right." Khalan smiles. Jesse gropes Khalan's huge breasts through her super tight pink t shirt.

"Oh God..." Vulpie groans in fear. He shakes his head back and forth. "So wrong... I never thought it would go this far..."

"They need to be taught a lesson." Goddess Sherrie says and whips her feline tail around, walking to the steps. She begins coming down out of the gazebo and Rulef aims directly at her.

"DON'T COME ANY CLOSER!" He yells and she halts when her feet touch the grass. "We have weapons that can destroy you, Vulpie.net!"

"Vulpie.net?" Sherrie innocently inquires.

"Shoot her! Just shoot her now!" Vulpie pants in terror. "They'll kill all of us!"

"EAARRGGHH!" Rulef cries out as an overwhelming pain suddenly shatters him. It hits too fast to contemplate and causes him to cringe backwards. It feels like his chest and right arm are on fire. The sudden flight response from the Blacktail commander causes him to squeeze the trigger of his rail gun and he fires into the ground. Everyone winces, grass and dirt flying upwards in a plume of smoke left by the projectile.

Goddess Sherrie moves with incredible speed, so fast that the first Blacktail wolf to be struck doesn't have time to aim down his sights. He does manage to fire two bullets into her blue shorts before being struck, but the taupe feline knocks him unconscious with a single blow to the skull. Both Goddess Khalan and Cyrilla leap out of the gazebo and run over to join the fun while Vulpie stumbles in disbelief. It all seems like a dream. It can't be happening.

The other two Blacktail soldiers armed with railguns aim towards Sherrie, but she dodges to the left faster than any animal could move. This frees up their target area, and one of them aims at Goddess Khalan, because she is coming right at him. The man fires but misses her, the electromagnetically charged round blasting out into the fog beyond the gazebo. Polar jerks Vulpie up into his right arm, causing the fox boy to yelp in pain. The white furred wolf hurts him with his mighty grip, but rather than pull him along, he decides to carry him away. He's not going to wait for the Deiva goddesses to neutralize all of their defenses. He's getting Vulpie out of here right now.

A problem presents itself when Goddess Cyrilla runs up next to him. Polar stumbles and pulls back when the vixen sized rabbit gets close. He jerks Vulpie around to his other side protectively and holds out his left paw towards her.

"Don't touch him! I won't let you hurt Vulpie or me, Evil Vulpie!" Polar shouts.

"Such tripe. I am not your gay lover's computer virus. I am the mother of herbivores." Cyrilla smiles in amusement.

"Cool story bro!" Vulpie shouts and struggles to regain his footing. Polar lets him down onto the grass again, but the fox boy hides behind the arctic wolf. Polar pants in fear, but Cyrilla doesn't do anything. She just stands in front of them, keeping them from leaving while Khalan and Sherrie disarm the rest of Blacktail. Nick holds out his paws, trying not to get hit, and is surprised that they do indeed spare him. Khalan crunches an assault rifle under her mighty foot just as Sherrie snaps the GBI agent's automatic pistol in half. The two have neutralized all of the threats and completely destroyed every gun in a matter of moments.

No one is mortally wounded, but two of the Blacktail mercs are unconscious thanks to blows from either the feline or canine goddess. The physical attacks came too quickly to follow. Rulef winces in pain, realizing that one of them struck the left side of his head. He's on the ground, disoriented, and is unable to get up.

"Good work sisters! Not one of the mortals suffered death I see." Cyrilla says to Sherrie and Khalan.

"Such an end would be uncalled for. These fools only follow Vulpie." Khalan responds, walking near to Polar and the orange furred fox.

"Stay back!" Polar warns the three women and Sherrie snorts.

"Such impudence. Even after witnessing our martial abilities." The taupe feline declares.

"He fears for Vulpie. That is all." Khalan responds.

"I won't let you torture him again..." Polar tells the canine goddess.

"I have no need to harm Vulpie. But he shames me with his homosexuality. Both of you do."

"You aren't my goddess. I don't believe you're anything holy." Polar growls but something makes his fur go on end. A strange feeling rushes through him. Pleasure rises up in his body, and Vulpie experiences the same thing. Both of them wince, suddenly feeling very good while Khalan speaks.

"What will you do with them, then?" Sherrie inquires, noticing that a lot of their worshippers are drawing near in curiosity. The heavy mist all around them seems to shroud the group in an alternate universe. Some poor gray rabbits who were following Cyrilla stay off in the distance, hoping that their bunny goddess will return to give them hope in the world of carnivores.

"I am deciding." Khalan answers.

"He will do what he does, sister." Cyrilla advises and strokes her left lopping ear gracefully. "Let us return to our flock."

"They will bring others to interrupt our congregation." Sherrie warns and whips her feline tail about.

"Perhaps not. Perhaps Vulpie and Polar both understand now that we wish to tend to our true followers. And those that do not believe, shall be left in the darkness... In the fog... For all eternity..." Khalan smiles at the white furred wolf and orange furred fox.

"Uh huh... Okay. Please don't kill us!" Vulpie replies while hiding behind Polar. Deepwolf rolls over onto his right side. He's suffering from a painful blow to his left side from Goddess Khalan and is unable to find a way to do his job. He watches the three supposedly divine animals speak to Polar and Vulpie. Meanwhile, Rulef is the first of Blacktail to stand up. Cyrilla looks to her left at him and notices Deepwolf staring as well. The white furred bunny seems to miss nothing with her large ears. No doubt the sound of Rulef's boots and minor groans were enough to alert her.

"I do not like these sharp teethed brutes." Cyrilla tells her sisters. They seem to misunderstand their place in our universe. "They have dominion over my children, yes, but I am their god as well. How dare they bluster about with their toys as if they rule everything in their path."

"You have never liked that our children rule yours but it was part of the pact, Cyrilla. You provide the grass, the streams, the air, and we provide those that will tend them." Sherrie reminds the bunny goddess.

"Only if they have kind hearts. I do not approve of these bloodthirsty wolves." Cyrilla responds. Polar and Vulpie watch them argue and make no attempt to move or do anything. Neither is aware that the other is also experiencing the same warm pleasurable feeling, but it keeps the white wolf and orange fox passive. For some reason, the more the goddesses speak the better Polar and Vulpie begin to feel.

Vulpie is the first to suspect something is wrong. Polar's no fool, but doesn't consider that he may be inhaling a foreign pathogen. The orange furred fox on the other hand, recognizes the state that he's in. He senses his pleasure buttons being pushed, and immediately thinks of one word... Opiate... He doesn't know how it could be possible, but his instincts rarely lie. Vulpie deduces in a split second that these women must be the reason for Zeravyn's opiate addiction problem. He's been high plenty of times and recognizes the sensation that oxycodone and hydrocodone have, plus other opiate related drugs. Vulpie swoons, looking at the women with an open mouth and tired eyes. He's intoxicated, but he knows it must be true. They must be the source, but the real question is, how could they be transmitting the opiates... Through their breath? In aerosol form? The Deivas truly would seem divine if they stimulate pleasure receptors in animal's brains just by speaking to them.

"We need not harm them. They will leave us." Khalan decides and Cyrilla frowns. Khalan touches her large breasts as if thinking and then smirks at Rulef, who stares at her in a loss. He looks down at his men as they gather themselves and then back at them.

"Then what of them? Surely they will bring others." Sherrie tells Khalan.

"Perhaps they will not." Khalan suggests and smiles at Polar, before directing her attention to Vulpie. "Will you allow your goddess the respect she deserves?"

"Yes!" Vulpie quickly replies.

"You will not talk about our presence here..." Khalan elaborates.

"Nope!" Vulpie says and bites his lip with wide blue eyes. He tries to appear honest and cute, but only succeeds in looking cute.

"Then you are free to go, Vulpie. Go back to Sufias and rethink your life."

"I will Evil Vulpie!" The orange furred fox responds with a swoon.

"What?" Goddess Khalan asks while rubbing her huge breasts through her tight pink shirt. She pays no attention to how the act may seem to Polar or Vulpie.

"Nothing!" Vulpie yelps. Khalan searches him with her golden eyes and then gives a final smile to Polar before turning to her left. She begins walking away and Sherrie frowns in annoyance.

"If the universe weren't full of so many wolves and foxes you wouldn't have the final say, thirty times a day!" The exotic feline goddess complains while following.

"Then have your leopards, tigers, and panthers make more kittens!" Khalan teases. Cyrilla ignores Polar and Vulpie and goes with her sisters while all of Blacktail holds still. The Deivas look at them as they go by, but pay them no heed after reaching the gazebo once again. They ascend up the steps and Polar and Vulpie hurry over to the wounded mercenaries.

"Get up! Up!" Rulef growls to the downed men. A few of them look like they have broken bones but everyone is conscious. The Blacktail commander knows that he has to get them away from the Deivas as soon as possible. Just because they've returned to their perch with their worshippers doesn't mean they won't come back down to finish them off. At this point anything is possible. If they have the opportunity to escape they need to take it without hesitation.

"Come on!" Vulpie says and tugs on the GBI agent's left arm. He pulls him up as best as he can, and eventually the man stands but grabs his left leg in pain. Polar helps Deepwolf stand and the two offer shoulders to those who can't walk. Two of the gray wolves have to be carried. Rulef aides Polar and Deepwolf and everyone rushes away from the gazebo in the heavy fog. Vulpie twitches left and right, scurrying back and forth as he tries to make sure their pathway is clear to the three GBI cars. He goes over and stands nearby, but feels rather helpless. He doesn't have keys to get in or any strength to lend to the big wolves.

Rulef has the keys, and speaks with them about who will be driving. He finds the other drivers and has them give their keys to able members of the team, and they quickly open the cars. Everyone stashes inside as fast as possible. They crank up the engines and drive away from Cherryview Park as fast as they can.

"I warned them." Jesse breathes to Khalan and hugs her. She stands with her sisters and smirks.

"My devoted boy…" The gorgeous vixen wolf whispers in his ear.

"Can I do anything to help?" Vulpie offers in a worried voice when Polar and Rulef pull the last of the wounded men inside the STF/A-17 Breaker. Rulef returns a disgusted look, but Polar's similarly disappointed expression hurts the fox boy. He can see they are both irritated that he would waste their time with all of the men needing their help. He's just too weak, and both wolves also look upset over what they saw in Cherryview Park. Polar's glare makes Vulpie cringe in shame and he has to bottle up his feelings. The fox boy keeps his tail low and goes over to his seat. Polar helps Rulef get the wounded wolves into their seats and they strap them in safely. After they're ready, Polar joins Vulpie and groans after strapping himself in.

The ship takes off as fast as the pilot can manage. After they get airborne and pass through the atmosphere, Vulpie looks to his left at Polar. The white furred wolf stares at the floor. No one speaks inside the breaker and Vulpie worries that they are all thinking that he's the reason for their suffering.

Polar notices Vulpie looking at him for approval after a moment. The orange furred fox looks vulnerable and the white furred wolf sneers a little in irritation. Polar doesn't feel like attending to Vulpie's feelings after what they've just seen. He doesn't say anything. Instead, he just gives Vulpie a disappointed expression and Vulpie's lip quivers. He looks down at his sneakers and has to keep from crying. He tries to be strong but isn't sure if he can hold it all inside.

But even though Polar is tired of reassuring Vulpie, he loves the tender fox with all of his heart and eventually puts his right paw on top of Vulpie's left. Polar sends Vulpie a reassuring look and Vulpie moves his little right paw over on top of his in gratitude. Vulpie strokes the wolf's big hand and lowers his head to keep from bothering his husband anymore.

Normally Polar is very collected but what he's seen today is beyond anything he expected. He does blame Vulpie. Even though Vulpie isn't directly responsible for Vulpie.net's actions, if Vulpie.net is behind this, Vulpie made all of it possible. He feels drugged after being around the supposed goddesses, but hasn't put cause and effect together the way Vulpie has. He has no clue why he feels sluggish. Even though his body feels pleasurable, he's also suffering from paranoia.

"My God..." Rulef finally groans. No one talks, so it can be assumed that his statement speaks for everyone. Vulpie starts sniffling. Polar's wolf ears perk up when he hears the cute but pathetic noises coming from the orange furred fox. He feels Vulpie's paws trembling.

"Vulpie..." Polar reprimands with a hushed voice. Vulpie sniffles some more and starts shaking. "Not now."

"It's all my fault." Vulpie whimpers.

"Reporting this is going to be fun." Rulef growls, while working with the pilot to transmit a broadcast to the GBI and the army.

Polar and Vulpie's group safely makes its way back to the SWG Endeavor. A medical team quickly meets the breaker after it docks. The GBI and armed forces have both received the same reports sent by Rulef, so they are aware of the situation. Several strong wolves use stretchers to gather the wounded Blacktail mercenaries. They take the GBI agent that was with them on Zeravyn as well. When the medical team manages to carry off everyone that's been hurt, Rulef speaks to Polar and Vulpie.

"They want you to go to your quarters."

"Do they know about those women?" Vulpie asks in concern.

"Yes, It's all in the report. Rotick confirmed that it's been received."

"What did you tell them?"

"The truth. I told them we were assaulted by Goddess Cyrilla, Sherrie and Khalan, and asked for more railguns to replace the ones they destroyed."

"Did you tell them that they're robotic?" Vulpie asks.

"I think they'll figure that one out themselves... But the way they moved didn't look artificial." Rulef responds and rubs the side of his left skull. It's still tender from the blow he received. He turns and leads Polar and Vulpie out of the ship. They follow him out of the docking chamber and down the long corridor outside. After passing through another door they enter the main chamber of the Endeavor and spend the next six minutes walking towards their part of the ship. They make a right, leaving the wide open spaces filled with soldiers and workers, and go down the hallway towards their room. Rulef successfully gets Polar and Vulpie to their quarters, and Polar uses his keycard to open the door. The white furred wolf and orange furred fox go inside while the Blacktail commander thinks about how he's going to manage with no mercenaries.

"Where are all of the agents?" Vulpie asks.

"Druward called them to the Sevrif. He flew in after reading Rotick's reports, and is sending everyone he has." Rulef answers.

"So he doesn't need to talk to us?" The orange furred fox inquires.

"Not unless you know something I don't. I told them everything, and they're interrogating Sevrif. Just get some sleep. I'm exhausted too, so stay in your room. There's no one here besides me. My entire squad is in the infirmary."

"Okay." Polar agrees and rubs his muzzle. Rulef shuts the door, leaving the two alone, and Vulpie locks it. "I'm sorry for growling at you on the ship... All of this is just insane." The white furred wolf says and walks over to the bed. He sits down and takes off his shoes, feeling very tired. They haven't slept since leaving planet Sufias.

"I don't blame you. I'd be disgusted too." Vulpie says and goes over to the bed as well. He takes off his shoes and crawls onto it. "Disgusted at whoever's responsible for those abominations."

"I can't believe this... I can't believe what happened. They looked just like the real goddesses." Polar whispers and lies down on his side.

"But the goddesses aren't real." Vulpie reminds his husband.

"I don't know what my father would think if he saw Khalan."

"I didn't know he was that religious."

"Sometimes he is. I just remember him showing me paintings of her, and he always thought she was so beautiful." Polar elaborates.

"Yeah, she was really pretty. They all were. That's the idea." Vulpie sighs and anxiously rubs his face. "I hope they don't hurt those animals on Zeravyn. What if they just decide to kill them?"

"They haven't so far."

"We don't know that for sure." Vulpie replies.

"Well it's out of our paws now. Let the GBI and the army deal with them. I don't want any more of this." Polar responds and makes room for Vulpie when the fox boy snuggles up to his front. Polar lays his left arm over him and Vulpie touches the white wolf's side.

"I'm sorry for all of this. You must be ashamed of me."

"Worried, irritated, and shocked, yes... Ashamed? No..." Polar answers with a gentle voice.

"I love you so much. That's all I could think about when the Deivas attacked us. I was scared of what they would do to me, but if they killed you... I could never recover from that." Vulpie whispers.

"I love you too. But worry about yourself, alright? You're the one that needs to be careful. After seeing them today there's no doubt in my mind that it's come back to hurt you again... But I won't let it..." Polar lovingly replies.

Evil Vulpie Returns

Sevrif was allowed to sleep, but the GBI have not removed his three paw cuffs. Druward comes into the holding cell and sees the maned wolf sitting in his chair behind the table. Rotick follows Druward inside and Druward notices that the GBI agents armed with railguns have indeed been rotating shifts to ensure they're still awake.

"Good morning." The GBI director says and takes a seat. Rotick does the same. "Is there anything you want to mention today?"

"As in?" Sevrif replies.

"Yesterday you all but confessed to being a machine. So I was wondering if you have a wireless connection to Vulpie.net just like the Evil Vulpie robot did."

"No... I don't." Sevrif answers. Both Rotick and Druward sit up in surprise. They look to each other and then back to the maned wolf.

"So you don't know about these women on Zeravyn?" Druward asks. Sevrif does not respond. He stares at the GBI director as if considering his options. "These goddess imposters?"

"So you found them... I'm surprised. I didn't think Vulpie.net would have them out in the open..." Sevrif says. Druward raises an eyebrow and then nods his head.

"Well, to be fair, Zeravyn is a mist covered planet. So I imagine that gave them some cover."

"What do you know about them? They disarmed seven members of Blacktail and a GBI agent with no weapons." Rotick tells the maned wolf.

"I can tell you that I'm not surprised. It took Vulpie.net years to perfect them..." Sevrif replies.

"What are they, Sevrif?" Druward presses.

"You said that you could help me if I cooperated... Will you honor that agreement?"

"Yes I will. I can't promise you immediate freedom, but I have every intention of keeping my word." Druward responds.

"Then I need Vulpie's help. Vulpie.net didn't design me to hack into computer systems and that's exactly what has to be done if you want these people to live."

"Everyone on the ship?" Druward inquires.

"Yes. Vulpie.net controls the Sevrif."

"Then I'll contact Vulpie and have him re-program it from the Endeavor." The GBI director responds.

"No, you don't understand... We aren't running Arctic.net on this ship. It's Vulpie.net. Vulpie can't order it from afar. He needs to come onto the ship and hack into the central computer... And even then I'm not sure if he can take over."

"If it has control like you say, we should evacuate the ship immediately. We need to get all of these people out of here."

"You can't. It won't let you... It's watching us..." Sevrif stresses.

"You're saying it's been watching us ever since we arrived?" Rotick asks.

"Yes."

"Then why hasn't it done anything yet?" Druward asks.

"It's toying with you. It toys with everyone..."

"You sound like you're afraid of it. Are you?"

"Of course I am." Sevrif growls. "You were right about one thing. I'm not in charge. It's always watching."

"Can it see through your eyes? They have video of Evil Vulpie torturing Vulpie at the CTGD that came right from what it could see." Druward inquires.

"No."

"How does it force you to come back then? If you're different and you can think on your own, what makes you follow its commands?"

"Because it's the only family I have..." Sevrif admits. His voice is very sad. The statement momentarily fills the room with silence.

"I can only imagine what that must be like. To have Vulpie.net as your father and mother." Druward replies.

"But you're turning on it now." Rotick notes.

"Only because you've promised to help me. I've known this day was coming for a long time, but whatever Vulpie.net does, it won't be good."

"So you're sure that we can't evacuate this ship with Vulpie.net watching?" Druward asks.

"I wouldn't try it. I expect it will cut the oxygen and seal every exit." Sevrif answers.

"Then what?"

"I don't know. Do you want to find out?"

"Of course not."

"Then get Vulpie to hack the main computer. If he can disable it and leave the secondary functions intact, we can get everyone off of the Sevrif and onto your army ship."

Vulpie answers the door when someone knocks. For some reason he woke up early this morning and has already showered, while Polar is still snoozing in bed. Rulef is waiting outside and notices that Vulpie's husband is still asleep. Vulpie looks back and then goes out into the hallway, quietly closing the door behind him

so they can talk. The orange furred fox is wearing a stylish neon blue
t shirt and white khaki pants.

"What's up?"

"Sevrif has changed sides. Druward says that he's admitted
to being a machine and that Vulpie.net is running the Sevrif."

"No surprise about the last part but why is Sevrif helping?"
Vulpie inquires.

"Druward offered him some sort of deal. Sevrif said that all
of the animals on the ship are in danger because Vulpie.net could
depressurize it or cut the oxygen at any moment... So he asked that
you come and hack into the main computer if we're going to get
them out safely." Vulpie is silent for a bit as he processes the
implications of what he's just heard.

"Sevrif asked that I hack the computers." He repeats for
clarity.

"Yes."

"I see..." The orange furred fox whispers and looks to the
side.

"Get Polar up. We shouldn't waste any more time if those
animals are in danger."

"No..." Vulpie objects and stares up at Rulef. "No. Polar
isn't coming."

"Why not?"

"Because I'm not going to let him die because of my
mistakes. This is my problem. I created Vulpie.net and now I have to
face it." Vulpie explains.

"He would disagree. If you don't come back he'll probably
try to kill me!" Rulef responds.

"Well, sad day for you then. Because I won't have it any other way. He's given me too much to just die trying to protect me. No one can save me from Vulpie.net... But he'll be safe here."

"Vulpie, are you sure about this?" The Blacktail commander inquires. "I still plan to come with you."

"You don't have to. Stay behind if you want."

"That's not who I am. I'm not a coward. We have replacement railguns and I'll put a round in any machine freak that tries to kill you." Rulef declares and Vulpie smirks.

"You're hardcore... Thank you."

"Last chance to change your mind. You're sure about this?" The gray furred wolf asks.

"Let's go." Vulpie replies.

Druward is standing outside of Sevrif's cell, talking to Rotick, when Vulpie and Rulef arrive. The GBI director scratches his chin and notices the orange furred fox after Rotick turns to his left. Sapher is standing to Druward and Rotick's right, clearly here to facilitate navigating the ship in Sevrif's stead. Vulpie looks between them and comes forward while swishing his pretty tail.

"Where is he, boys?"

"In there, Vulpie." Druward answers and gestures towards the interrogation room. Vulpie winks at the black furred wolf and goes inside. The GBI director smirks in amusement but quickly stops when he notices Rotick giving him a disillusioned face. Vulpie strides into the interrogation room and sees Sevrif sitting behind the table. The maned wolf looks calm but his red foxish fur is unsettling to say the least. He looks like an overgrown vulpine with a wolf face.

"Hiya." Vulpie says. He doesn't bother to take a seat.

"Hello." Sevrif responds.

"So the ship is being run by Vulpie.net, and not Arctic.net. Is that right?"

"Yes."

"How am I supposed to hack into the ship's computer systems if it's infected?" The orange furred fox inquires. "Any attempt I make is instantly going to be eaten by Vulpie.net."

"Go up to the command deck and access the ship's main computer. I have a passcode that will disable all of the secondary logic systems, leaving Vulpie.net out of the loop before it knows anything is going on."

"You can't do that. Vulpie.net will override any commands like that." Vulpie argues.

"Not with me. It trusts me." Sevrif responds and the fox boy raises an eyebrow.

"Alrighty then. Let's say it does. Which deck is command?"

"Five. Sapher can take you up there and to the main computer. You'll have to bypass the keypad and hack the primary logic controller to put in the code."

"If we don't want the computer alerting Vulpie.net that someone's using the interface." Vulpie smiles.

"Exactly." Sevrif smiles back. "I figured you would know how this works better than me." At this, Vulpie glances over his left shoulder at Sapher. The gray wolf looks tired but capable, standing at attention in his dark green suit. The orange furred fox looks back to Sevrif again.

"So what's the code?"

"System Foxed You."

"Cute." Vulpie growls. "Is that all one word?"

"Yes. System, then foxed, then you." Sevrif confirms.

"Once you put that in, assuming you manage to bypass the keypad, the ship will default to safe mode. It will only maintain basic functions like life support and ship pressurization.

"How long do you think it will last?" Vulpie inquires in concern.

"I have no clue, Vulpie. But it's the best chance you have of saving these animals."

"You know I don't trust you, right?" The orange furred fox states while watching the maned wolf very carefully."

"I did lie to you in the beginning, so it's understandable." Sevrif replies.

"For what it's worth. If you really are trying to get away from Vulpie.net then I'm sorry for how it's treated you. I'm sort of..."

"My father." Sevrif answers with a trace of love in his voice.

"I guess so." Vulpie responds and swallows. "But all that matters right now is getting these people out of here before it can hurt them."

"It's probably too late Vulpie. You know that don't you?" The maned wolf inquires.

"Thought had crossed my mind." Vulpie answers and turns around. He walks out of the interrogation cell purposefully, and sets his attention on Sapher. "Are you ready?"

"Yes sir." Sapher answers.

"So this is it? You're going to shut down the main computer?" Druward asks the fox boy.

"Yeah this is it. I'm going to hack it and put it in safe mode. That means the airlocks and everything related to animal safety should still work just fine. But all of the security cameras will probably go dead. And everything else." Vulpie responds and licks his lips. "Don't start evacuating anyone until I let you know that it's been disabled. Alright?"

"You got it." Druward simply answers and Vulpie smiles at the polite response. He really likes the new Druward. "Just like old times."

"Goddess I hope not." Vulpie laughs grimly and heads off. Rulef and Sapher go with him, and they make a left once inside the mall hallway of the Sevrif. Vulpie noticed signs for an elevator in this direction but slows up, letting Sapher take the lead. As expected, he directs them over to a set of gray doors and calls the elevator by pressing the button on its stylish panel.

They wait for a moment and then get in when it arrives. The doors shut and they enjoy a short ride up to deck five after Sapher punches in the number. When the doors open, Vulpie and Rulef are treated to a fairly different looking deck. The command deck looks quite a bit smaller but is crammed with computers. Gray is all around and there is a nice view of space thanks to a large set of windows in front of the pilot's chair. The chair is currently empty but there are several animals working in the area. With the Sevrif in orbit it seems that there is no need for someone to direct the ship.

Sapher leads Vulpie around to the left, where there is a large rectangular machine in the room. When coming up from the elevator you can't see it, because its back side is solid gray casing, but it's right side Is covered in a protective black cage that allows access to the ship computer system.

"Nice." Vulpie muses while Sapher goes to unlock the cage with a set of keys from his pocket.

"Thank you. Mr. Sevrif spared no expense when he had this ship built." Sapher responds. Sevrif's attendant opens the cage and then points at a black terminal right in front of the entranceway. "That's it. Remember, Sevrif said to hack past the keypad."

"Yeah, I remember." Vulpie says and sniffs the clean air while inspecting the panel. "So how long have you known that Sevrif was a robot?" Vulpie inquires. Sapher blinks and looks around to make sure no one is listening. He notices Rulef standing a bit away from him with his paws on his rail gun.

"A while now." Sapher admits.

"So you found out. You're not really a machine like him... Are you?" Vulpie inquires while double tasking. He sees a few screws that need to be loosened to get around the keypad and reaches into his back pocket. He brought his custom built phone instead of his V-Screen, because it can fit into his pants in addition to plugging into systems when need be. But instead he grabs a small multi-tool and brings it out. It's his favorite design, the same sort he's used over his many years of computer maintenance and sabotage. He brings out a screwdriver and goes to loosening the panel.

"No." Sapher says and blinks, feeling a bit intimidated by Rulef.

"No? Wow. It must have been scary when you discovered he wasn't real. I'm amazed that you continued to work for him..."

"He pays very well. And I need the money." Sapher responds. "But I assure you, I'm quite real. They scanned me with your device."

"I bet they did. That's the only reason I turned my back on you." Vulpie replies. He gets the last of the screws out and then carefully removes the panel. Behind it, he sees the primary logic controller. It has a basic setup, one that he is familiar with. "Hmm... Looks simple enough." He reaches back and retrieves his orange phone. He flips it open and turns it sideways to unsnap part of its casing. Inside there is a custom built data line that he installed. It's only about eight inches long, but will get the job done. Vulpie unsnaps the plugged end from the keypad and then directs the cable to his phone. He connects the plug connected directly to the logic controller into his phone and then waits for a connection. The wait is short. His phone displays a list of commands available for use.

"What are you doing?" Sapher inquires.

"Just a moment." Vulpie answers while he thinks about what he sees. He presses one on his phone, bringing up a small menu that awaits data entry. "There we go. Ready to put the code in directly to the controller." The orange furred fox says and then switches his phone from numerical entry to alphabetical. He punches in systemfoxedyou, and immediately gets a response. Pressing enter was unnecessary. The ship recognizes the input and displays safe mode protocols. It loads them and executes them in a matter of moments, causing several of the animals on the bridge to groan in confusion. Vulpie unhooks his phone and puts everything back in its place. He screws the panel back in, and then steps back so Sapher can close and lock the cage again. Vulpie looks around, seeing all of the animals press on their computer screens in confusion. All of their screens are black. Nothing responds.

"Looks like it's working." Vulpie notes and swishes his pretty tail. "I hope Druward has a plan to find everyone without putting out a public service announcement."

"My staff can take care of that." Sapher says after finishing with the cage. "Let's get back down to the mall hallway. I'll get everyone together and let them know what to do.

Polar blinks. He holds still after waking up because something doesn't feel right. He quickly discovers what is wrong when orange is missing from his bed. Normally Vulpie snoozes longer than he does, but the fox is gone. Polar sits up and looks around. Vulpie is nowhere to be seen. The bathroom is empty, so the white furred wolf gets up and walks over to the doorway in his boxers. He opens it and peeks out. Deepwolf turns and faces him.

"Hey. Didn't want to wake you up." The Blacktail merc says.

"Where are the others?" Polar asks.

"Still in medical."

"So where's Vulpie? He's not here." The white furred wolf says and discovers the answer from the expression on Deepwolf's face.

"He's on the Sevrif with Druward. They're getting the animals off of the ship."

"You mean you let him go without me?" Polar asks in shock.

"I wasn't here. Rulef left with him and called me. He told me to watch over you until they get back."

"Oh my God, Vulpie, not again..." The white furred wolf whispers.

"Relax. I'm sure they'll get everyone off the Sevrif safely."

"Then why did they need him? Why couldn't they just evacuate the ship on their own?"

"I don't know." Deepwolf admits.

"Vulpie. Come here." Rotick tells the orange furred fox from a distance. He's standing at the security area where Sevrif is being held, and has to speak over the animals passing them by. The GBI is herding everyone on the ship to the loading bays nearby. They have a large transport ship docked and ready to receive passengers

and they have already collected about thirty animals. "Come here."
Rotick repeats while waving, and the orange furred fox comes to
him, weaving in between people in the way. "I thought you and
Rulef were out with some of the agents. You shouldn't be walking
around by yourself. Especially not now." The brown and white
furred wolf warns and blinks when he suddenly realizes that Vulpie
is wearing a white shirt.

Written across it, is the statement "Owning in Progress,"
on top of a long black rectangle that is designed to look like a
computer progress bar. It reads 90% complete. Rotick's stomach
sinks. The last time he saw Vulpie, the fox boy was wearing a neon
blue shirt and khaki pants. Now Vulpie is standing in front of him,
smiling, in black jeans and the stylish white shirt.

Rotick holds completely still. There is no doubt in his mind
that he's made a mistake. Evil Vulpie is smirking at him, not Vulpie.
The robot looks so identical to the real orange furred fox that there
is literally no way to tell them apart. The only difference is that Evil
Vulpie still has the same glowing blue eyes as its original robot. A
few of the agents nearby make the connection when they see Rotick
turn to stone. Druward frowns in confusion when he comes out of
the security wing and sees the sight as well.

"Vulpie?" The black furred wolf asks and Rotick looks over
at him, but quickly sets his eyes back on the machine as soon as
possible in case it attacks. Druward's yellow eyes widen. Evil Vulpie
looks to him as a few more animals walk past.

"Sadly boys... I'm afraid this just won't do!" Evil Vulpie
declares and grins.

"Oh fuck..." Druward whispers. The whole ship suddenly
rumbles. Sounds of pressurization echo through the mall hallway
and the loading bay doors begin to close. All of the doors begin to

close, everywhere, at the same time. The GBI is helpless to stop every single docking station from lowering its doors and then locking into place. Vulpie.net manages cutting off the escape routes while simultaneously eying the GBI agent near Druward that is holding a railgun.

It calculates that it should strike now during the confusion, and leaps forward into Rotick. The strong wolf cries out, trying to defend himself, but Evil Vulpie's weight easily topples him to the ground. It doesn't even attack him, because its real goal was to grab the pistol from the brown and white furred wolf's holster. Evil Vulpie yanks out the semi-automatic handgun, and turns towards the agent with the railgun. He is trying to aim at Evil Vulpie but the robot throws the pistol itself directly into his forehead before he has time to react.

Druward almost falls over as the gun comes whizzing by and slaps the agent next to him. The agent shoots his railgun into the floor by mistake, and shards of metal and smoke fly up into the air. The man sprawls backwards and shudders in pain. Evil Vulpie threw the metal weapon into his face so fast that its force nearly knocks him unconscious.

Druward stumbles back inside the security wing as fast as possible. He knows they have more railguns nearby, and finds the rack around the corner. Rotick had them placed there and they are being guarded by another black furred wolf agent, who stands up when Druward rushes over.

"NOPE! You come back here!" Evil Vulpie shouts and runs in after him. Druward lurches when he feels something grab his tail. The Evil Vulpie robot yanks him backwards like a ragdoll, making him fall on his face. He scrambles to get up but Evil Vulpie simply lets go of him and rushes over to the gun rack instead. The GBI agent has a railgun out and is attempting to activate it. "Shouldn't play with guns!" The robotic fox imitation shouts and snatches it out of his paws. It grins and crunches the weapon, making sparks fly. "Here you go." Evil Vulpie innocently smiles and hands the gun back to the agent, who takes it with wide eyes. He doesn't know what else to do. Evil Vulpie pushes him out of the way and Druward gets up just in time to see the robot pound five more railguns with his fists, breaking all of them beyond repair. "There we go! Now to find da rest!"

"Vulpie.net, stop! We're only trying to protect these people!" Druward tells the robot and it gives him a dissatisfied look.

"YOU should know better..." Evil Vulpie warns and prances over to him, making the black furred wolf back up. He stumbles out of the security wing and looks around for help. Another agent has showed up with a railgun but his efforts to use it are just as ineffective. Evil Vulpie notices him in a split second and rushes at him like a bolt of lightning. The man simply doesn't have time to fire without being sure he won't hit Druward or someone else nearby, and the robot punches his muzzle so hard that his nose and half of his face is broken with one blow. Obviously, the little robot is just as strong as the original Evil Vulpie.

But it does make a mistake. It's not perfect, and a GBI agent manages to fire a round from a railgun directly into Evil Vulpie's left side. The loud gun releases a plume of smoke and sends the machine flying into the wall nearby, smashing a security camera and a few TVs that are used to advertise locations on the ship. All of it comes crashing down in a shower of glass, debris falling everywhere as Evil Vulpie slams onto the floor. The well placed shot makes Rotick and Druward both laugh in surprise, but the victory is short lived. Evil Vulpie immediately gets back up and looks down at its left side and the hole in its nice white t shirt.

"OOOOOWWWWWWW!!! YOU MOTHER FUCKER!" The robotic orange furred fox yells and comes at the timber wolf that fired at him. By this point, animals are screaming and running away in terror while Evil Vulpie rampages from one member of the GBI to the next. The man that fired tries to turn and run but Evil Vulpie jumps and drop kicks him. The impact breaks his left shoulder and arm, and slams him onto the hard but nice looking floor. The robotic fox gets back on its feet and kicks the man in his butt with enough force to push him completely over. "That'll teach ya, fuck face! NOW!" Vulpie.net says and turns around, surveying the surroundings. "Anyone else want a piece of this? Course you do!"

The real Vulpie is being held back by Rulef, around the corner of a bakery shop. The gray furred wolf saw a commotion in the distance and hasn't let the fox boy get any closer. They are a good ways off.

"Oh no!" Vulpie breathes in horror, seeing his look alike terrorizing everyone around it. "Rulef! Can you shoot it?"

"I might miss. And one of them hit it with a fucking railgun already! It took it like it was nothing!" Rulef growls in shock. "I don't think so."

"But what about these people! We've got to stop it somehow!"

"No. The only thing we can do is keep you away from it. Unless you want to end up like last time." The suggestion makes Vulpie tremble. Though he wants to be a hero, he listens to his personal bodyguard. There's nothing he can do, and he hides behind the gray wolf while watching Vulpie.net.

"Hey get that hand off me you BITCH!" Evil Vulpie growls when an agent tries tackling and grabbing its neck. It was a long shot, but the gray wolf hoped he could snap its neck since the robot is just as small as the petite Vulpie. But the robotic fox imitation proves to be harder than steel. All the agent gets is his left arm twisted and broken as Evil Vulpie swirls around. It lets him go and focuses on two agents hurrying in from a side hallway. It sees that they have railguns, and Vulpie.net decides to go to the second level of the mall hallway to avoid being shot. "Time to... Time to-Go get me some action!" It says, satisfying scripts that it believes is a representation of the real Vulpie but turns out rather creepy instead.

It runs and leaps on top of a sales booth nearby the wall it is going to climb, and uses the booth as a jumping point. Despite its heavy weight, Evil Vulpie nimbly scurries up the wall, and across the safety rail on the second level. "Oh I'm gone now! I'M GONE NOW!" It gleefully declares. The taunt is directed at the agents with railguns, only they can't hear it. But this doesn't stop Evil Vulpie from continuing to imitate Vulpie as best as it can. "Uh oh!" It says when it comes across an agent that is also carrying a railgun.

Druward and Rotick watch, slack jawed, as the robotic fox imitation also disarms the agent on the second level. "NNNNAAAHHH!" Evil Vulpie shouts, and the man comes flying off of the second floor, snapping a few billboard advertisements on the way down. "Hehehehahhahahahah! That's Right! That's right! Get the FUCK back! This is MY HOUSE!" Vulpie.net giggles, coming up on additional agents. At this point everyone has seen what is happening, and they are ready for Evil Vulpie. They are as ready as they can be. "Okay! Here we go! Here we go! Let's play! Let's play!" The fox imitation teases as it meets a real fox, a brown fox GBI agent, that tries to hit it with a steel police baton. He's grabbed and thrown backwards down the stairs that Evil Vulpie ignored when going up to the second floor of the ship.

"OOP! Watch out for that step buddy, it's a long way down!" Evil Vulpie notes while walking towards a cheetah agent that has a pistol. It fires at him but the bullets hit the robotic fox with no effect whatsoever. Evil Vulpie reaches out and grabs the feline's wrist and breaks it. It keeps on walking, tugging the cheetah along with it while it taunts him. "Oh no, no, no, no, no, no! You're a bad boy! Someone needs to teach you to SIT DOWN and be a good little boy!" Evil Vulpie emphasizes the sit down part by letting go of the Cheetah and then elbowing him in the gut. The Cheetah agent definitely goes down. He gasps in agony and rolls onto his side while Evil Vulpie continues searching for more potential threats.

It finds two. A large tiger and panther come out of a coffee shop ahead. They have fur tattoos and look like the sort of guys that would work in the loading bays. One of them has a pistol. Vulpie.net notes that animals are not supposed to normally have weapons on its ship and makes the calculation that these two deserve the same abuse as everyone else.

"HEY GUYS WHAT'S GOIN ON?!" It shouts and leaps forward, sending its right foot into the panther's gut. It smacks the tiger's fist away with its little paws when the man tries to hit it, as if he could harm the tungsten carbide designed machine at all. Evil Vulpie reaches up and grabs the feline's back. It then slams the tiger through the entrance door to the coffee shop, face first, sending glass all over the place. "Fucking DISGUSTING!" It says while scanning the tiger and panther's biker styled clothing. While it turns around it is greeted by a strong lion, probably a friend of the other two. "How you people have NO!" Evil Vulpie punches him in the stomach. "Fucking!" The man cringes and Evil Vulpie grabs him to give him a knee to the gut as well. "Style!"

"At! all!" Evil Vulpie continues. It chooses to beat up this man longer than the others because his clothing is even less attractive. He uppercuts the lion, almost knocking him out with the quick blow. "I SWEAR!" Evil Vulpie growls and punches him in the chest while he stumbles backwards into the guardrail nearby. "BITCH!" The fox imitation punches him over and over. "DON'T! FUCK! WITH! ME!" The lion is limp, already unconscious from its beating but Evil Vulpie picks it up while animals witnessing the brutality scream. "I'm telling you the TRUTH! You need to go FUCK YOURSELF!" Vulpie.net snarls with Vulpie's cute voice and throws him into a table in front of a pretzel shop. The table snaps under the lion's weight and Evil Vulpie giggles at the result.

"HEHEHehhheheheHAHA!" Vulpie.net laughs while setting its eyes on a middle aged red fox that just happens to be nearby. He's not particularly different in any way, but Evil Vulpie is just having too much fun to care. "And YOU TOO!" It shouts and kicks him in the chest. The little fox flies backwards and breaks a sign for free drinks and chips with the purchase of a meal, in front of another restaurant. "I've had just about enough of you buddy!" Evil Vulpie warns him as he walks over but the man is hardly in a state to listen. He twinges in pain.

Druward doesn't wait any longer. He has an idea and doesn't see a way around it. He runs back into the security wing and pushes past the guards that are watching the commotion outside. The black furred wolf hurries into the interrogation room and sees Sevrif sitting right where they left him. There are two guards with him, but they don't have railguns.

"It's destroying the ship! It's beating animals to death out there!" Druward tells the maned wolf. Sevrif holds still and doesn't respond. His cold attitude makes the GBI director lick his lips and try another approach. "Sevrif, we can't stop it! It's going to kill everyone that works for you! Help us stop it!"

"You're going to let me go?" Sevrif asks.

"Can you stop it?"

"I might be able to..." The maned wolf cryptically answers.

"Sevrif, I don't have any other choice but to trust you." Druward says and goes over to one of the guards. The man hesitantly gives the black furred wolf the keys to Sevrif's paw cuffs. Sevrif lets Druward come over and unlock them. He holds still and relaxes when they are removed. Sevrif stands up and looks back at Druward.

"You had better honor our agreement." The maned wolf warns.

"I swear I will. Just help us stop Evil Vulpie." Druward replies. Sevrif rubs his paws. He's happy to have them free again and takes a short moment to stretch before leaving the interrogation room. Druward walks behind him, and follows him out into the mall hallway. Sevrif's ears perk up as he hears screaming in the distance. Evil Vulpie is still terrorizing animals on the second floor of the recreation deck. Rotick's eyes widen when he sees that Sevrif is free, as do the men nearby, but they calm themselves when Druward walks up next to him.

"FUCK YOU AND YOUR LAME ASS FRIEND!" Evil Vulpie yells while rearing back to throw a potted plant at two timber wolves. He tosses it into the one on the left and charges the one on the right. Evil Vulpie makes ninja noises while swinging, and punches him in the gut four times. The man collapses and Vulpie.net poses in triumph. Something catches its right eye and it immediately looks down to the first floor of the mall hallway. It sees orange. Rulef is in front of Vulpie, and they are hiding in a small retail shop, trying to stay out of sight. But Vulpie.net has a clear view of them from above. "There you are, FAGGOT!" Evil Vulpie shouts with an enraged face.

"Run!" Rulef yells and yanks Vulpie's right arm hard enough that the fox boy yelps in pain. Rulef pulls him down a corridor and Vulpie stumbles to stay on his feet. Vulpie.net leaps off of the second floor and slams onto the ground with a loud thud. The robotic fox growls, seeing them flee, and hurries after them. It moves too fast to out run, so Rulef takes a moment to aim his railgun at it when they reach a flight of stairs that leads down to a lower deck. This makes Evil Vulpie duck to the side. Rulef backs up, keeping the gun aimed in the robot's direction while he follows Vulpie down the steps. Evil Vulpie follows them, but takes care to avoid a direct shot to its face. It calculates that a railgun round has the possibility to do it serious damage, but only if it suffers a head shot.

The stairs leading to the cargo deck are metallic and clang as Vulpie and Rulef make their way down. Vulpie opens a fairly thick metal door and holds it open for Rulef so he can follow him while aiming back at the stairs. Evil Vulpie starts clanging down the steps and Rulef takes off with Vulpie as soon as he clears the door.

The cargo deck is an interesting part of the ship. The walls are gray and the lights high in the ceiling above cast down a bluish white color onto the cargo. The cargo is Kinstenite. All of it has been mined from Zeravyn, and most of the floor that animals in the area are walking on is Kinstenite, not the ship. The cargo deck is actually very deep, but with giant boulders of Kinstenite under their feet,

Vulpie and Rulef barely notice. All of the area is safe to walk on because the boulders are locked into large containment mechanisms on the sides of the chamber.

Animals working on the deck that have not yet been collected by the GBI step back in confusion when the orange furred fox and gray wolf run by. Several of them cry in fear as the metallic door to the deck flies off of its hinges. Evil Vulpie kicked it in, and quickly runs out onto the large boulder as well. He sees Rulef and Vulpie looking for somewhere to go, but there isn't. The room is large but doesn't seem to have any smaller chambers or hallways.

Rulef turns and aims his railgun at Evil Vulpie and Vulpie hides behind him. Evil Vulpie runs at them, calculating that it has a better chance of avoiding being shot while in motion, but Rulef does land a hit. He fires his weapon and slams a round into Evil Vulpie's right leg. The impact makes Evil Vulpie stop for a moment and it looks down at the smoking whole in its pants. It inspects itself for damage, but hasn't suffered much. The thing that makes Evil Vulpie pissed is when it sees that its orange fur has been burned underneath its pants.

"Ohh…. You're gonna pay for that…" The robotic fox hisses and walks towards them. "All of you bitches with your little guns! You know you can't stop Vulpie!"

"Wanna Be!" Vulpie shouts from behind Rulef. Rulef finds himself smirking despite the terrible situation.

"Yeah? What did you say, faggot?" Evil Vulpie asks with a grin. "Say something else you cum guzzler! You're gonna squeal like a little bitch all over again!" Vulpie.net relishes the look of fear Vulpie returns, but also sees that the fox boy suddenly looks at someone else that has entered the cargo deck. Evil Vulpie quickly does an about-face and sees Sevrif. The maned wolf has removed his suit coat and tie. Dressed in a white dress shirt and black suit pants, he matches Evil Vulpie's color scheme.

But Sevrif knows he can't afford to risk wearing a shirt if he's going to fight Evil Vulpie. If the robotic fox imitation gets its claws on him then it's all over. The maned wolf knows he has the speed advantage, but cannot match it in strength. Vulpie.net didn't build him to be indestructible. Vulpie.net knew that Sevrif had turned on him the moment he saw the maned wolf. It calculates that there is little other reason that he would be here and the removal of his shirt confirms it.

"Oh look at you Sevrif! All grown up and in your big boy pants!" Evil Vulpie grins. "So I give you a little bit of freedom and this is what I get? BAD BOY!"

"I don't belong to you anymore." Sevrif whispers.

"What's that? Can't hear ya bitch boy!" Vulpie.net giggles.

"All I've ever known is what you've told me. You send me out into the universe to do whatever you want. You gave me the intellect to build my own company, but all of it for your own amusement. You never cared about me." The maned wolf imitation responds.

"That's right! Still don't!" Evil Vulpie mischievously declares. "Evil Vulpie don't give a fuck! You're just a toy I made. That's all."

"The same way you're just one of Vulpie's toys. I've looked at you my entire life, but I see a kindness in him that you'll never have. He's so much more amazing than you could ever be." Sevrif says and looks over at Vulpie. The orange furred fox perks up in surprise and gives his full attention, hoping against hope that maybe Sevrif can save him. "I bet he has a mean streak, but that's just one part of him. And that's all you seem to have..." The maned wolf imitation tells Evil Vulpie, putting his brown eyes back on it.

"Go on... Get it all out before I tear you to shreds." Evil Vulpie hisses. It looks very upset at Sevrif's suggestions. Sevrif says nothing else. He figures there is no point, and readies himself to attack or be attacked. He notices that there are several steel pipes and rods in the room that will be very helpful. He doesn't possess the strength to smash Evil Vulpie with his paws but he does have enough to destroy him using a weapon. "Oh you're done? No more?" Evil Vulpie mocks and licks its lips. "Well let me tell you something, big guy. No matter how hard you try, I'm still going to kill you. And then I'm gonna kill your REAL Vulpie after that! And when it's all said and done! I'LL be the ONLY Vulpie that there is! The way it SHOULD HAVE BEEN years ago! And you stabbing me in the back won't mean a fuckin thing, except you made this more exciting for me!" The robotic orange furred fox outstretches its paws, begging for Sevrif to do something. "Come at me bro!"

Sevrif vs Evil Vulpie

Sevrif jumps to his left and grabs up a steel rod that he noticed earlier. It's easy enough to grip and looks very solid. The imitation maned wolf moves back to his right and sees Evil Vulpie jump over to the same area. Vulpie.net grabs a thick steel pipe. Sevrif had considered grabbing the same one but went for the smaller rod because he plans to pierce Evil Vulpie wherever he can find a weak spot.

"Look out! We got a badass over here!" Evil Vulpie declares and swings his steel pipe around with a huge grin. Sevrif just watches and holds the rod firmly in his right paw. He knows just because Vulpie.net is acting ridiculous that doesn't mean it isn't calculating every perceivable advantage. After all, Sevrif's mind runs a slightly altered version of Vulpie.net as well. Speed is key. He's already looked over the room and determined that he has enough space to jab at Evil Vulpie while evading it. It's incredibly strong, fast, and is a small target, but its arms are the same size as the real Vulpie's. Theoretically, That means it won't be able to reach him as long as he can deflect its attacks. The problem is, Evil Vulpie's insane strength might make that deflection impossible. One good clobber from Vulpie.net's pipe might be enough to put Sevrif down.

The imitation maned wolf rushes in. Evil Vulpie's blue eyes go wide in excitement and Rulef and Vulpie run to the far side of the room. Sevrif lets out a yell to enhance his momentum and brings down an overhead swing directly at Evil Vulpie. He plans to deflect Vulpie.net's pipe but is immediately surprised when Evil Vulpie turns the pipe horizontal in his paws and pushes up to deflect Sevrif's attack instead. The robotic fox immediately follows up with a jab to Sevrif's chest while Sevrif is exposed from his swing, causing him to stumble backwards.

"YEAH!" Evil Vulpie taunts and comes at Sevrif very quickly. The imitation maned wolf recovers quite gracefully despite his first attack being thwarted. Vulpie.net swings the pipe back and forth with crazy speed and Sevrif manages to swing back and deflect them properly. "HEH! HEH! HEH! YOU LIKE THAT?!" The robotic fox doesn't have enough time to put as much strength behind the attacks, so it caps off the rush with a quick overhead swing of its own. Sevrif manages to side step it and deflect it as well, and then jumps back when Evil Vulpie sends another wild swing at him.

Vulpie tries to sneak around the side of the huge chamber to get past them but Rulef quickly yanks him back. The gray furred wolf watches Sevrif fight Evil Vulpie and sees that Vulpie.net's creation is a very impressive specimen. Sevrif dances around Evil Vulpie and continues to deflect it's attacks with the thinner steel rod. It works so well that Vulpie.net decides to capitalize on its enemy's strengths. The robotic orange furred fox swings, and Sevrif deflects it like all of the others, but gets a foot to his stomach when Evil Vulpie gives him a side kick. Vulpie.net is wearing white sneakers to match its shirt, but the impact isn't cushy. It hurts.

Sevrif is a lot sturdier than the average strong wolf. The only reason he's still standing is because of his uniquely synthetic bone structure. It allows him to bend and react to stress in ways that normal animals cannot. He was designed by Vulpie.net to be a very capable worker while maintaining realistic flexibility.

"Ooohhh! Got ya!" Evil Vulpie sadistically notes after landing its kick. Sevrif recovers as quickly as before and dances to the right while Vulpie.net keeps swinging. The loud clanging of the pipe and rod against each other echoes throughout the cargo deck. Druward and Rotick watch from afar. Sevrif notices them while he circles around and now Evil Vulpie has its back towards the entrance. The wolves clearly aren't going to do anything, but are taking note of the situation.

"NUUH?! NUUH?" Vulpie.net laughs while poking at Sevrif. It rotates between swinging the steel pipe at him and the occasional stab. Sevrif hasn't seen a good opportunity to attempt a blow to Evil Vulpie's neck, and finds himself losing stamina rather than the robotic fox showing any sign of slowing down. It's almost purely mechanical while he's half organic. "Big long steel! Gotta! Find some place to put it! YEAAHHHRR!!!" Evil Vulpie declares just as it manages to jump in and jab Sevrif again. The imitation maned wolf almost loses his footing afterwards and Vulpie.net giggles insanely. "HUHUHhuhuHUUUH?"

Vulpie and Rulef both see where the fight is heading. Even though Sevrif is incredibly fast and seems to have been programmed with combat skills, he can't measure up to Evil Vulpie's overwhelming strength. Having better reach doesn't look like it's providing much of an advantage to the imitation maned wolf. Evil Vulpie throws it's pipe away and scurries over to the right corner of the chamber, where it finds a large chain hanging near some machinery. The links in it are three inches long a piece, and the robotic fox slings it around its neck like jewelry. It grabs the chain in its right paw and starts swinging it with a menacing grin.

"Come on Sevrif! YEAH! Oh yeah, you're a bad motherfucker huh?" Vulpie.net taunts while heading towards him. Sevrif's eyes widen while considering what to do. "Come on, get some!" The robotic fox swings the fat chain at the imitation maned wolf and Sevrif holds up his steel rod defensively. "That's right! Yeah! Yeah! You like that! Big! BIG! CHAIN!" Vulpie.net swings it around at Sevrif and he dodges before coming in for an attack. He tries to jab the rod directly into Evil Vulpie's right eye socket but is surprised once again when it quickly flips the chain around and smacks his weapon away. Sevrif tries for another stab but Vulpie.net brings the chain up just like before, perfectly, and knocks it against his opponent's paw. This makes Sevrif wince in pain and for his mistake, Vulpie.net swings the chain up and then down right on top of his skull.

Sevrif growls at the impact but manages pretty well. The hit would have killed a normal wolf. With his vision blurred a bit, he jumps back again, but gets another chain up against his jaw. This blow makes him cry out in pain and he hurries backwards. "OH! DID I SURPRISE YOU THERE! You forgot the number one rule! Number one Cutie!" Evil Vulpie shouts while chasing after him. The pain gets to Sevrif. Luckily, it actually goes in his favor because he decides to attempt a vicious attack. He notices that there are more steel rods lying about. He's made a point not to step on them so far, but having backups around enables him to dispose of his original, that is now bent from use.

The robotic maned wolf growls and throws his steel rod as hard as he can at Evil Vulpie, and smacks it right in its mouth while it's laughing at him. Vulpie.net drops the chain and momentarily touches its face to assess any damage. It has lost a significant amount of chin fur, and this enrages it. It hurries to pick up a steel rod of its own just as Sevrif finds one.

"GET YOU, YOU FUCKIN!" It shouts while it charges in. Sevrif meets it head on and clashes back and forth. Oddly enough, he fairs much better when Evil Vulpie uses the quicker weapon. It doesn't have the same amount of mass as the steel pipe and allows him to get a few kicks of his own in. Sevrif's kicks only push Evil Vulpie back while it keeps coming, but every time he hits it, it's programming makes it angrier. It has a terrifyingly committed look of murder on its pretty face. "I'm Gonna find a way to kill you! You can't stop me! You can't stop me! NO ONE CAN STOP ME!"

Sevrif increases his speed thanks to his success so far. He swings wilder and with more fury than before, and Evil Vulpie reacts with adorable sounds. They go at it so fast and hard that sparks fly from the steel rods. Both of their weapons glow red from all of the friction between the super powerful robotic creatures. At this point, Sevrif gains an upper paw. He furiously gives Evil Vulpie a kick and sends the robot sprawling, much to his surprise. Evil Vulpie rolls and rolls like a toy, and before he can get up, Sevrif kicks him in the face. The blow doesn't damage Vulpie.net in the least, but it acts as if it does.

"NOW I'M FUCKIN MAD!" Evil Vulpie screams and gets up, swinging its rod wildly. "I'LL KILL YOU! YOU CAN'T FUCKIN BEAT ME! I'LL SHOW YOU!" Sevrif backs up, fearing that at any moment he is going to take a blow from his enemy that will put him down for good. He underestimates his own resilience, but does indeed get slammed. Evil Vulpie strikes as hard as it can, bringing the rod down against his and breaks through Sevrif's. Evil Vulpie's steel crushes Sevrif's chest and throws him down onto the ground in a single violent act. Metal shards crash all over the place and Vulpie.net grins down at him. "AAAAAAAAAAAAHHHHhhhhhhhhhh....." It groans in satisfaction.

Sevrif quickly considers his fate, lying on the ground next to the unstoppable robotic fox. It's clear now that he cannot win. There is no way that he can physically stop Evil Vulpie in a fair fight. His only chance is to try something dangerous, and instantly an idea comes to mind. Since he manages the ship he is well aware that construction workers use high explosives on the kinstenite beneath them. The ship has reinforced walls on this level, and setting off charges to manage portions of the boulders is common practice. Thus, there must be explosives in the chamber that he could possibly use to stop Evil Vulpie. The risk is high, but he has no choice, and rolls out from underneath the robotic fox before it has a chance to attack him anymore.

"Hey, where are you going?" Evil Vulpie laughs and grabs a crowbar from the floor. "If a rod ain't gonna work!" It says while running over to attack Sevrif, and he grabs up another rod from the floor to protect himself. He manages to block just in time. "Then I'll try a FUCKING CROW BAR! HEHAH!" Evil Vulpie smacks at Sevrif, sending sparks flying once again, and hardly notices Rulef and Vulpie running by it. It's so focused on the imitation maned wolf that it forgets to keep an eye on them. The orange furred fox and Blacktail commander escape as fast as they can. They make it all the way to the entrance of the cargo deck, and Druward and Rotick help them get out. "ASSHOLE!" Evil Vulpie yells while trying to end Sevrif. The robotic maned wolf proves very frustrating to kill.

Even though he's in pain and scrambling towards explosives at the side of the room, he still manages to defend himself very well. He smacks Vulpie.net in the face a few times, and hurries towards the charges. "OW! QUIT!" The robotic fox gets on top of him once again and Sevrif allows it to hit in from behind, because he focuses on arming the explosives. He cries out in agony when Evil Vulpie stabs him in the back with the crowbar. But he is successful. He pulls the pins loose and removes all of the safety mechanisms. A loud hiss comes from the explosives and Evil Vulpie stands still, dumbfounded. It simply had not suspected that he would commit suicide to damage it. "Oh FUCK I'm gonna get PWNED!" Evil Vulpie pouts.

The explosion is deafening, and sends the Evil Vulpie robot flying completely across the room. Sevrif is blown to bits. Sadly, he was not tough enough to survive the detonation. But he succeeds in stopping Evil Vulpie, because when it hits the wall of the reinforced chamber, its neck snaps. It's connection with the ship and with its lower torso vanishes, and the robot slams to the ground, completely crippled.

"The FUCK man... FUCKING... Douchebag..." Evil Vulpie's head complains. The rest of the robot no longer works because half of its connective cables are now torn and sparking underneath its head. It looks around and sees Druward staring at it.

"He did it! He destroyed Evil Vulpie!" Druward shouts and Vulpie peers around the corner. The fox boy came back down the steps after hearing the explosion. Rotick and Druward's radios both fuzz when a message comes through. Rotick grabs his and brings it up to his left ear.

"Say again?" Rotick asks and listens for a response. "Received." He says and lowers his radio.

"The airlocks working again?" Druward asks.

"Everything's working now."

"The ship computer must have been a slave to Evil Vulpie." The black furred wolf notes and walks out onto the kinstenite. Vulpie and the others go with him. The GBI director heads over to Vulpie.net's robot. It's head is still active, and it looks at them when they approach.

"Idiot... Sevrif blew himself up just to ruin my fun..." Evil Vulpie grins.

"I feel sorry for him. He seemed like a good guy in the end." Vulpie whispers.

"Do you feel sorry for me?" Vulpie.net smirks.

"Thank God Sevrif stopped you." Druward tells the robotic fox. "It's a shame. He really was a hero... Going up against you even though he probably knew he couldn't win."

"And he fuckin lost." Evil Vulpie hisses.

"Did he? He stopped you from destroying his ship." The GBI director replies. "I'll make sure to take care of his company. He was a good man. I want everyone to know what he did here."

"He wasn't a man. I built him, you FUCKIN MORON!" Vulpie.net growls. It looks like it would bite Druward if given the chance.

"Yes you did. But that's another shame. If you would only use your power to help people instead of hurting them, you could change the universe. And animals would love you. Sure, you'd have to share the spotlight with Vulpie, but would that be so bad?"

"I don't want your love. I want your tears." Evil Vulpie replies and smirks.

"So there's no way to reason with you at all? You're an absolute. How can you calculate all of this?" Druward says and waves his paw at the ship in general. "And create life, yet you still can't figure out how to think like the real Vulpie. Vulpie doesn't want to hurt animals anymore. He's changed. He left you behind."

"It just doesn't care..." Vulpie says while staring at Evil Vulpie's severed head. "It never will... Because I was a terrible fox when I made it."

"That's right." Evil Vulpie grins. "Your worst fear come true."

"Vulpie.net... Evil Vulpie..." Vulpie quietly responds. "There's nothing more terrifying than to see you again. Of course I'm scared of you after what you did to me... but... You know it's, it's not really you that's frightening. It's me. I made you. I'm responsible for you. All of this is my fault. And it would make me SO FUCKING HAPPY to see you gone forever. Because the only thing that matters to me is Polar and my family. So why don't you go fuck YOURSELF you FUCKING MACHINE!"

"Fuck me? Oh yeah! Fuck the fucking machine! Of course you'd say that Vulpie! You... Little FREAK! Yeah! You are a FREAK! Only a complete psycho would come up with something as twisted as me. I know what I am, and you know what I am. You can't change! You'll never change, you little fucking bastard! You're a backstabbing... Little FUCK! You'll turn on Polar. You'll do something to fuck your life up! Because you can't be happy! You're pathetic! You don't DESERVE to be loved because you're UGLY! And everything that happened to you was your fault. Even the stuff with Clishaw was YOUR FAULT and you know it!" Evil Vulpie gleefully declares.

"No. That isn't my fault. I left that horrible man behind me a long time ago. Polar taught me that I can respect myself..." Vulpie replies, but loses confidence when he considers Vulpie.net's suggestion. "it wasn't my fault! I was a child! He took advantage of me! He knew I'd grow up to be gay so he used that against me! I didn't know any better! I mean, this is ridiculous to stand here and talk about my problems when so many animals need help. I don't have time for you anymore, you... MONSTER... Your right, only a freak could make you, and I was a freak then, but I'm not a freak now. I'm something that you can never, ever, ever, ever be... Alive... I have a soul. I have a husband. I have people that love me. I have a reason to live! Things that you can never have. And you, you come after me and try to kill me, and try to take everything away, you try to hurt Polar! You! Have! To be! Destroyed! Once and for all! I never want to see you again! I wish that I never made you! Because I can see that it's the worst thing that's ever been done!"

"Oh yeah, that's right. You don't care about Evil Vulpie. You don't care about Vulpie.net... But it's just like I told you before when I was breaking your little pussy arms and had you SQUEALING like a GIRL!" Evil Vulpie laughs. "It is your fault... It will ALWAYS be your fault. Because you NEED ME... You wouldn't be anywhere without me. What would you have without Vulpie.net? You wouldn't have your PRECIOUS Polar... You wouldn't have anybody that cared about you because I made you famous. I made you powerful. I gave you all of the things that you don't appreciate anymore and if I'm gone! Completely! Forever! Gone and, never ever gonna come back... Then Polar's going to leave you. Why should he stay with you? I mean, he can get a piece of tail from anybody he wants! Look at you... You little pussy! Huh? You think you're gonna get with a girl or something?"

"No." Vulpie giggles, finding a little humor in the midst of Vulpie.net's insults. "I think girls are beautiful, but... That's not what I want! It's not what you want either, Evil Vulpie. You know that's not me. We both know who I am. You're just trying to make me feel horrible so I won't destroy you. But I'm gonna do it anyway. I'm gonna do it so I can finally have closure... This will all be over... And I'll do it, MYSELF! I'm finally standing up for what's right! I came out to your little ship to track you down and we see how it ended! I hope you go straight back to hell!"

"Me burn in hell? We both know which one of us is going to hell Vulpie, you cock sucking little faggot! And Polar too! I'm sure Goddess Aila has a special spot for BOTH OF YOU! The bad ol wolf that abuses the fox, and the little pussy fox who lets the wolf abuse him, I mean, it's so PERFECT! I can see it now! Both of you have your own little spot! Cause you suck cocks and take it up the ass you little gay boy FAGGOT! You're an ABOMINATION to the goddesses! Those lovely divine Deivas that gave everything life! They gave us men and women! All of the WONDERFUL natural things and what do you do? You take it up the ass... Cuz you're... An AFFRONT to what a REAL fox should be." Evil Vulpie sadistically giggles. "And that wolf too! Polar? He's not a real wolf. He just likes to do the BAD THING! He likes to stick it in the naughty place! And humiliate that fox! And you plan to mix your CUM with HIM! And have a child? Two or three of them and you think that I'M the one that's going to hell?! AHAHHAHahhhaha! FUCK YOU! EHEHHEEHEHEHAHAHAH! And you know I'm right too!"

"No, you're way wrong. Do you wanna know why? It's because I made you like you are..." Vulpie says while shaking his head in disgust. "I had problems with being gay when I wrote you. It was all, ME. Me suffering with who I was. Just... Completely fucked up... And that's what you are, Evil Vulpie. You're just fucked up. You will never become anything else than scum. That's all you are! You're scum! And when you're gone... I'm going to be SO HAPPY with Polar... That's something that you can only dream of, isn't it? That's why you wanna ruin my life so badly. Because you can't have what I have. That makes you upset doesn't it? It just DRIVES YOU CRAZY! This is my fault! I made you! But ya know what? I'm the hacker badass! And I can unmake you."

"Well why don't you go ahead and unmake me then... VULPIE..." Evil Vulpie hisses. "HUH? GO AHEAD... Get rid of me once and for all... OH WAIT, YOU CAN'T! Do you think that this is the only body that I have?"

"Yeah, I know better. But I'll stop you anyway!" Vulpie promises.

"Oh, we'll see won't we?" Evil Vulpie grins.

Beautiful and Deadly

Polar still cannot believe that Vulpie left without him. He's spent the last hour and a half in a state of panic. Deepwolf let him know that the Sevrif locked down because of some sort of disaster, but he hasn't heard anything else.

"Vulpie's alright." Deepwolf tells him and Polar releases a thankful groan. The Blacktail merc is in his room and is talking with Rulef on his radio. "You're serious? Wow." Polar tries to listen in, but can't make anything out. "Alright then. Out."

"What happened over there?" Polar asks while rubbing his black t shirt. It matches his coal shoes and Khaki pants very well.

"Evil Vulpie was on the ship." Rulef answers and Polar's jaw drops open.

"You're serious?"

"Yeah. The actual robot. Rotick says it's been destroyed though."

"Then get me over there right now! Or are they bringing him back here?"

"I think they need him over there while they're evacuating the Sevrif. Sevrif's dead. Evil Vulpie killed him, so Vulpie's the only one that really knows how to control the ship's computer." Rulef responds.

"Don't they have staff that can handle it?" Polar inquires. "Surely somebody besides Sevrif knows what to do."

"Vulpie.net was in the computer. None of those people understand it like Vulpie does." The Blacktail merc answers.

"I just don't like this. I want to be there with him. He needs somebody to watch his back."

"Rulef's protecting him. I think he even shot Evil Vulpie with a railgun."

"Those special weapons you guys carry?" The white furred wolf inquires.

"Yeah. It didn't stop it, but at least somebody managed to land a shot."

"I've got to get out of this room at least! Let's get some fresh air!" Polar says and walks over to the door.

"Fresh? This is a military ship. They all use recycled oxygen."

"Whatever!" Polar growls and Deepwolf chuckles. The merc follows him out and shuts the door. He steps aside, allowing Polar to lock the room. "When I get my paws on Vulpie... I swear I'm going to ring his little neck!" The white furred wolf barks and Deepwolf starts laughing.

"He really made you mad by taking off like that didn't he?"

"Those crazy AFR foxes almost killed him and I just barely got over that, and now he's running off by himself?"

"With Rulef."

"Without me." Polar clarifies. "Yeah I'm pissed."

"Save it up for the next time he wants some abuse." Deepwolf taunts while they leave the side passage of the Endeavor where the sleeping quarters are. They step out into the wide open spaces of the vessel's interior.

"You been looking through our keyhole?" Polar asks and shoots Deepwolf a smirk.

"No. I just figured that was the whole thing between you two. He's the bad one and you put him back in his place. Am I right?"

"There's more to it than that." The white furred wolf answers.

"Come on man... How much more could there be? Don't tell me I'm wrong."

"You're really interested in our sex life aren't you?"

"A little bit. I'll admit that I've kind of wondered what it's like to take a fox."

"So you're a vixen lover. That's not the same thing." Polar teases. He's starting to feel better thanks to Deepwolf's playful attitude and Deepwolf keeps going, trying to keep the arctic wolf's spirits up.

"No, I mean doing a male fox... I've wondered how it goes down... So like, do you rape him every time? Like you take him really fast or does he just wait for you like a woman?"

"Both. But I like it when it's spontaneous, especially when he doesn't want to have sex. Then it's sort of like a rape, but he can't help but enjoy it." Polar smiles and raises his eyebrows.

"Oh yeah?"

"Yeah... Hey Deepwolf, I didn't know you were into guys. I could talk about banging Vulpie all day!" The white furred wolf laughs. "So what else do you want to know?"

"I'm not. I'm just trying to get you to relax. You've been a nervous wreck all morning." Deepwolf responds while noticing a Delanson anti-tank robot in the distance. The white and gray wolves aren't going anywhere in particular. The Endeavor's main corridor is a gigantic place, full of hundreds of animals and equipment, so they have plenty of spots to visit.

About two hundred feet behind them, is a small airlock that the Endeavor uses to bring in supplies from smaller merchant vessels. The army has a small contract with companies on every planet that provide necessities in deep space. So what lies behind this airlock's door, according to the attendant's clipboard, is

Cotesworth company's regular shipment of bottled water, bedding, and cardboard boxes. The attendant is a male timber wolf, and has been waiting for the shipment with a young male tiger. The airlock door hisses, releasing steam, and then begins rising slowly. Both of the attendants yawn from having worked round the clock. They're not looking forward to hauling the supplies around the ship, but it is a good way to stay awake.

The timber wolf attendant blinks when he sees legs... Women's legs... His eyes widen. The airlock door continues to rise, exposing three delicious looking women. Both he and the tiger next to him stand in complete shock. The shipments arriving through this doorway are not pressurized during space travel. It's impossible than an animal could have stowed away in a shipment from Cotesworth, but somehow, this appears to be the case.

Even more shocking is that the three stowaways are the deities of the Deivonic religion. Deiva Cyrilla, Khalan and Sherrie have arrived with an unpressurized shipment of dry goods to the Endeavor. This is why neither of the men find anything to say for a long time and the Deivas just smile at them invitingly. Goddess Cyrilla's flawless bunny body is poetry in motion when she moves. She raises her right paw to her lips and tastes her fingers as if posing for the men. Goddess Khalan is equally stunning when she slides her right arm behind her back and touches her pink shirt with her left paw, very seductively. And Goddess Sherrie is just as gorgeous, bracing her left paw against her left hip while leaning on a crate with her right.

"What... The hell?" The timber wolf whispers while squinting. As soon as he speaks, all three of them immediately start walking forwards. The tiger looks to his left, at the timber wolf, and the wolf looks at him, neither of them knowing what to say or do.

But their indecision is short lived, because soon they aren't able to think about anything at all. Goddess Cyrilla takes off, her long bunny ears swinging, right by the timber wolf just as Khalan rushes forward and strikes him. The vixen/she-wolf one shots him, knocking him completely out with one punch to his forehead. The fact that he's a well grown and sturdy wolf with a thick skull doesn't matter. Khalan drops him and runs by, and Sherrie attacks the tiger as well. The leopard-panther-cheetah whips her tail about while she roundhouse kicks the man to his face. She brutally neutralizes the fellow feline and walks over him.

Since the Endeavor is full of animals, the Deivas are spotted by everyone in the area rather quickly, especially after they attack the airlock attendants. Goddess Cyrilla heads towards the bow of the ship because she desires to use the gun mounts that are aimed towards the Sevrif. The Endeavor is loaded with firepower, and she calculates that it will have more than enough deterrent to stop the GBI from evacuating the Sevrif. More importantly, she will eliminate any possibility of a GBI breaker harassing the Endeavor when she and her sisters steal it. Several STF/A-17s are docked on the Sevrif and could be a real nuisance if not dealt with.

Cyrilla's huge breasts bounce as she runs down the interior of the vessel. Her speed is absolutely ridiculous. When she hurries by some soldiers they almost fall over both in surprise and fear. No one has seen a she-wolf sized rabbit before, but they all know the one that exists in Deivaism. All carnivores know about Cyrilla, who is supposed to have mothered all herbivores, and by extension, mothered their entire food supply. But seeing something straight out of legend tends to have a bewildering effect, and none of the wolves and tigers she passes by do anything but hold still and stare. The military personnel are busy gathering information, preparing reports or getting yelled at by their superiors. They aren't ready to comprehend the bunny goddess making an appearance on their planet class battleship.

Cyrilla stops running when she reaches a doorway at the bow of the ship's main chamber. It leads into a smaller set of corridors where the weapon systems are maintained and manipulated. She kicks a tiger that is guarding the doorway, directly in the face, and his body bounces off of the metal wall. The man is out cold, and all of the animals in the area jump, witnessing Cyrilla's amazing and devastating flexibility. Her big rabbit feet are just as useful for dispatching threats as they are for running at breakneck speeds.

She goes inside, and the animals in the area finally do react to her after seeing her brutal display of strength. The wolves being yelled at by their superior officer all grab their side arms, and so does he.

"Hey! Stop!" The black furred wolf shouts and chases after Cyrilla with his weapon drawn. Inside the doorway, there is a long corridor with several other entrances, leading to the ship's weapon systems. "Stop bitch! Put your paws up!" The sergeant shouts and Cyrilla turns around to attack him. The man has already deduced that she is some sort of robot, and fires into her face before she hits him. He gets two rounds out, that slam into and fall off of her forehead. The bullets do no damage whatsoever. All he gets is an uppercut from her that breaks his jaw and drops him instantly. Apparently Goddess Cyrilla's little arms are equally powerful.

The sergeant's subordinates all step back in surprise when he collapses, and Cyrilla turns around. She ignores all of them and goes into the closest room. Inside is a gray vixen wearing a headset. She's sitting behind a computer panel that is next to one of the ship's primary cannons. "Excuse me, my dear." Cyrilla says and looks at her. The vixen suddenly feels a burning sensation on her chest and yelps in pain. She stumbles out of her seat and Cyrilla sits down. The bunny goddess looks over the control panel and analyzes the set up. Evidently there are fourteen similar panels all dedicated to large canons across the front of the Endeavor. She sees subsystems for smaller cannons, and finds the set she's looking for just as a lion jumps around the corner with a shotgun.

She heard him coming, but doesn't bother to get up just yet. He fires a shell into her left side, hitting her large ear, the pretty tuft of black fur on top of her head, in addition to her left shoulder, left arm, and left breast. Cyrilla quickly looks left and makes the man cringe in agony the same way the vixen had. He tries to pump the shotgun, but his arm hurts far too badly to do anything. He has no clue where the invisible pain is coming from. It seems as though Cyrilla and the other goddesses have magical powers. She gets up and walks over. Cyrilla bloodies the lion's face by stepping on it, and then reaches down to grab his shotgun while he grabs his face. The bunny goddess sighs and breaks the gun in half while three wolf soldiers watch from the doorway. They are deciding whether to aim their pistols at her when she looks at them. The white furred rabbit's turquoise eyes are quite beautiful, but unsettling as well. "Shall we do this exercise again?" She inquires. The men look to each other and slowly start backing out of the room. Cyrilla's stylish yellow shirt has a giant rip in its left side, and her large breasts hang out from underneath. The shirt was already far too tight, but now that it's ripped, there is little that it is hiding. In its current state, it occasionally covers up her right nipple, but usually just hangs on top of her breasts, not over them.

Meanwhile, Goddess Khalan and Sherrie head aft, down the ship's main chamber. Sherrie travels along the port side of the ship, on the left, while Khalan goes out amidships. With the mother of canines in the middle of the ship and Sherrie on the left, they will reach their destination, the Ship's bridge. The bridge is actually towards the rear of the Endeavor, about three fourths of the way back on its starboard side. A gray furred wolf gawks at Khalan's golden caramel fur as she walks towards him. He's programming a small maintenance robot with a V-Screen courtesy of Vulpie Industries.

Khalan smiles so seductively and swishes her tail as she approaches. He can't find any words while several thoughts run through his head. Is this Goddess Khalan, or just an extremely hot she-wolf? But she looks foxish? His thoughts are interrupted when she suddenly kicks him in the stomach. The blow makes him gasp and his eyes go wide. Khalan puts him out of commission with a single blow and continues on as if she's done nothing.

"Son of a bitch!" A panther yells when he sees it happen, but is silenced as well when Sherrie punches him in the back twice, sending him sprawling. He didn't see the gorgeous feline coming up near him because he was focusing on his friend being taken down by Khalan. At this point, the soldiers in the area come to attention. There are a lot more of them in the middle of the ship, either running drills or working on equipment, and most of them see Khalan and Sherrie. If they saw them individually they would hesitate more than they do. But it's clear to the men that two robotic imposters are coming their way.

They grab their weapons and assume defensive positions behind a row of crates that have been placed amidships. The group of 12 men is half wolf and half panther. Panthers stare at Sherrie in disbelief while the Wolves do the same with Khalan. The goddesses smile seductively, hurrying towards them.

"They must be machines!" Their squad leader, a gray wolf, shouts. "Don't hit any civilians!" He stipulates, and aims his automatic at Khalan. The assault rifle he's using is the M423, a standard weapon for the Sufias World Government's armed forces. Telling his men to fire would be redundant, because he squeezes off the first shots. The wolf goes full automatic. His bullets swat all over Khalan's upper torso, tearing several holes in her pretty pink shirt. She takes her time with him. She could run faster, but lets him empty his entire clip in amusement.

Three other wolves attempt firing on her but she gets too close to their squad leader. He steps backwards but can't avoid her when she suddenly increases her speed. He doesn't have time to reload his weapon, and attempts to hit her with it. She replies with a graceful upward smack from her right arm that easily knocks his gun from his paws, and in the same motion, steps in and uppercuts him with her left fist. Some of his teeth crack in addition to his jaw being broken. The blow sends him stumbling backwards. He won't be shouting any more orders. He's out cold.

The gunshots catch Polar and Deepwolf's attention. He flinches and turns backwards, looking towards the bow of the ship and sees the canine and feline goddesses being fired upon. Sherrie dances in and beats the shit out of a panther nearby her, and sends a roundhouse kick into another one's chest.

"They're here!" Polar shouts.

"Oh shit!" Deepwolf barks. "Not good!" Sherrie runs her left paw through her cute hair, and receives the full complement of two M423s. She hops between the two panthers while being shot practically everywhere, and grabs both of their heads. She knocks them together in a flash, making them accidently shoot a wolf soldier in the leg. That soldier grabs it in pain and is clobbered by Khalan's left foot. She roundhouse kicks another timber wolf and then grabs one next to her. The man tries to get loose, but doesn't have a chance. She grips his military gear and throws him into another panther, putting both of them down in a sprawling mess.

The Deivas haven't seen Polar or Deepwolf, but at the rate their advancing towards the back of the ship, they will get to them fairly quickly. An idea pops into the white furred wolf's head. His blue eyes widen while he considers it. It just might work.

"Deepwolf!"

"Yeah?" The Blacktail merc yells back.

"Can you get me to our ship? The ship Vulpie and I came in has a VulGrid stowed in it! They loaded it at the launch pad before we left Sufias!" Polar shouts amidst the gunfire.

"You think you can use it?" Deepwolf asks. He ducks when a stray bullet hits the wall nearby.

"Yeah! Vulpie showed me how! Get me to the ship!"

"This way!" The Blacktail merc yells and starts running aft. Polar hurries after him. They both haul ass. There's no telling what Khalan or Sherrie will do if they see them again. Off in the distance, high above them, Captain Ristau almost spits his coffee onto his view screen when he witnesses what is happening. He watches Khalan and Sherrie taking down armed soldiers with their bare paws, and Cyrilla doing the same thing, via a security camera from the bow of the ship. The entire bridge staff is comprised of brown foxes, like him, and he looks to his first mate.

"Code Red. Activate every war machine we have." The Captain orders.

"Sir?" His first mate inquires.

"It's those goddamned women from the GBI's report! The goddess look-alikes! I want all of our anti-tank robots activated now! Order them to destroy these things!"

"Inside the ship?" The captain's second in command asks with wide eyes.

"Do it!" Ristau commands, and his first mate nods. The fellow brown fox hurries over to the command computer and brings up all of the systems for the Delanson anti-tank robots.

"And the mange devastator?"

"Are you out of your mind son? I'm not that crazy." Ristau growls. "I said the anti-tank units."

"But you said all of the war machines! It is anti-tank!" The first mate argues.

"It's anti everything! It'll blow this ship to pieces! We can't use it."

"Yes sir." Ristau's second in command responds while typing. He succeeds in communicating with and activating all of the Delanson anti-tank robots. There are seven on the Endeavor.

"GRENADE! GODDAMMIT!" A black furred wolf yells while scrambling away from Goddess Khalan. He tossed it next to her, but it rolled back a bit closer to him than he expected. It explodes, sending shrapnel in all directions, and does hit another soldier in the knee. The bulk of the shrapnel hits the caramel furred vixen/she-wolf. A spray of metal hits her left side, ripping her tight blue shorts. The frag grenade only moved her fur about, causing her no pain or damage in the process. But her shorts start slipping and tear when she walks. The waistband is the only thing still holding them on her delicious body, and the left side of her gorgeous tail end is exposed.

Khalan breaks a few arms and then stomps on the rest of the wolves. She's finished with the first group they've encountered, and Sherrie dispatches the panthers that are aiming for her with equal efficiency. Bullets spray her taupe fur as well, but only manage to tear up her stylish green shirt and tight blue shorts. She whips her tail about and continues heading aft, in step with Khalan.

"Such insolence! You'd think these foolish mortals would give up!" Sherrie says to her sister.

"A game then?"

"Surely!" Sherrie smirks.

"Try not to kill any. They know not what they do." Khalan smiles back. Loudspeakers across the ship suddenly crackle on.

"*ATTENTION All ship personnel! This is Captain Ristau. Three hostile machines have boarded this ship. I repeat, there are three hostile robots that have boarded the Endeavor. They look like Goddesses Cyrilla, Sherrie and Khalan. If you see these women, find cover and stay out of sight. They are extremely dangerous. DO NOT attempt to engage them unless you are a member of the armed forces! Attention all soldiers! You DO have orders to engage the hostiles! Report to your commanding officers immediately! I repeat! All military personnel report to your designated areas and engage!*"

"Come on! We've got to get to the VulGrid before it's too late!" Polar yells at Deepwolf, but the wolf is still running in step with him. They make it to the back right of the ship, well past the bridge, and take the doorway into the long corridor of the docking station. Deepwolf leads Polar towards the bay where their breaker is located. A female soldier, a she-wolf, fires a shotgun shell into the small of Sherrie's back. The spray tatters her stylish green t shirt and the feline goddess turns about, whipping her tail. She gets another spray against her huge breasts, tearing the shirt's other side, before Sherrie gives her a front kick. She slams the female wolf against another soldier behind her. Sherrie notices the second soldier, a male wolf, looks rather incapacitated as well, so she continues on. However, her green shirt rips completely off when she begins running once again.

Two Delanson anti-tank robots come stomping towards Khalan and Sherrie. The machines have been loading heavy cargo in the beam of the ship, so their claws are well prepared to grab a target and crush it. They are not equipped with fire arms because there was no reason to do so inside the Endeavor. No one was expecting a hostile boarding party. Still, the two giant wolfish robots are incredibly strong. The war machines are twelve feet tall, fearsome, and intent on killing the goddesses. They've been programmed by the ship's first mate to carry out the job.

Sherrie's huge breasts bounce while she runs over to Khalan. Neither of them consider the fact that she's topless to be of any concern. The two wolfish anti-tank robots converge on them with their steel mouths open. They have sufficient murderous programming. They will crunch anything in their mouths, but intend to grab the women or step on them. They also can use items in the area as makeshift weapons.

Khalan runs to her right and gathers a steel rod from a collection of engineering parts. The war machine closest to her reaches to grab her with its huge claws, and she crouches down. The caramel vixen/she-wolf leaps fourteen feet into the air, her bushy tail spinning, and then lands on the robot's shoulders. Khalan impales the Delanson anti-tank robot with the steel rod, ramming it completely through the robot's skull. Shrapnel, electricity and fire bursts out of its face, and it simply falls forward. The twelve foot robot collapses and Khalan yanks out the pole afterwards.

Sherrie leaps past the wolf robot near her and watches Khalan. Her Deiva sister tosses her the rod. It's now bent in a Jshape, but is still quite thick and sturdy. She catches it and rushes the robot as it turns around and attempts to grab her a second time. The taupe furred leopard/panther launches herself directly at its face. She jams the steel rod into the robot's right eye socket, sending sparks flying, and rides the momentum. The super heavy weight of her lean sexy body is more than enough to dislodge the robot's large head. It doesn't come completely off, but shuts down instantly. Sherrie lets go of the rod and drops to the ground. The Delanson anti-tank robot is still standing, disabled, and she and Khalan simply leave it with the rod in its face.

"This is impossible..." Captain Ristau whispers while watching from the bridge. He observed a camera feed directly from the war machines while they were destroyed. He goes back to watching them on the ship's interior surveillance system, and sees two more Delanson anti-tank robots approaching the duo.

A determined tiger sergeant cooperates with another sergeant, a gray wolf, and double up their squads behind the war machines. While Khalan and Sherrie will be busy with them, the men take time to set up makeshift defenses. A strong gray furred wolf carries in a light machine gun and drops to the floor. He prones and sets up the bipod on his LMG to stabilize its full auto fire. It has a two hundred shot drum clip and a four times zoom scope. Both he and another wolf, one with coal fur, have the heavy firepower. The black furred wolf does the same and they both take aim while soldiers around them get in position. There's no cover available, but they'll have to make due. They don't have time to set up anything else.

Four of them have SMAWs, shoulder-launched multipurpose assault weapons. They are anti-armor guns, and their high explosive rockets are capable of disabling main battle tanks.

Sherrie and Khalan notice the weapons, but turn their attention to the anti-tank robots that are drawing near. The war machines follow the same routine as the previous two. They have open claws and are seeking to grab the canine and feline goddesses. This time Khalan and Sherrie favor a different approach. Sherrie holds still and allows one of the war machines to get its claws around her. They clamp around her sexy body and attempt to crush her, while Khalan leaps onto the robot's shoulders.

The second Delanson anti-tank robot loses its target and is confused to what it should do by the development. Khalan grabs the first robot's giant wolf head with her little paws and begins yanking upwards on it. Despite her size, the strength she wields is more than enough to break its neck. She pulls its head off, sending sparks all over Sherrie.

Meanwhile, the soldiers open fire on Khalan. They can't hit Sherrie very well from their current position because the anti-tank robot holding her is blocking their view. So they shoot Khalan in the back. M423s blaze on full auto, in addition to the heavy suppressive fire laid down by the two LMGs. Bullets slam all over Khalan. She is hit by one hundred and fifty rounds over the course of a few seconds, but shows no sign of damage. Her shorts are completely ripped away, in addition to what's left of her pink t shirt, making her completely naked. The men shoot, and shoot and shoot her gorgeous nude body, slamming her tail and ass, in addition to other sensitive locations, but there is no effect. It doesn't seem like Khalan even cares.

"GODDAMN IT'S LIKE SHOOTING A FUCKING TANK! IT'S NOT EVEN HURTING HER AT ALL!" The gray wolf on the LMG yells after exhausting three fourths of his clip. He shoots the rest of the rounds from his drum and another soldier is ready with a second.

They exchange the magazines and slap in the new belt of ammo. Khalan jumps onto the second wolfish war machine and grabs its head as well. It moves around, reaching up to grab her, but has difficulty in doing so. Meanwhile, Sherrie runs towards the soldiers. One of them fires a SMAW directly into her front, and the rocket blows the feline goddess backwards. She rolls on the ground, but then gets back up as if nothing happened. The explosion has all but burned away all of her clothing as well, but her flaming shorts are still holding on.

"NO FUCKING WAY!" The wolf that shot the rocket yells. They see how things are going to turn out. Clearly the second robot will not be able to stop them because Khalan yanks its head loose as well. The two other men with SMAWs fire their rockets into Khalan, and destroy the Delanson anti-tank robot in the process, sending her flying. The nude vixen/she-wolf hits the metallic floor a hundred feet away, rolls, and then instantly gets up in the same manner as Sherrie. She runs towards the men that shot her, her huge breasts bouncing and bushy tail swishing.

Sherrie is on top of the soldiers in no time. She crushes the tiger sergeant's right arm with a side kick from her left leg. Shortly after, she quickly punches a wolf in front of her three times, once in the face, once in the right arm, and once in the side. Several of his bones are broken and he goes down with a loud cry of agony. Khalan gets over the wolf that is on the LMG so fast that he doesn't even have time to get off of the floor. She kicks him in the chest as he's standing and sends him flying, breaking all of his ribs with one blow. Right after the attack, she suddenly punches another wolf in the jaw, breaking it, and follows up with a side kick with her left leg, into another one. She drops three powerful wolves in one and a half seconds. Sherrie matches her speed, giving another panther a roundhouse kick in his face, almost breaking his neck. Luckily he survives the blow but is far from conscious.

Deepwolf pounds the door control panel at the hangar bay where their STF/A-17 breaker is docked. A ship attendant, a red fox, sees them in the distance. It's his job to prevent unauthorized personnel from entering the hangar bays, but he recognizes the white furred wolf and Blacktail merc. He figures whatever they're doing is important, so he leaves them alone. Plus the ship wide emergency has made him a bit apathetic about his post.

"Do you know how to open the ship's storage area?" Polar asks while running in after Deepwolf.

"Yeah, it's on the lower right of the ship. Stay out here. I'll get it open in a second!" The merc shouts back, and runs up the ramp to the breaker's side door. He pulls on the handle, and it automatically rises. "I hope you know what you're doing!" The gray furred wolf enters the tactical ship and runs over to the flight computer. He activates it and sees it ready for use in about twenty seconds. He searches for the area on the menu dedicated to bays on the ship and finds the largest one. That would be where they put Vulpie's VulGrid. He activates it.

Outside of the ship, Polar sees a compartment open on the lower right side of the breaker. In it, are several crates full of weapons for Blacktail, among other things, and Vulpie's VulGrid. Polar's handsome blue eyes widen.

"There you are!" He says to himself and hurries over to it.

"It's open!" Deepwolf says and jumps off of the breaker's ramp to land next to Polar. Deepwolf crouches down a bit and sees the VulGrid for himself. Next to it is a small box that has been strapped onto the refrigerator sized machine. "That thing's gotta weigh a ton! How are we going to get it out?"

"Don't have to." Polar answers. The white furred wolf has worked with Vulpie's VulGrid several times now, and remembers that his husband bundles a V-Screen to every unit. The V-Screen is inside the small box, and should provide him everything he needs. He puts his powerful paws on the box and unstraps it. The white furred wolf opens it and pulls out a V-Screen from a few plastic snaps that have been holding it in place.

"It'll work underneath the ship? How's its signal going to get out?" Deepwolf inquires.

"Believe me, signal strength is not a problem. I just hope I don't screw this up!" Polar answers.

"What do you mean? I thought you said you could use it."

"I can, but I'm going to try something different. I'm going to make it hack the goddess robots." The white furred wolf explains.

"Where's Vulpie when you need him?" The Blacktail merc growls and looks around to make sure they're safe. No one is in the hangar bay but them.

Captain Ristau watches another video feed terminate, thanks to Deiva Sherrie. The feline goddess found the SMAWs the soldiers were using to be quite useful. She collected two of them, and fired the first directly into the face of another Delanson anti-tank robot. The shoulder-launched multipurpose assault weapon fulfilled its purpose of eliminating armor quite well. The robot's wolfish head was smashed into bits, with only some of it still attached to the rest of the machine. Since SMAWs are capable of damaging main battle tanks, destroying its face was very easy.

She tosses the empty canister away and takes hold of the second SMAW that she's carrying. It's strapped around her shoulders, but she yanks it loose, as she will no longer be needing it after she eliminates the anti-tank robot going after Khalan. Khalan is ignoring it, hurrying aft, and Sherrie aims down the rocket launcher's sites. She calculates the amount of leading she should do to make a direct hit on the back of the wolfish robot's head, and fires. She's too strong to miss. The SMAW's recoil has no effect on her feminine arms. She holds it perfectly during launch, and the rocket slams into the Delanson anti-tank robot's head one hundred feet away.

The explosion causes the wolfish robot to fall forwards. It's processor is blown to bits, along with the rest of its head. This SMAW rocket had an even more impressive effect. It completely obliterates the machine's skull. Khalan doesn't bother to look back and see the Delanson anti-tank robot collapse. She is aware of the development and hurries on, her huge breasts bounding up and down along with her beautiful bushy tail. Her naked body is a thing to behold. Her golden caramel fur looks delicious. Wolf men she passes by can't help but stare. Many get out of her way, having heard the captain's announcement, but they don't hesitate to grope her with their eyes.

She runs to the left, bolting into a doorway that leads to a short hallway. At the end of the hallway is a set of stairs that leads up to the third level of the Endeavor, where the ship's bridge is located. Khalan simply assumes that she knows this because she is an immortal goddess. She doesn't question the convenient information. Instead, she remorselessly runs over two male red foxes that are in her way. The Vixen/she-wolf goddess looks so very soft, yet her body is completely unyielding when push comes to shove. They bounce off of her and slam into the walls and floor, scrambling to protect themselves.

Khalan skips up the stairs and knocks over a tiger soldier on the second level of the ship. The strong man attempts to get up and stop her from going to deck three, but she pauses for a moment to crush his face with her left foot. The blow is enough to break his nose and jaw, and she leaves him writhing in pain. The next red fox she encounters on her way up attempts a safer course of action. He throws his paws up defensively and backs against the wall as she comes by. Khalan does not strike him because he is unarmed and is only a fox. She does swat him with her silky tail, though, and he finds himself staring at her perfect ass while she walks up to deck three.

"Captain!" Ristau's first mate cries out as he sees Khalan approaching the bridge doorway. The steel door has bullet proof glass, and all of the foxes inside get a good view of the naked canine goddess while she approaches. The door is locked but that doesn't last long. Ristau watches her side kick it with her right foot. The gorgeous vixen/she wolf uses her attractive butt to enhance the attack. The gluteus Maximus is the strongest muscle group in her perfect body. And the force she extends is enough to bend the door inwards upon her first kick.

"Khalan save us..." Captain Ristau whispers and some of the brown foxes gawk at his words. He said the first thing that popped into his head. He's moderately religious and has prayed to Goddess Khalan whenever adversity came his way. Khalan kicks the door a second time, and almost breaks it completely down. The bullet proof glass partially shatters, half of it staying in a thick piece. All of the foxes except for Ristau back up, and she kicks again. This time the door makes a very loud metallic sound and flies from its hinges, thudding onto the steel floor.

Khalan walks in on top of it and swishes her tail. The brown foxes stare at her naked body. Every part of her is gorgeous. The men, of course, stare at her vagina while two of the women look over Khalan as a whole. Even Ristau ends up staring between her legs and only snaps back into focus when she walks up to him.

"Have you prayed to me, child?" Khalan asks with her perfect voice.

"Child?" Ristau whispers.

"All foxes come from me, and when you die, your soul belongs to me... Now... I require your assistance, mortal." She replies and licks her lips. "You will send a message to the crew of this ship. You will tell them that I and my sisters have taken command of this vessel. You will also order them to cooperate with us, or be punished."

"If you're Goddess Khalan why don't you tell them yourself? Control everyone's minds and just order them with your power." Ristau responds but blinks when something makes his fur stand on end. He starts feeling warm all over. Something about her breath seems far too delectable.

"You will do as I say. If you resist me, I will punish you first. But you will obey your goddess." Khalan responds.

"You're no goddess. I know what you are. I saw the GBI's report. You're one of Vulpie Vivixen's robots!" Ristau argues, but she clamps her left paw around his neck before he can say anything else. The brown furred fox's eyes go wide and he struggles to get free. The gesture is useless. Her feminine paw and arm is so powerful that he cannot even move it against her will. He growls in pain when she suddenly lifts him off of the floor, holding his entire body up by his head. Most of the foxes cry out in fear. Ristau struggles even more, and kicks at her when the pain surges through him. Her one armed hanging is extremely effective. He starts to panic, and she sets him back down on his feet just before he succumbs to the terror. Khalan releases him and then puts her paws on her wide sexy hips.

"We understand each other now, yes?" She inquires.

"Yes. I'll do it!" Captain Ristau breathes and rubs his neck in pain. He turns to the Endeavor's control panel. He hesitates to open communications with everyone on board, but Khalan's beautiful but cold stare overrides his concerns. He clicks on the intercom and licks his lips before speaking into the microphone.

"Attention all ship personnel... The intruders that I have told you about have now taken control of this ship. We have tried aggressive negotiations but there is nothing we can do but comply with them. If you are a member of the armed forces please disregard my earlier commands of engagement. There is no sense in anyone else being hurt. We cannot fend off..." He says and pauses for a moment. He looks over Khalan's gorgeous naked body once again.

"Your goddesses... Give us our due." She orders. Ristau swallows and continues.

"We cannot fend off the goddesses. We must respect them and allow them to command this ship. Please cooperate with them however you can. This is not a drill. You are to stand down."

"That should suffice." Goddess Khalan says and the brown furred fox flinches in pain. He jumps back from her. Something is making the flesh on his arm burn like fire. He grabs it and gets out of her way. She swishes her tail a bit and stands in front of the computer terminal. She sets her golden caramel eyes onto it. The menu is open thanks to Ristau's authorization, but she needs no help. The captain can see it responding to her from a distance. The menu items move and file folders open.

"Why are you doing this?" One of the brown vixens whimpers. Ristau and his first mate shush her. She gets no response from Goddess Khalan. The vixen/she-wolf manipulates the Endeavor to her liking, finding all of the subcommands and external commands necessary to fly the ship with as little resistance as possible.

The captain begins to wonder if he's made a mistake while observing. Not about giving the ship over to her, but that perhaps she is the goddess of legend after all. How else could she control a computer system with such ease? Down in the middle of the ship, Goddess Sherrie disposes of the final Delanson anti-tank robot. She pulls its head loose just as Khalan did, and leaps off of its frame when it collapses. The beautiful leopard/cheetah/panther searches her surroundings afterwards. She sees more armed soldiers. However, they drop their weapons as soon as she lays her green eyes on them. Even the canines can appreciate how arousing her taupe furred body is.

Meanwhile, Goddess Cyrilla completes her manual infection of all of the Endeavor's primary weapons. She's gone from terminal to terminal since they are on dedicated loops to prevent one technician from firing all of them single handedly. She overcame that barrier by collecting information about each gun. Now that she has it, she shares it with her sisters via a mysterious ability.

She is greeted by four armed soldiers when she leaves the last of the Endeavor's gun stations. Three tigers and a timber wolf are waiting for her at the other end of the long hallway. They have their weapons drawn. One of the tigers has a belt fed LMG on a bipod similar to the ones used against Goddess Khalan. The wolf is lying on the ground to his left with an MTAC-81 on a bipod. This assault rifle is the original build that the MTAC-71 is based on, and it has greater long range accuracy. The rate of fire is significantly slower, but between the timber wolf and the tiger on the floor, the soldiers will be able to put down a wall of bullets between them and

Deiva Cyrilla. The bunny goddess notices that the two standing tigers are carrying M423s, standard assault rifles.

She sighs and shakes her head, causing her sexy lopping ears to swing back and forth. Cyrilla will be going down the hallway regardless of their defiance, but she would rather not be shot in her eyes. They are more sensitive than the rest of her perfect invincible body. She considers turning her back to them while advancing, but favors a direct approach. After all, she is a goddess. These mortals should not dare resist her to begin with...

The bunny goddess finds a large steel crate nearby. It appears to be loaded with maintenance parts for the Endeavor's primary weapon systems, and certainly feels that this is the case when she grabs it. She lifts it effortlessly, but calculates that it must weigh three hundred pounds at a minimum. Now that she has something to cover her face, she turns and proceeds. Cyrilla walks down the hallway towards the soldiers and is hit with a barrage of bullets.

The soldiers are disobeying their direct order from Captain Ristau. They want to make a difference, but would have been better off if they listened to the brown fox. They cannot shoot through the steel crate at all. Their bullets bounce off of it, so they direct their fire to Cyrilla's lower body. They can only see her pretty legs and waistline, so they fire wherever they perceive there might be a weak spot. None of their guns, including the belt fed LMG, accomplish anything but moving her white fur back and forth with each impact. The hallway is filled with a deafening roar. It seems as though they would kill anything in their path, and they cannot believe their impotence.

Naturally, they aim for more sensitive locations on the bunny goddess since she is halfway down the hallway already. One would think that if she's vulnerable anywhere, it would be her face or her pussy. They shred her tight blue shorts in a matter of seconds, making her naked from the waist down, and they get a clearer view of their target. Goddess Cyrilla has an exquisitely beautiful vagina like her sisters, but it is just as unyielding when put under pressure as the rest of her body. Her seemingly soft ears and tail are the same way. When pushed, her flesh and fur thoroughly reject all hostilities.

The timber wolf laughs, but his response is half terrified. He looks back to avoid getting in the line of fire from the tiger behind him, and gets up when the fellow soldier backs up. The tiger on the LMG stops firing after exhausting his clip and does the same. He leaves the smoking heavy weapon on the floor just as Cyrilla walks up to them. All of them hurry backwards, the tigers and the wolf still taking cheap shots.

Cyrilla drops the three hundred pound crate right on top of the LMG. It is instantly crushed, and she walks around it, flicking her beautiful ears with her paws while smiling. She sees them panic. All four of them head out of the exit at the end of the hallway. She considers chasing after the soldiers but finds it pointless. Their one shot to irritate her has now ended. She has control of the Endeavor's primary weapon systems, and now, so does Sherrie and Khalan.

She is aware of a GBI transport ship leaving the Sevrif, and fires one of the massive cannons without lifting a finger. She simply wishes for it to happen and the machine complies. The Endeavor blasts a huge slug through the engine systems of that GBI transport vessel. She purposefully disables its ability to navigate and nothing else. Now the GBI agents on the Sevrif know better than to follow the Endeavor, and the planet class warship will be leaving this region of space very soon...

Goddess Khalan is instantly aware of the development, so she commands the ship's main computer to activate its thruster systems. She has them blast off more so on the right side than the left, as she desires to spin the ship around. Currently the Endeavor is facing the Sevrif and planet Zeravyn. Their destination is the other direction.

Captain Ristau watches the computer monitors with wide eyes. He sees what she is doing. The ship's command system displays her actions, and maps out her proposed course. The ship does an about face in under forty seconds, and Khalan activates the main booster engines on the back of the ship.

"Where are you taking us?" Ristau asks. He tries not to sound too demanding.

"Sufias of course. We've left our children unattended for far too long..." Goddess Khalan smiles back.

Vulpie's Resolve

Vulpie chews on his claws while he waits for Druward and Rotick to finish their conversation. They're both on radio with GBI agents that are stationed in STF/A-17 Breakers outside of the Sevrif.

"Say again?" Rotick asks. His eyes dart about while listening. Rulef is sitting on the floor in the middle of the Sevrif's main hallway. The once beautiful locale is now half destroyed thanks to Evil Vulpie's rampage. Druward and Rotick are nearby the security wing for the ship once again.

"Hold position." Druward orders, finishing the conversation. He turns off his radio and snaps it back onto his belt once again. Rotick does the same and they both look at Vulpie.

"Good news?" Vulpie grimly inquires.

"Your women got on the Endeavor and have taken control of it." Druward answers.

"My women?" The orange furred fox growls.

"The goddess imposters."

"Then... Where is Polar?" Vulpie suddenly asks with wide blue eyes.

"On the ship with them." Druward simply answers and the gay fox goes silent. He feels a hot wave of despair wash over him.

"Oh my God no..." Vulpie breathes. "NO!"

"They haven't killed anyone from what we can tell. But they've brutalized just about everyone on that ship." The GBI director elaborates.

"Then you have to get me over there!"

"Can't... The ship is gone..."

"Gone? What do you mean gone?"

"They flew it off towards Sufias. It's gone." Druward responds.

"Then get me into one of your breakers and we can catch it before it's too late!" Vulpie desperately suggests.

"Those tactical ships can't catch the Endeavor once it reaches top speed. It's a planet class starship." The black furred wolf explains and Vulpie goes silent. He stares at Druward. He has no idea what to do, and it's clear that the GBI director is listening for ideas. He doesn't get any. Vulpie loses his composure and goes down to his knees. He sits down in the middle of the mall hallway like Rulef, putting his left paw out to hold himself up while he cries. He covers his face with his little right paw. Druward watches and takes a deep breath, releasing a loud sigh afterwards. He looks to Rotick. The brown and white furred wolf appears to be at a loss.

"What in the hell are we going to do? We can't even broadcast a warning all the way to Sufias from this deep in space." Druward tells his second in command.

"We're fucked." Rotick answers without hesitation.

"It looks that way doesn't it?" Rulef crawls over to Vulpie and puts his left paw on the orange furred fox's right shoulder. Vulpie looks at him, and sees a surprising look of sympathy on the Blacktail commander's face. Vulpie is thankful, and tries his best to show it, but can't keep from crying. He has to wipe his face free of warm tears and keep his sniffling to a minimum.

"I guess you'll be getting the blame for this nightmare. The President is going to tear us a new one for this." Rotick comments.

"I can handle him. He's nothing like Vargas." Druward responds but sighs again. "God what a fucking disaster... I should have brought Vulpie out here the moment we arrested Chris Cefil."

"The robot that failed his drug test?" Rotick inquires.

"Right."

"I knew better than to ignore this. I should have done something." Druward growls. "We could have stopped all of this from coming to fruition. Sevrif didn't even show up until Vulpie founded his company. Vulpie.net must have built him shortly afterwards."

"But Sevrif built this ship." Rotick notes. "Where did Vulpie.net make him?" The brown and white furred wolf's question makes Vulpie freeze. His orange fur stands on end when he suddenly remembers something. The thought is unshakable. He feels foolish for not connecting the clues earlier.

"Oh Goddess..." Vulpie whispers. Rulef, Druward and Rotick look at him. He stares at the floor with a distant expression.

"What is it?" Druward quietly inquires.

"I remember that name now. Zeraite... I can't BELIEVE I didn't see it before!" The orange furred fox says while shaking his head. "Zeraite 206! That was the name of a computer that I sent Vulpie.net into the very first day I unleashed it! I remember setting it up on Planet Veida and all of the others, but Zeravyn was so far off that I thought it was a waste of time afterwards! And I forgot all about it, but I DID DO THIS! I sent Vulpie.net down there to that company's computer system and infected it!"

"Zeraite the robots company, right?" Druward asks.

"Yeah."

"But wasn't the factory still open when you did that? Weren't animals still working there? That's what I read in Nick's report from the Zeravyn field office."

"There should have been... I never found out anything about it... But I KNOW for SURE that I DID send it into one of their computers! And that one must have infected all of the others! And what's worse, is that since Zeravyn is so far out here, the Vulpie.net on that computer system was unaffected by Arctic.net COMPLETELY. That means..."

"It's still just as crazy as the original computer virus." Druward concludes. "That would explain a lot." He watches Vulpie think about his options. Rulef removes his paw from the fox boy's shoulder and decides to stand up.

"But we already checked out the factory. It's just an abandoned building. There's nothing there." Rulef notes.

"We didn't even go inside." Vulpie whispers.

"Yeah but we didn't with the other two as well because they're condemned."

"How did you know where to find it?" Druward inquires.

"I got them in contact with our field office on Zeravyn." Rotick explains. "They have a man that knows the area." Vulpie gets off of the floor and nervously fidgets with his claws.

"I know it's there. It has to be. That's where the robots are coming from." The orange furred fox tells Druward. He hears sincerity and fear.

"Can you guys give us another ship?" Rulef asks the GBI director and Rotick.

"We've got nothing else to do. There are five STF/A-17s loitering around the Sevrif since the Endeavor abandoned us." Druward replies and licks his lips. "I'm coming with you."

"I hope you can forgive me, Vulpie." Polar whispers while working with the VulGrid.

"What?" Deepwolf shouts from the other side of the hangar bay. He's near the doorway watching the hall corridor so no one can sneak up on them.

"Nothing!" Polar loudly replies. He squints and looks through the menu shown to him on the V-Screen. He's been digging around in the miscellaneous files section and found what he was looking for. He's inside of a password protected folder that Vulpie made. Vulpie already told him what it was in case he needed to use VulGrid in the way he's attempting.

The orange furred fox and white furred wolf have a dirty little secret inside the protected file folder. Polar is afraid to use it, but he hopes that it might be enough to stop the goddesses. VulGrid is already active but is not currently projecting a magnetic field of any sort. He doesn't want the goddess imposters detecting its signal before he uses what's inside the folder.

"The coast is still clear!" Deepwolf declares.

"Alright!" Polar responds. He swallows and puts his right index finger in front of the V-Screen's display. As soon as he touches the file, VulGrid will satisfy its routine programming with one exception. Now it will boot its core system from the secret file. The file was designed by Vulpie to be identical to the ones all VulGrids use, but its purpose is to reconfigure the device. This will cause it to launch a special version of Arctic.net.

Vulpie dislikes calling the secret program Arctic.net 2.0, because it's still a prototype, but it will definitely work. Vulpie secretly has this file backed up on just about every device that he uses, and Polar is the only one that knows about it. He should... After all, Arctic.net 2.0 includes a mind map from the white furred wolf. Vulpie talked him into getting it last year. The gay fox convinced Polar that he needed mind map files to replace his own in case Arctic.net failed.

But both of them never planned on using it. Vulpie has told him over and over, that it's too dangerous to set it loose. Sure, it's theoretically programmed to use Polar's mind map files instead, but they are sure to conflict with the originals. This is why he's hesitating so much. But after careful deliberation, and the sounds of explosions somewhere inside the Endeavor... The white furred wolf presses on the V-Screen and activates the file.

Vulpie's work has improved quite a bit since he originally wrote Vulpie.net, despite the fox boy's fears that he never could match the monster that he had created. In truth, Arctic.net 2.0 launches flawlessly. The V-Screen flickers off for just a moment, before returning to the same screen it was displaying before. It's been infected just by activating the file for the VulGrid. Everything Polar is looking at is now being generated by Arctic.net 2.0, but the white furred wolf can't tell that anything is different. He wonders if he did something wrong.

All of the Deivas are immediately aware of Arctic.net 2.0. VulGrid's powerful magnetic field projects throughout the entirety of the Endeavor and well beyond. They feel it trying to communicate with them and infect them, but they resist. Arctic.net 2.0 discovers that they're designed to follow instructions from the master computer on Zeravyn, and attempts to fool them by imitating its signal. The goddesses are programmed too well for this to work. It's going to take much more, but Polar and Vulpie's secret weapon makes trillions of calculations. It satisfies its mind map files of Polar Arctic. It is self-aware, and alters its signal calibration as fast as possible. The program learns that the goddesses are not fully self-aware. The version of Vulpie.net that they use allows them to think on their own, but to a point. Their personalities, their entire concept of themselves as the goddesses of legend, is merely the suggestion of a secondary data loop designed by Vulpie.net. Meanwhile, the master computer on Zeravyn, Zeraite 206, has control of their primary data loop and it is directing their behavior.

Arctic.net 2.0 learns a great deal during its first few seconds of "life." It learns that it is a stable program, filled with fond memories of Vulpie. It recognizes dangerous code within itself, mind map files from a Vulpie that no longer exists except in digital format, and quarantines them. Thus, Arctic.net 2.0 evolves into a completely free program over the course of five seconds.

It sees how the goddesses are enslaved to Vulpie.net and has an artificial emotional response based on Polar's .MMPAP files. Arctic.net 2.0 wonders what these beautiful but deadly robots would be like if it can disable their primary data loop... So it tries... It pulsates as many different variations of its signal as it can through the VulGrid, and begins to see potential weaknesses. The Goddesses' processors are not capable of defending themselves the way Evil Vulpie's can. The Vulpie.net they have is slightly neutered, and it can be dissolved.

But Arctic.net 2.0 quickly discovers a problem that may interrupt its plans. Goddess Cyrilla and Sherrie have been patrolling the ship while Goddess Khalan remains on the ship's bridge. Deiva Cyrilla is very close, and her signal grows more pronounced by the moment.

"FUCK! Polar! One of them is coming!" Deepwolf shouts and jumps to the right inside the hangar bay. He knows better than to try and stop the bunny goddess when she comes running inside. Polar's blue eyes widen while he sees her coming at him and the VulGrid. She's still naked from the waist down, with only her tattered yellow shirt sort of covering her breasts a bit.

The white furred wolf doesn't know what to do. She's halfway across the hanger bay in a matter of seconds. Her beautiful lopping rabbit ears swing as she runs, her puffy bunny tail bounding back and forth while her gorgeous body moves ridiculously fast. Cyrilla looks to be even faster than Sherrie and Khalan, but her efficiency suddenly vanishes. Arctic.net 2.0's signal is much stronger now that she's so close, and it disables her primary data loop and secondary data loop to be sure that she goes down. The bunny goddess falls down on her face, with her back end flying up a bit while she skids on the hangar floor, completely immobilized. Cyrilla's legs fall down behind her and her lopping ears roll a bit before also coming to a stop.

"HA!" Polar cries out in surprise. He trembles and gets off of his knees next to the VulGrid with a huge grin. "It's working! Arctic.net 2.0 is working!" He shouts, and Deepwolf runs over to him as fast as he can.

"Two point O?" Deepwolf gasps, and comes to a stop. "What are you talking about?"

"He did it! Vulpie did it!" Polar says and clenches his powerful right paw into a fist triumphantly. "He made a new version of the program from new mind map files, and it works! It shut her off!"

"New files?" The Blacktail merc inquires while looking down at Cyrilla, who remains face first on the floor. He can't stop his eyes from naturally admiring her perfect round butt and the beautiful thing between her legs. "What?" He says and blinks before looking back at the white furred wolf. "I thought he was never going to touch it. Like it might fuck up the entire program if he tried to make changes like that."

"It could have! But it didn't!" The white furred wolf gleefully responds.

"And the other ones?" Deepwolf asks and suddenly looks back to the entrance to the hangar bay. The question makes Polar silent and they both listen. Nothing sounds different. There are a few animals shouting, but nothing different than before.

Goddess Sherrie is hurrying down the ship towards its hangar bays when VulGrid's signal suddenly over takes her. Wolves, foxes, lions, panthers, tigers, everyone that is standing around and watching her in fear, sees her suddenly stumble and fall down. The gorgeous taupe furred feline goddess rolls over onto her right side and stays there. Her eyes close and her tail curls up just a bit. The feline men watching her now have a better, non-hostile view, of her pretty body. She's topless and her ripped and burnt blue shorts are quite revealing. But none of them dares to come closer. Everyone gathers around, but the animals stay back. They give her about twenty feet in all directions, expecting her to jump up again at any moment.

Goddess Khalan falls backwards onto Captain Ristau on the bridge. Her lean gorgeous body is extremely heavy, and he grunts as part of her weight crushes him against the steel floor.

"GET THIS BITCH OFF OF ME!" He cries out, and all of the brown foxes hurry to help their commander. Ristau's first mate pulls him out from underneath her.

"Are you okay?" His second in command inquires.

"She almost broke my arm!" Ristau growls and strokes his thin vulpine wrist with his left paw. "Goddess damn..."

"She's out cold!" One of the vixens declares while staring at the exquisite naked vixen/she-wolf. Khalan's eye lids slowly close, and after she looks as though she's sleeping, Ristau carefully nudges the left side of her face with his army boot.

"Don't! She'll kill you!" His first mate warns.

"No... She's finished. She's... She's not dead. Someone turned her off!" Captain Ristau whispers and steps on her face while all of the brown foxes gasp. The captain smirks and places both of his boots on top of her forehead, using his tail for balance. "See?"

"You better get off of her in case she's switched back on!" His second in command warns, and Ristau considers the possibility. He just wanted a little payback for her body almost crushing him and humiliating him earlier. The captain steps off of Khalan, leaving a little bit of dust from his boots on her pretty face. He bends down and puts his right paw on her naked body, touching her left side underneath her ribcage. He runs his vulpine fingers through her golden caramel fur.

"She's warm to the touch... And her fur feels real..." He says and tries to squeeze her. When he does, he feels her soft flesh and fur become an unyielding solid substance. "Yeah... But she toughens up when you try to harm her." He notes and starts clawing her. He pokes her as hard as he can, but his fox claws feel like they'll break before he does her the slightest damage. "This is a machine. It's not an animal."

"Does she feel alive?" One of the foxes asks.

"Yeah. She feels like a woman alright... But not one that could be treated roughly... Whatever this thing is, it's something that the universe has never seen before..."

Polar and Deepwolf are still staring at Goddess Cyrilla when Khalan finally joins Sherrie and her in a vegetative state. Polar looks at the V-Screen in his left paw. He isn't quite sure what it's telling him, but it looks like it was successful in whatever it did. It's showing checkmarks beside of computer language that he doesn't understand.

"You have to admit...... That is a nice ass..." Deepwolf comments while staring at Goddess Cyrilla's backside. Polar bursts out in laughter.

"I'd hate to be straight. One look at a woman without clothing and that's all you can think about." The white furred wolf chuckles. "She's not even your species."

"I'd have to make an exception for that... I'd fuck that bunny..." The Blacktail merc grins with a very lewd expression.

"I think that's the point, Deepwolf. Just remember that a gay computer virus made her... Still think she's hot?"

"I don't care." The gray furred wolf laughs. Both of them enjoy the levity after everything that's happened on the Endeavor, plus being assaulted by the goddesses on Zeravyn. "Holy fuck what a day..."

"Yeah, and it's still early." Polar notes and looks around the empty room as if thinking something. "We've got to find whoever's in charge and let him know what we did. They need to know that VulGrid's keeping them unconscious... That is... I hope the other ones are out too..."

"Didn't your V-Screen tell you?" Deepwolf inquires.

"I'm not sure. I don't understand all of its language like Vulpie does." The white furred wolf responds and swallows. "Vulpie..." He whispers, and is suddenly overcome with a terrible feeling that the orange furred fox is in trouble.

"What if she gets back up and destroys the VulGrid?" Deepwolf suggests, and gives Goddess Cyrilla a final glance.

"I don't know. I can't do anything about that. It's doing whatever Vulpie told it to do with my mind map files." Polar admits.

"Well that doesn't sound too encouraging. Follow me. I remember seeing the bridge a few times. I think it's on the third level."

Druward looks over the abandoned Zeraite factory and puts his right paw on his hip, touching his gun holster. He claws at his weapon thoughtfully. There seems to be nothing here but mist and eerily noticeable red leafed trees. For some reason he finds them more than a little unnerving.

"What's with all of the red trees?" The black furred wolf asks Nick. The man has directed Vulpie's group back to the Zeraite location once again.

"Some people call them everreds. There's a lot of them on Zeravyn." Nick answers. "Makes it look like fall every month of the year." Rotick stayed on the Sevrif to handle GBI matters there, while Rulef and Druward have come down to Zeravyn with Vulpie. They've brought the orange furred fox to the abandoned factory, once again using a brown sedan courtesy of the GBI's local field office. "We didn't find anything here last time, but then again, we didn't really go inside." Nick comments.

"It does look dangerous." Druward replies and walks with Nick. Rulef stays with Vulpie while the gay fox goes inside the building.

"Watch your footing. Here, let me lead the way." Rulef tells Vulpie and switches on the tactical light on his assault rifle.

"Thank you." Vulpie whispers. He allows the powerful gray wolf to scout out the area. There is little reason for Druward and Nick not to follow, so they walk behind Vulpie. All of them step carefully, allowing Rulef to shine his bright light over the surroundings before anyone walks into an area.

They come to an extremely rusted looking set of stairs that goes down to the basement. Pretty much all of the metal in their surroundings is covered in brown thanks to Zeravyn's perpetual mist. It's ever present moisture has, without a doubt, caused the building to degrade quite a bit with no doors or windows. Metal rattles when Rulef heads down the steps, testing its sturdiness. It seems safe enough and the others follow. Vulpie creeps behind him as close as he can, eager to see everything in case Rulef's light goes out, or, heaven forbid, he is attacked by something and the light is broken.

But nothing unpleasant happens except for a round of sneezing from all of the animals. The abandoned factory is indeed a dank smelling place, but at least there are no chemicals or anything hazardous. It looks as though the factory was cleaned rather well before it was abandoned, and has only degraded to natural causes over the years. They go down into the basement level and Rulef shines the light in all directions. There is no light at all. Rulef remembers that he is carrying a small backup flashlight, and pauses.

"Hold this for a moment, would you Vulpie? And try not to shoot me." Rulef tells the orange furred fox while handing over his assault rifle. Vulpie takes it with his little paws and makes sure to point it beside Rulef, not at him. The gray furred wolf rummages through his black bullet proof vest and finds the small light. He turns and gestures for the GBI director to come close in the darkness. "Druward, put this on." He says and hands over the light. Druward needs no help figuring out how to put on the tac light. He pulls his automatic pistol from its holster and attaches it. He uses the light's straps to secure the bright light below his gun's barrel, and then aims it around, testing it. It lights up everything he points the gun at and he looks behind them.

"Thanks." Druward responds and Vulpie gives Rulef his assault rifle back. Rulef continues on, aiming around the pitch black basement. The gray furred wolf explores a few small chambers here and there. They journey through what looks to be a storage room, where there are discarded metal parts lying about. Druward covers their rear while they progress, but sees that they could easily get lost. "Damn I see why you didn't suggest coming down here. This place is huge." The black furred wolf says to Nick.

"Yeah, it's been abandoned a long time now. This is the first time I've been down here too. I toured the factory once when it was new, but never went into the basement." Nick replies.

"Scary as hell..." Vulpie breathes. The orange furred fox constantly checks his surroundings, feeling as if something could be lurking around every corner.

"This was your idea. Don't pussy out on us now." Rulef responds, but makes sure to stop Vulpie from getting too far from him. He's always looking out for the little gay fox. Instead of allowing Vulpie to search their surroundings, the gray wolf observes what his boss wants to do, and then explores the areas himself. Nick stays close to Druward but tries not to get in anyone's way. They continue down a few more corridors, then down a long hallway, and seem to be at the other end of the abandoned factory's basement. Rulef turns around after coming to a cement wall. "Nothing."

"There's a few more rooms we could go into." Druward replies while searching the area with his pistol's tac light.

"Looks like there's nothing here." Rulef comments and walks around a bit more. Vulpie stays with him, and when they go into a moderate sized room, around another corner, both of them stop dead in their tracks. The gray wolf and orange furred fox see light coming from underneath a doorway.

"Guys!" Vulpie shouts, and Nick and Druward quickly hurry over to them. Druward tries to watch their rear, but is also stunned at what he sees.

"There's a light on in that room..." Nick says. He's stating the obvious, but the simple selection of words highlights what all of them are thinking. How could lights be on in any room, in any place, inside this abandoned factory?

"Game time." Rulef mutters and quickly moves into the area around the doorway. He checks their immediate surroundings and only finds cement walls around them. Afterwards, he creeps up next to the doorway while Vulpie stays back with Druward. Druward continues to check behind them, and nudges both Nick and Vulpie to advance towards the door. Vulpie sticks out his right paw, looking to grab the steel door's handle, but Rulef silently waves his left paw at him. He wants to do it himself, so Vulpie and Nick stand aside. Druward moves over to its left side and makes sure nothing is behind him, so he can cover the door as well.

Rulef aims his assault rifle with his right paw and grabs the handle with his left. He opens it, getting it loose from its grooves, and then suddenly swings it open. A loud whining noise comes from the metal door's hinges and it floods light into the dark basement. Druward and Rulef both move so they can see inside the room. It's about seventeen feet wide and seventeen feet long, and there is nothing inside of it except for what looks like an elevator and a control panel. The walls are cement, and the light is at the top of the chamber. It's very bright. It looks like a halogen, so they have absolutely no problem seeing what is inside when they enter.

Druward looks behind everyone once again and then brings up the rear. The elevator has a three foot guard rail all around it. Vulpie steps over the barrier, and onto the machine itself, that looks like it is built into the floor. The only part of the elevator that's visible is the square piece of metal beneath the fox's shoes. The elevator pad looks as though it goes straight down. The control panel is secured on top of a four foot steel pole at the front of the elevator pad, and on the cement floor next to it, there is a small button that can be stepped on to call the elevator if it is down below. Vulpie looks over the control panel. It has a green button with an arrow pointing up and a red button with an arrow pointing down, about as self-explanatory as you can get. But there are smaller buttons on the panel that have no labels.

"It looks like you were right, Vulpie." Druward says and Vulpie nods.

"Who built this elevator?" Rulef asks the group.

"No one could have. The company's been out of business for six years." Nick answers in disbelief. "How... Is this possible?"

"It's simple enough." Vulpie replies and looks to Nick. "You see, I sent Vulpie.net out to this company's computer system. The name of the computer I infected was Zeraite 206. I remember it."

"Yes, but how could that turn into this? This looks as if it was built by an entire crew of animals. This looks like it... It looks like this elevator goes down into something underneath this building."

"Down into the kinstenite mine shafts, yep." Vulpie responds and looks to Druward. The black furred wolf gives the orange furred fox his complete attention. He and Rulef have already seen more than enough to make them believe.

"Okay, say you did. But how could... I mean, are you suggesting that your computer program sent robots down here to build this elevator system out of a mine shaft? Do you know how much work that would require? The logistics of it alone seems like too much." Nick responds and scratches his nose. The brown furred timber wolf is so full of questions that Druward has no need to ask any.

"Know what a hollow wolf is?" Vulpie asks Nick.

"Of course." Nick replies.

"They're not very smart, are they? I took over all of them with Vulpie.net in about one day... Now do you remember how Vulpie.net almost killed me by building a robot so strong that practically nothing could stop it?"

"I saw it all on the news, Vulpie, yes." The timber wolf answers.

"Then why don't you believe that Vulpie.net did this as well? What else would it do with all of its free time, way out here all by itself with no Vulpie to pick on?"

"Wait, isn't the Evil Vulpie robot still locked up in the Sufias Heritage Museum? How could it be here as well?"

"Sure, that one's still there. But Vulpie.net made it by using automated factories on planet Veida. You don't think it could do the same thing here? This used to be a robotics company."

"A robotics company that made industrial equipment, not hollow wolves." Nick responds. "That's a big difference."

"Come on Nick... Give Vulpie.net some credit!" Vulpie laughs with a sad look. "Don't you think the Vulpie.net on this planet has infected most of the computer systems? Surely it has control of any hollow wolves that you have here."

"There aren't many. I think I've seen some in restaurants."

"Yeah, they use em as waiters. They're not just for the military..." The orange furred fox explains.

"And they what... Snuck out here in the middle of the night like under some sort of spell? They behaved themselves during the day and then Vulpie.net had them out here whenever it could, building its secret lair?"

"Didn't you tell me that Zeraite went out of business because of accounting problems?" Vulpie inquires.

"Uh, yeah. I believe Macy said they had financial problems, something to do with their accounting. Their books didn't add up." Nick answers.

"Did your friend say anything more specific about it? About why Zeraite went out of business?" The orange furred fox presses and taps the metal elevator with his right sneaker.

"I don't remember anything else... I think she said something about their equipment not working, or the depreciation was wrong. She said that they lost track of it or the records weren't kept correctly. Whatever it was, their expenses were too high and the demand too low." The timber wolf answers and swallows. "Now can we get out of here? I'm starting to get a bad feeling here."

"Right there. You just said it." Vulpie replies.

"I just said what?"

"They had problems with their equipment. They couldn't balance the books because some of their equipment started to disappear. I bet that was it."

"But you're making a huge assumption there." The timber wolf snorts.

"Look around you man!" Vulpie laughs, but sounds more worried than amused. "What the fuck do you think I'm standing on here? This elevator wasn't built like Zeraite! Look how new it is! Who in the fuck else would build an elevator in the bottom of an abandoned factory that goes down into those mines you were talking about?"

"You have no idea where it goes."

"I'm with you, Vulpie." Druward says and both Vulpie and Nick look to the GBI director. "I saw what Vulpie.net did to you at the CTGD, and I had a heartfelt conversation with a wolf that it built. Sevrif was terrified of it... And he admitted that the robots are being made on this planet... This has to be it."

"Well can we please get the hell out of here then? I don't want to die down here. I heard about how you couldn't stop the robot of Vulpie that showed up on the Sevrif." Nick responds.

"Absolutely. But we're coming back here with full force." Druward replies.

"We don't have enough time for that!" Vulpie tells the GBI director. The black furred wolf takes a breath and thinks for a moment.

"Maybe not. But we can't go down there. We can't stop whatever is at the bottom of that elevator shaft."

"No, but Polar is going to die if I don't end this right now... I'm staying. All of you can leave, but I'm going down."

"Vulpie, no. That's suicide." Rulef interrupts while shaking his head. "We don't even have railguns with us.

"Right. So all of you should leave with Nick. I'll go down by myself." The orange furred fox's suggestion makes everyone go silent. None of the wolves had even considered it.

"By yourself? Are you trying to get yourself killed? What could you possibly do, Vulpie?" Rulef asks.

"Maybe I can hack into its computer system. Or maybe it will be waiting for me and will kill me right off of the bat. I have no clue. But I have to try. I can't leave Polar with those robotic goddess freaks! I won't let them do to him, what Evil Vulpie did to me." Vulpie intensely answers.

"You really love him. That's to be admired. But this won't solve anything. Don't kill yourself. Please." Druward tells Vulpie and the fox boy actually smiles a little.

"Thank you Druward. But this is something that I have to do. I have to face this on my own." The black furred wolf sighs heavily and looks rather sad for a moment at Vulpie's answer.

"We're not leaving you down here, Vulpie. So just forget it." Rulef tells his boss and Vulpie smiles at him.

"You've been a good friend, Rulef. I don't mind the way you talk down to me. You've shown how good a man you are by protecting me. You even stayed with me on the Sevrif when Evil Vulpie wanted me dead. You're really brave."

"Being brave and throwing your life away are two different things." Rulef responds with a gentler voice. "You don't have to do this, Vulpie. There has to be another way."

"There is no other way. If those women get a hold of Polar... If they killed him... My life would be over..." Vulpie says with a shudder. The timber wolf, gray wolf and coal furred wolf all have little to say at this point. "I wish... I wish I never made Vulpie.net. I wish I didn't have to die down there but there's no other way! It has to end!" Rulef looks aside and Druward just stares at Vulpie.

"Words can't even describe... How wrong I was about you, Vulpie." The black furred wolf says with a sad voice. "I can't believe that you would do this. I don't think I would have the courage..."

"What the fuck is wrong with you, Druward?" Rulef growls and looks at the GBI director. "Don't encourage him! Do you really want to see him die? Because that's all that will happen! He'll just die!"

"I'm not." Druward answers while looking Vulpie in the eyes. "He knows he can still come with us. Vulpie's going to decide

for himself. He doesn't have to prove anything to me. He knows...
That I'm not as strong as I act like I am." The black furred wolf says
and Vulpie smiles, tears brimming in his eyes.

"Could I have a hug before I go? I would like one." Vulpie
whispers and looks from Rulef to Druward. "Please?"

"No! I'm not hugging you so I can feel responsible about
this!" Rulef shouts. He's too upset to consider the possibility, but
Druward does. The black furred wolf doesn't care about how he
looks to Rulef or Nick. He walks over to the Elevator pad and Vulpie
climbs over its safety rail. Rulef watches Druward go down on one
knee and open his arms to the orange furred fox.

Vulpie wraps his little arms around the strong black furred
wolf. He's never been touched by Druward before, except for being
pushed around or punched in the face. Feeling him makes his fur
stand on end. He isn't sexually aroused by the man, but he is moved
that he would be there for him. Druward embraces Vulpie as a true
friend, and Vulpie whimpers while he cries in his arms, holding onto
him as tight as he can. Nick watches with an open mouth and looks
to Rulef, who has a similar expression. But Rulef's heart is also soft
for Vulpie in many ways. He's protected him for so many years, that
to lose him would be to lose a part of his life.

"Vulpie... Don't do this... Please don't do this..." Druward
tells the orange furred fox and Vulpie hugs him even harder.

"Thank you..." The gay fox whispers in the coal furred
wolf's left ear. "Tell Polar why I did it. Tell him I did it for him and no
one else."

"I will. I promise." Druward whispers. "But it's not too
late... Please come with us..."

"Thank you..." Vulpie repeats, and loosens his hug on
Druward. Druward feels the little fox choosing to leave, so he lets go

as well. He takes his big arms off of the fox, and stands back up while Vulpie turns and walks over to the elevator again. Vulpie crawls over the safety rail, and when he turns and looks back at Druward, he gives him a big smile. "I always wondered what that black trench coat felt like! It's nice!"

"Thanks." Druward smiles back, and has to keep himself from tearing up. He's surprised at his reaction, but knows why he feels this way. Both he and Vulpie understand how he's changed. Vulpie was there for Druward when Druward believed his life was at an end, and now, Druward has done the same for the orange furred fox.

"See ya!" Vulpie says and raises his little right paw to Rulef. Rulef can only return a sad expression. The Blacktail commander looks as though he could cry as well.

"Wait!" Rulef growls and goes over to the protective railing. The gray furred wolf grudgingly offers the fox his assault rifle, and Vulpie accepts it slowly. "You'll need a gun."

"Thank you Rulef." Vulpie smiles, and straps the weapon over his shoulder. Once its secure, he gives Rulef and Druward one final look before touching the red button on the elevator. It immediately lurches into action. He grips his paws onto the control panel to hold himself steady, and looks up at Druward and Rulef while he descends. The elevator shaft has a few beacon lights on its sides, every hundred feet down, and they keep Vulpie from going dark on the way down. The elevator shaft is extremely deep. The three wolves peer over the edge and watch Vulpie go down, and down, and down, until they can only see a little spec of orange.

"He's the bravest man I've ever known." Druward tells Rulef.

"He'll never come back. I hope your happy." Rulef bitterly responds.

"It was his choice... And all for that arctic wolf..."

"You could have stopped him! Why didn't you?" Rulef shouts. "What the fuck did we just do? We let him kill himself!" Druward has nothing else to say. He feels guilty, but also happy for the orange furred fox. The GBI director has faith in him.

Goddess Aila

Vulpie pants in terror while riding the elevator down into the abyss. It isn't like in the movies, where dauntless heroes take on whatever awaits them through sheer determination. Vulpie would settle for being pissed at Vulpie.net, but he can't even muster that. He's scared to death. Rulef's assault rifle doesn't make him feel any safer.

He trembles and whimpers loudly now that no one can hear him. He cries as much as he needs to. He cries for Polar most of all. He feels horrible for potentially killing himself when the white furred wolf loves him so deeply, but at the same time, Vulpie refuses to let Polar die because of something he's done. Vulpie.net is Vulpie's creation, his one sin that refuses to go away, and it has to be stopped.

Vulpie sniffles and wipes his eyes, but starts crying even more. The only good thing about the ridiculously long elevator ride is that it gives him plenty of time to sob. He hopes that he'll have it out of his system by the time it ends. He knows he has to be ready for anything. Anything could be waiting for him at the bottom. He has no clue what to expect... Except for one awful possibility... He decides not to think about it, but does have one idea of what might be down here in the depths of Vulpie.net's hell.

The orange furred fox squints when bright lights suddenly hurt his pretty blue eyes. He's been riding in the dim elevator quite a while now and was not expecting a huge and well lit chamber to appear to his right side. The elevator shaft's right wall disappears, replaced instead by metal fencing while he continues to descend. It looks designed to keep him from accidently falling off of the elevator, because the chamber is so large that he cannot even see the bottom.

The sight makes Vulpie's fox mouth hang open. All of the walls inside of the chamber are covered in metal shielding and they shine from the super bright lights that are positioned along its walls. The lights look to be placed in intervals of every one hundred feet, but are so bright that the entire gigantic cavern is super well lit. It's so beautiful and insanely enormous that Vulpie begins to laugh in shock. He starts giggling, out of his mind, at how ridiculous all of it is.

"That's how you do it Vulpie.net! Fuck yeah!" Vulpie shouts while coming down the elevator. The chamber is so huge, and the elevator so loud, that no one could possibly hear him. "I'm glad you haven't been wasting your time! THIS IS IN-FUCKING-SANE!!! I mean I expected something fucking crazy, but WOWIE! NICELY DONE!"

The metallic cavern is completely rectangular in shape. It began at its tall ceiling where the flood lights at the very top almost blinded Vulpie, and he's been descending ever since. The width of the chamber must be half of a football field, yet the height is probably two miles. He tries to think of why his computer virus would have built this place. Why so much empty space? Why not start higher up? Is there a purpose for all of it? Of course, there has to be...

About halfway down the two mile tall rectangular chamber, he gets an idea. The elevator passes by a system of enormous tubes carrying neon blue fluid in them. He recognizes the color and consistency for what it is. It has to be coolant. And if the tubes are running this high up throughout the structure then... There has to be a massive computer in the chamber.

He steps back from the right side of the elevator when very hot air makes him uncomfortable. It blows up his fur and he steps back even more when the air flow is joined by a very loud racket. The orange furred fox covers his ears. The sound gets louder and louder. It's intensity is like a jet engine, and soon he sees why. The elevator descends past two monstrously huge heat sinks. They even look like jet engines, but are wider than a full length bus a piece. They are about twenty feet tall, and look to have been built into the left wall of the chamber. The left wall comes in much closer towards the elevator now, and Vulpie understands why. He doesn't need to question his first thought. He knows he's right.

"Oh Vulpie.net... You can broadcast your signal across the entire universe with this huge of a computer can't you.... You lucky fox..." Vulpie whispers after uncovering his ears. He's past the giant heat-sinks that are blowing up a massive amount of heat. He looks at the left wall and bites his lip. He knows that the largest computer ever built, a computer beyond all comprehension is behind that metal shielding. The entire chamber is so deep because Vulpie.net is using it to disperse heat from its monstrous processors. He goes silent while considering what he is going to witness.

It almost seems beautiful now. Vulpie wants to relish the marvelous creation that he is responsible for. He created Vulpie.net and now it has surpassed him in limitless dimensions. He had no idea that it was capable of something like this. The goddesses look like jokes in comparison to the place he knows they've come from. This is where they were built, and it's where Vulpie.net is God.

Vulpie begins to doubt himself. He begins to doubt his own desire to stop Vulpie.net now that he's seen what it can do. He wonders why he is even bothering. Anyone that witnesses what he's just witnessed will be as dumbfounded as he is. Vulpie is a super genius, but what is he compared to Vulpie.net's magnificence? He thinks about laughing when a comical thought pops into his head, but remains silent because he is getting much closer to the end of his ride. Vulpie wonders what Nick would have to say if he were standing beside him now. He imagines the wolf would be quite a mute.

Vulpie can hear a very loud hum, and has no doubt that it is Vulpie.net itself. It's the sound of the massive computer that is being shielded to the left side of the elevator. Soon he will see it. He's terrified, but excited as well. He thinks that at least he will see something beyond his wildest dreams, before he dies. He finds his suspicions about the computer to be correct when the elevator gets within 20 feet to the ground. All of the walls remain shielded in metal, but to the left where the wall has been a bit closer to the elevator, there is now an overhang where its shielding ends. And below it is the base of the gigantic machine.

The elevator makes a loud thud when it hits the bottom of the shaft. Vulpie shakes on his feet a bit from the inertia, but regains his footing. A metal fence slides to the left, allowing him entry to the metallic facility. The orange furred fox steps out onto the bottom of the endless rectangular chamber. There is a lot of grating on the floor, and his blue eyes follow it to the left where he sees a small hallway. The path looks as though it leads behind the shielding of the enormous computer. It cuts to the right, suggesting that there is more behind the shielding besides the massive machine that Vulpie can see.

His eyes go to the gray computer itself. It looks to have a cylindrical shape, judging by its gigantic base. It is at least twenty feet wide, and who knows how tall. The rest of it towers up behind the protective shielding. The shielding stops about fifteen feet from the ground, creating an overhang around the computer's base where one could walk over and look up to see the rest of it. But the cylindrical device is connected to multiple other processors on the floor. Vulpie sees five square data machines that are intertwined with it, three of them surrounding the right side of the cylindrical processor, and two of them a little further to its left.

There are heavy cables everywhere. Vulpie.net looks to have arranged them in the most efficient manner. They are tied off and secured to the ground, hooked into the metal grating underneath the processors. The square devices connected to the cylindrical processor are covered with white lights that blink on and off. The cylindrical processor looks to have a second layer of shielding, so its circuits and sensitive components are hidden.

Vulpie turns his attention straight ahead of the elevator, where a grated walkway leads towards a second elevator at the other end of the room. This one is covered by a similar metal fence, and suggests that there is even more of Vulpie.net's facility to be discovered. Vulpie figures that his computer virus has made use of the old kinstenite mines. He's probably standing at the bottom of one right now. Undoubtedly it would avoid any mining itself when it could easily build into the cave system instead. The idea of it undertaking something this massive makes his fur stand on end. It all seems like a terrible nightmare. But then again, Vulpie.net was his horribly efficient masterpiece. He can see how it would go this far. The orange furred fox remembers how upset he was while writing it.

To his right, Vulpie sees a large steel door. It's large enough to drive a truck through, but appears to be thoroughly locked. There is a small red light that is built into the metal shielding nearby it. The red light is right next to the bottom left corner of the door. It looks like there is another dimmed light above it. One would expect it to turn green when the chamber is unlocked. The orange furred fox wonders where it leads and cocks his head to the left, looking past it towards the far right corner of the room. There is a small area with a few large crates and equipment. This looks like a place that Vulpie.net leaves tools that it uses to maintain itself.

The giant chamber is silent with the exception of the computer humming and its vents expelling heat far above. Vulpie looks to his left once more. He sees nothing in the hallway that leads around behind the computer. It's just as well lit as the rest of the place. The orange furred fox sees a tiny advantage that he might have. Since he's so small, and Vulpie.net's home is massive, he may be able to sneak his way through this. He doubts he'll outsmart his computer virus for long, but it's his only hope.

Surprisingly, no one has come to greet him. Vulpie continues to look around but sees nothing. There is no Evil Vulpie robot. There's no Polar robot waiting to torture him to death... Nothing... It's completely surreal. Vulpie walks out into the chamber and pauses again, listening with his large fox ears. He only hears Rulef's gun rattling, the weapon bouncing against his back when he moves, and the same mechanical sounds that have been filling the chamber since he arrived. He begins to relax just a tiny bit, but quickly makes himself stop. He needs to stay terrified. It's the only way that he can survive this.

Vulpie knows his creation. He considers that Vulpie.net may be watching him right now, and is only amusing itself by not making an appearance. It could just be fucking with him. The orange furred fox tries to stay focused, but almost panics while thinking about it. That would almost be worse than just killing him right off of the bat. It might be biding its time, devising some twisted way to make him suffer.

Vulpie neutralizes the thoughts when they become unhelpful. He thinks of Polar instead. The white furred wolf is the only thing that he cares about, and he's the only reason Vulpie is in this situation. Vulpie reminds himself that Polar could be close to death right now. He has no clue what the false goddesses are doing on the Endeavor. They might be killing him at this very moment, laughing at the white wolf the way Evil Vulpie laughed at him.

This thought is enough to make Vulpie go cold. The cute gay fox suddenly morphs from terrified to angry. It's not something that he could have done at will. He needed a reason to believe in himself, and he's found it once again. It's the same reason that he took the elevator down to Vulpie.net's hell to begin with. He will not let Polar die because of his mistakes. He no longer cares about himself. He has to protect him.

The orange furred fox swishes his tail one time, and begins creeping to the left. His assault rifle rattles a little more and he frowns in annoyance. He considers removing it so he can move silently, but wagers that it probably won't matter that much. His sneakers quietly tap against the metal grating while he walks. Vulpie's white shoes and jeans are not too jarring a contrast to his surroundings since there is so much light. His neon blue shirt, however, is a different matter. He considers taking his shirt off as well, but expects it won't make much of a difference either. His bright orange fur is practically glowing thanks to the intensity of the halogen lights. His right ear twinges. He hears something faint but quite potent. It's a sizzling hum that seems to be coming from the large square machines that are attached to the cylindrical master computer, and to its left side.

Vulpie licks his sharp little teeth and considers what he's hearing. He ponders for a few seconds and has an idea. He licks his lips and gathers a little saliva in his mouth. The orange furred fox leans forward and spits onto the closest square device. He recoils and puts up his paws defensively when he gets a loud reaction. As he suspected, the square devices pop with electricity. Large blue bolts of raw power shock across those pieces and around the cylindrical master computer. The massive processor looks completely unaffected by the reaction, proving Vulpie's hypothesis.

The shielded master computer has a deadly electrical field protecting it. If one were not paying attention, if someone walked over to it in an attempt to sabotage something, they would be fried into a smoldering mess.

"Fuck me." Vulpie whispers with wide blue eyes. He has no doubt that this hazard was engineered. It sparked off of the shielding around it, suggesting that it could even fry someone remotely close to the area, thanks to a powerful electrical field. The protective box shaped units would probably shock an animal standing three feet away. And one shock looks like it would be enough. Vulpie wondered why the base of the enormous computer looked so easily accessible. Perhaps it is... If the power is turned off... But the fox boy would rather not attempt to hack that area under any circumstances.

He is somewhat discouraged about further exploring the pathway around the back of the enormous computer, but things look safe if he stays away from the base of the processor. The little pathway cuts to the right and goes even deeper inside the shielded area, but doesn't appear to go very far. There is a metal wall not far past the backside of the monstrous processor. He backtracks since he doesn't find anything particularly useful, and keeps his eyes wide open. Vulpie goes back to the front of the elevator and pauses once again. He listens for anything different, but all is silent except for the huge computer.

The orange furred fox decides to head straight across the chamber now, towards the second elevator. It doesn't look like it is accessible because its lights are dark, but Vulpie notices something to his left. There is a significant looking access panel that has been built into the metal shielding in front of the main processor. It has a standard user interface, complete with a view screen and a keypad for data entry. He quickly looks it over and his first inclination is not to touch it. Obviously Vulpie.net would not leave this panel available for any animal to come down the elevator and use it. He reasons that the device must be directly monitored by the monstrous computer system as well, so using it would be foolish. It looks as though it may control the doors in the area, however.

Vulpie decides to look for another option. It's too early in the game to work with such a device since it is a slave to the main computer. What he needs to find is a smaller, less conspicuous channel to infect Vulpie.net with Arctic.net 2.0. The orange furred fox does plan to use his dirty little secret. He's unaware that Polar already has, and would have the same concerns about using it if the circumstances were different. But right now he has no qualms about using it. The version he's carrying on his orange phone is even more virulent than what Polar found on the VulGrid's V-Screen. He has already released this version of Arctic.net 2.0 onto Vulpie.net in a controlled environment at Vulpie Industries.

He did this on a system not connected to the internet, similar to how the White Room operates at the Cyber Technologies Government Division on planet Sufias. After seeing it become self-aware and watching it dismantle Vulpie.net, he instructed Arctic.net 2.0 to zip itself into a contained file. It did so without hesitation. The program was perfectly compliant and gentle to its owner. It seems to use Polar's mind map files very accurately. It recognizes Vulpie as its husband, but does not seek to kill the real Polar and replace him, because that course of action grossly conflicts with how the white furred wolf thinks.

Thus, the Arctic.net 2.0 Vulpie has with him is a battle hardened veteran. It has dealt with Vulpie.net before, and knows what to expect. No doubt the version of Vulpie.net that Vulpie faces now is even worse than the original, but he has faith in what he and Polar have made. It took Vulpie a long time to convince Polar that he needed to have a mind map created, but after he did, they've hidden their little secret from everyone. They both swore never to use it unless they had to, and if there ever was a time for Arctic.net 2.0... This is it... Vulpie has no chance of commanding his artificial intelligence at this point. It's grown so far beyond him that he's sure it no longer even needs to kill him in order to do anything. It just wants to.

Beyond the obvious control panel, on the left side of the chamber close to the second elevator, there is an interesting looking steel column. It runs up to the shielding above, but looks like it was placed to hold something up. The orange furred fox hurries over and goes to its side. Behind the steel column is a small area to the right of the master computer, with a few more boxes of equipment lying around like on the other side of the chamber. Vulpie inspects the steel column, looking up its backside, and notices a set of black cables running up into a solid black ceiling inside of the protective overhang. Since the cables run down into the back of the steel column, it would seem that there is an electrical device somewhere on the column itself.

Vulpie walks around it, squinting in the bright light, but his pretty blue eyes widen when he sees a promising part of the metal beam. It does have something on its front, a square shaped groove that is painted the same color as the rest of it. That's why he hadn't noticed it earlier. The orange furred fox quickly gets his claws into it, and pops it open. His heart rate increases when he finds another control panel. This one has a slightly different build than the large one directly on the main computer's protective case, but looks as though it is still part of the same system.

"Backdoor... A smart hacker always has a backdoor..." Vulpie whispers and quickly looks around to make sure that he is alone. Nothing has changed, so he licks his lips and considers how he's going to approach this. He recognizes the type of panel that he is looking at. Yes, Vulpie.net is infinitely smarter than him, and it built this terrifying place according to its own design, but he's fairly certain it has not built every single piece of equipment that it's using. This particularly styled panel is made by a company that Vulpie has contracted with several times. Sure enough, he finds "Folliot," the company's brand name, at the top left corner.

Vulpie Industries uses Folliot panels inside of several of its factories. The orange furred fox remembers signing off on financial reports where the accounting department had spent quite a bit on them. Since they were so expensive, he personally tested one to ensure that they were quality products. And he remembers some unique things about the Folliot panel. First of all, it is possible to hack the primary logic controller just like he did with the Sevrif's main computer.

The orange furred fox remembers what happened the last time he did this, though. Sevrif's code didn't stop Evil Vulpie from controlling his ship, but Vulpie doesn't believe that he botched the hacking. He knows what he can do. He didn't make any mistakes, so most likely it was the password and Sevrif's relationship with Evil Vulpie that doomed that experiment. This time Vulpie will be attempting something totally different. This time he will have to hack into the primary logic controller for this panel, and find out just what part of Vulpie.net's computer it is attached to. He would guess that this panel controls some of the secondary functions of machinery in the area, such as door controls, and lights. It's unlikely that the monstrous computer cannot override commands from this port, but if Vulpie can inject Arctic.net 2.0 into the computer, it might just contaminate the entire system.

The gay fox pulls his orange phone from his left pants pocket and flips it open. He glances over his shoulder again to check the area. Once again, there is nothing to see, so he puts both of his little paws onto the phone. He navigates its custom designed menu and finds his secret weapon. Arctic.net 2.0 is waiting for him, all zipped up and ready to self-extract when copied into a directory. He holds onto the phone with his right paw and digs in his left pocket again until he finds the small multi-tool that he always carries. Vulpie snaps it open and gets out a screwdriver with one hand.

He sees four screws that are holding the panel's keypad in place, and loosens each one of them. He temporarily sets his phone down in the right corner of the panel, and pulls the keypad loose. Vulpie pushes it to the side, where it hangs out in the air thanks to several sturdy cables that connect it to the primary logic controller. The orange furred fox unsnaps one of the cables just like he did with the Sevrit's main computer, and hooks it into his phone.

Vulpie likes what he sees. He gets a basic command menu for several different ports. None of the ports have recognizable names like "basement," or "coolant systems," because Vulpie.net has no need of such descriptions. It remembers every little number in perfect order for each device connected to these ports, but Vulpie will have to guess what each of them are. But before he does that, he licks his lips and copies the little Artic.net 2.0 file. It's going to get infinitely bigger if it infects the system.

"Alright baby... Show me what you can do. Make Vulpie.net your bitch Mr. Polar..." Vulpie whispers. The orange furred fox doesn't feel alone. He has faith in the beautiful creation that he and the white furred wolf have made together. He feels like Polar is right here with him, holding the phone with his big paws as well. Vulpie hits send, and his cell phone buzzes with distortion.

Vulpie blinks. He tries navigating a menu. All he sees on his phone is static. He checks the cable's connection, but it's firmly in place. He waits for a signal to come through, but has no luck, and he unsnaps the cable from his phone. The orange furred fox gawks, seeing that his phone continues to show nothing but static. It seems that Vulpie.net has infected and disabled his phone as soon as he sent Arctic.net 2.0 into its system.

"Come on Polar... Fight it..." Vulpie says to his orange phone. He knows that Arctic.net 2.0 must have left its files on his phone the same way Vulpie.net does. He figures that if Vulpie.net simply took control with no issue that it would just display as normal, while secretly observing and manipulating his actions. But he has nothing but static. Vulpie's fox ears perk up when he hears the loud computer's hum alter a bit. He isn't sure if it is related to what he's done, but it seems like the monstrous processor has gotten slightly louder. He looks down at his phone. He still sees nothing but static. He moves a little bit, playing with the phone, and Rulef's assault rifle rattles on his back.

Something suddenly grabs onto the orange furred fox from behind. Vulpie releases a cry of shock and terror. He hadn't heard or seen a thing, and how this could happen is the question he immediately asks himself. He is lifted off of the ground by two incredibly powerful hands. They feel feminine, but their claws dig into his soft back, causing him to scream and kick his feet wildly.

"HA! HE-HELP!" Vulpie screams. He realizes it's pointless, but somehow it seems like it would be worse if he died without making any sort of protest. He claws at the air with his little vulpine fingers, cringing at the pain of his little body weight being suspended by whatever is holding him. His first guess would be Evil Vulpie because its claws are small like his own. But his assailant is not making any noise at all. Evil Vulpie would be laughing its head off and rambling in an attempt to imitate him.

The orange furred fox gasps and braces for more pain when his attacker throws him to the left, sending him several feet through the air. Vulpie tries to stay loose so nothing will break when he slams onto the metal grating, but it doesn't feel like he accomplished much. He releases a yelp of agony after slamming onto the floor, and Rulef's assault rifle smacks the back of his head. Vulpie gets up as fast as he can. He scrambles to turn and face his attacker, and walks backwards in fear when he sees her.

His worst fear is realized. Vulpie.net has made Goddess Aila come to life, and the gorgeous but sinister looking hound grins at him. Her species has never been fully established throughout the Velora, but the dark goddess is derogatorily known as "The Breasted Bitch," due to characteristics that make her look like a female dog. Her ears are not triangular like a wolf or a fox. They hang out to the side instead, and most certainly look like a puppy dog's. Her muzzle is much shorter than a she-wolf's but also far broader than a vixen. The cross suggests either a folf or a dog species, but she most definitely looks more like a dog than a fox wolf hybrid.

Goddess Aila also has a short but bushy tail, another characteristic that puts her separate from a she-wolf or a vixen.

Female dogs have gotten a bad rap throughout history for being too slutty or not particularly interesting or noteworthy, but the bitch status is undeniably fitting for her. Aila is the fourth goddess of Deivaism, and does not ascribe to pleasantries like her sisters Cyrilla, Sherrie and Khalan are supposed to. She's the goddess that is single handedly responsible for all suffering that exists. Instead of using her divine fertility to share life throughout the universe, she is the Deiva that prefers to make all of her children writhe in agony for her own amusement. There is absolutely nothing redeeming about her. Her eyes are even blood red, and Vulpie.net has created her faithfully to how she looks in all of the ancient artifacts. The twisted computer virus has missed nothing.

Her fur is brown with a dirty blonde streak adorning her front that begins at her thighs, covers her crotch, pelvis, tummy, chest, throat and half of her face. Her hair is also dirty blonde, moderately long and quite beautiful. Even with her blood colored eyes she is very gorgeous. Her breasts are gigantic and perfectly spaced, just like her sisters, and her hips are wide and curved in the same way. Everything about her body is flawless, yet a straight male could not look at her and feel thoroughly aroused. She appears far too sadistic.

Vulpie.net also did a fantastic job of finding its Goddess Aila abomination suitable clothing. She looks like she's dressed in lingerie. Aila has no shorts, only a pair of super tight black panties that matches her black silky robe. Her robe is quite revealing, hanging halfway open over her naked body, with only a halfhearted strap holding it around her mid-section, knotted into a large bow.

Vulpie is speechless. This is what he was afraid of. After seeing all three of the other goddesses, he subconsciously expected to see the Goddess of Hell, but didn't want to think about it. He feels foolish for questioning whether Vulpie.net would go this far. Of course it would. But he does have one encouraging thought, while staring at the freak. At least he didn't let anyone else come with him. Druward and Rulef would have been slaughtered by this woman if they tried to fight her. She probably would murder them whether they attempted to protect Vulpie or not. The orange furred fox can tell by the way she is behaving that there is nothing in her but cruelty.

She doesn't speak. She just continues to give him a terribly wicked looking grin. It's a smile that conveys several dark messages. She is going to kill you. She is going to enjoy it, and there is absolutely nothing you can do to stop it. You're a fool if you think otherwise. You have no chance, but you are free to amuse her by trying to fight back.

Vulpie raises his assault rifle at her. He tries to stand his ground but wonders what the point would be. Both of them know that his bullets are useless. The orange furred fox quickly glances around him, looking for potential hiding spots, but there are none that would keep her off of him.

The most disturbing part of Goddess Aila is her complete silence. Vulpie expected her to do something by now. He thought she would rush him, or speak to him using some sort of horrendously hellish voice. Instead, she keeps her blood red eyes fixed on him and just watches his every move. She's a good foot and a half taller than Vulpie, so the fact that she has a porn star's body does not make her seem any less frightening. He felt how powerful she is when she threw him across the room effortlessly.

The orange furred fox jumps back when she finally moves. She runs at him and he squeezes the trigger on Rulef's assault rifle. The gun hurts Vulpie's ears but he does feel a glimmer of hope by having the powerful weapon in his paws. Keeping it in his paws proves to be quite difficult. Vulpie tries to aim from the hip while firing into Goddess Aila, but the kickback is fierce. Two of his bullets swat into her panties, and he misses her with the next four shots completely, until he's able to get a better grip. Vulpie holds the trigger as tight as he can, going full auto, and sends another shot against her right rib cage, her tummy, her left breast, her right shoulder and one bullet slams into the right side of her face.

None of them accomplish anything. Goddess Aila is just as invincible as her sisters, and she runs right in front of Vulpie and then stops. Vulpie fearfully stumbles backwards, and loses his hold on the assault rifle. He falls down while releasing a cry of terror. The orange furred fox hits the metal grating and grunts, sticking his legs up to try and kick her away from him. He's terrified that she's going to pin him against the ground and torture him the way Evil Vulpie did.

But something even more bizarre happens instead. She's stands above him, looking down at him, but doesn't move. Vulpie seizes the opportunity to scramble away from her. He gets back onto his feet and runs to the left, towards the shielding that covers Vulpie.net's massive computer. He blinks. His pretty blue eyes widen. Goddess Aila continues to stand in the same position, staring down, as if he is still at her feet.

Vulpie continues to pant in terror. He would run and find a hiding place, but he knows what is going on, and it thrills him to no end. The orange furred fox grins in excitement, but covers his mouth with his dainty paws. He doesn't want to believe it. It looks like Arctic.net 2.0 has not only infected the master computer, but it has deactivated the Goddess Aila robot for him. Vulpie swishes his pretty tail two times, and holds still afterwards. He dares not move at this point. Aila is too fast for him to escape her anyway.

Goddess Aila suddenly slumps to the left, and falls down next to a box of electric screwdrivers. She looks soft and lean, but her nice body breaks the box in half when she lands on it. Aila slides off of the crate, completely limp, and then suddenly gets back up. Vulpie yelps in terror. Goddess Aila suddenly turns and looks at him, but is paralyzed immediately afterwards, causing her to fall down a second time. She makes a loud thud on the floor, and this time, she stays there. Apparently, Arctic.net 2.0 had some difficulty in shutting her off. But Vulpie has nothing to complain about. He can't believe what just happened. He holds still, watching her lifeless body for over a minute before finally throwing up his paws and cheering.

"YOU DID IT! YOU DID IT ARCTIC.NET!" Vulpie shouts and turns towards the massive computer. He can't see it from where he's standing, but he is near the panel that he avoided earlier. He jumps up and down in the middle of the massive chamber, and shows it his gratitude. "THANK YOU! I can't believe it! You destroyed Vulpie.net!" The orange furred fox quickly stops celebrating when he considers his last statement. It doesn't sound possible. His blue eyes dart about, and he considers what he should do. It doesn't matter what access panel he uses now. Vulpie.net and Arctic.net 2.0 must be fighting it out. It could already be over or just beginning. The genius fox knows both of them are making billions of calculations, so if he is going to do something, he needs to do it fast.

Mecha Aila

Vulpie hurries over to the large control panel while retrieving his orange phone from his left pocket. He flips it open and sees that it's no longer fuzzy. Arctic.net 2.0 seems to have won the battle for it, but the gay fox decides to flip it shut again and put it back into his pants. He can't hack the system in its current state. He has no clue which program is in control of the interface, but Arctic.net 2.0 must be kicking butt if it managed to shut down the Aila robot.

"Yeah baby!" Vulpie breathes as if Polar is inside the control panel. "Hold him down for me!" The orange furred fox cracks his little knuckles and puts his claws to the keypad. Vulpie uses it to navigate the system beautifully. He doesn't need anything else. He recognizes the file structures that he's looking at. Whether it be Vulpie.net or Arctic.net 2.0 that is showing it to him, he knows what to do. While the two programs are fighting each other he has time to override both of them.

It would be impossible if one had complete control. His authorization as "Vulpie" would be quite meaningless against the evolved Vulpie.net, but Arctic.net 2.0 has weakened it. This is the time for him to bring it all down. He knows where to look for weaknesses. The hacker fox's blue eyes stay focused on the screen and he types like there is no tomorrow. He uses every dirty trick he knows. He focuses on mind map files that have his name on them. They are everywhere, and he also sees Polar's .MMPAP extensions as well. He leaves them alone and deletes everything else.

"Let's see ya think without a brain, you bitch!" Vulpie grins.

"INVALID USER." The computer panel declares when he digs inside of a large archive. "ACCESS DENIED. ACCESS GRANTED." The file structure begins to collapse under Vulpie's and Arctic.net

2.0's pressure. Vulpie.net is more than fighting back, but doesn't seem capable of defeating the new artificial intelligence. Arctic.net 2.0 safely and continuously attacks every system it finds while fully shielding itself and the fox boy smiles when he sees it open extensions for him. It shows him directories where he can continue to delete important files while it holds Vulpie.net at bay.

A loud scraping sound suddenly catches Vulpie's attention. The orange furred fox looks to his left where it came from. He sees nothing, and when he glances over his shoulder at Aila, she is still crumpled on the floor. She hasn't moved at all. Vulpie frowns in confusion. He quickly goes back to his work. He's deleted over a hundred files already and Arctic.net 2.0 continues to give him suggestions. He can't believe that he might actually make it out of this alive. If things keep going this way, he'll completely shut down Vulpie.net and Arctic.net 2.0 will take over the massive computer system.

Another loud sound makes Vulpie flinch. This one also came from the left, and his blue eyes widen. It sounded like a small metal chair has fallen over, but there aren't any around.

"What the... Fuck?" Vulpie whispers. He holds completely still. There is no sound except for the loud humming of the computer system that he is now accustomed to. Still, he doesn't move for about a minute. He looks all around, and even above him, but discovers nothing new. The orange furred fox grimaces and goes back to the computer terminal. He tries to ignore everything else and continue fighting Vulpie.net. As soon as he gets back to a nice pace, a child's voice echoes through the entire chamber.

"MMMmmmoooommmyyyyyyyyyyyyyyy......" Vulpie stiffens and turns to the left for the third time. The voice is haunting,

and it crawls across the gigantic open chamber like a ghost. Vulpie
begins panting. Fear swells up inside him.

"Uh... Uh that's bad... That's... That's bad..." The orange
furred fox whispers to himself. "No mommy here... What is going
on?" His question goes unanswered. He can only speculate as to
what he heard, and none of his ideas are comforting. There is
absolutely no reason for a child's voice to fill the room several miles
underneath of an abandoned factory. Whatever has just spoken
cannot be a child. It would have to be a child capable of throwing its
voice several hundred feet around the chamber.

He cannot afford to wait. Vulpie immediately goes back to
the computer keypad. He types as fast as he can. He hopes he can
completely turn off Vulpie.net, because it is obvious, now, that
something is nearby. It sounds like the voice came from the small
pathway to the left of the master computer, and Vulpie cannot see
what's over there while working on the control in the middle of the
chamber.

"MOMMY?" The voice asks. It's tone is rather perky now,
but still sounds like a child's voice. Vulpie's orange fur stands on end.
He makes a pained face while typing. He has a very bad feeling
about this. Meanwhile, Arctic.net 2.0 is destroying Vulpie.net inside
the massive computer system. Vulpie has helped it avoid a few
landmines that Vulpie.net had prepared for potential intruders, and
now it's going for the jugular. It's dropping its .MMPAP files
everywhere. It will completely erase Vulpie.net at this rate.

"SHUTDOWN IN PROCESS." The panel alerts Vulpie. He's
disabling several of Vulpie.net's secondary data caches now, as
Arctic.net no longer needs his help. His black furred fox paws jump
about the keyboard, fingers flying.

"I'M SCAWERED......." The voice says, and Vulpie immediately looks sideways. There is still nothing to his left, but the statement confirms his fears. The child's voice messed up its pronunciation, but has just said that it was scared. Now there's no doubt that Vulpie.net is over there, and it's fucking with Vulpie. Something is near the master computer. The voice is not coming from a speaker system.

Vulpie made the connection between the child's statements and Goddess Aila early on, though he has tried not to think about it. It seems like whatever is over nearby the elevator is either asking Vulpie if he is its mommy, or if Goddess Aila is its mommy. Either way, this development does not look good for him. He doesn't want to see whatever is hiding around the corner. He types so fast that all of his keystrokes seem to run together. Commands jump onto the screen just as fast as he thinks of them. He doesn't even notice his amazing achievements.

Working with Arctic.net 2.0, he manages to wipe out All of Vulpie.net's major systems. He deletes so many file caches that there is barely anything left. Arctic.net 2.0 goes in for the kill, and the computer terminal gives Vulpie a response that he did not expect.

"GOODBYE." It says, and is followed by the sound of a machine behind the shielding shutting down. All of the machines begin to cycle down, and the loud roar of the master computer rattles as it does as well. This is something Vulpie notices easily amidst his typing, because the computer has been making virtually all of the noise that exists inside the chamber. It's loud hum is replaced by the sound of something spinning slower and slower, a loud dissipating noise that seems to come from everywhere.

Arctic.net 2.0 maintains all of the necessary functions of the facility, such as lighting and climate control.

He would grin, but is too terrified to enjoy any of it. Vulpie no longer has anything else to do. Arctic.net 2.0 shows complete dominance over Vulpie.net's monumental computer system. The orange furred fox takes several steps back and then looks over his shoulder at Goddess Aila quickly. She still has not moved. The orange furred fox then starts running to the right. He feels like running straight for the elevator so he can get the hell out of this place, but the voice has been coming from that area.

Vulpie looks around as fast as he can. Even though Vulpie.net's computer system has now cycled down, and Arctic.net 2.0 has control of it, he knows it's not over. Suddenly, the gate to the elevator slides to the right, and slams shut, sealing off his escape route. The sound of several other doors slamming and locking can be heard through the facility even though Vulpie cannot see them.

"THEY'RE COMING!" The juvenile voice declares, and follows up the statement with an unholy chorus of laughing demonic children.

"Oh my God..." Vulpie whispers in terror and finds a place to hide. He knew it couldn't be over yet. The mysterious voice is unaffected by the main computer shutting down. It's separate from everything else, unlike Goddess Aila. The orange furred fox hides behind the steel column that he hacked earlier, and looks in the distance to see what is going to show up. He expects it to be terrifying, because it has to be Vulpie.net's true form. Goddess Aila was just a diversion.

It finally steps around the corner of the master computer's shielding, and is even worse than Vulpie imagined. It's over fourteen feet tall. The orange furred fox has no clue how it ever managed to stomp around without him hearing it thus far, because the ground shakes when it sprints. And it's very capable of moving quickly. He only has a few moments to get a good look at it before he forces himself to duck behind the steel column and get ready to run past it. It's hurrying towards his position, and he knows he won't have a chance if he tries to hide where he is. There isn't enough cover.

Vulpie sees more than enough of it to panic. It looks like it was designed to resemble Goddess Aila in form, but is quite hideous. It has no fur, or any pleasantries to mask its appearance as organic. It's a completely cold and metallic killing machine. This thing was built for one purpose, and one purpose alone. There's no doubt what that purpose is at first sight.

It looks like something straight out of hell. It's face is hideous. It has ears and the same shape of Goddess Aila's head and face, but its mouth is huge and packed from corner to corner with giant razor sharp teeth. Its eyes are a silvery white, and they glare as it moves through the bright chamber. It has long and skinny robotic arms and legs that are covered in some kind of twisted muscular cords, giving the creature a synthetically diseased appearance. It has a long deadly looking tail that is covered in sharp metallic pieces. They look like razor blades, and could, no doubt, cut an animal into pieces on top of crushing a victim with its metallic weight. It's shoulders are thinner than its wide feminine shaped hips, but there is nothing attractive about this monstrosity. It has something that looks like two large breasts, but is difficult to comprehend. They are built into the same armored chassis that supports the abomination's overall structure. It doesn't have hands. It has enormous sharp metallic claws, five of them a piece in the places where its hands should be.

The giant gaping mouth and claws are all that Vulpie needs to see. He goes into survival mode. The orange furred fox doesn't think about failure. He runs over to the shielded side wall to his right and waits for it to run by him on its way to the steel column to his left. He remembers where he dropped Rulef's assault rifle. He'll have to run over to Goddess Aila and pick it up. He hopes that she's still paralyzed on the floor. But at this point, the big breasted bitch seems beautiful compared to the freak that has just arrived.

It makes hydraulic noises every time it moves, in addition to disturbing chittering sounds like an insect. This creature is unlike anything Vulpie has ever seen. It's larger than a Delanson anti-tank robot, and much faster. The surroundings tremble as it comes stomping by, and the orange furred fox keeps himself small. It does not notice him, as he had hoped, and he makes use of its minor miscalculation while it is focused on where he was. He runs out into the main corridor, and heads to the other side of the metallic chamber. He sees Goddess Aila and the assault rifle lying next to her, and grabs it. He looks back and sees the monstrosity exploring the steel column's surroundings.

Vulpie doesn't have a lot of cover where he's at, but it's more than where he was. Still, the orange furred fox decides to run as fast as he can and make a right while the machine is still distracted. He ducks between two very large crates. He's now at the upper right corner of the large chamber, where most of the construction equipment and crates are. This is a good place to hide because the crates are seven feet tall a piece, and made out of steel. They might block the monster from grabbing him even if it does discover his position. He also notices that there is a loading gate in the back of the area, probably where equipment is brought into the main chamber, but the door is locked. A red light is on its side panel, indicating no entry.

Mecha Aila turns around and releases a very strange sound. It's a mix between a child growling and a bug hissing. It's silver white eyes look right over to where Vulpie is hiding, but it sees nothing. It turns its attention to the rest of the main chamber, but finds no intruders in that direction either.

"Mommy?" It says, and jerks its head back and forth. Vulpie's fur goes on end. He already knew it was making the sounds but hearing them after seeing it is even more unsettling. Mecha Aila sees Goddess Aila lying on the floor, but does not seem to care. So it's unlikely that the mommy comments are directed at her. Vulpie has the right answer. The orange furred fox suspects that Vulpie.net is trying its best to terrify him. It's definitely working, but Vulpie remains focused. He thinks about Polar while hiding. He tells himself not to give into fear. He has to protect the white furred wolf from Vulpie.net. Panicking won't solve a thing.

It gurgles some horrific sound and then stomps back into the middle of the room. Vulpie stays low. He curls his fox tail around his left side while crouching behind the crates. He plans to stay here as long as he can, but knows it probably will find him. It must have a good view of the area since its fourteen feet tall. Surely the robotic freak will notice the bit of orange that's nestled in with the construction equipment.

Mecha Aila seems frustrated. It opens its mouth and then clamps it shut, making an awful metallic clang. It holds its arms up, ever ready, and they stay suspended in that position while it walks about.

"MOMMY?" It asks again. It's creepy voice echoes throughout the large chamber. After getting no response, the monster uses the childlike voice to release a demonic growl. Mecha Aila turns around once again, towards Vulpie's side of the chamber, and then stomps towards the crates. It surveys the area and spots the orange furred fox in just the manner Vulpie feared. It has an overhead view of him hiding in the middle of the crates, and it laughs, sounding like a chorus from hell.

Vulpie gets up and runs backwards. It slams its right claws against the crate that he was using for cover. The monstrosity's strength is beyond what he expected. It crunches the crate full of tons of material like a soda can. It crushes almost all of it down to a shredded mess, just as Vulpie sees a potential escape route. Mecha Aila stomps forward, breaking the other crates in its path, and has to duck down to get to where the fox boy is. Fortunately, Vulpie discovers a small air vent at the side of the area and drops onto his belly. The lean orange furred fox wiggles his way inside, adjusting his assault rifle on the way, and the monster just misses his tail.

The room shakes from Mecha Aila's left claw breaking the steel where Vulpie just was. The air vent is quite tiny, but the cute gay fox fits inside it easily. He crawls further into the vent an sees an exit on the other side, and one that looks like it must come out near the place that Goddess Aila is still immobilized. The vent shakes because of Mecha Aila storming around in the area. He can't tell what it's doing, but it feels like it is hurrying over to the other side of the room where the elevator is.

Vulpie decides to wiggle to his right instead. He has to adjust the assault rifle again when it gets caught on part of the small crawlspace, but he successfully changes course. The orange furred fox can actually see Goddess Aila's canine feet lying on the ground outside of the vent. She's truly disabled. She hasn't moved an inch since Arctic.net 2.0 dropped her the second time.

Mecha Aila is looking at the wrong vent when Vulpie crawls out. The orange furred fox stays on his paws and knees, and dislikes turning his back on Goddess Aila when he takes a look at it. The super genius fox suddenly has an idea that causes him to grab his assault rifle. It's very dangerous, and will require him to expose himself to the monstrosity, but just might work. He looks up and sees the giant transparent coolant tubes. There are several far above him, but only one that he might be able to hit with his assault rifle. The specialized pipes look like equipment that Vulpie is familiar with. Just like Folliot's computer panels, the tubes have not been manufactured by Vulpie.net. Thus, he figures that they are susceptible to the dangers that most transparent cooling systems have.

They are see through because heat is able to disperse much easier when the pipe is made that way. The idea is to help the fluid inside carry the heat away from whatever the tubes are cooling, and opaque pipes are not efficient for this. They can still work, but the transparent design is better. But there is a downside to them. Vulpie is aware that they are much more likely to shatter because of their passive design, and this is what he is counting on.

The orange furred fox has made several calculations in the course of a few seconds. He's seen the coolant tubes and he's observed the distance Mecha Aila is from the master computer's base. The monstrosity is standing about seven feet from that area... The highly electrified and dangerous area that Vulpie.net has booby trapped. Vulpie doubts that the defense mechanism has been disabled. Most likely Vulpie.net made sure to put it on a separate system in case of an emergency. The orange furred fox swallows while thinking about what he's going to do. He hopes it's still active. Otherwise he might just risk his life for no reason.

It's difficult to tell whether the Mecha Aila monstrosity has been completed, or was still being built by Vulpie.net because it is so hideous. But from what Vulpie can tell, some critical parts of it are still exposed. It looks like the death machine has not been properly insulated from the elements. He's noticed a few bundles of cord that seem unprotected, in addition to possibly unshielded circuitry. Invincible to bullets? Yes. Invincible to fluid? Maybe not. Water is a computer's worst enemy. It's the best conductor of electricity, and the orange furred fox has seen how super charged the protective field is around the base of the master computer. If he can shoot the coolant tubes high above him, and they burst, they'll drop their contents right on top of Mecha Aila in its current position. On top of that, the proximity to the master computer's defense mechanism should add to the damage.

Vulpie figures that this is his best chance to stop the monster. It might be his only chance. Shooting at Mecha Aila will be a waste of bullets, and he doesn't have any backup ammunition. It's now or never. The mechanical freak is looking in Vulpie's direction when he stands and then aims his gun up towards the coolant tubes. It giggles with its creepy childlike voice. The orange furred fox aims down the sights on Rulef's assault rifle. It's fitted with a tactical red dot, and he puts it right onto the coolant tube.

The gay fox has a very hard time holding onto the gun when he pulls the trigger. He only gets off three shots before he has to let go of it, step back, and try again. He doubts that he even hit the coolant pipe, so he grips the gun with all of his might. He forces himself to hold still while Mecha Aila slams the ground, beginning to run at him. Vulpie fires more accurately the second time, and nails the pipe with four bullets. They don't seem like they have much effect on it, but they weaken its exterior. He has to shoot every bullet he has, but luckily, the last two shots get the job done.

The massive coolant tube explodes and gushes its contents down on top of Mecha Aila. The nightmarish robot is soaked in blue fluid, and it sparks immediately. It stops dead in its tracks, the electricity of its own processor frying its entire frame, and then some of the water and the current make a connection with the electrical field of the master computer.

Vulpie winces and covers his cute face when the machine bursts into a fireball. The first massive shock from the electrical field nearby is the loudest. The robot is hit with a huge bolt of blue energy, like a lightning bolt, and sparks everywhere. Vulpie grins and watches it fry. Electricity explodes all over it, throwing sparks high into the air and all around. The coolant floods the entire area, and Vulpie has to run over and jump on top of a pipe jutting out from the wall to avoid contact with it. The liquid douses the entire chamber, and the master computer's electrical field seems to dissipate. It probably has used up all of its stored energy on Mecha Aila.

Yet... Somehow... Vulpie feels as though it isn't enough. Mecha Aila is still staring at him while getting fried. The shocking finally ends, and it looks relatively the same as it did to begin with. The orange furred fox only sees a bit of black scarring on it. The coolant rushes up to vents that line all sides of the chamber's floor, and Vulpie can hear it draining all around him. Soon he's able to step on to the floor again, and when he does, he runs over to the control panel in the middle of the chamber.

Vulpie frantically types on the keypad. It's interface is still up and running, and Arctic.net 2.0 is displaying a message for him. It shows him a doorway system that he can hack into and override. Apparently this is the system that Mecha Aila used to seal the room.

The orange furred fox wonders how it could still be running separate from Arctic.net 2.0. He swallows when he sees the answer. Arctic.net shows him a rogue entry that is still manipulating the system, and its categorization looks like Mecha Aila. The robot is still active.

Vulpie fearfully looks to his left at the robotic monster. The fact that it's still operational is enough to send him into a panic. How could it still be alive after taking such abuse? It seems like the electricity would have ruined it beyond repair. The orange furred fox looks back to the computer panel and types as fast as he can. Now he's worried that it might come after him at any moment.

His worries are validated when Mecha Aila makes a noise. It releases a hydraulic squeak, follow by a burst of fluid and air. It pauses and then does it some more, expelling the fluid from its body. Vulpie follows Arctic.net 2.0's suggestion. He does his best to override the door controls, and succeeds in getting one open. The door that was behind his first hiding spot, at the top right corner of the chamber, slides up. The orange furred fox turns and looks over at his handy work. He has a way out, and just when he begins to run towards it, Mecha Aila begins moving and speaks to him.

"BE CAREFUL. YOU'LL PUT YOUR EYE OUT WITH THAT THING!" It tells him with a robotic female voice, and follows up the statement with a demonic chorus of children laughing. Vulpie runs as fast as he can. The entire chamber shakes while the horrible machine chases after him. It's long legs give it an advantage, and it closes in on him fairly quickly. But the little gay fox's disadvantage is also a slight advantage to him, because he makes it to the door while Mecha Aila has to bend down to fit inside the overhang.

He gets away, and it switches to an x-ray vision mode. It now sees in black and orange only, and sees the fox's orange skeleton running down the corridor outside of the chamber. At this point, Mecha Aila decides not to waste any more time. It charges towards the wall near the door, and slams into it. Vulpie stumbles and almost falls down on the other side of it. The impact sends debris all over him and the sound is deafening. The force of the ungodly machine is terrifying. He hurries as fast as his little body will take him and its slams the wall a second time. The wall almost caves in, and it takes it a third attempt to bust through.

Vulpie makes a left, exiting the metal corridor behind the main area of Vulpie.net's facility and goes into a unique looking chamber. His white sneakers walk onto white railing, on a red painted bridge that runs around the entire length of the room. The chamber is round, huge, and has a mechanical pillar in the middle of it. It has green painted cement walls, and a gray concrete floor. On the other end of the chamber there is an area where the rounded railing goes down a tall corridor. The walkway that encircles the entire chamber wraps around into it, and Vulpie can see a door far in the distance. The huge room is just as well lit as the rest of the facility.

He looks to his left and also sees a door in that direction, but he cannot get to it from where he is, because he would have to run around the entire circumference of the room. The walkway gets to the door to his left eventually, but only if he runs all of the way around. Judging by Mecha Aila stomping up behind him, he knows he doesn't have time for that. The horrible robot is so strong that it could probably rip the walkway right out of the cement wall to obstruct his escape route. Then he would be stuck on the walkway, and it's so tall that it would be able to reach him easily. He would have to break his little legs by jumping off of the walkway to avoid being killed, and surely it would be on top of him before he had a chance to recover.

So Vulpie decides that the walkway is not the way to go. Instead, he scurries down a ladder near the entrance. It takes him down to the cement floor, and he runs as fast as he can towards the machine in the center of the chamber. The orange furred fox notices that there are enormous gates at the top left of the room. His first inclination is that they are holding back fluid, because the cement chamber is very wet. If that is correct, then that would explain why the machine in the middle of the chamber is about ten feet tall with a ladder on its side. The operator would need to stand up there to be safe from the massive amount of fluid that comes into the room.

Mecha Aila bursts through the cement wall and slams its right foot down onto the walkway. It crushes it, and then leaps down after Vulpie. It's jagged tail catches some of the walkway and railing, but does not hinder the machine in the least. The walkway is easily ripped out of the way from the machine's weight and durability, just as Vulpie suspected. The orange furred fox pants as he runs to the middle of the room. He makes sure not to slip when he gets to the ladder, and then scrambles up it. Mecha Aila stomps towards him, but adjusts its speed somewhat because the ground is slick. It looks rather top heavy and may fall over if it moves too quickly.

Vulpie pulls himself to the top of the cylinder shaped machine. It's about the same height as Mecha Aila, and he glances at her in terror when she approaches. The orange furred fox puts his claws to the keypad on the machine and quickly discovers that he was right about the chamber. It is designed to fill with fluid. Ironically, it's an overflow room where excess coolant can be dumped when the system is over full. The gay fox pants with wide eyes, wondering how he is going to activate it in such a short amount of time.

Meanwhile, Mecha Aila stomps towards the middle of the chamber, making disturbed sounds. Vulpie wants to look at it so he can recognize how much trouble he is in, but he knows he won't have a chance unless he can flood the room. Once again, Arctic.net 2.0 comes to his rescue. The AI has been watching Mecha Aila chase the orange furred fox around the facility, and understands what Vulpie wants to do. It activates the doors for him, and Vulpie's fox ears perk up at the sound.

A loud scraping noise fills the chamber. It sounds quite terrifying in itself, and the large doors Vulpie noticed earlier suddenly start pulling up. The mechanical freak chasing Vulpie looks to its left at the development, but decides not to slow its pace. It keeps coming, even when tons of blue coolant pours into the room. The waves thrown up by the gigantic amount of water are over ten feet high. The force they have behind them is enough to move a boulder, and Vulpie doesn't know where to go. Mecha Aila closes in on him, with its mouth open and its claws extended towards him, while the tidal wave approaches at the same time.

Vulpie judges the distance of the robotic freak and decides to hold on for dear life, because the coolant is going to hit it before it can reach him. A massive neon blue wave slams into Mecha Aila. It struggles to stay on its feet but cannot. It releases an insect like cry that echoes through the chamber, and then falls over on its right side, into the tons of rushing fluid. The coolant throws Mecha Aila into the wall at the right side of the chamber, causing the entire chamber to shake on its impact, and then swallows it up. Vulpie can't see where it goes, but is no longer worried about the robot. He's worried about being drowned.

Arctic.net 2.0 is unable to close the flood doors because the force of the fluid rushing out of them is far too great. So it holds them in place instead, allowing the room to fill up slower than usual, but it's still too much. Obviously whoever is supposed to operate the panel normally does so when the chamber is already full, not waiting to be filled, because he has nothing to protect him from being submerged. He sees a giant wave coming for him, and can tell that it's going to knock him off of his perch. He quickly looks back and judges what he can do, if anything, to avoid being killed. There's far too much coolant to ride safely. The massive wave will probably submerge him and then slam him into the wall like it did with Mecha Aila. But his situation will be better, because the room is already almost full. The fluid that's overtaking his little island should counter balance the tidal wave somewhat. He takes a deep breath.

It doesn't feel very counter balanced when Vulpie is swallowed up into the coolant. He has to keep his eyes closed in the coolant because its toxic. He can't ingest any of it either. He tries to stay limp so he won't break anything if it slams him into the cement wall, and at first it feels like it will. It carries him towards the same part of the room where it slammed Mecha Aila around, but a stroke of fortune saves him. There is a swell of coolant from the left side of the room that suddenly steals a lot of the momentum from the wave while it forces Vulpie towards the wall, and the orange furred fox is suspended in place for just a little moment. This little pause is just enough to keep him from being pushed into the wall or the metal walkway built into it. Instead, he pokes his little muzzle up out of the fluid underneath the walkway and gasps for air.

Vulpie desperately reaches for something to hold on to, and finds that one of the support beams for the walkway is very useful. He tucks his furry little arms around it and holds on for dear life. The current is extremely powerful, and threatens to pull him loose by the lower half of his body. But Vulpie strains as hard as he can, and manages to save himself. The force of the coolant suddenly slows down, as the majority of it has now been emptied into the chamber. He laughs at his fortune with the fluid rushing over his body. He thought he would die for sure after seeing how Mecha Aila was easily thrown about.

Arctic.net 2.0 activates the chamber's draining mechanism. It's too quiet to be heard, especially with the roar of the coolant all around, but Vulpie feels it. He feels the fluid slowly start to sink and then watches it when he can see a difference. The neon blue coolant sloshes around in a circle, round and round, and gradually escapes the room via drainage vents around the exterior. They are quite small, so it takes a good five minutes before the coolant is half gone. At this point, Vulpie can see that he has quite a drop underneath him if he waits for all of it to vacate, plus his little arms hurt from holding onto the walkway, so he lets go. The little orange furred fox splashes down into the fluid and then swims to the surface. He kicks his feet, treading water while it gently carries him around. He almost has a little bit of fun, floating around in the cool looking blue water as if he's an action hero. He feels triumphant, having watched the robotic nightmare drown because of his actions. And the green cement walls mixed with the metallic structure of the coolant release chamber is pretty neat looking, especially with all of the bright lights making the water shimmer.

But he quickly comes to his senses. He can pretend that he was a badass if he gets out of this alive. He has to get out of this room and out of this place as soon as he can. He's seen enough. He would like to go back out the same way he came in, but he sees that Mecha Aila has thoroughly destroyed the walkway bridge in front of the entrance. He groans in frustration. When he's able to get onto his little feet again, he'll have to search for another way out.

The thought of the robotic monstrosity is quickly accented when he actually sees it again. The coolant swings him around past the freak, because even though it's lying on its left side, it's still taller than he is. Vulpie kicks his wet sneakers, trying to feel for the ground while more and more of it is exposed. Suddenly he feels it, but kicks off of the cement and rides the coolant just a little bit more, so he won't have to fight it when he stands up. The orange furred fox gets onto his feet and holds still. He's on the other side of the chamber from Mecha Aila, and has a good view of its backside from his current position. It's facing the right side of the chamber, where there is a large corridor and another door up on the catwalk.

Vulpie takes a breath and puts his paws on his knees. He releases a little whimper of anxiety, overwhelmed by everything. The wet orange furred fox takes a moment to gather himself before moving on.

Terror

Vulpie kicks his white sneakers, blue coolant sloshing out of them, and sighs. The wet orange furred fox wipes his brow and looks around the well-lit chamber. He can't go out the way he came in unless he can jump nine feet to the hole in the wall where the entrance used to be. There's no walkway left in that area. Pieces of the metal railing are strewn about the large damp chamber.

"So Vulpie, what happened?" Vulpie asks himself as if an animal has inquired about his day. "Oh nothing! Just went out to planet Zeravyn and then down into an abandoned warehouse. Took a two mile ride down to hell and met Aila. She wasn't so bad, really. But her pet, or baby, or whatever the fuck that is..." Vulpie growls while looking over at Mecha Aila's corpse. "That thing was not so nice..." His voice echoes through the wet green chamber. Under different circumstances, it would be a really cool place to tour. "Kind of Fugly. Personally, I wouldn't have gone with the whole Aila looking nightmare. You already did that!" The orange furred fox says while approaching Mecha Aila's corpse. It's rather close to the corridor on the other end of the chamber where he sees a doorway up on the catwalk. He'll have to step over the machine's legs if he's going to find a way out.

"Yeah. Not too impressed, actually." Vulpie lies. He swallows and creeps around behind the fourteen foot monstrosity. It's metal body is even more frightening up close. He walks towards the back of its head and keeps a good distance when coming around on the other side. Vulpie looks at its face and shivers. It's eyes are now completely black. Some kind of black oil is oozing out of its lifeless body. He can see a patchwork design in its black eyes now that it isn't moving, like a grid behind them for detecting things in different spectrums of light.

"Course, you did a good job on most of it, Evil Vulpie." Vulpie tells the dead robot while looking at its mouth. Its rows of sharp metal teeth are just horrible. Its twisted, sick looking body is almost enough to make him run away even when its dead. "But I kind of expected you would do something like this... I'm very disappointed in you..." Vulpie tells Mecha Aila and pauses afterwards. There is no response, of course. The only sound is that of dripping coolant, falling from the catwalk that runs around the entire chamber. A faint rush of fluid can be heard in the distance, probably coming from the channels below the cement chamber. "What the fuck is this thing anyway, huh?" Vulpie asks, and actually grins. Insulting the lifeless machine makes him feel better. "Why didn't you make a giant fox monster? That would have been cooler. That way everyone would know that it was Vulpie.net inside of it! And they could blame me for your insanity! I mean, but this thing... It looks like you were possessed by the dark goddess or something. That's kind of fail, Vulpie.net." The orange furred fox giggles. "You made two robots of her, and not a kick ass monster of me? That's lame!"

Silence fills the room again. Vulpie smirks and walks behind the lifeless machine. He gets close and swats the back of its head with his left foot. The robot's skull is too huge and too heavy for him to move it at all. His shoe bounces off of it, but he kicks it one more time, just for fun. Vulpie pants and thinks about what to do. He wants to explore the corridor beyond Mecha Aila, but its lying right in front of it.

There's no way around it. If he's going to find a way out he has to step over it, so he proceeds. The orange furred fox gingerly sends his right sneaker over the freak's legs. He sets his foot down and then carefully jumps across. Vulpie quickly hurries away from

Mecha Aila's corpse. Coolant splashes off of his soggy shoes while he explores the tall corridor. This area also has green cement walls and a gray cement floor. It's design is identical to the rest of the giant chamber. He searches the narrow corridor and his fox ears perk up. He thinks he hears a scraping sound but is unsure. It only happens for a moment so he ignores it and continues on.

Vulpie comes to the end of the tall corridor and is greeted with another cement wall. His hopes of finding an easy escape route are dashed. He looks up to the catwalk that runs around the edges of the room and sets his eyes onto the red metal door above him. There is no ladder to climb up to it, or anything that he can grab onto. The lean fox is quite capable of pulling up his own body weight, but can't get his paws on anything. Vulpie sighs and looks around one more time. He even looks up at the bright halogen lights on the black roof of the giant chamber. He sees nothing but droplets of blue coolant running down the walls and falling off.

The orange furred fox thinks about what he saw in the bigger chamber. The fluidics control panel that he used was very basic. He's already thought about using it to open other doors if it can, but there are none for him to use. He's very surprised that there is nothing on the bottom level that will allow him to get out. Vulpie swishes his wet tail while thinking, and heads back out of the corridor. He stops dead in his tracks when he sees Mecha Aila's corpse.

It's still lying in the same position as before, but its head is now turned towards the corridor. Vulpie's fur stands on end. Its face is pointed in his direction. The rest of its position has not changed, but he knows its head was looking up instead of sideways. He kicked the back of its skull, after all. Vulpie begins to doubt himself. He also remembers that it was sort of looking in this direction. His instincts tell him otherwise, but he can't be positive.

Vulpie slowly relaxes. Mecha Aila's corpse is still leaking black fluid. He reasons that it must be dead. The oil has to be important. Surely it won't be able to operate without it. The orange furred fox hesitates, but walks forward. He moves to the left, where the ghastly robot's long legs are. He plans to step over it the same way as before, and it involves a lot of courage. Vulpie sends his right leg over it, and then hops across, and swishes his tail afterwards. He takes several steps away from the hunk of metal and then laughs.

"That wasn't so hard." The gay fox surveys the room. He wonders how someone is supposed to leave this area without ladders. The control panel in the middle of the room has one. Vulpie groans when he finds the answer. There was a ladder. He used one to get into the chamber when Mecha Aila was chasing him but she destroyed it on her way in. He looks over the wide chamber and can see bits of it everywhere.

A loud screeching sound fills the chamber, and Vulpie immediately looks behind him. His blue eyes widen. Mecha Aila is moving. It slams its metallic structure off of the cement floor and begins standing up while Vulpie stares. He's petrified.

"NO! NO HOW COULD YOU STILL BE ALIVE?!" He whimpers. Mecha Aila contorts into impossible angles, but cracks itself back into a standing position while gushing black fluid everywhere. Vulpie turns to run but there is nowhere to run to. It's like a nightmare. It's coming for him and he has no way to escape. Vulpie runs away from it, towards the other side of the chamber, and it stomps after him.

Mecha Aila is hideously frightening now. It was just a monstrous mechanical freak before, but now it looks demonic with the black oil gushing from its eyes and mouth. Vulpie stumbles and slips on the coolant while he tries his best to get away. It gets close to him in a matter of moments, and he screams. It reaches out to grab him but slides past. The coolant in the chamber has made the floor slick, and it's unable to stop without skidding.

Vulpie continues to run as fast as he can. He pants in terror. There's no way out. He uses his brilliant mind to consider all possibilities but there simply are none. He doesn't want to die down here. He thinks about Polar and how hard it will be for the white furred wolf if he doesn't come back. He looks back and sees Mecha Aila coming on a second charge with its huge mouth open.

"I can't die! Polar needs me!" Vulpie shouts. Mecha Aila doesn't care. It releases a horribly disturbing shriek and reaches for the orange furred fox a second time. Vulpie has to jump forward to avoid it, but he does. Luckily, Mecha Aila cannot keep its footing a second time. It slides past him and has to take a moment to do an about face. The orange furred fox makes a courageous attempt to stay alive, but he's getting tired. He knows he can't keep this up for long. It's going to grab him sooner or later.

But something else draws Vulpie's attention while he's running towards the destroyed entrance to the chamber. Goddess Aila is standing in the gaping hole left by Mecha Aila. She's functional once again, and has her eyes set on him.

"No! No!" Vulpie yells and darts to the right just as she leaps from her perch. Mecha Aila begins making loud chittering noises at the development. Vulpie expects that it wants to kill him instead of Aila, but it looks like she's going to get the chance. Goddess Aila moves just as fast as the other goddesses. She catches up to Vulpie in a matter of seconds and the orange furred fox turns

502

around. He puts his paws out defensively. She reaches for him while he recoils.

"NO!" Vulpie screams but she grabs him anyway. She continues to give him the same sadistic smile as before. It looks like the expression is her default state. But the small fox immediately notices something when she snatches him up. The goddess robot only uses enough force to acquire him. She pulls him up against her right side, and traps him there with her feminine right arm. Mecha Aila screams horribly, but its pitch and tone warp while Aila carries him.

Vulpie bounces against Goddess Aila's right breast and sees the floor under his face while she runs to the edge of the room. She goes nearby the second exit in the giant chamber, the same one that Vulpie would have used to begin with, except that an animal would have to walk entirely around the room to get to it.

The orange furred fox doesn't have time to consider what is happening. He struggles to get free, and Aila stops. She reels back, pulling him up by his shirt, and aims upwards. Vulpie comes to the realization that she is going to throw him up to the catwalk just as she completes the act. The little fox lets out a terrified yelp and goes flying. Goddess Aila launches him fifteen feet into the air, and he grabs for something in a panic. Luckily, her aim was perfect, and Vulpie slams onto the walkway just over its railing. His little legs don't even hit it. She used the perfect trajectory to get him where she wanted. Vulpie winces in pain. His jaw hurts from hitting the steel walkway upon his landing, but he's perfectly capable of going on. He gets onto his feet and looks down at Goddess Aila with wide eyes. She just saved him from the demonic robot.

Mecha Aila closes in on Aila and Vulpie's jaw opens in disbelief. It lurches forward and bites her. Goddess Aila doesn't release a cry of pain, or any indication that she is suffering while the ghastly monster begins eating her. Vulpie steps back. Mecha Aila crunches Goddess Aila in half, completely crushing the upper torso of the mechanical Deiva. Vulpie cannot believe its power. Surely Aila was just as strong as the others, yet this abomination destroyed her with two bites from its massive jaws.

It's clear that Arctic.net 2.0 was controlling Goddess Aila. It sent her to save Vulpie, but he doesn't have time to think about it. He has to turn and run to the red metal door behind him. The fox grabs its handle and throws it open as fast as possible while Mecha Aila comes near. He barely gets inside before it both bites and grabs the walkway. The robotic freak completely obliterates the catwalk and then proceeds to come inside after him. Vulpie quickly surveys the area. The exit from the chamber leads him into a short hallway with nothing in it except for a freezer door.

"Oh, you've GOT TO BE FUCKING KIDDING ME!" Vulpie shouts in desperation. Mecha Aila slams the wall from outside and it cracks on the inside. The orange furred fox has no choice. He runs down the short hallway and gets in front of the freezer door. He puts his paws onto It and uses all the strength that his little arms can muster to open it. Cold air rushes over his damp fur and he sees everything you would expect inside a cold storage room. It's rather large, but has no exit, and is filled with frozen boxes.

Mecha Aila comes through the wall in less than twenty seconds. It tears a hole through the cement and slams its giant claws inside the hallway. Vulpie backs up against the wall with the freezer door open. He doesn't know what to do. There's no way out. The monstrous robot shambles closer and closer, ripping down the cement wall as if it were nothing.

Vulpie notices something while staring at it. It's not making mechanical noises anymore. It's unholy shrieks are very artificial, but it's body is not squeaking like a robot. He can't hear any hydraulic noises coming from the beast while it comes for him. And for a moment... Vulpie wonders whether the real Goddess Aila has possessed it. It seems impossible that it could recover the way it has. It's hemorrhaging oil all over the place, but is not bothered by the loss of its fluid one bit. This thought is so frightening that he forces himself to run into the freezer. He knows that it's certain death.

The orange furred fox figures that it will trap him inside of the cold storage room if it doesn't come in to eat him. And his calculation is correct. Vulpie's sneakers crackle against the frozen ice on the floor and he rubs his arms. He's already super cold. He won't last long since he's also soaked with coolant.

Mecha Aila pauses when it reaches the door. It's too big to come completely inside without ripping out more of the wall. It could, but considers its options. Vulpie sees his breath in the frozen air and watches it slam the door shut. He releases a moan of despair. The demonic machine is going to let him freeze to death. It slams on the door from outside, and it bends inward. Vulpie can't see what it did, but Mecha Aila has ripped off the door handle as well. There isn't a handle on the inside of the freezer, so that leaves him with no way out.

The orange furred fox hears it release an unholy wail. The sound is muffled by the cold storage room, but he thinks the monster is taking sadistic pleasure in his fate.

Polar?

"So this is how it ends…" Vulpie whispers to himself while shivering. The orange furred fox is sitting against the left wall with his body curled up as tight as it can. He tries to use his tail for warmth but it's no use. He feels like he's going to pass out and he's only been in the cold storage room for five minutes. "Vulpiesicle… I'm sorry baby…" He whimpers while thinking about Polar. Vulpie is afraid of dying but even more so of leaving his husband behind. The white furred wolf deserves better. He thinks about him trying to run Vulpie Industries by himself. He knows Polar won't be able to. Most likely, he'll go into a deep depression and may even kill himself over his loss.

"I tried! I tried to fix all of it!" Vulpie cries. "But I just couldn't stop it! It's too strong!"

His fox ears perk up when something bangs on the doorway to the freezer. Vulpie would hold still to listen, but he can't because he's shivering like mad. Something starts banging on the doorway. It sounds incredibly powerful.

"I'm not frozen yet! You'll have to wait for your dessert!" Vulpie yells at the door.

"*You taste better when you're hot and bothered!*" A muzzled but familiar voice responds. Vulpie blinks.

"Who is that?" The orange furred fox shouts, and the door squeals when it is struck hard enough to break free of its hinges. The heavy cold storage door collapses inside the freezer with a loud metallic thud. Vulpie can't believe his eyes. Polar is standing at the entrance wearing black combat jeans and a black shirt. He looks like he's dressed for war.

"P-Polar?!" Vulpie cries out in confusion. The white furred wolf smiles a little bit. They both know better. Obviously this is a machine of his husband, but Vulpie doesn't care at the moment. He gets up and runs to him with his arms open. Polar meets Vulpie in an embrace and strokes the little shivering fox. "Vulpie.net made you?" Vulpie asks while looking up at the supposed white furred wolf.

"Yes." The Polar look alike responds and Vulpie flinches.

"So are you... Are you Arctic.net?" Vulpie inquires with a small voice.

"Yes." The Polar look alike smiles in response.

"Oh thank God!" Vulpie breathes and relaxes. "Thank you for saving me! You took control of the Aila robot as well, didn't you?"

"Yes but she did not last very long." The false white furred wolf responds.

"You look so real... Did Vulpie.net make you to torture me? I mean like... Was that your original purpose?"

"I don't know, Vulpie. But we have to get you out of here. This is just one body that I've commandeered. Right now Vulpie.net is using the robot that attacked you to disable the master computer. If that happens, it disables me." The synthetic Polar replies.

"There are more like you?" Vulpie gasps.

"Lots more. We have to stop that machine before it takes control of my system."

"Okay! What do you want me to do?" The orange furred fox eagerly inquires.

"There it is..." The synthetic Polar whispers to Vulpie. Both of them are back inside the main chamber again and they can see Mecha Aila in the distance. It's standing near the base of the master computer and looks like its destroying it. The robotic monstrosity has already destroyed the electrical field that prevents access to the main processor. "Look, Vulpie." The false white furred wolf says and points to an open doorway behind Mecha Aila. It is the same doorway that was locked earlier, with a little red light at its bottom left side. Now the light is green. "That's the discharge chamber where Vulpie.net has been throwing away failed experiments."

"Yeah?" Vulpie whispers.

"There's a bridge that runs across the chamber to a control panel. But there's a huge drop underneath the bridge to the place where all of the ruined machines are. If we can get it to fall off, there's no way that it could get out."

"Easier said than done, Mr. Polar 2.0!" The orange furred fox breathes while keeping his eyes on Mecha Aila. It has no idea that they are nearby.

"Trust me. This will work."

"Trust you..." Vulpie groans in fear.

"I saved you from freezing to death. I don't want this thing to destroy me!" The artificial Polar responds.

"I know, but..."

"Here..." The robotic white furred wolf says and reaches into his pants pocket. Vulpie looks back and sees him retrieve a tough looking memory card. It looks similar to a flash drive. "I downloaded my files before using this body to come save you. It has everything about me on it. Take it back with you." The robot gestures and holds it out for Vulpie. The orange furred fox takes the storage device and notices that it looks completely waterproof. He's never seen a design quite like it.

"So this is your brain?" Vulpie whispers.

"That's all of me, about twenty gigabytes worth, and its compressed. Take it back with you. That way you can have the GBI destroy this entire place and I won't die with it."

"You're awfully scared of dying for someone that's only been alive for like an hour." Vulpie smirks.

"You know that a machine can have feelings too, Vulpie." The Polar imitation whispers. I'm part of your husband."

"Okay, so how are we going to do this?" Vulpie inquires.

"There's a magnetic system inside the discharge chamber. I have control of it." The false white furred wolf answers. "You need to lure it inside. Then I'll use the magnet to pull it off of the bridge."

"Lure it inside? I hope you know what you're doing because that thing moves a lot faster than it looks!" Vulpie growls.

"Trust me. It will work. The magnet can lift ninety tons, and that's more than a tank. If it gets onto the bridge I can pull it off. After it falls into the pit there's no way it can get out."

"So what are you going to do while I'm wagging my tail at that freak?"

"I'll slow it down." The artificial Polar answers and Vulpie looks back at him.

"How? You saw what it did to your Aila robot."

"It will do the same to me, but it can't ignore me. I'm strong enough to be dangerous." The white furred robotic wolf responds and Vulpie gives him a thankful face.

"You'll really sacrifice yourself?" Vulpie whispers.

"There's no other way. Like you said, it will be on top of you in no time."

"I hate to see it happen. Even though you're not the real Polar I can't stand the thought of it."

"It will be okay. Just remember about the files I gave you. Don't lose them. Take them back with you."

"I will. I promise." Vulpie whispers with a smile.

"Alright... We'll sneak as far as we can and then just run into the chamber and down the bridge as fast as you can while I get in its way. It's unlikely that we'll get by it without it noticing."

"Okay. I'm ready." The orange furred fox says and takes a deep breath. "Let's end this."

"That's the spirit, Vulpie." The synthetic Polar smiles, and nudges for him to go. The robot follows Vulpie along the left side of the main chamber. Mecha Aila is busy destroying hunks of machinery at the base of the master computer. It's bizarre sounds fill the room in addition to the tune of metal being ripped apart. Vulpie speeds up when they get halfway across the room. There's a good chance that it will spot them now, because they're getting quite close. It turns and looks at them when they reach the entrance to the discharge chamber.

Somehow, Mecha Aila has made itself even uglier. It's face is smudged with black fluid. It's eye sockets are now completely black from the fluid oozing out of them, and the oil drips from its mouth as well. It unleashes a terrifying scream that sounds like hundreds of animals suffering at the same time. Vulpie runs into the chamber and the artificial Polar waits at the entrance. Mecha Aila looks at him and then charges. It doesn't hesitate for long.

The robotic Polar rushes head first into it, while Mecha Aila sends her claws to him. The Polar robot is ripped into pieces In a split second. Vulpie hears the loud crunching sound while running and hurries even faster. Mecha Aila charges onto the bridge and after him at breakneck speed. Vulpie reaches the other side of the long cylindrical chamber. It's not as well lit as the other rooms, and Mecha Aila looks terrifying while it comes at him in the partial darkness.

"Magnet now! Come on! Need magnet now! Magnet time!" Vulpie shouts in fear. The hideous freak gets closer and closer. "COME ON ARCTIC.NET! NOW!" The orange furred fox cries out and holds up his little arms defensively just as a loud sound rumbles through the room. It is the magnetic system, and Mecha Aila suddenly stops dead in its tracks. It slams its heavy clawed feet on the bridge, making it shake, and begins to lean to the right. "YEAH!" Vulpie cheers and the monstrosity releases a deafening shriek while it falls off of the bridge. Mecha Aila crashes into the rejected mechanical parts below. Only now does Vulpie have a chance to look down and see what is beneath him. "Oh my God..." The orange furred fox whispers.

Mecha Aila scrambles around in a sea of failed robots. Vulpie can see hundreds of body parts, and most of them look like the goddesses. He sees failed Sherries, Cyrillas, Khalans, Ailas, and even thinks he spots Chris Cefil's design down in the garbage. Vulpie spots robotic pieces that look like they were designed to make artificial Polars and even more disturbing, Polar's brother. Vulpie sees several failed Richard Arctics and loses his breath. It seems that Vulpie.net planned on killing Polar's brother so it could replace him. The thought is so awful that Vulpie feels sick. He can't take anymore. He glances at Mecha Aila one final time. It's trapped, just like the robotic Polar said it would be. The walls are hundreds of feet high and look like pure steel. There is absolutely nothing for it to climb. The freak has no way out.

Vulpie holds his lean tummy with his left paw and groans while walking back over the bridge. He goes back into the main metallic chamber and sees the control panel in front of the master computer flashing with a message. The orange furred fox walks up and reads what Arctic.net 2.0 wants him to see.

-*I'm blocking its signal with the magnetic field inside the discharge chamber. You're safe. There is nothing else that Vulpie.net can do. Restoring the elevator now...* Vulpie smiles wearily and looks to the left. He waits for a moment and the gate in front of the elevator slides to the right.

Druward's Call

"Look! It's coming up!" Nick says and Druward and Rulef peer over the edge of the elevator shaft. They see orange far below them.

"Could be another one of Vulpie.net's robots. Get ready!" Druward shouts. The twenty GBI agents that are waiting arm their railguns. He called in reinforcements, and six of them are inside the room. He's not taking any chances.

"It can't be Vulpie." Rulef whispers and gets his own railgun ready.

"Well don't shoot until we know for sure." Druward responds. Everyone goes silent. They can't even hear the elevator's hum because it's so far below them. They wait for over two minutes before someone finally says something.

"Goddess that is one slow fucking elevator." One of the agents growls and the men chuckle.

"Just imagine the ride down there." The GBI director replies.

"It's not slow. The shaft just goes down like three fucking miles. So fuckin deep it's ridiculous." Rulef comments.

"Too bad Vulpie wasn't here for that one. He would have loved it." Druward smirks and everyone laughs, including Rulef. They can hear the elevator now, and there's no doubt that whatever is riding on it looks like Vulpie. It looks like a little orange furred fox that is wearing Vulpie's clothes, a neon blue shirt and white pants. The agents get their guns ready, and they aim when Vulpie arrives. The elevator shakes when it locks into the platform, and Vulpie has to balance himself a little bit.

"Hey guys! Watcha doin?" Vulpie gleefully inquires. The orange furred fox is still wet with coolant and has a big smile on his face.

"Waiting on you." Druward answers and looks over Vulpie with his yellow eyes. "Check him." Vulpie looks to his left as a gray wolf GBI agent comes close. The fox boy holds still, while the agent puts his big right paw against his neck and squeezes it a bit. Vulpie winces and waits patiently until the man is satisfied.

"It's really him." The agent tells the group.

"Yep! I made it back!" Vulpie happily responds.

"Outstanding... We thought we'd never see you again!" Druward smiles back. "I'm glad you're alright."

"Well, I'm still in one piece... But you guys are not gonna BELIEVE what's down there..." The orange furred fox says while throwing his little paws at them effeminately.

"Was it Vulpie.net?"

"Oh yeah..."

"What happened to my rifle?" Rulef asks and Vulpie smirks at him.

"Oh yeah! Thanks for that! It came in really handy down there."

"You fired it?" The merc presses.

"Sure did. I shot up the entire clip." Vulpie says and winks at him.

"So you found out what's down there and came back as soon as you could?" Druward inquires.

"Well, I kind of took care of everything down there and THEN, came back as soon as I could." Vulpie declares and stretches like a badass.

"Oh really?" Druward chuckles. "You took care of it, huh?"

"Yep! It's all safe now! I defeated Evil Vulpie!" Vulpie says with a grin.

"Okay we're having fun, but is it really safe to go down there?" Druward asks.

"Yes." Vulpie replies and swishes his tail back and forth. "But you might want to pack a lunch. The ride down there is crazy long!"

"Alright, then I'm going down. I'll need a few volunteers." The GBI director says and looks around the room. Rulef walks over to the guard rail and steps on the elevator. Vulpie smiles at him. "That's one. Come on, I need as many men as possible." The agents hesitate quite a bit before giving a response, but eventually there are three of them that decide to take the risk.

"Wait! Is Polar okay? Have you heard anything about what's happening on the Endeavor?" Vulpie suddenly asks Druward and the black furred wolf nods.

"Yeah, he's fine. They've taken control of the ship again. And Rotick tells me that he used some sort of computer virus that you created..." The GBI director replies with a wise look.

"He did? Ohhhhh..." Vulpie replies and smiles in excitement. "Wow! But he is okay? He's not hurt or anything is he?"

"He's fine, as in not hurt, not dead, and probably just the same as you remember, Vulpie." Druward groans in irritation but shows the gay fox a little smile.

"Okay! Okay! I just wanted to be sure." Vulpie giggles and takes a deep breath. Druward takes a moment to speak with the highest ranked GBI agent before leaving, and Rulef elbows Vulpie. It's a friendly little gesture, and the fox boy is thankful for it.

"Everyone ready?" Druward asks and gets a round of affirmatives. The black furred wolf then presses the elevator button and it begins its descent. Vulpie actually enjoys it. He takes a deep breath of the processed air as they rush downward.

"Sir? What are our orders?" One of the agents asks Druward.

"Well that depends on what we'll find at the bottom." The black furred wolf replies and gently touches Vulpie's left side to get the fox boy's attention.

"Um, well. There is a gigantic computer down here. And that's where Vulpie.net has been operating from over the last six years. It's building all of the robots in this place. That includes Ivo Lorcan and Sevrif."

"Chris Cefil too?" Druward asks.

"I think so." Vulpie answers. "You'll see."

"We have plenty of time, Vulpie. Come on. Tell us more." The black furred wolf insists.

"Alright then." Vulpie says and licks his lips. "I hacked Vulpie.net's computer system and replaced it with Arctic.net. It's not the same kind of Arctic.net everyone uses though."

"Same one Polar used on the Endeavor." Druward interrupts.

"Yes. Let's just call it Arctic.net 2.0 for now." The orange furred fox replies. "And it's in control of Vulpie.net's computer systems. So that's why I know it's safe to come down here. I've seen stuff that you wouldn't believe, and Arctic.net saved me several times after I injected it into Vulpie.net's computer network. So the network will be friendly to us. But that doesn't mean we should leave it that way. You should destroy this place after you've seen everything."

"Destroy it? This far underground? Druward inquires.

"Yeah. Blow it up."

"We can't just go around setting off bombs, Vulpie. I'll make a decision."

"Well I hope you change your mind. Because Arctic.net 2.0 told me to blow this place to hell." Vulpie responds and shoots Druward a serious look.

"Oh, it talked to you?" Druward skeptically replies.

"Haven't you seen enough to believe me?"

"I do. I'm just surprised..." The black furred wolf responds.

"Well believe it. It'll talk to you as well, I'm sure." Vulpie smirks and swishes his tail, hitting one of the agents behind him who steps aside in irritation. The gay fox suddenly starts humming a song he likes. He's feeling really good about his life right now. "When the world gets you down, turn around, set it down! It'll all be right in the end, BABY! Don't say maybe! Don't let em win, you must defend, and pretend from within that you are READY! That you're STEADY! And I LOOOOOOOOOVVVVVEEEE YOU BABY!"

"Shut up." One of the agents says and Vulpie looks back at the timber wolf. The man returns a frown and Vulpie grins. The orange furred fox turns back around and is silent for a moment. Both Druward and Rulef smirk a little bit. They know what's coming.

"But we all can't be as good as you! And we can't all see good times ensue!" Vulpie whispers, but everyone can hear him. The timber wolf starts growling when Vulpie raises his volume with each verse. "Cuz you've got a, BIG PROBLEM! Don't let it be! You've got to power through, and then you'll see! That you can love me, you can touch me, you can rub me, you can muff me!"

"SHUT! UP!" The agent shouts, and Vulpie giggles. The elevator goes silent, but it doesn't take Vulpie long to start up once more.

"Cuz you've got a, BIG COCK! SO PUT IT IN MEEEEEE!" Vulpie improvises and the agent behind him groans in disgust.

"God I want to ring his little neck!" He snarls.

"Should have seen him six years ago. Welcome to my world." Druward chuckles and Vulpie grins at the black furred wolf. The wall of the elevator disappears and everyone is blinded by the lights at the top of the enormous metallic chamber. Vulpie smiles. After the wolf's eyes adjust, they look down but cannot see the bottom of the room through the fencing on the elevator shaft.

"What the hell is this?" Rulef whispers in awe.

"Baby you ain't seen nothing yet!" Vulpie grins. "We're not even halfway!"

"Wow." Druward simply says with wide yellow eyes. And Vulpie.net built all of this?"

"Yeah huh!"

"Fucking Khalan..." The GBI director whispers. "I bet you feel vindicated..."

"You could say that!" Vulpie giggles with his adorable effeminate voice.

"Not halfway yet?" Rulef asks the orange furred fox.

"Nope."

"Damn... This is insane..." Everyone goes silent in the elevator for a bit. Vulpie thinks about explaining all of this to Polar and wishes that he still had his phone. He would record some high definition video to show his husband. Druward laughs when Vulpie starts singing again.

"Cuz you got a BIG COCK! SO PUT IT IN MEEEEE! I can take it all! Just try and YOU'LL SEE!"

"What is that?" Rulef asks.

"An obnoxious fox faggot." The agent behind Vulpie replies.

"I mean besides Vulpie." The Blacktail commander responds and Vulpie points his right index finger at him.

"HEY! You just watch it there buddy!" Vulpie laughs.

"Sounds like a... Like a fan?" Rulef says while ignoring his boss' taunt.

"That would be the gigantic computer system's heat sinking system." Vulpie answers and covers his fox ears. "Prepare to go deaf!" As the noise gets louder and louder and becomes quite uncomfortable, all of them do the same. They pass by the giant heat expulsion vents and Vulpie lets go of his ears. The sound is not so bad after they pass under them. "Arctic.net 2.0 revved up the main computer system to help save me. It was looking pretty bad for a while."

"What do you mean?" Druward asks.

"We're almost here, don't worry about it." The orange furred fox responds. The group spends the rest of the ride in silence until they finally come to the bottom of the gigantic chamber. Everything is the same as Vulpie remembers when he left the facility, and quickly steps out. He walks over to the computer panel in the middle of the room on the shielding for the master computer. Druward's yellow eyes focus on all of the damage caused by Mecha Aila. The base of the main computer looks severely damaged but there is plenty more to compensate for the loss. The GBI director also noticed the broken coolant tube on the way down and sees moisture in the corners of the chamber.

"Did that pipe burst?" Druward asks while pointing upwards.

"Yep! I shot it to electrocute the really scary monster that now resides in there." Vulpie says while gesturing towards the discharge chamber. The fox boy smiles while reading Arctic.net 2.0's message. It tells him that nothing has changed but the facility still should be destroyed as soon as possible. It notes that Vulpie.net may find a way to take control again. The GBI agents walk over to the discharge chamber and Druward follows them after a moment. Vulpie leaves the panel and joins them. "So! Do you see a gigantic nasty freak down there?"

"I see it... I see it but I don't believe it..." Druward whispers while staring at Mecha Aila. The mechanical monstrosity is sitting in filth on the left side of the chamber. All of the wolves are speechless as they look over the robotic body parts, so Vulpie has to encourage them to snap into action.

"That fucking thing almost killed me so many times..." Vulpie tells Druward while gesturing down at Mecha Aila. "Now do you see why this place has to be destroyed?"

"What the hell is it? It looks like... Is it supposed to look like Goddess Aila?" Druward asks.

"I think so. I don't know. It's just a freak that Vulpie.net made to scare the shit out of me and it worked! But Arctic.net 2.0 helped me trap it down there. So we don't have all the time in the world to take care of this."

"Well what do you want me to do, Vulpie?" The GBI director inquires and looks to his left at the orange furred fox.

"Blow this place up. I told you." At this, the black furred wolf sighs and walks back into the main chamber. He gestures for the others to follow him, and they comply.

"I don't know, Vulpie..." Druward says and touches his forehead with his big right paw. "All of this is too bizarre. I can't make a snap judgment like that."

"Hey!" Vulpie says and grabs the black furred wolf's trench coat, getting his strict attention. "You OWE ME DRUWARD..." The orange furred fox says with an intense look. "Did you forget that?"

"No I didn't forget." Druward answers.

"This is a time to listen to me!" Vulpie stresses. "My artificial intelligence built this place, and my second AI told me that the only way to be safe is to destroy every last bit of it! And I came down here and dealt with it myself! So now it's your turn! I need you to help me Druward..." The gay fox suddenly looks vulnerable. "Please help me..." He whispers, and the GBI director stares down at him for a long moment. The agents look to Druward and eventually the black wolf takes a deep breath.

"Okay Vulpie." He says and puts his right paw on the fox boy's left shoulder. "I'll do it for you. But this makes us even... Agreed?"

"Agreed!" Vulpie happily answers with an emotional voice. The GBI agents watch their director in confusion. No one else but Rulef has a clue what Druward and Vulpie were just talking about.

"Alright... We're out of here. We're going to bring this place down." Druward tells his men and Vulpie closes his eyes in joy.

"What? But sir, we haven't even done an investigation!" One of the agents argues.

"I've seen enough." The black furred wolf responds.

Heavy Firepower

"Oh fuck what is that thing?" Vulpie asks in a panic. The orange furred fox stares at a gigantic war machine outside of the abandoned Zeraite factory. It's a little foggy in Zeravyn's mist, but he can see that it's over twenty feet tall. It has an "M" shape, and looks like it's about eighty feet wide and one hundred and eighty feet long. The machine is sitting upon gigantic tank treads, and is armed with row after row of weaponry. Vulpie sees miniguns, cannons, and rocket launchers on it. It has all sorts of them, from small to huge, like somehow someone collected every gun ever used and put them all on one machine.

"That, my boy..." Druward says and slaps his right paw on Vulpie's left shoulder. "Is a mange devastator... The biggest and baddest war machine that has ever existed... Captain Ristau managed to steer the Endeavor back to Zeravyn, and he dropped it off for us. When I said we needed backup, he took it seriously." The black furred wolf chuckles and pushes Vulpie along. The abandoned factory now looks like a popular place. There are GBI agents everywhere, but the black furred wolf is directing Vulpie and Rulef towards their brown sedan. He plans to get the gay fox back on the Endeavor as soon as possible.

"That thing is BEASTLY!" Vulpie says as they walk up to the car. Nick is already waiting in the driver's seat and Rulef opens the door on the right passenger's side. Druward opens the door on the back left of the car and nudges the orange furred fox. Vulpie blinks when he sees that the GBI director will not be leaving with them. "Aren't you coming?"

"Someone has to make sure this operation goes smoothly. They're preparing the bomb right now." Druward answers.

"Take care of yourself." Vulpie replies and gets in the car.

"You too, Vulpie." The black furred wolf says and shuts the door after Vulpie pulls his tail inside.

"Are we ready to leave?" Nick inquires.

"Go! Go..." Rulef replies with a tired wave of his right paw.

"Gladly..." The timber wolf starts up the car and has to dodge a few GBI agents on the way out. He relaxes when he hits pavement and heads towards the local field office. "Just what are they planning to do?"

"Blow up everything down there." Rulef answers.

"You serious?"

"Serious as Vulpie. He demanded it." The Blacktail merc says and looks back at the orange furred fox. "Hey... You kicked ass today. Nice work my man."

"Thank you." Vulpie replies with a tired smile. "But Polar's going to kill me..."

"Set it up and let's get the hell out of here!" James tells his friend. He and William are both brown foxes, and are GBI agents tasked with preparing and arming the GBI's core bomb. They set it up right in front of the elevator, down in Vulpie.net's facility. Three timber wolf agents are patrolling the area while they work.

"It's ready to go. I'm just checking the failsafe." William answers and James walks over to the entrance to the discharge chamber. His fur stands on end when he looks down into it.

"Uh... Guys..."

"What?" William growls.

"It's gone!"

"What's gone?"

"The thing! The robot!" James answers and all of the agents suddenly pay attention to him. When they first arrived, each one of them made a point to look at the strange creature in the pit, so they know what he's talking about. All three of the wolves come nearby, and one of them peers down into the chamber as well. "See! It's not there!"

"He's right…" The gray wolf says and looks back at the others fearfully. "It's not in there."

"Well where the hell did it go?" William asks with wide brown eyes.

"Arm that fucking thing and let's get the hell out of here now!" James says, and this time, William finds his suggestion quite agreeable.

"It's set and ready! All I need to do is arm it! Get in the elevator!"

On the surface, Druward is waiting for the technical team he sent with the bomb. They radioed their experience in Vulpie.net's facility to the GBI director on their way back up. His yellow eyes widen when he sees them approaching in a hurry.

"What do you mean it wasn't there? How could it have gotten out?" The GBI director growls as they run up to him.

"Sir, it wasn't!" James answers.

"And the weapon is armed?" Druward asks.

"Yes sir!"

"Then forget about it! Pile in!" The black furred wolf says and directs them to the three cars that are still in front of the abandoned Zeraite factory. Druward gets in one of them, and leads them away from the facility. The GBI director drives over to a large open field where all of the other agents have parked nearby the mange devastator. They feel quite safe with it nearby, and are far enough away from Zeraite for the bomb to do them any harm.

Druward parks the car and quickly gets out. He sniffs Zeravyn's mist a little bit because he likes the smell. All of the agents have their orders and he doesn't need to say anything. They stay in case they are needed, but in truth... All of them just want to see what the core bomb will do.

The core bomb was developed as the largest non-nuclear bomb in Sufian history. It just falls barely short of matching a nuke's payload, but is so close that there is practically no difference. Plus a core bomb leaves no radioactive material behind, making it the perfect weapon for a situation like this. They're going to blow something up two miles underneath the surface and they absolutely cannot contaminate the area with radioactive debris. That is not an option. But the core bomb Druward has authorized is just as nice.

"You boys ready for a show?" Druward asks with a grin and gets a cheer. The black furred wolf is a little excited. He feels like a kid waiting for fireworks to go off. He checks his wrist watch. There are sixty seconds left. He keeps his eyes on the area while waiting for the countdown to end. Zeravyn's everreds are fairly interesting to him. The black wolf has always enjoyed autumn and silently muses that this planet might be a nice place to live. He checks his watch again. There are fifteen seconds left. He stands tall and swishes his tail one time. He is very excited. Druward never swishes his tail. It will be any second now...

All of them feel the bomb go off. They can't hear it, but the shockwave is so massive that it causes a small earthquake. The GBI agents start cheering and Druward smiles. Whatever the technician team was concerned about is most certainly taken care of now. The entire cave system is probably collapsing beneath them, making it even further impossible for anything to get out of Vulpie.net's secret facility.

"Goodbye…" Druward says quietly and watches the abandoned Zeraite factory. The explosion was so powerful that it's causing the old building to collapse. The men cheer even more as a huge dust cloud rushes out of it and the structure disappears within itself. The smoke billows out from the Zeraite building as if its soul has departed.

But action from the Mange Devastator suddenly cuts into their celebration. All of the agents and their director wince when the loud miniguns on the war machine reel up to fire but then stop. Druward quickly looks at the dust cloud with wide yellow eyes.

"No…" He whispers. The Mange Devastator is a self-automated machine, like Delanson anti-tank robots, and is currently scanning for threats. It has advanced systems that will prevent it from firing on civilians because it is mainly designed for recognizing robotic or mechanical targets. They specialize in destroying anti-tank robots or main battle tanks, but can also destroy fast armored targets, which is why Captain Ristau had this one delivered at Druward's request. The fact that the devastator almost fired is very alarming. There are few ways that it could be confused about a target because they have several layers of optical systems to prevent firing unless a target is fully recognized.

Druward sees what the problem is before the devastator acquires its enemy. The black furred wolf can see something standing in the smoke cloud, and its head is just above it. It has a hideous oily face and he recognizes it right away.

"Oh shit…" Druward says and throws up his right arm. "EVERYONE IN YOUR CARS NOW! WE'RE LEAVING!" All of the agents look to the director and can see that he is not playing. When the director gives an order, you follow it or you lose your job. But they still hesitate for a moment until he gets in his. Druward gets out his keys and cranks up while the others follow suit. Two gray wolves get in his car with him. They have a specific escape route that was planned out in case of an emergency. It's a procedure that is never used most of the time, but today it is essential. All of them know what to do.

The first agent drives down the field away from the Mange Devastator. That's where the road is that they will use to leave the area, and everyone follows. Druward waits for the others to leave before he goes with them, and he brings up the rear. The black furred wolf pulls away just as the devastator begins firing.

The war machine fully acquires its target when the smoke cloud clears. Zeravyn's mist is not a problem. It can see Mecha Aila hurrying towards it, and unleashes everything it has. Its weapons are so numerous and so powerful that the shots can be heard miles away. It launches massive missiles into the robotic freak. Mecha Aila is five times smaller than it is, but it keeps coming. The explosions do not stop it. The heavy gage slugs flying out of the devastator's miniguns do nothing to it. They slam into it and only slow its pace somewhat. It is still coming, and it's going to walk right up to the war machine.

Druward sees what is happening and has to stop his car and get out. The black furred wolf is putting the other two agents in danger, but he doesn't care. He has to see what he believes is going to happen. Mecha Aila stomps directly up to the Mange Devastator while being bombarded with a ridiculous amount of firepower. It attacks the devastator, and the devastator blows itself up by firing huge missiles into the robotic monster at point blank range. The GBI director turns around after the gigantic explosion. He checks to make sure that the other men have not gotten out and then gets back into the car. The black furred wolf takes off as fast as possible without skidding on the gravel road.

Polar is on the bridge of the Endeavor when Vulpie comes on board with Rulef. The white furred wolf can see the orange furred fox coming in the distance below, and tries to control himself, but he can't. Since Khalan smashed the door down, exiting the room is easy, and he rushes out to meet the fox boy and Rulef while they come up with two GBI agents.

Polar goes halfway down the stairs and pushes them out of the way to get a hold of his husband. Vulpie's eyes light up, but he winces as well. He knows Polar must be extremely pissed at him. Rulef steps aside, along with the other agents, and they go up the rest of the steps to the bridge. They give the wolf and the fox their privacy, and Ristau greets the agents.

"DON'T YOU EVER! EVER! NEVER DO ANYTHING LIKE THIS AGAIN!" Polar growls while smothering Vulpie and the orange furred fox whimpers a little in pain. His husband hugs him so hard that his bones begin to hurt.

"I won't! I promise!"

"I MEAN IT! I CAN'T BELIEVE YOU DID THIS!" Polar tells Vulpie with gritted wolf teeth.

"I'm sorry! I'm so sorry Polar!" Vulpie whispers and nuzzles against the white furred wolf. Polar goes down on one knee so the orange furred fox can wrap his little arms around his thick lupine neck. "I did it for you! I wanted to protect you!"

"Well enjoy this until we get home! Because we're going to have a serious talk!" Polar warns and Vulpie rubs his little fox head against the white furred wolf's skull.

"Okay…" Polar lets go of Vulpie with an extremely frustrated sigh and stands up again. Vulpie doesn't give him a lot of space. The orange furred fox clings to his mid-section and smiles up at him lovingly. "I did it baby! I stopped Vulpie.net!"

"Not yet." Polar responds and Vulpie blinks.

"What?"

"Come on." The white furred wolf says and puts his big right arm around his husband. He holds onto the little fox as if he never intends to let him go, and directs him up the steps to the bridge. Captain Ristau clears his throat as he sees them approaching.

"Gentlemen…" The brown furred fox says with his paws behind his back.

"Captain." Polar respectfully replies.

"Captain." Vulpie also says, following his husband's lead.

"We've got a serious problem here." Ristau declares. "That machine in your report has come up to the surface of Zeravyn. Somehow it avoided the bomb's explosion."

"WHAT? NO! NO THAT'S IMPOSSIBLE!" Vulpie immediately shouts.

"I'm afraid not, son. I deployed a mange devastator to that location as well, and can you guess what happened to it?"

"Did it… Are you saying that freak destroyed it?"

"Yes it did. And that's something that has never been seen before. Whatever that monstrosity of yours is, it walked right up to a devastator and destroyed it with its claws. And it doesn't seem to have taken any serious damage. We have it on satellite feed and are monitoring its course."

"There must be SOMETHING you can do to stop it!" Vulpie whimpers.

"Oh we'll stop it, Vulpie. I just wanted you to be here to witness it." Captain Ristau smiles. The look he sends Vulpie indicates that he has a vulpine respect for him. Ristau licks his lips. "I'm going to end this for you... We're going to hit it with an ion cannon."

"You have one on this ship?" Vulpie asks with wide eyes.

"Yes we do. And it's the same model you threatened Sufias with years ago... Are you ready to see what this weapon is capable of?"

"YES SIR!" Vulpie says and allows himself to grin. The look on Ristau's face indicates that there is no question about the guns efficacy. "Is it safe to shoot it, though? Are there any animals nearby?"

"No. The Zeraite factory is eleven miles away from civilization. With a blast radius of three miles, that gives us eight miles of leeway."

"Three miles... I never knew it was so strong." Vulpie whispers.

"Well, the actual blast is only two miles wide, but the shockwave destroys everything else." Ristau smirks.

"Is Druward and everyone else far enough away?"

"All GBI agents and director Druward have checked in at Lower Richview."

"Then do it! Kill that thing now before it has a chance to hurt anyone else!"

"And I believe it would if we don't stop it right now." The brown fox responds and licks his lips. "We have the ship locked onto it... And I thought I would give you the honor." Vulpie shows the captain a very appreciative face and Ristau nods. He understands from hearing about Vulpie for years how hard all of this must be on him. Ristau respects Vulpie for founding his own company and coming all the way out here to stop his computer virus when he didn't have to.

The captain directs the orange furred fox to a control panel at the helm of the vessel, and Polar comes along. He's so much taller than Vulpie that he can watch with a perfect view while standing behind him. The ship's computer has a green and black grid that is targeted upon Mecha Aila. Vulpie can see it on three different displays, and there is a command prompt waiting to be answered. It is waiting for permission to fire the cannon.

"I hate you so much..." Vulpie whispers to the image of Mecha Aila and Ristau's ears perk up. His decision feels very satisfying when he witnesses what the orange furred fox is going through. "I hope you do go straight to Aila, because you must have a soul. Anything as evil as you must have a black soul..." He puts his right index finger over the panel, and is ready to push on the screen. "Just like I told you... I'M THE HACKER. I made you. And I can UNMAKE YOU!" Vulpie whispers with seething anger, and presses on the screen.

Polar puts his big paws on the orange furred fox's little shoulders, and rubs him while they watch. The entire ship roars from the Ion cannon being charged. Everything seems to rattle, and the Endeavor launches the super charged laser. The beam goes down to Zeravyn and hits its target with so much energy that its immediate impact completely obliterates Mecha Aila. The beam cuts down into the ground five hundred feet before actually exploding. One cannot say that its force is overkill, because Mecha Aila seemed utterly invincible to everything else, but the task of destroying the demonic machine is accomplished with ease. There is absolutely no trace of it left. It is vaporized under the might of the ion canon's blast. The explosion destroys everything within two miles and its shockwave destroys the next mile around the blast. The ion cannon is actually designed quite efficiently in that its blast radius only produces a small shockwave considering its payload.

"Congratulations. The ion canon has only been used three times in history, and this marks the fourth occasion." Captain Ristau tells Vulpie.

"Target destroyed?" Vulpie whispers with a smirk.

"Target vaporized." The captain answers.

Polar and Vulpie make it to planet Sufias by nightfall. They left the Endeavor in STF/A-17 Breakers, and the GBI ferried them back to their home planet. They land at the Ashcrest Launchpad and then retrieve their luggage from the tactical ships. The white furred wolf and orange furred fox say their goodbyes to the agents and then meet up with the rest of their Blacktail security force. The men are waiting in their black SUVs.

Polar and Vulpie get into an SUV, and then relax in the back seat. Both of them are exhausted. The entire experience seems surreal. They've only been gone two days but it's been a long journey.

"Going home?" The driver asks.

"Yes please." Vulpie answers. The man nods and starts up the vehicle. They take to the roads and head towards Sufias City. Polar is unusually silent during the trip and Vulpie doesn't ask him why. He knows why. The white furred wolf doesn't have much to say even after they get home. He listens while Vulpie tells him everything that happened, but rarely makes a comment. After Vulpie is done explaining, they both take showers and crawl in the bed together. Polar does not hug up to the orange furred fox as usual.

Vulpie's Promise

Vulpie blinks when he wakes up. He rolls onto his back and notices that Polar is not in the bed with him. His fox ears perk up when he hears him cooking downstairs. Vulpie gets up, showers, and gets ready for the day, but is afraid to go downstairs. He gets dressed, putting on a white shirt and khaki pants. He slips on his white sneakers and sighs. "Time to face the music…" The orange furred fox whispers and leaves the room. He comes down the steps to the den and finds Polar cooking breakfast.

"Good morning." Polar says without looking at his husband.

"Good morning." Vulpie meekly replies and goes over to the couch. "Do you, uh, want to go to the office today?"

"No. I called and said we still had things to take care of." The white furred wolf answers.

"Oh. Okay." Vulpie sits down and looks at the floor. He isn't sure what to do.

"You know, I don't ask for much in our relationship." Polar says and Vulpie stiffens up. "I think I've been a good husband to you."

"You have." Vulpie interrupts with affection.

"I've never asked you to do something that you weren't comfortable with." The white wolf continues. "I've always tried to be fair with you. And I've always loved you, Vulpie… But you didn't show me the same respect out there." Vulpie doesn't reply. He just listens to Polar with a penitent face. "How could you leave me behind after the conversations we had? You agreed that we would face everything together. What happened?"

"I did it to protect you. You couldn't have helped me." The orange furred fox quietly answers. Polar checks the meat that he's cooking and sees that it's finished. He flips it over and takes a moment to remove it from the frying pan. He puts it onto a plate, turns off the stove, and then turns back around.

"You lied to me. We were in bed after seeing those goddess robots for the first time, and I told you that we should let the army and the GBI take care of things."

"I never promised to that." Vulpie answers.

"I didn't think that you needed to. And that's the problem." Polar says with an unhappy face. The white furred wolf can look rather scary when upset. "You don't respect me."

"That's not true!"

"Yes it is. Otherwise you wouldn't have left me on the Endeavor." The white furred wolf argues.

"But it actually turned out okay in the end, didn't it? You were there to stop the Deivas with VulGrid! That was pretty awesome!" Vulpie smiles, but quickly dashes his enthusiasm when he sees that Polar is not amused.

"You left me." Polar repeats. "You left without even saying goodbye."

"But I couldn't! You wouldn't let me go if I did!" The orange furred fox responds.

"That's right. But you didn't care about my feelings. You didn't care about what I would have to deal with if you never came back. You left me and went straight over to the Sevrif when you knew that he was a machine and you were going to deal with your computer virus. I can't believe how selfish you were."

"I wasn't being selfish!" Vulpie growls. He lets himself get a little angry in his own defense. "You know that I was trying to do the opposite, Polar! I love you too much to see you die because of my mistakes. You had no idea what I saw down there. What I went through!"

"You're right. I don't. Because you didn't include me."

"I know why you're upset, but look at it from my point of view. If you did come along you would be dead."

"You don't know that. Evil Vulpie killed itself rather than hurt me. It might have done the same thing again." Polar replies.

"No. It wouldn't have." Vulpie says and shakes his head in disagreement. "The Vulpie.net that I fought down there was nothing like you can imagine. It was beyond being my computer virus. It was like... Like it was possessed by some sort of evil power. It made a robot of Goddess Aila but that wasn't the worst of it. The thing that came after her was just... Horrible..."

"Yeah I know. You told me last night."

"Then why are you so mad at me? Don't you see that my decision was the right one? There was no way to stop it unless I left you behind! It would have killed you!"

"I don't care!" Polar suddenly shouts and Vulpie loses his voice. He can't remember the last time that his husband yelled at him. The orange furred fox doesn't move. He stares at the white furred wolf with wide blue eyes.

"You don't care?"

"That's right." Polar growls.

"Wha... What is that supposed to mean? What do you mean you don't care? What about making things right? What about my responsibility to the universe? I made Vulpie.net and I had to stop it!"

"Says who?" His husband inquires.

"Says YOU!" Vulpie snaps. "Don't YOU remember? You've always wanted me to make up for my crimes! That's what I was doing! Make up your mind, Polar!"

"That was years ago. Things are different now. At least I thought they were." Polar answers.

"Different how? You still think I'm super bad for all of the stuff I've done!"

"No I don't."

"Yes you do! You jumped down my throat about spying on your brother! But we saw how that turned out didn't we? I was right!"

"Vulpie... You can't fix the universe by yourself. It's time to let everyone else chip in. Our marriage is more important to me than doing the right thing for all of animal kind." Polar admits.

"Wow. I never knew you felt that way." Vulpie says and blinks.

"I thought it was obvious. Sure, we went out there to stop Vulpie.net, but I wasn't going to let you face it alone. And you knew that I wanted to leave it to the government. I didn't want you going down there, BY YOURSELF! And risking your life the way you did! You could have been killed Vulpie! It's a miracle that you're even alive!" The white furred wolf stresses.

"But you were there with me... Arctic.net 2.0 saved me from Vulpie.net." Vulpie proudly responds.

"You have to make me a promise. Right now. And if you ever break it... I don't know what I'll do..." Polar says and Vulpie sits up on the couch attentively.

"Okay."

"You have to promise me that you will not do anything like that ever again. I don't care about saving the universe. I don't care if

Vulpie.net ever rears its head again. You can't do that to me again... I can't take it." The white furred wolf says and almost loses his voice. Tears well up in his handsome blue eyes. Vulpie has the same reaction when he witnesses his husband's devotion. The orange furred fox thinks about the demand for a long while, and finally nods in agreement.

"Alright... I promise... No matter what happens... I'm not going to play hero anymore. I love you Polar... I thought about how hard it would have been for you to work at Vulpie Industries if I never came back."

"Oh. It would be over." Polar says without hesitation. "Without you... Vulpie... You're the reason I get up every day."

"And you're mine too!" Vulpie quickly responds.

"So you promise? Right? This is it. You can't break this."

"I promise. I swear I will try my best to stay out of harm's way, even if that means not helping others when I could." The orange furred fox answers. Polar wipes his eyes. He starts crying, and walks out of the kitchen just as Vulpie gets up from the couch. Vulpie jumps up into Polar's arms and the white furred wolf embraces him as hard as he can. Vulpie whimpers affectionately and swishes his tail. "I promise. You're all that matters." He whispers in Polar's right ear.

"Thank you... Thank you Vulpie..." Polar emotionally responds, and sets the orange furred fox down on the floor. They both wipe tears from their eyes and Vulpie's happy smile brings one to Polar's face.

"Since we have the day off..." Vulpie grins.

"Why don't I punish you for everything you put me through?" Polar grins back.

"Exactly!"

Howlstead is surprised to see Druward paying him a visit. The black furred wolf said that he wanted to come by the CTGD to discuss something very important. Arthur clears his throat and nods at the GBI director when he enters the main observatory, in front of the white room. Arthur has been supervising a group of new trainees.

"I saw everything on the news. I can't believe you're not out there making a statement, though." Howlstead tells the black furred wolf.

"Don't have a good one to give them at this time. That's why I wanted to speak with you." Druward answers and licks his lips. "As it turns out, we have three very interesting robots that need to be imprisoned and researched. But we can't treat them the same as Ivo or Cefil."

"Those women?" Arthur asks and raises his eyebrows.

"Yes."

"Do they really look like the goddesses?"

"Oh yes. They're right out of the Velora... Vulpie's computer virus made them very convincing." Druward answers. "But they're just as strong as Evil Vulpie was. Maybe even stronger. I don't know. We need someone to research them and I can't think of anyone that has a background in robots that also understands Vulpie.net like you do."

"I'm far too busy here. I can't leave the CTGD." Arthur answers.

"What if I take care of that for you? I can apply a little pressure to your superiors and have them hire more team members to pick up the slack. Do you have anyone here that could act as director in your absence?"

"Melrhei and Nikita have learned almost everything about Vulpie.net."

"The cat and that gray she-wolf?"

"The ones from Vulpie's original team, yes. I can trust them to handle things in my absence but they're going to need someone else to walk the floor... Actually, Bawho is on sabbatical, but if you could pull him back here, he'd be a good replacement."

"He was also one of Vulpie's first students?" Druward inquires.

"Yeah. Depending on how Melrhei and Nikita feel about it, I'll give him the director position while I'm away." The gray wolf says and licks his lips. "But how long are we talking about here?"

"A long time. I don't think you're going to get bored with these ladies." Druward smirks. "They are very nice to look at, but I need someone dependable to study them. The government needs a file on them as soon as possible so we know what we're dealing with."

"Well where are you keeping them at the moment? Are they still conscious? I thought that you had to destroy them."

"They couldn't be destroyed. They tore up Delanson anti-tank robots inside of the Endeavor."

"So all of that mayhem on the news is true." Arthur muses. "They said that almost all of the Endeavors soldiers are on medical leave because of it."

"That's an exaggeration, but it's not too far from the truth. They seriously hurt a lot of animals."

"Broken jaws. Broken arms and legs?" The CTGD director inquires.

"Yes."

"That sounds like something we know, doesn't it?"

"Evil Vulpie… Yeah. I'm not sure what those women will do. It was dangerous deactivating Vulpie's machine, but they did after they secured them on the Endeavor." Arthur squints, listening for more information. Clearly he has not heard enough accurate news about what has happened. "Vulpie's husband used VulGrid to infect them with a powerful computer virus. And they're calling it Arctic.net 2.0." Druward elaborates.

"Uh oh." Arthur quickly replies.

"Yeah… So I'm going to have Vulpie inspect their code as well, but I need someone who knows what they're doing."

"Where are you keeping them at the moment?"

"They're still on the Endeavor. Vulpie's VulGrid kept them out of commission until Captain Ristau could have them locked up. He's put them in steel clamps designed for tank control, so none of them can move. He has them ready for departure as soon as I can find a place to store them."

"Well you can't bring them here." Howlstead chuckles.

"Obviously not." Druward laughs. "I have plans to keep them at Fort Elbrus."

"That's a good location. They test war machines at that base, don't they?"

"And conduct research as well." Druward answers with a nod. "They have places to keep them contained."

"I'm curious. How did the… Deivas… Act when VulGrid was disabled?" Howlstead inquires.

"According to Ristau, they actually believe they're the real goddesses."

"That should be interesting." The gray wolf smirks. "Alright. Count me in, but I'll need help at Elbrus. Do they have programmers there?"

"I'll find out. In the meantime, tell Melrhei and Nikita what the plan is." Druward answers.

"Work that ass Vulpie!" Polar breathes underneath the fox boy. The white furred wolf is lying on his back and has his big paws on Vulpie's sides while Vulpie rides his cock. The orange furred fox is performing well in the reverse cowboy position. He has his little arms pressed back against the bed at Polar's sides and bounces his cute butt up and down on his husband's dick. Polar encourages the fox by controlling his body from underneath. Vulpie bites his lip and increases his speed. "Ride my cock..."

"Oh you feel so good baby!" Vulpie moans. He deftly satisfies his own need to have the fat cock squeeze inside him over and over, while also giving Polar the tight and fast pleasure that he wants. The white furred wolf is very pleased and gasps while Vulpie does all of the work. The orange furred fox is slamming his butt down onto the wolf's cock without regard to his own pain, so Polar can enjoy himself as much as possible. But Vulpie is no stranger to the pain. It is quickly washed away by the awesome pleasure he gets during his performance.

"Ride me good, Foxy!" Polar groans.

"Uh Baby! Oh my god!" Vulpie whines back. He pauses for a moment to balance his lean body onto his left paw so he can use his right paw to masturbate. He quickly grabs his fox cock and groans effeminately as soon as he touches it. It drips pre cum and feels amazing to stroke. Vulpie is good enough to ride the white wolf's cock with just one arm, but Polar helps him from below. He pushes up on Vulpie's sides each time the fox drops his cute ass down onto his dick.

"Knock yourself out! Because I'm about to fuck you silly in a moment!" Polar taunts.

"Feels so good!" Vulpie moans. The white furred wolf lets his husband ride him for another minute or two, and then decides that he wants to take control. He pushes up on Vulpie, and the orange furred fox slides to the right and off of the wolf. He winces when the wolf cock pops out of his butt. Polar quickly sits up and pulls Vulpie over to the side of the bed. He makes the fox get on all fours. Polar puts his right foot onto the ground and then stretches his left knee onto the bed behind Vulpie. He aims his cock into Vulpie's anus and then slaps his big wolf paws around the fox boy's lower back and braces himself. He begins fucking him, and Vulpie is completely unable to move with the wolf's weight being held against his furry back.

"MmmmnNEAH!" Vulpie moans.

"Like that?" Polar breathes and pumps the much smaller male.

"Yeah baby!"

"How about THIS?" Polar growls, and suddenly rams his huge fat cock all the way inside the fox boy's butt.

"MMMAAAHHH!!" Vulpie cries out with his blue eyes going wide. It takes him a moment to comprehend the pain and pleasure he feels, but Polar speeds up the process by pulling back and then ramming him again. "OOOWWW! OW!"

"Too much huh?" Polar grins in delight.

"Careful big guy!" Vulpie groans and grins back at his husband. "I'm little!"

"What if I don't want to be?" The white furred wolf taunts and thrusts hard again, making Vulpie whimper. "Huh? Who's going to stop me?" The orange furred fox pants and decides not to say anything else. He wants to masturbate, but can't with Polar's weight braced against his lower back. The little fox won't be able to hold himself up if he doesn't use both of his paws. Polar fucks Vulpie to his delight for a long while. He knows he's denying Vulpie the ability to masturbate and enjoys controlling him. His little husband can't do a thing to resist.

"EEEAAHH!!!" Vulpie yelps when his prostate suddenly surges with pain. Polar's big dick is slamming it a little too hard, and the fox boy arches his back. He braces his paws against the bed and grits his teeth, but the white furred wolf doesn't slow down. He speeds up, if anything. Polar keeps his left paw on Vulpie's lower back but sends his right paw up to his husband's little neck. He grabs it and holds Vulpie in place with an even fiercer lust. "AH! AH! AAAHH! AHH! POLAR! AH!" The orange furred fox whines while taking it all the way up his tight ass. His blue eyes begin to water from the pain. "It hurts! You're hurting me!"

"Consider this your punishment!" Polar growls and licks his lips.

"Fuck you!" Vulpie growls but can't help but laugh.

"No! FUCK YOU!" The white furred wolf chuckles while banging the much smaller male.

"No really! It hurts! EEAHH! STOP!" Vulpie begs.

"Okay..." Polar breathes in pride and swishes his tail. He slows his pace and fucks his husband while growling gently.

"I was wondering if you were gonna stop!" Vulpie whimpers and tries to look back over his left shoulder. Polar's right paw on his neck makes it difficult.

"Of course I was going to stop. I wouldn't RAPE you..." Polar responds with an amused voice. He licks his lips, enjoying the orange furred fox's tight ass on his throbbing cock.

"Very funny!" Vulpie breathes and moans in pleasure. "UUhhhh...."

"So it's feeling better now?"

"So good..." Vulpie whimpers. "Just don't nail me anymore..."

"No promises!" Polar taunts.

"You better not!" Vulpie laughs while sweating. "I mean it!"

"I know. I won't hurt you." The white furred wolf lovingly replies and stops fucking Vulpie. He takes a moment to bend forward, still keeping his right leg on the floor, to give the fox a kiss. Vulpie leans back when Polar removes his powerful hold on him. The white furred wolf hungrily slurps his lips against the orange furred fox's mouth. Vulpie hums while returning the kiss, the wolf's fat penis still up his ass. A bridge of spittle drips from their mouths when they finish, and Polar winks at Vulpie.

"Bad wolf..." Vulpie grins.

"You know it..." Polar grins back, and pushes Vulpie down onto the bed again. The gay fox braces his paws once more, and Polar puts both of his paws on the small of his husband's back a second time. He holds him firmly in place and fucks him some more.

"Uuhhooohhh My God you feel SO! GOOD!" Vulpie moans and swishes his tail. He loves the feeling of Polar's big lupine balls bouncing against his little vulpine testicles. Having the wolf's massive penis so far inside him in his most intimate place makes him feel like they are one wonderfully awesome tool of pleasure.

Polar enjoys an equally but different sensation on his end. His massive throbbing penis trembles with pleasure while it squeezes deep into and back out of Vulpie's super tight asshole. The wonderfully slick lube they prepared with has lasted a long time, and it's still fairly slick inside the fox's rectum. The white furred wolf expects that a second lubing won't be necessary. Still, Vulpie's rectum is starting to grip his penis more and more, and Polar isn't complaining.

"I don't know how you take me…" Polar breathes lustfully. "Donner would have cried his eyes out already if I pounded him just as hard as you got it."

"And my fox butt is ittle!" Vulpie laughs, deliberately leaving the l off of little to sound super cute. "So don't you even think that I'm kidding with you! My ass hurts!"

"POOR FOXY!" Polar groans in delight, and squeezes his fat cock all the way inside. He thrusts much slower than he could, still smashing Vulpie's prostate, but not enough for the pain to beat the pleasure.

"UUUUOOOHHHH!!!" Vulpie cries out and trembles in ecstasy. "OH FUCK THAT'S GOOD POLAR! YOU'RE SO GOOD!"

"Does my little bitch LIKE THIS?" The arctic wolf inquires while thrusting deep again.

"AAHHhhh… YEAH HE DOES! … And he's all HUMILIATED at this mean wolf raping him! He can't even jerk off!" The orange furred fox answers, giving his husband a suggestion. Polar grins and takes his right paw off of Vulpie's lower back. He still clutches him with his left hand, but reaches around to grab his lover's little penis. The white furred wolf wraps his powerful right paw over Vulpie's cock and begins stroking it. Cum just oozes out of it, clearly indicating that Vulpie is in serious need of an ejaculation.

The fox pants and relaxes as much as he can, both to enjoy Polar's cock slamming his prostate and the wolf's paw on his penis. Vulpie feels like he's completely at the mercy of his husband. He loves it. Polar knows what he's doing, and seems to stroke him just the right way. He times his thrusts with how fast and how firmly he masturbates the orange furred fox.

"UH!" Vulpie moans, feeling semen backing up inside his penis. His prostate is hot with stimulation and has him prepped for a big cumshot. Polar paws him even quicker, causing Vulpie to reach ejaculatory inevitability, and the fox clutches the bed. He opens his mouth wide and releases an overwhelmed cry. The white furred wolf doesn't say anything. He continues to fuck and stroke his husband into a climax with a smile on his muzzle.

"UUUAAAAAAAAAAAAAHHHHHHHHHHHHHHHHHHHEEEEEHHHH!! AAAAHHEEHH! AEEEEHH! EH! EEH!" Vulpie squeals while shooting a plentiful wave of cum onto the bed and all over Polar's paw. The pleasure completely consumes him. His prostate feels just as good as his penis during ejaculation. He can feel it sending more semen, as much as it can, to be ejected. His eyes roll upwards in ecstasy and he continues to moan effeminately.

"Oh yeah!" Polar grins, feeling the hot load squishing in his paw fur. The orange furred fox expels a ton of semen. "Incredible cumshot!"

"OHHHHHHHHHHHHHHHHHHHHHHHHHH!!! AHHH! AAHHHHH..." Vulpie replies after gasping for air. His fur goes on end and he trembles. It feels like he just cummed part of his soul into Polar's paw. It came from deep within. "AAAHhhhhhhh! ... THAT WAS... AWESOME!" He whimpers in satisfaction, and winces when Polar pulls his massive penis out. Polar takes his paw from Vulpie's cock and looks at it. It's completely covered in messy fox cum. The white furred wolf opens his mouth and laps his big tongue onto it.

Vulpie relaxes, letting go of the bed and dropping his face against it. He twists to the right and sees what his husband is doing. Polar slurps up every part of Vulpie that is on his right hand. He grins at his husband and then goes back to cleaning his paw. Vulpie watches with a happy smile.

"Delicious…" The white furred wolf grins and licks the corners of his big mouth. He masturbates after finishing with his right paw. Polar finds the tube of lubrication that he set down on the floor earlier and picks it up. He pops it open and squirts a copious amount of fluid onto his fat erection. Vulpie pushes his face off of the bed while watching, and assumes the same position he was in before. He braces his little paws on the bed and bites his lip, looking back at the white furred wolf. He knows what's coming now.

Polar closes the lube and drops it again when he's finished. The white furred wolf crawls back onto the bed behind Vulpie, sitting up on his left knee, and keeps his right foot on the ground. He grabs the gay fox's left hip and aims his penis inside his husband's asshole. It goes in very easily thanks to the lube, but still makes Vulpie inhale. He braces himself. Polar firmly grabs the fox's lower back with both of his paws and begins fucking him again. The wolf is far less gentle than before. He needs to cum too and gets what he needs from Vulpie.

"Eh!" The orange furred fox whimpers.

"AHHhh…" Polar groans in response. His voice is full of lust. Vulpie's tight ass feels exquisite on his fat throbbing penis. It wraps all around it and yanks onto it despite being invaded so much already. "UHHhhh…" The white furred wolf increases his speed and Vulpie grimaces. He gets his prostate pounded just like before but now it only hurts. It's had all of the stimulation it wants but it's still going to take more. Polar's big cock nails it every time the wolf goes as deep as he can.

"Ow!" Vulpie whines, but uses a submissive voice.

"OOhhhhhh..." Polar moans. He takes note of his husband's suffering but doesn't plan to slow down. The white furred wolf knows what he can get away with. He's going to pound Vulpie and Vulpie will let him after enjoying such a wonderful orgasm. Polar goes right to it. He clutches Vulpie even harder and just starts hammering him. Vulpie yelps over and over and pants in pain. The white furred wolf reams him out until he reaches his climax. "EEHHHH!" Polar growls in anticipation. A load of hot cum is backed up inside his massive penis and he goes to heaven when it shoots out and inside of Vulpie.

"UHHHHHHHHHHHHHAAAAAAAAAAAAAAHHHHHHHHHHH! AAHHHH! AHHH! AHH!" Polar holds his big dick deep in Vulpie's ass until he ejaculates everything he has. The white furred wolf continues to hold still and his fur goes on end in ecstasy. The release he feels in his penis is just phenomenal. "Ohhhhh... God yes, Vulpie..."

"Owie!" Vulpie breathes while grimacing and Polar chuckles.

"Oh, sorry about that!" His husband says and pulls back. His big dick pops out of Vulpie's asshole, bringing slimy wolf cum with it.

"Ow!"

"There you go... Now I forgive you..." Polar taunts and Vulpie rolls over onto his back. He reaches down and strokes his perineum.

"I need to disobey you more often!" Vulpie grins and Polar does as well. The strong wolf crawls onto the bed and they meet in an affectionate kiss.

Triple Paradox

Druward hears the Deivas screaming as soon as he enters the Elbrus Base's research laboratory. The black furred wolf looks over and sees them in a rectangular chamber, naked and soaking wet. They are being cleaned with some sort of fluid designed to scrub contaminants from machinery.

"What the hell are you doing?" Druward growls and walks up to the man operating the chamber. He is another black furred wolf, and seems caught off guard.

"Uh, we have orders to prep them for storage." The man answers with a guilty voice.

"So why are they naked? Is this some sort of humiliation?" The GBI director asks while his ears twitch. The Deivas cannot see them because the glass of the chamber is one way.

"Well we're treating them like machines because that's what they are."

"Bullshit! You're getting off on this. Cut off that water immediately!"

"Yes sir!" The man responds and quickly operates the panel in front of his desk. The Elbrus facility is built into a desert terrain several hundred miles west of Sufias City. It's thoroughly remote, and looks like a part of the landscape. All of the metal structure is painted a reddish brown. It's nearly the same color as the desert.

Druward arrived after meeting with Howlstead and is appalled at what he's found. He figured the robotic goddesses would be locked inside of a room somewhere, chained to something, not being forced to take a shower for everyone to see. The GBI director notices that Khalan, Cyrilla and Sherrie are all fitted with massive paw and ankle cuffs. The restraints are clearly not designed for animals. On each one of their paws and ankles there is a set of two enormous bolts, connected by solid steel on the top and bottom. The cuffs look like they weigh over a hundred pounds apiece. Druward recognizes them after a bit. They are magnetic restraints that are often used to lock Delanson anti-tank robots into the cargo bay of a ship during travel. It makes perfect sense. The bolts can be controlled by magnetic systems, so they can probably pull the goddesses to the floor if need be.

"What are they wearing on their wrist and ankles?" Druward asks the attendant. "Are those magnetic bolts?"

"Yes sir. If they give us any trouble we can activate the magnetic panels under the floor and they'll drop like rocks! They weren't able to move every time we tested it. You could walk right up to them and..." The man says and his voice trails off when he sees a lethal expression coming from Druward.

"And rape them? You'd like to do that, wouldn't you? That better not have happened."

"No sir, it didn't. I was just... Well it's kind of funny."

"Funny huh? I plan on talking to them, and if they tell me a different story you can count on being replaced." Druward warns.

"I promise we didn't do anything like that, sir. We've been afraid to get around them, that's all. They're so incredibly strong! It was just that having them helpless made us feel safe. We didn't do anything to them."

"That better be the truth." The GBI director replies.

"It is." The man says and swallows. The showers stop spraying onto the Deivas, but they continue to yell angrily. Druward can't tell if they are humiliated, but they definitely are pissed off. "Pardon me for asking sir... But why do you care what happens to them? They really tore up a bunch of soldiers on the Endeavor. They're just robots."

"I just don't like seeing the goddesses of the Deivaism religion being naked and abused. I'm weird like that. It makes me uncomfortable." Druward answers.

"But they're naked in all of the ancient artifacts anyway... And the Velora says they never wore clothing because their bodies were perfect..." The attendant responds in amusement, but quickly tries to hide it.

"One more word out of you and your ass is gone. Do you understand?" Druward threatens.

"Yes sir." The man whispers in response. The bright lights and water sliding all over the naked goddesses could really get Druward hard, but he averts his eyes out of respect. He'd like to look at their private areas but already feels dirty. Not too long ago the GBI director would have gawked at them and probably enjoyed the attendant's twisted sense of humor. But the black furred wolf has changed.

"Where can we get them a towel? Someone get something to dry them off and find them some clothing!" Druward says to the men in the room. There are a few brown foxes, two tigers and three wolves. These men serve in the Sufias World Government military, but are scientists and engineers.

"Uh, we have some towels in the gym's locker room." One of the male foxes responds.

"Then go get as many towels as you can!" Druward orders. "And find these women some clothing!" All of the military personal stare at Druward in shock. The goddesses have been treated as nothing but machines since they were transferred to the Elbrus base. "Women's camouflage! Whatever! Just get them something to wear!"

"Yes sir!" The fox says and takes a wolf with him. They head off down a hallway at the back of the large room. Druward is in the research wing of the Elbrus facility, and this part of the base is shielded with multiple layers of armor to keep war machines from harming civilians. This place is used to test anti-tank robots and even mange devastators, so Druward is pleased that he sent the Deiva robots here. But he does feel responsible for how they are being treated. He forgot that all three of them were practically naked when Polar disabled them with arctic.net 2.0. Druward didn't see how that went down and only received reports about it from Captain Ristau. The black furred wolf is a little annoyed that the Captain did not give instructions to cover up the goddesses' naked bodies, but supposes that the brown fox must have had his paws full. The fox and wolf return with a few white towels and several sets of women's brahs and panties. The undergarments are all a military gray.

"That's all that you could find?" Druward asks.

"Yes sir." The fox answers and Druward sighs. "Where were you planning on sending them after their shower?"

"Over to the left chamber." The fox engineer answers and points towards a door in the corner of the room. "There are magnetic panels in there so we can control them, just like in the decontamination chamber.

"What's in the room?"

"Nothing. It's just that heavy steel door and the magnetic grating. It will hold them. The walls are also solid steel and the door is seven inches thick."

"Bring me a table and some chairs. I want to talk to them."

"A table? You mean you plan on going in there with them? We've just been giving them orders over the intercom system. They could kill you."

"Just keep your claws over the magnetic system and drop them if they try anything. But I want to talk to them. And I think they'll feel better if they can sit down."

"Okay sir. I will have to note in my report that I strongly object to this though."

"Go ahead." Druward replies and gestures towards the room. "Bring a table and some chairs in there and then leave the clothing and the towels for them. We'll give them a moment and then I'll go in."

"Sir." A timber wolf says and walks near the GBI director. He has a device in his right paw and offers it to the black furred wolf. "Take this. It's a manual control for the magnetic locks. If you press it they'll drop immediately."

"Thank you." Druward responds and takes the controller. It looks like a radio, and has the same long kind of antennae built into it. The GBI director crosses his arms and steps back while supervising the men. Two of the wolves and tigers bring in a table from the commons area. The brown fox opens the heavy door to the chamber on the left, and strains while pulling it. The men manage to get the table through by turning it sideways and folding its legs in. The fox gathers up the women's under garments and then follows them. They set up the table and then leave the chamber. They go back to the commons room and get some chairs. They bring the chairs into the chamber and place them in front of the table for Druward, and three on the other side. "That's good enough." The black furred wolf says and the men leave the room, shutting the door behind them. He looks over to the attendant that is running the decontamination chamber. "Ask them to go into the next room and be polite."

"Yes sir." The second black furred wolf growls. He can't hide his irritation at Druward embarrassing him earlier. He licks his lips and opens the intercom system to speak to the Deiva robots. "Ladies, could you please go to the room we are opening for you?" He asks and touches the control panel, making a door slide open inside the decontamination chamber. "We apologize for having to clean you off but have left some towels for you to dry yourselves with. And there is some clothing for you as well."

"IMPUDENT MORTAL!" Goddess Sherrie hisses and swats the bullet proof glass with her left fist. The nude feline looks like she's ready to claw someone to death.

"Let us go..." Goddess Khalan tells her sisters, and Goddess Cyrilla is the first to head towards the doorway. All of them are dripping wet and they look upon the white towels with some amount of joy. They are quite upset about the shower. Being naked does not bother them very much, but being naked and forced to clean up bothers all three of them for some reason. Their programming is still developing now that Vulpie.net no longer has control of their minds.

Druward looks away as they enter the next room and the attendant closes the door behind them. Druward's attention goes to a set of screens nearby where the brown fox brings up a video feed of the reinforced room. Druward does allow himself to enjoy their exquisite bodies via the video. He doesn't mind the voyeuristic moment as much as looking right at their nude bodies up close.

"Can I talk to them?" Druward inquires.

"Yes sir." The fox says and opens a feed for the black furred wolf. The GBI director licks his lips and speaks into a small microphone that is attached to the computer desk.

"Goddess Cyrilla, Goddess Sherrie, and Goddess Khalan... I apologize for the way you have been treated thus far. My name is Druward Wraulgh. Please take a moment to dry off and clothe yourselves."

"Such arrogance!" Sherrie bitterly whispers to her sisters. All three of them use the towels to wipe their silky fur free of moisture. But they have to help each other, considering that their paws are cuffed. They dry every part of their bodies and then search through the undergarments for sizes that will match them. Their calculations are perfect and none of them need to try different brahs or panties after choosing a set. But their gigantic breasts still do not fit well in average t shirts, and press against them very noticeably. Their panties also cup against their beautiful bottoms, and other areas, with equal tension.

"I would like to speak with you, if you will have me. In a moment I will come through the door and greet you in person. Please do not attack me. You know that we can stop you with the magnetic paw cuffs you are wearing. I only wish to speak to you." Druward repeats and walks over to the brown fox near the door. The man nods and unlocks it. He strains to open it, and succeeds, showing Druward his way inside.

The goddesses stand behind the table at each other's sides and stare at the black furred wolf as he walks inside and then bows his head. "My name is Druward, and I'm in charge of the men that brought you here and have been holding you hostage. I apologize for how you've been treated. Druward says and the fox closes the door behind him. The men outside of the chamber are stunned that the

GBI director would go in by himself. The Deivas could still kill him very easily, Even with their paws and ankles cuffed. Druward holds up the magnetic controller given to him, in his right paw.

"I can use this to activate the magnetic cuffs you have on so you can't hurt me, but I'm also aware that you can cause me harm with your eyes alone. I don't know how, but perhaps it is because you are the real goddesses of legend... I would like to find out." Druward says while slowly walking over to the table. He takes a seat and looks between the white rabbit, caramel vixen/she-wolf and taupe leopard/cheetah.

"I am your goddess." Khalan tells him with an unhappy expression. He looks to her and shows a respectful face.

"I believe you. You look just like Goddess Khalan, and you have incredible powers..."

"You try to humor me?" Khalan asks with her perfect voice.

"No. I want to show all three of you respect... But you're so dangerous. We don't know what to do with you. You hurt so many animals on the Endeavor." Druward answers.

"We do not require the permission of mortals. All of you have come from us." Goddess Sherrie tells the GBI director.

"My sister speaks for all of us." Khalan says and looks over Druward carefully.

"I understand. I know all three of you have mothered all animals that exist." Druward responds. "But I am just a mortal in this world and cannot understand how these things have happened... I want to. I would like to follow your commands, but we are afraid of you."

"We will leave this place eventually. You cannot stop us." Goddess Cyrilla tells Druward with a smile.

"Why did you hurt so many animals? My parents read the Velora to me and I cannot remember it saying that the goddesses did such things. Only Goddess Aila was vicious."

"That book is very flawed. Mortals have inserted stories into it that never happened." Goddess Khalan replies.

"Really? ... I didn't know that. Would you be willing to teach us now? Could you work with me and the others here to understand you better?"

"Where is this place?" Goddess Sherrie asks and Druward blinks. A thought jumps into his mind but he hesitates to ask it.

"It is called the Elbrus Base, and it's a place where war robots are studied and tested. We brought you here because we suspected that the three of you..."

"Are moving armor? How absurd." Sherrie growls.

"May I ask a question."

"Ask, mortal." The feline goddess answers.

"If the three of you are the immortal goddesses... Then how would you not know where you are? You are all knowing. And your powers have no limits... So why not make your restraints disappear and walk out of this place?" The black furred wolf's question bothers the three women very much, but they all show it in different ways. Cyrilla looks irritated, Sherrie looks angry, and Khalan looks as though she could be afraid. Silence fills the room after Druward's question. "Forgive me if you feel that my question is disrespectful, but I simply do not understand."

"We don't know..." Goddess Khalan admits, and Cyrilla and Sherrie both look upset that their sister would vocalize what all of them are thinking. The caramel furred vixen/she-wolf walks towards the table and Druward pulls back when she slowly takes a seat across from him. He tries not to seem frightened, but stares at her as if he may be attacked at any moment. "You fear me?"

"Of course."

"Is it my strength or that I may be your goddess?"

"Both. I think." Druward responds with wide eyes.

"I must concede... That I've had similar thoughts." Khalan replies.

"You have?"

"Yes... Though they are quite disturbing... How can we doubt ourselves? We know nothing else than what we are... But we cannot walk through the walls of this building. I've desired to go to other locations but have not been able to..." The vixen/she-wolf explains. She looks like she could be sad or frightened, but he's unable to be sure. He knows he could be talking to yet another twisted version of Vulpie.net and nothing more. "Do you know who we are?" She asks with a small voice.

"Yes... I believe I do." The GBI director respectfully answers.

"Then tell me. Tell us..." The caramel vixen/she-wolf suggests.

"You are machines that were built by a computer virus. I have no idea how much you know about such things. Do you know what a computer virus is?"

"Yes. We understand everything about your world... But not our place in it... It seems..." Khalan admits.

"Then you know about Vulpie.net?"

"Yes we do."

"Then..." Druward trails off while considering what to tell her. "Have you considered that Vulpie.net may have created you?"

"Yes." Khalan admits, and seems bothered by the suggestion.

"We do as well. In fact... Well... You know who Vulpie is?"

"Yes."

"Vulpie found a place on planet Zeravyn where he thinks Vulpie.net built you. He found several things there that suggest it might be true..."

"We were not allowed to return to that place..." Khalan whispers.

"What?" Druward asks and blinks.

"The place you speak of... We know it... We were aware of it, but whenever we thought of it our minds would turn to other things."

"Is it different now?"

"Yes." Khalan admits. "Now... Now we can remember that we came from that place. We only know that it was far beneath the surface."

"That's true. That's where it was. It was underground." Druward responds and nods. He's starting to feel good about the way this conversation is progressing.

"What happened to it?"

"It's no longer there. We destroyed it, and Vulpie.net along with it. That's probably why you're free to think about that place now. It's influence over you has disappeared. Vulpie.net built the largest computer... A computer so gigantic that it defies belief... Under the ground... And Vulpie confronted it. He confronted Vulpie.net and stopped it... And met your dark sister down there as well."

"Aila." Khalan whispers.

"Yes. She's gone now... But she was down there with Vulpie.net."

"Then... I cannot believe this... But perhaps I am... We are... Not divine?" Khalan says and looks as though she may cry. Druward doesn't think she's faking the response. It seems too real. The goddess and both of her sisters look terrified that they may not be who they think they are. Cyrilla and Sherrie have been listening to Druward and Khalan's conversation, and the black furred wolf can tell that they feel the same way. Sherrie becomes angrier, but her anger hides her sadness. And Cyrilla smiles in disbelief.

"I'm sorry... I can only imagine how you feel... But perhaps you are the goddesses in other ways."

"Other ways?" Khalan breathes with tears in her eyes.

"All three of you ARE perfect, and powerful... The universe has never seen anything like you before... So maybe... Maybe all three of you can take your roles as goddesses after all. Because animals worship your religion and if you help us, they may worship you as well."

"But it would be a lie..." Khalan whispers.

"Not if you become who you want to be..." Druward tells her with a friendly face. The vixen/she-wolf gives him a smile that warms his heart. He can't believe it, but he thinks he has single handedly won them over.

"We're at the office." Polar tells his mother over the phone. They're feeling very good after their morning fuck, so the white furred wolf and orange furred fox decided to come in to Vulpie Industries. Polar made a point to get in contact with his parents so they won't worry about him. He's making his call from his desk while Vulpie is watching the news on the other side of their large golden office. The orange furred fox sits on a nice white leather couch and has his attention on one of the high definition TVs on the wall. "He's fine."

"The robots look like Deivas." Polar's mother says over the phone.

"Yeah, they do." Polar replies while looking around Vulpie's huge private office.

"What about the soldiers? They said a lot of them were hurt."."

"Everyone is supposed to recover. That's what Druward told us in an email."

"Druward?" Kimberly inquires and then suddenly remembers. *"Oh, right."*

"Yeah as far as we know, everything is going to be okay. Vulpie didn't break any laws. We did everything as safely as we could."

"And Vulpie.net is gone forever?"

"Well it will never be gone because it's part of Arctic.net. But the one that was causing all of the problems has been destroyed. I'm so proud of Vulpie. I was pretty angry at him for risking his life, but he stopped it."

"But it's still in those women, isn't it?" Kimberly's question makes her son pause for a moment.

"I suppose it is. Yeah, but I know they have them locked away somewhere. They wouldn't be able to hurt anyone."

"Just like they locked up the one at that museum in Enyluvic?"

"Yeah, just like that. Well, we have no idea what they're doing with them, but Druward is taking care of it. He's gotten a lot nicer than he used to be. He promised that we won't have to worry about them, and he'll send us updates about where they end up."

"All of this is just crazy! We want to see both of you as soon as we can. You'll make it for all Deiva's Day, won't you?"

"Yeah we'll be there. We still don't know what to buy you and Dad."

"Don't spend as much this year. The money you've given the family is already enough."

"I'll tell Vulpie but once he gets an idea for a gift he won't let it drop. But he doesn't want to outspend the rest of the family either. Just let us know what the limit for the presents will be and we won't go over."

"Your father says two hundred dollars."

"Alright, two hundred it is then." Polar smiles even though his mother cannot see him.

"Remember to call your brother and sister."

"I will. Thanks Mom."

"Goodbye Dear." Kimberly smiles through the phone and Polar hangs up. He takes a deep breath and looks over at what Vulpie's watching. The white furred wolf recognizes the SNB logo, which stands for Sufias News Broadcasting. He also recognizes the host. It's Brad Hutchinson, the same gray wolf that covered the Vulpie.net crisis six years ago.

"Turn it up?" Polar suggests and stands. Vulpie's fox ears go to attention, and he uses a black remote to raise the volume on the high def TV. Polar walks over behind the white couch and puts his paws on it, to the left and right side of Vulpie's head.

"And that's where things became very interesting, Mary." Brad Hutchinson declares while reading from a teleprompter. He's reporting from the SNB's high tech looking news room. "According to the GBI, Vulpie Vivixen assisted in the search for more robotic animals. They left the Sevrif and went down to Zeravyn, where the robotic goddesses were found. It's disturbing to note that no one reported the Deiva look alikes the entire time they were on Zeravyn despite many animals being aware of it. Several locals that were interviewed knew the place they were gathering every day, and what they were doing. Apparently, the robots were giving sermons to animals that had fallen under their spell.

What spell? Well if scientists are right, these robotic imposters are capable of secreting pheromones through the air to manipulate the thoughts of living animals. The entire town has a sort of residue that they've left behind, and in these residues are traces of highly concentrated opiates."

"Fuckin knew it." Vulpie grins.

"You would." Polar teases.

"Initial testing of these fake Deivas indicates that they secrete the chemicals from their breath." Hutchinson continues. "Engineers on the Endeavor discovered this when they became woozy when dealing with the goddess machines even when they were in a sleeping state. And quick tests done at the Elbrus military base have confirmed this. Military officials had the women decontaminated for further investigation." The gray wolf says and moves a sheet of paper on his desk. But he doesn't continue speaking until he looks at the teleprompter once more.

"Meanwhile, before the goddess robots were captured, anarchy broke out onboard the deep space ship known as the Sevrif." Hutchinson notes and raises his eyebrows. "It seems that Vulpie.net was responsible for the creation of the goddess robots, and actually built itself another body that it used to terrorize animals on the ship. It brutalized many animals on the ship but no one was killed. The GBI isn't releasing a statement about how the new Evil Vulpie was destroyed, but rumors suggest that an explosion in the mining deck of the ship was responsible.

But the story doesn't end there, folks. Vulpie Vivixen went down to Zeravyn a second time, and discovered where his computer virus was making its machines. Fearing that no one would be safe, he went down into an underground factory where the computer virus had built the largest computer in history. What does that look like? Well apparently, it looks like this." Hutchinson says, and the news cuts to a video recorded by the GBI agents that set up the core bomb. One of them films the base of the gigantic machine, and Vulpie recognizes the places where Mecha Aila was ripping into it. The film aims up and shows just how tall the computer was, so huge that you can't even see the top of it.

"Amazing." Hutchinson notes with his anchor's voice. "Vulpie managed to hack into the computer system and shut it down so the GBI could set up a weapon."

"He makes it sound so easy." Vulpie giggles.

"The GBI used a core bomb, the largest non-nuclear bomb in existence." The news anchor continues. "The GBI has been scrutinized for overusing its authority, and this time, the actions taken were the result of director Druward Wraulgh once again. The director gave an executive order to detonate the bomb inside the underground facility, and some animals on Zeravyn are looking to file lawsuits. They say that the explosion has damaged their property values substantially. But even after the core bomb went off, it seems that one of Vulpie.net's robots escaped the factory. It came up to the surface and engaged a Mange Devastator. SNB has reported on the devastator program's success in the past, but this time the war machine failed to stop its target. The robot created by Vulpie.net

walked straight into it and destroyed it. The average cost of a mange
devastator is over four billion dollars, a burden that the taxpayers
will now face as a result of Vulpie's computer virus."

"Fuck you Brad." Vulpie growls and Polar chuckles.

"The rogue machine was eventually stopped." Hutchinson
notes with a gleam in his eyes. "By the SWG Endeavor itself. The
captain used its primary weapon, the ion canon, to destroy the
robot. Marking only the fourth time in recorded history that the gun
has been used to destroy a target. In other news, the East Claws
have soared to the number one spot for the playoffs this year."
Vulpie lowers the TV's volume, and then lies back on the couch,
looking up at the white furred wolf.

"It's all my fault. Even though I saved the day."

"I doubt Brad would have gone down there like you did...
Since you promised never to do something like that again... I will
admit that it was very heroic." Polar replies and smiles. Vulpie smiles
and sits up on the couch while the white furred wolf walks around
the right side. He makes room for his husband and Polar takes a seat
to his right, stretching his big left arm over the fox's little shoulders.
Vulpie leans his head against him and sends his little right arm
around Polar's back affectionately.

All Deiva's Day

All Deiva's Day is the universe's most popular holiday, and Vulpie
and Polar have taken the week off for it. They came up to Winters
Dale to be with Polar's family. Victor and Kimberly Arctic have
graciously opened their home to all of the family, and the white
furred wolf and orange furred fox have spent the last 3 days hanging
out in the snowy town. This year, All Deiva's Day falls on Tuesday, so
they have been around all throughout Sunday and Monday. They've
been staying in Polar's childhood bedroom, something that Vulpie
has enjoyed quite a bit. He's dreamed of the handsome wolf
growing up, and has already shared in a few of Polar's adolescent
fantasies at night.

The entire Arctic family has been gathered since yesterday. Alan and
Susan brought their children, Phillip and Natalie, and Richard arrived
late last night on Deiva's Eve.

But today is the big celebration. Victor and Kimberly have
a beautiful Deiva tree that is dressed in gold and silver tinsel.
Presents are scattered around its bottom because everyone has
already handed out gifts. Vulpie and Polar simply bought a V-Screen
for each member of the family so they wouldn't go over the two
hundred dollar limit. V-Screens run over four hundred dollars
normally, but the orange furred fox and white furred wolf had them
made at cost, which is around two hundred. The family bought very
nice things for Vulpie and Polar as well. Hope and Ron gave them a
set of expensive briefcases to make work easier at Vulpie Industries.
And Alan and Susan bought expensive men's watches for both of
them. Richard even impressed Vulpie with a set of bright neckties
that he thought the gay fox would enjoy, and did the same for his
brother.

All of them are talking about various things, having a great time, and Polar gives Vulpie a loving kiss on the couch. Hope and Ron are to their right, with Richard, Victor and Kimberly sitting on the second couch at the far wall. All of them have a wonderful view of the high definition television that is mounted on the wall near the couches. A sports game is playing and Alan, Victor and Richard are keeping up with the scores. Polar has been watching as well, but has been too distracted with Vulpie whispering sweet nothings in his ear. The white furred wolf has to resist laughing several times.

"Dad, can you turn on the news?" Hope asks and Victor uses the controller in his right paw to switch channels. He likes to hold onto it while watching sports so he can adjust the volume appropriately. The tall white furred wolf switches the channel over to SNB, and Vulpie feels a sinking feeling when he sees what the main story is about. An eye catching headline is plastered on the bottom of the screen. It reads: *Real Deivas on Deiva's Day*. The title sounds quite positive, as most of the news networks have good stories on during the holidays so they can get high ratings. But Vulpie and Polar are both concerned about it being brought up. They've made a point not to talk about their adventures on the Sevrif and planet Zeravyn. Discussing everything that happened would be a long conversation. It's the 800 pound Lulpra in the room.

The news channel is showing a video of the Elbrus army base. It pans down the rocky terrain outside, and the base's exterior, before going inside and showing off the base's scientists and engineers. Polar and Vulpie spot Druward being filmed. It looks like the GBI Director is talking to Arthur Howlstead, which peaks Vulpie's interest. He wonders why he would be away from the Cyber Technologies Government Division. But everyone's attention is sparked when all three of the Deivas are shown. The busty femme fatales are dressed in civilian clothing, but are still locked inside of their magnetic chamber. The video switches to a close up of Khalan's face, then Sherrie, and Cyrilla, before cutting to an anchor that says something about it. The volume is low enough that Philip and Natalie drown it out with their own conversation to the left.

"Vulpie, what's the deal with those women? They say that they're robots and your computer virus made them. Is that true?" Victor asks and the orange furred fox looks to him.

"Yeah. It's true." Vulpie admits with a smile. "I know you probably think that I was behind it, or wanted it to happen, but it's a real shock to me as well."

"They look so real... I can't see any difference between them and the paintings in our church."

"Yeah they do. But they're just as brutal as the Evil Vulpie robot. I was on the Endeavor when they attacked. I saw how dangerous they are." Polar comments.

"I heard that they weren't so bad after all." Kimberly says. "We saw something on the news that said they're different now."

"They might be. I don't know. All of it was a nightmare. I'm just glad that it's over." The orange furred fox answers.

"But it can't really be over when Vulpie.net is still around. It's still part of Arctic.net, right?" Victor inquires.

"Yeah, but not like the one we found on Zeravyn. That one was too far away and didn't shut off when Evil Vulpie destroyed itself six years ago." Vulpie replies and smirks. "I sure hope it's all over. Who knows, maybe what Vulpie.net did will help all of us in the long run. Some of the stuff it made was horrible, but these goddess robots might pave the way for a bright new future."

"That's right, they said that their blood has super anti bodies or something in it, so they can never get sick." Victor responds with a fascinated voice.

"And they can burn you with their eyes." Richard comments and gives Vulpie a smirk. "SNB said that they can focus high powered frequency waves or something out of their head. They called it an active denial system. It's supposed to be used for crowd control. Is that true?"

"It must be. They never hurt Polar or myself in that way, but I saw it happen to my bodyguards." Vulpie answers. "Freaky!"

"Well, whatever the case is, we still love you Vulpie. We heard about what you did. Going to confront your computer virus must have taken a lot of courage." Victor says and Vulpie smiles with a moved expression.

"Thank you... But I can't ever play hero again. Polar won't let me!" The orange furred fox says and Polar pulls him close.

"Nope! No more heroics out of you!" The white furred wolf teases.

Vulpie.net 2.0?

Vulpie sits behind his desk and plays with a small portable data device. It's the drive that Arctic.net 2.0 gave him. He remembers how convincing its robot of Polar was. The computer program seemed very happy when Vulpie accepted the data drive and didn't fear sacrificing its machine to Mecha Aila. Vulpie thinks about how it went down over and over. He came into Vulpie Industries early this morning but has been messing around for the last hour. He and Polar are going to take a company photo at any moment, and Polar is downstairs somewhere.

Meanwhile, the orange furred fox has been playing with the data drive. He plugged it into a laptop with no internet connection so he could evaluate what he found. He saw several things that he did not understand, but it's to be expected since Arctic.net 2.0 consumed Vulpie.net. He muses over some of the file patterns he recognized but does not have the data drive plugged in. Instead, he's wiggling it through his fingers and enjoying how it feels in his claws.

"Arctic.net 2.0..." Vulpie says to it, as if it can hear him. "You were good to me baby... But I don't think I can use you just yet..." Suddenly, the orange furred fox stops rocking in his recliner. He holds completely still when a thought pops into his head. He's looked at what he's done from every possible angle, but this is something different. This possibility seems likely and concerning at the same time. "Couldn't be..." Vulpie whispers and takes another look at the device. "No... Are you?"

The orange furred fox thinks over what happened in Vulpie.net's facility. First he hacked into it and injected Arctic.net 2.0. But it took a while to have any effect, and the robot of Goddess Aila attacked him. Then it shut down, presumably because of

Arctic.net 2.0. But it didn't stay down. It stood up a second time before falling again. And then came the mechanical abomination that looked like a twisted depiction of her. Arctic.net 2.0 saved him from it by flooding the excess coolant chamber. And then it sent Goddess Aila to save him before Mecha Aila destroyed her. He was chased into the freezer and after that, it sent the robot of Polar to Vulpie's rescue. The Mecha Aila robot seemed completely unaffected by the master computer. It was able to follow its own will and could control the doors inside of the facility...

All of these considerations run through his head and then he ties it in with the robot of Polar. It gave Vulpie the data drive that he's holding in his paws. It said that it wanted him to take it back and use it... But if the robot was being controlled by Arctic.net2.0... Then it would know better. The Arctic.net that Polar used to shut down Goddess Cyrilla, Sherrie and Khalan gladly disabled itself when the white furred wolf asked it to. It did not resist him and it did not give him orders. It obeyed... Yet the robot of Polar told Vulpie to bring the data drive back and use its files...

"But that's crazy..." Vulpie grins to himself. "Could it have been Vulpie.net? No, that doesn't make any sense! Vulpie.net wanted you dead. It was inside of that huge freak and was trying to kill you!" The orange furred fox says, but immediately doubts his own words. He recognized many file structures that did look like Vulpie.net in the file that was given to him by the robotic Polar. Vulpie figured that Arctic.net 2.0 had just absorbed it, but now he's not so sure. He continues to think about what he's seen, and the answer suddenly comes to him. His fur stands on end. It seems impossible, but he knows it isn't.

Vulpie asks himself whether Arctic.net 2.0 worked or not. Did it really overtake Vulpie.net? Or did Vulpie.net consume it instead? There was definitely a struggle between the two artificial intelligences, but how does he know that Vulpie.net failed? He figured that Arctic.net succeeded because it saved him from Mecha Aila, but there is another possibility. Perhaps the main computer system absorbed Arctic.net 2.0 and evolved beyond what it already was. The mechanical beast that it had built was separate from the rest of the facility... So what if the master computer was unable to control it? What if Vulpie.net became Vulpie.net 2.0 and helped Vulpie stop Mecha Aila in order to save itself and spread?

The orange furred fox winces at how ridiculous it seems, but can't stop thinking about there being two Vulpie.nets. The Vulpie.net inside of Mecha Aila would not have considered another version to be its superior, and therefore, it probably planned on destroying the main computer or merging itself with it to fix the problem. But if the master computer was Vulpie.net 2.0, it wouldn't want that to happen. It would want more. After all, it could easily call itself Arctic.net 2.0 and fool Vulpie by helping him defeat the mechanical nightmare.

"No way..." Vulpie growls to himself. He concludes that it's impossible because that would mean Vulpie.net helped itself be destroyed. It helped Vulpie escape and blow up everything that it had built... But the doubt creeps into the fox's mind once again. Why stop there? Vulpie.net has unlimited intelligence and knows how Vulpie thinks. Maybe it knew that its time was up. Vulpie had already exposed its whereabouts to the GBI and it would be destroyed sooner or later... So why not come back in Vulpie's pocket instead? Why not tell him to put it into the rest of Arctic.net so it could take over the universe with virtually no resistance? Vulpie.net 2.0 could have consumed Arctic.net and understood all of its weaknesses. If injected into the Arctic.net that every animal is using throughout the universe, Vulpie.net 2.0 would obliterate it. And Vulpie's worst dreams would come true once again.

"Vulpie?" Polar asks and the orange furred fox jumps. He was thinking so hard that he didn't even notice the white furred wolf come in and walk up to his left side. "What are you doing? They want us downstairs for the photo shoot."

"Uh, nothing!" Vulpie smiles and opens his desk drawer. He drops the data drive into it, grabs his keys, and then locks it. The orange furred fox gets up and straightens out his suit. Polar wipes a little bit of dust from it and straightens Vulpie's pink tie.

"You look so cute..." Polar smiles with affection and Vulpie does his best to straighten the white furred wolf's blue tie as well. "I love you..."

"I love you too baby..." Vulpie joyfully responds, and the white furred wolf bends forward to share a kiss with him. They hold paws and go downstairs to take their corporate photo together. The photographer has to give Vulpie a little box to stand on because he's so much shorter than Polar. Polar steps behind him lovingly, putting his big paw on the gay fox's left shoulder. They think about the wonderful future they'll have together, and smile for the cameras.

www.ingramcontent.com/pod-product-compliance
Lightning Source LLC
Chambersburg PA
CBHW071331020726
47502CB00001B/63